Democracies endure until the citizens care more for what the state can give them than for its ability to defend rich and poor alike; until they care more for their privileges than their responsibilities; until they learn they can vote themselves largess from the public treasury and use the state as an instrument for plundering, first, those who have wealth, then those who create it.

The American people seem to be learning that fatal lesson. The last forty years have seen the United States reject the temptations of empire, but nearly succumb to the seductions of democracy. We have reached the abyss, but not yet taken the last step over it. The survival of freedom itself is at stake; and that future is by no means certain.

CREATED BY
JERRY POURNELLE

IMPERIAL STARS

VOL. 2

REPUBLIC AND EMPIRE

[signature: Jerry Pournelle]

with John F. Carr

BAEN BOOKS

REPUBLIC AND EMPIRE

This is a work of fiction. All the characters and events portrayed in this book are fictional, and any resemblance to real people or incidents is purely coincidental.

A Baen Books Original

Baen Publishing Enterprises
260 Fifth Avenue
New York, N.Y. 10001

First printing, October 1987

ISBN: 0-671-65359-8

Cover art by Alan Gutierrez

Printed in the United States of America

Distributed by
SIMON & SCHUSTER
1230 Avenue of the Americas
New York, N.Y. 10020

DEDICATION

For Sir Rodney Hartwell, who keeps alive
the notions of honor in an age that has forgotten.

ACKNOWLEDGMENTS

REPUBLIC AND EMPIRE was written by J.E. Pournelle especially for this volume and appears here for the first time. Published by arrangement with the author and the author's agent, Kirby McCauley Ltd. Copyright © 1987 by J.E. Pournelle.

OUTWARD BOUND by Norman Spinrad first appeared in *Analog Science Fiction* magazine. It appears here by permission of the author. Copyright © 1964 by Condé Nast Publications.

IN THE REALM OF THE HEART, IN THE WORLD OF THE KNIFE by Wayne Wightman was published originally in the August 1985 issue of *Isaac Asimov's Science Fiction Magazine*. Copyright © 1985 by Davis Publications.

DOING WELL BY DOING GOOD by Hayford Peirce was first published in the August 1975 issue of *Analog Science Fiction* magazine. Copyright © 1975 by Condé Nast Publications.

CONSTITUTION FOR UTOPIA by John W. Campbell was first published under the title "Constitution" in the March 1961 issue of *Analog Science Fiction*. Copyright © 1961 by Street & Smith Publications.

MINOR INGREDIENT by Eric Frank Russell was published in the March 1956 issue of *Astounding Science Fiction*. Published here by special arrangement with the author's estate and Scott Meredith Inc. Copyright © 1956 by Street & Smith Publications.

THE TURNING WHEEL by Philip K. Dick first appeared in *Science Fiction Stories* #2 in 1954. It appears here by arrangement with the author's agent, Scott Meredith Inc. Copyright © 1987 by Philip K. Dick.

REACTIONARY UTOPIAS by Gregory Benford was first published in the Winter issue of *Far Frontiers* in 1985. It appears here by special arrangement with the author. Copyright © 1985 by Gregory Benford.

THESE SHALL NOT BE LOST by E.B. Cole appeared in the January 1953 issue of *Astounding Science Fiction*. Copyright © 1953 by Street & Smith Publications.

Research for certain nonfiction in this book was supported in part by grants from the Vaughn Foundation and the L-5 Society Promoting Space Development, 1060 E. Elm St., Tucson AZ 85709. Opinions expressed in this book are the sole responsibility of the authors.

CONTENTS

REPUBLIC AND EMPIRE
Jerry Pournelle

As it was in the past, so shall it be in future: the history
of the world has been the struggle of empire and republic.
Each has its champions.

It used to be fashionable to say "the Republic of the
United States," and our Pledge of Allegiance preserves
that language. The name of republic holds magic no less
than does the name of empire.

Some of that magic has been lost. In this enlightened
time, we are all officially in favor of democracy, and we are
pleased to call this the era of democracy. We are taught
not only that all democracies are good, but that the worth
of a government depends on how democratic it is. The
notion that a government can be "good" but not democratic will strike many as bizarre.

It has not always been thus. If we believe, with Thomas
Jefferson, that the purpose of government is to assure the
rights of life, liberty, and the pursuit of happiness, we
might do well to recall what Acton said in tracing the
history of freedom in Athens:

"Two men's lives span the interval from the first admission of popular influence, under Solon, to the downfall of

1

the State. Their history furnishes the classic example of the peril of democracy under conditions singularly favourable. For the Athenians were not only brave and patriotic and capable of generous sacrifice, but they were the most religious of the Greeks. They venerated the Constitution which had given them prosperity, and equality, and freedom, and never questioned the fundamental laws which regulated the enormous power of the Assembly. They tolerated considerable variety of opinion and great license of speech; and their humanity towards their slaves roused the indignation even of the most intelligent partisan of aristocracy. Thus they became the only people of antiquity that grew great by democratic institutions. But the possession of unlimited power, which corrodes the conscience, hardens the heart, and confounds the understanding of monarchs, exercised its demoralising influence on the illustrious democracy of Athens. It is bad to be oppressed by a minority, but it is worse to be oppressed by a majority. For there is a reserve of latent power in the masses which, if it is called into play, the minority can seldom resist. But from the absolute will of an entire people there is no appeal, no redemption, no refuge but treason. The humblest and most numerous class of the Athenians united the legislative, the judicial, and, in part, the executive power. The philosophy that was then in the ascendant taught them that there is no law superior to that of the State—the lawgiver is above the law.

"It followed that the sovereign people had a right to do whatever was within its power, and was bound by no rule of right or wrong but its own judgment of expediency. On a memorable occasion the assembled Athenians declared it monstrous that they should be prevented from doing whatever they chose. No force that existed could restrain them, and they resolved that no duty should restrain them, and that they would be bound by no laws that were not of their own making. In this way the emancipated people of Athens became a tyrant, and their government, the pioneer of European freedom, stands condemned with a terrible unanimity by all the wisest of the ancients.

"They ruined their city by attempting to conduct war by debate in the marketplace. Like the French Republic, they put their unsuccessful commanders to death. They treated their dependencies with such injustice that they lost their maritime Empire. They plundered the rich until the rich conspired with the public enemy, and they crowned their guilt by the martyrdom of Socrates.

"The repentance of the Athenians came too late to save the Republic. But the lesson of their experience endures for all time, for it teaches that government by the whole people, being the government of the most numerous and most powerful class, is an evil of the same nature as unmixed monarchy, and requires, for nearly the same reasons, institutions that shall protect it against itself, and shall uphold the permanent reign of law against arbitrary revolutions of opinion."

—John Emerich Edward Dalberg, Lord Acton
"The History of Freedom in Antiquity"

Classical writers spent much time analyzing the forms of government. Machiavelli put it better than most:

"I must at the beginning observe that some of the writers on politics distinguished three kinds of government, viz., the monarchical, the aristocratic, and the democratic; and maintain that the legislators of a people must choose from these three the one that seems most suitable. Other authors, wiser according to the opinion of many, count six kinds of government, three of which are very bad, and three good in themselves, but so liable to be corrupted that they become absolutely bad. The three good ones are those we just named; the three bad ones result from the degradation of the other three, and each of them resembles its corresponding original, so that the transition from the one to the other is very easy.

"Thus monarchy becomes tyranny; aristocracy degenerates into oligarchy; and the popular government lapses readily into licentiousness. So that a legislator who gives to a state which he founds, either of these three forms of government, constitutes it but for a brief time; for no precautions can prevent either one of the three that are reputed good, from degenerating into its opposite kind; so great are in these attractions and resemblances between the good and the evil.

—Niccolo Machiavelli, *The Discourses*

This view of government was held universally among writers on history and politics from Aristotle to very nearly the present day. And if we no longer believe that the pure forms of government are inevitably doomed, it is only because we have come to hold, with little evidence, greater faith in democracy than either the ancients or the founding fathers of the United States ever had.

Now, when the classical writers say that a government, whether monarchy, aristocracy, or democracy, is good, this means that the governors put the interest of the state ahead of their own narrow interests; that law, and freedom, and justice, were sovereign.

This, alas, is by no means inevitable in these days of partisan politics; there are politicos in plenty who would chance ruining the state to gain political advantage. Thus, the trend of the U.S. from Republic to Democracy may not deserve the enthusiasm it receives. None of this would have surprised the ancients. To them, human history was no more than the endlessly sad tale of the cycle from tyranny to aristocracy, aristocracy to oligarchy, oligarchy to democracy, and democracy to a chaos ended only by the imposition of an emperor, whose successor will be a tyrant; and on, *per omnia secula seculorem*.

However, there might be a remedy to the tragedy of the cycles. Cicero puts it this way:

"When there is a king, everybody except the king has too few rights, and too small a share in what is decided; whereas under an oligarchy, freedom scarcely extends to the populace, since they are not consulted and are excluded from power. When, on the other hand, there is thoroughgoing democracy, however fairly and moderately it is conducted, its egalitarianism is unfair since it does not make it possible for one man to rise above another.

"I am speaking about these three forms of government—monarchy, oligarchy, democracy—when they retain their specific character, not when they are merged and confused with one another. In addition to their liability to the flaws I have just mentioned, each of them suffers from further ruinous defects. For in front of every one of these constitutional forms stands a headlong slippery path to another and more evil one. Thus beneath the endurable, or if you like, lovable Cyrus—to take him as an example—lurks the cruel tyrant Phalaris, influencing him towards the arbitrary transformation of his own nature: for any autocracy readily and easily changes into that sort of tyranny. Then the government of Marseille, conducted by a few leading men, is very close to that clique of the Thirty which once tyrannized Athens. And as for the Athenian democracy, its absolute power turned into rule by the masses; that is to say, into manic irresponsibility.

"You may well ask which of them I like best, for I do not approve of any of them when it is by itself and unmodified: my own preference is for a form of government which is a combination of all three."

—Cicero, "Dialogues on Government"

Cicero believed that the Roman Republic had achieved that mixed form; that the Roman constitution was as near perfection as mankind could achieve. Yet even as he wrote, the Republic was falling, and Cicero was eventually murdered by agents of Octavius Caesar, later called Augustus. A single lifetime was sufficient to witness the glory of the Republic extinguished in civil war; the dictatorship of Julius Caesar; and the monarchy of Augustus.

Hundreds of books attempt to explain the fall of the Republic. Here is one of the best:

"Let us compare the situation around 150 BC [when the Republic was strong] with that around 50 [just before the end]. The transformation is astonishing. In a hundred years, the character of political competition—as well as its potential rewards—changed dramatically. In the 50s, at the very top of the political tree, the prize was total indefinite dominance. Caesar and Pompey fought to rule the Roman world. Contrast the 150s. Then the prizes were of limited character and duration . . ."

—Mary Beard and Michael Crawford,
Rome in the Late Republic

In a word, the scope of politics had changed. Moreover, the place of Rome in the world had changed. In 150 BC, Rome was a regional power. By 50 BC, she was the greatest power on Earth, with no rival but Persia.

Santayana tells us that those who cannot remember the past are condemned to repeat it.

In the nineteenth century, theorists might delude themselves into the notion that the cycles were ended, and progress had come at last. Marxism was one such philosophy that predicted that government and society would evolve from lower to higher forms.

Inmates of Auschwitz and the Gulag found otherwise. Not only is progress not inevitable; things can and do get worse, as well as better. If we wish to avoid catastrophe, we had best be aware of history.

Certainly, we have much to learn from the fate of Rome and Athens. In our enlightened time we may not kill our unsuccessful generals, but we allow the media to humiliate them. We may not conduct our foreign policy by debate in the marketplace, but is television much different? We are well aware that to tell anything to the Congress is to tell it to the world; yet the Congress, in the name of the people, demands to know all our military and diplomatic secrets.

The top prize in politics may not be unlimited power forever, but it is certainly fame and fortune. Lyndon Johnson never held any but public jobs, from Texas schoolteacher to President, and left a fortune anyone might envy. Nixon may have resigned in disgrace, but he will never go hungry. Contrast that to Jefferson, who put up

Monticello as a lottery prize in order to pay debts incurred when he was President.

In the last century, a Secretary of State could say, "Wherever the standard of freedom and independence has been or shall be unfurled, there will be America's heart, her benediction, and her prayers. But she goes not abroad in search of monsters to destroy. She is the well-wisher to the freedom and independence of all. She is the champion and vindicator only of her own."

In this century, John F. Kennedy could say that America would "pay any price, bear any burden, meet any hardship, support any friend, oppose any foe, to ensure the survival and success of liberty." We may not, in fact, have fulfilled all of Kennedy's promises, but we have gone abroad in search of monsters, which, alas, we failed to destroy.

During the hot summer of 1787, as remarkable a group of men as was ever assembled met in Philadelphia to write a Constitution for the newly independent United Colonies. All had some kind of political influence, but many were scholars, and most were much more familiar with history than would be any collection of that many politicians we might assemble today. They were all well aware of the cycles, and they were determined to found a nation that might escape them. "A new day now begins," they said, and so it was written onto the Great Seal of the United States. Our New Order would be neither democracy nor monarchy, but a mixed form—one that might endure so long as we were worthy of it.

"What have we?" an onlooker asked of Ben Franklin when the work was done. "A republic or a monarchy?"

"A republic, Madam, if we can keep it."

Many believed, and time seems to have proved, that the Philadelphia Constitution was the most perfect instrument of government ever devised by mankind. Certainly, it brought relative peace and absolute prosperity, and endured practically unchanged for generations; in fact, until the present.

This generation has seen more fundamental change in the nature of our Republic than any previous one. We have come a long way from the mixed Republic, and a long way toward a pure democracy. We have changed from a public philosophy of reliance on individual responsibility to a preference for collectivism. We have not so much disparaged liberty, but we have made security, not liberty, the highest goal of the state.

"Those who would give up essential liberty for a little temporary safety deserve neither liberty nor safety," Franklin warned us. We have come perilously close to doing that.

"The state was the great gainer of the twentieth century, and the central failure. Up to 1914, it was rare for the public sector to embrace more than 10 percent of the economy. By the 1970s, even in liberal countries, the state took up to 45 percent of the GNP. But whereas, at the time of the Versailles Treaty, most intelligent people believed that an enlarged stage could increase the sum total of human happiness, by the 1980s, the view was held by no one outside a small, diminishing, and dispirited band of zealots. The experiment had been tried in innumerable ways, and it had failed in nearly all of them. The state had proven itself to be an insatiable spender, an unrivaled waster. Indeed, in the twentieth century, it had proven itself the great killer of all time. By the 1980s, state action had been responsible for the violent or unnatural deaths of over 100 million people—more perhaps than it had hitherto succeeded in destroying during the whole of human history up to 1900. Its inhuman malevolence had more than kept pace with its growing size and expanding means.

"What was not clear was whether the fall from grace of the state would likewise discredit its agents, the activist politicians, whose phenomenal rise in numbers and authority was the most important development of modern times. As we have noted, by the turn of the century, politics was replacing religion as the chief form of zealotry. To archetypes of the new class, such as Lenin, Hitler, and

Mao Tse-tung, politics—by which they meant the engineering of society for lofty purposes—was the one legitimate form of moral activity, the only sure means of improving humanity. This view, which would have struck an earlier age as fantastic, became to some extent the orthodoxy everywhere . . ."

—Paul Johnson, *Modern Times*

In 1940, the people of the United States believed in individual responsibility. They might look to government for a helping hand, even for temporary assistance to get past a crisis, but the notion that the government might be responsible for feeding and clothing and housing the citizens would have been rejected as socialism. Today, things are a bit different.

In 1945, the forces of freedom and liberty held dominant power over the world. The Republic of the United States had a monopoly on nuclear weapons, an enormous army in Europe and another in Japan, and a war economy. We might have imposed imperial rule over the world. Instead, we dismantled our army, brought the soldiers home, and used our economy to help our former enemies. We were given the choice between republic and empire, and we opted to remain true to our republican heritage.

Five years later, we were engaged in war in Korea—war that somehow, for all our might, we couldn't win. Within a generation, a president who had pledged to bear any burden and fight any foe stood below the Berlin Wall and could do no more than shout defiance. Within two generations, more than half the people of the world lived under tyranny, and we were still not done.

"In the days that followed Brezhnev's death in November 1982, the multitude of British and American Sovietologists and political figures interviewed from morning to night by the media urged that we "seize the opportunity" to give the Soviet Union proof of our good will. Most of them specifically recommended that the Americans immediately lift their embargo on technological transfers to the U.S.S.R.—even those with possible military applications (this was done at once)—and that we postpone for one year the deployment of the Euromissiles that were to comprise Western Europe's counterweight to the intermediate-range SS-20s Russia had already positioned on its Western frontiers.

"Just what was this 'opportunity' to be seized? The death of one leader and his replacement by another do not necessarily mean the country's policy will change. Only the new man's actions can show if he has taken a different tack. In the seven years preceding Brezhnev's death, it was Soviet foreign policy that was aggressive, not the West's. So it was up to Moscow to take the first step, not the West. There was no sign in Andropov's past of liberalism or pacifism. So why offer him unilateral concessions before he had given the slightest indication of his good will or uttered a single word that sounded conciliatory?

"Why? Because deep down, whatever they may say and write to the contrary, Westerners accept the Soviet Union's idea of them. They very nearly agree that they are at fault for the collapse of detente. We see ourselves through Moscow's eyes, we accept the myth of the Communists' desire for peace, and acknowledge that it is we who are guilty of aggressivity endangering the world's stability."

—Jean-Francois Revel, *How Democracies Perish*

Democracies endure until the citizens care more for what the state can give them than for its ability to defend rich and poor alike; until they care more for their privileges than their responsibilities; until they learn they can vote themselves largess from the public treasury and use the state as an instrument for plundering, first, those who have wealth, then those who create it.

The American people seem to be learning that fatal lesson. The last forty years have seen the United States reject the temptations of empire, but nearly succumb to the seductions of democracy. We have reached the abyss, but not yet taken the last step over it. The survival of freedom itself is at stake, and that future is by no means certain.

Herewith, stories of republic and empire in the near and far future.

Editor's Introduction To:

OUTWARD BOUND
Norman Spinrad

Norman Spinrad lives just up the hill from me, but we don't see each other nearly as often as we'd like. Writing can be a lonely business.

Spinrad was once considered a "new wave" writer, but since I haven't any notion of what that means, I can't comment. I do know that he pays attention to character as well as technical detail, but then, so do a lot of writers who aren't thought "new wave" at all. One thing is certain. He can tell stories that you'll remember a while.

In conventional thought, Democracies are preferable to Empires, because they are more humane and ethical, and more likely to adhere to the rule of law. The facts are different. Polities conventionally described as Republics have had imperial ambitions, and have often enforced their imperial rule over others. The Athenians converted from Republic to Democracy, but continued to act as colonial masters over their former allies in the Aegean. And as C. Northcote Parkinson points out, they enforced their rule with a cynical ferocity matched only by the most ruthless of dictators.

On one occasion, Mytilene wished to withdraw from the alliance and cease paying tribute to Athens. The Athenians blockaded the city and brought about its surrender, after which Cleon got the popular assembly to decree that the entire military-age population of Mytilene should be massacred, and everyone else sold into slavery. A galley was dispatched to deliver the order to the Athenian military commander at Mytilene.

The issue was debated again the next day. When Diodotus called for mercy, Cleon demanded justice: he warned the Athenians that the maintenance of empire demanded that the subjects be kept in a constant state of fear, and the empire would pass away if the Athenians were guided by compassion.

The moderates won, and another ship was dispatched to rescind the orders of the first. On that happy occasion, the first ship, bearing the dreadful news, was slow, while the second was rowed by men eager to arrive on time.

Athens was hardly the last state, republic or empire, to sacrifice principle to expediency. For all the power of the state, though, the decrees of Republic and Empire alike must be carried out by men.

OUTWARD BOUND
Norman Spinrad

Captain Peter Reed floated closer to the big central viewport of the conning globe.

Before him, filling half his field of vision, was the planet Maxwell, green continents and blue seas reminding him of Earth.

He shook his white-haired head. Earth was fifty light-years off, or to put it another way, seventy years ago, or in another way, only four months.

Reed shrugged, not an easy task for a seventy-year-old

man in free fall. Or to put it another way, an eight-hundred-year-old man.

Reed could not help laughing aloud. Fifty subjective years in space, he thought, eight hundred years in objective time, and still it has its wonder for me.

As he watched, a mote of light detached itself from the disk of Maxwell, and arced upward.

That would be Director Horvath's ship, thought Reed. Last time the *Outward Bound* was at Maxwell, it had been ruled by a hereditary king. But that was three hundred years ago. King La Farge, thought Reed sadly, dead and gone three hundred years.

This Lazlo Horvath, now. He seems to be a different proposition. Ambitious, dangerous.

Reed smiled wryly. If he keeps up this way, he may soon be honored by a visit from Jacob ben Ezra.

The captain spoke into the communicator. "Rog, get the reception room ready. Our customer's on the way."

He paddled awkwardly to the rear of the conning globe, grabbed a guard rail, and pulled himself through the rotating doorway, into the main cylinder of the *Outward Bound*.

Immediately, he felt the tug of gravity. The *Outward Bound* was an untidy collection of cylinders and globes, held together by spars. While in orbit, the whole conglomeration spun about a central axis, creating an artificial gravity. But, of course, it was necessary that the conning globe be stationary, so it hung in front of the main cylinder, mounted on frictionless bearings, so that it alone did not share the ship's rotation.

Captain Reed made his way to the reception room. Lazlo Horvath should be an eager customer. The last tradeship to hit Maxwell had been the *Stargod*, one hundred years ago, and that was still in the days of the Kingdom.

Director Horvath was new and ambitious, and like all planetary leaders, he chafed under the yoke of Earth. An ideal customer.

Roger Reed was already in the reception room when his father arrived. There was some family resemblance. He had his father's large frame, but on him it was well-muscled, not hung with loose flesh. His hair was a flamboyant red, and he was going through one of his periods of experimentation with mustaches. This one was only a week old, and its ultimate nature could not yet be discerned.

"Horvath's on board, Dad," he said.

"Please, Roger," said the old man, with a weariness born of endless repetition, "at least when there is a customer aboard, *don't* call me 'Dad'."

"Sorry, sir."

Captain Reed looked about the reception room. It was the one area of calculated ostentation on the ship. It was paneled in real knotty pine. A genuine wool carpet lined it from wall to wall. The captain sat behind a huge mahogany desk, on a genuine red leather covered chair. Three other such chairs were scattered about the room. A viewer was built into one wall.

The room always made Peter Reed feel uncomfortable.

"Well, Roger," said the captain, "do you think this'll be a good haul?"

"Don't see why not, da . . . *sir*. The Directory of Maxwell seems to be at that stage when they think that with a *little* help, they can break the Terran hegemony. They ought to go quite high for the force field, for instance."

The old man sighed. "They never learn, do they?" he said. "No doubt Horvath will think that the force field is an ultimate weapon. He'll never stop to realize that on Earth, it's already seventy years old."

"Why so glum, *captain*?" said the younger Reed. "After all, it's our stock in trade."

"So it is, so it is."

An orderly appeared at the door. "Captain Peter Reed," he said formally, "it is my honor to present Lazlo Horvath, Director of Maxwell."

A short, squat man, of about fifty, stalked into the room. He was dressed in a black uniform, with gold trim, encircled by a wide Sam Browne belt. He wore heavy black boots.

Oh, no, thought Peter Reed, not one of *them!*

Nevertheless, he rose politely, wryly aware of the plainness of his simple light-green coveralls. "Director Horvath."

"Captain Reed."

"My second, Roger Reed."

"Mr. Reed."

"Sit down, Director," said the captain.

Horvath perched himself on the edge of one of the chairs.

"It has been a while since a starship visited Maxwell," he said. His voice was deep and crisp.

"Yes, I know. The trader *Stargod*, one hundred years ago."

For a moment, there was a flicker of puzzlement on Horvath's tough face. "Ah, yes, the *Stargod*," he said smoothly. "Well, Captain Reed, what have you to offer?"

"Several new concepts," said Peter Reed, studying the Director. It was obvious that the man had let something slip. But what?

"Such as?"

"For one thing, an amusing new concept in drinks. Roger, the refreshments."

Roger Reed waved his hand, and a panel slid aside, revealing a pitcher of red liquid, and three glasses on a tray. He poured the drinks.

Captain Reed smiled as he saw the perplexed look on Horvath's face. The drink was made up of two different wines, one hot, one cold, kept separate by a new chemical technique so that one tasted alternately hot and cold liquid. It was a strange feeling.

"Very amusing, Captain Reed," said Norvath. "But surely you don't expect Maxwell to pay good radioactives for such a parlor trick."

Reed grinned. The hot-and-cold liquid technique was just a come-on, of course. The really big commodity he had to sell was the force field.

"Director," he said, "as you know, traders don't sell *products*, except radioactives, at times. What we sell is science, knowledge, techniques. Now the drink may be a parlor trick, but there can be practical applications for the technique."

"Perhaps, perhaps," said Horvath shortly, "but what else do you have? Perhaps . . . perhaps you at last have the secret of Overdrive?"

Peter Reed laughed. "Maybe I have the Philosopher's Stone, as well?" He saw that Horvath was not amused. "I'm sorry, Director," he said. "It's just that we've never made port on any planet, in the eight hundred years that the *Outward Bound* has been in space, where they didn't ask that question. No, we don't have the secret of Overdrive. It is my opinion that there never will be an Overdrive. Man will never travel faster than light. It's a chimera, a schizophrenic compulsion to leave the limiting realm of the real universe, to find a never-never land called Hyperspace, or what have you, where reality is suspended, and the Galaxy belongs to Man."

Horvath frowned. "A very pretty little speech," he said. "So easy for *you* to say. But then, you are not under the heel of Earth. You starmen are by nature free agents. But we, we *colonials*, we know what it is to suffer the tyranny of time. Maxwell is fifty light-years from Earth. Therefore, since we were settled from Earth, from an Earth that was already sixty years ahead of us when we emerged from Deep Sleep, we will *always* be sixty years behind Earth, just as the outer ring will always be two hundred years behind. To you, an Overdrive would be just one more thing to peddle, although it would bring the best price in history. To us, an Overdrive would mean freedom."

"Of course, you are right, Director," said Captain Reed. "Nevertheless, that doesn't make Overdrive any more possible. However"—he noticed Horvath's anticipation with satisfaction—"we do have something new, something big. I suppose they've been looking for this as long as they've been looking for an Overdrive—*a force field*."

Horvath's eyes widened. "*A force field?*"

"Ah, you are interested."

"Of course. It would be idiotic to try and hide it. *This*, Maxwell wants."

"And what have *you* to offer?" asked Peter Reed softly.

"One ton of thorium."

"Oh really, Director!" said Reed. "That's all right for the hot-cold technique, but—"

"Two tons!"

"Come, come, Mr. Horvath. A force field is the ultimate defensive weapon, after all. Two measly tons—"

"Ten tons!"

"Now, what are we going to do with all that thorium? Can't you do better? We deal in knowledge, you know. Perhaps you have something in that area—"

"Well," said Horvath, his hard eyes narrowing, "there was another ship here, only three years ago."

"Oh?"

"Colonizer, heading for the outer ring. Direct from Earth."

"So what?"

"Well, captain, there was a *passenger* aboard."

"*A passenger?*"

"Yes, a Dr. Ching pen Yee. Had to leave Earth quickly, so it seems, some kind of mathematical physicist. We're holding him."

"I don't see what this has to do with *us*," said Peter Reed.

Horvath smiled crookedly. "Grand Admiral Jacob ben Ezra is on his way to Maxwell. In fact, he's decelerating already. Should be here in about a month."

Captain Reed stroked his nose. If Earth was sending ben Ezra himself after Dr. Ching, the man must be someone really important. Earth virtually *never* pursued a fugitive beyond the twenty-five light-year radius of the Integral Control Zone. And Horvath knew it.

"So what are you offering?" he said slowly.

"Ben Ezra can't know that he was put off here," said Horvath. "He'll be eager to get away. I propose that I trade you Ching for the force-field theory."

"But neither of us knows whether Ching has anything of

alue," said Reed, knowing that anyone who was being
ursued by Jacob ben Ezra over fifty light-years must
now something *very* valuable indeed.

But Horvath knew it too. "Come, captain. We both
now that Earth would not send ben Ezra, unless Ching
was very important indeed. Ching and one ton of thorium
or the force field."

"Ching and three tons," said Reed, with a little smile.

"Ching and two tons."

Peter Reed laughed. "Ching and three tons for the force
eld *and* the hot-cold technique."

"Very well, captain," said Horvath, rising and sticking
ut his hand, "you've got a deal."

The two men shook hands.

"Have your men begin bringing up the thorium imme-
iately," said Reed, "and get your scientists up here quick,
o learn the techniques. I certainly don't want to be in this
ystem when ben Ezra gets here."

"Of course not," said Horvath, with a grin. "Rest as-
ured, captain, I'm a very good liar. And believe me when
say it has been a pleasure doing business with you."

"The same, Director. Mr. Reed will show you to the air
ock."

As Roger Reed opened the door, Horvath stopped and
urned.

"Captain," he said, "one thing. If you ever do get hold
f an Overdrive, Maxwell will match anyone's price for it.
ou can write your own bill of sale."

Captain Reed frowned. "You know as well as I do, that
e traders sell the same knowledge to every planet we
uch."

Horvath eyed him thinly. "I am aware of the practice,"
e said. "However, in the case of an Overdrive, Maxwell
ould make it well worth your while to make it an *exclusive*
le."

Reed shook his head, and grinned. "I'll keep it in mind,
irector," he said.

* * *

Grand Admiral Jacob ben Ezra finished his fourth cigarette of the morning. On a starship, with its own self-contained atmosphere to maintain, smoking was a hideous luxury. But Admiral ben Ezra was a man with privileges. A small, frail old man of eighty subjective years, he had been in space for over seven hundred objective years, and was something of a living legend.

Right now, he was nervous. He turned to his aide. "David," he said, "can't we cut a week or two off the time?"

"No, sir," replied the younger commander. "We're using maximum deceleration as it is. Photon sails, plus ion drive."

"What about using the atomic reaction rockets as well?" asked the admiral, knowing full well what the answer would be.

"We just don't have the reaction mass to spare," said the commander. "Photon sails, of course, cost no fuel, and the ion rockets use very little, but with the ion drive going, and three weeks left till planetfall, we can't use the rockets for even an hour. Besides—"

"Besides, our course is already plotted, and we'd undershoot," said ben Ezra. "David, David, don't you know when an old man is talking just to let off steam?"

The young commander fidgeted with embarrassment.

"Nevertheless," said the Grand Admiral, rubbing the end of his long nose, "I wish we could. It's going to be a close thing."

"Why, sir?"

Jacob ben Ezra lit a fifth cigarette. "The *Outward Bound* left Earth just about when we did. They're scheduled to stop at Maxwell. No doubt, the *SS–185* will put Ching off somewhere before they get to Toehold. My guess is that it'll be Maxwell."

"So, sir?"

Ben Ezra exhaled a great cloud of smoke.

"Sorry, David," he said. "Somehow, I'm beginning to find it difficult to remember that not everyone is as old as I am. The *Outward Bound* is one of the oldest tradeships

round; in fact, if my memory serves me correctly, it was
 e *first* one built specifically for the purpose. Her captain
 Peter Reed. He's been in space longer than *I* have."

"Longer than *you*, sir?"

Ben Ezra laughed. It was not the laugh of an old man. It
 lt good to laugh, especially under the circumstances.

"Yes, my incredulous young friend," he said, "longer
 an I have. Reed is one of the cleverest captains in space.
 lso, don't forget, he has the force field to sell, this trip."

"You mean you think Maxwell will trade *Ching* for the
 rce field? But, sir, once they find out why Ching's out
 ere, *no one* would trade him for *anything*."

Jacob ben Ezra puckered his leathery lips. "You are
 suming that Dr. Ching will talk. I doubt that very much.
 e knows that we'd follow him to Andromeda, if we had
 . My guess is that he'll figure his only hope is to change
 ips as often as possible, and not tell *anyone* why he's on
 e run."

"Then why would Captain Reed accept him in trade?"

"Because," said the Grand Admiral, raising his bushy
 hite eyebrows, "Reed is clever *and* experienced. He will
 now that anyone who is being pursued by us, all the way
 om Earth, is someone who has something of vital
 nportance."

Jacob ben Ezra crushed his cigarette against the bulk-
 ead. He shook his head violently.

"If only he knew," he said, "if only he *knew*."

The *Outward Bound* orbited low over Maxwell. She was
 untidy spectacle—one great central cylinder, around
 hose girth the space gigs were clustered; three lesser
 linders, connected to the main body only by spars; the
 nning globe; and, far astern, the propulsion reactor, a
 ll black globe, behind which sprouted two set of rockets—
 e small, almost inconspicuous ion drive, and the great
 action rockets, which fed off whatever reaction mass
 ppened to be in the huge fuel tanks, located just for-
 ard of the reactor.

To make the whole thing even more messy looking, the

main cylinder and its auxiliaries were pocked with globes, tubes and blisters, looking for all the world like budding yeast under a microscope. Like Topsy, the successful tradeship just *grew*, adding a cylinder here, a globe there, a blister in another place, as the ship's fortune waxed. In deep space, where friction was no factor, this wild messiness was a status symbol, a sign of prosperity.

Now, Maxwellian ships were coming and going constantly, bringing thorium, food, water, scientists. They had one great navigational hazard to overcome. Four mile-long spars sprouted from amidships on the main cylinder. During acceleration away from a sun, or deceleration towards a sun, four immense triangles of ten-molecule-thick plastic would stretch from the spars, catching the energy of photon packets outward bound from light sources. By grams per-square-yard, the solar sails provided negligible thrust, but cumulatively, over two square miles of surface area, they were good for a steady, if mild acceleration. Besides, the energy they provided was free.

But now, since the spars were empty, and the ship was spinning about its central axis, the spars were the arms of a monstrous windmill, which the Maxwellian ships had to avoid.

Captain Reed smiled as he watched the ships thread their way gingerly toward the *Outward Bound*. No doubt, there were simple ways of making the spars stationary while the ship spun, perhaps using the same circle-in-circle bearings that served to immobilize the conning globe. But no starship *he* had ever heard of had bothered to try. It was just too amusing watching the planethogs dodge the whirling spars.

Well, this would be the last day they'd have to brave the whirlwind. The last of the thorium was aboard, the Maxwellians had their force field and hot-cold technique, and Ching would be coming aboard on the last ship.

None too soon, either, thought Peter Reed. Ben Ezra will be here in another ten days. Ten days to get here, perhaps a week or two to break Horvath. Captain Reed had few illusions about *that* individual. Within three weeks at the outside, Jacob ben Ezra would know that Ching pen Yee was aboard the *Outward Bound.*

Ben Ezra would be able to close the gap to a week or less, at the next planetfall, Nuova Italia, only ten light-years away.

But by that time, thought Reed, I'll know whether Ching's worth keeping. If he isn't, ben Ezra can have him at Nuova Italia. But if he is . . . well, ben Ezra will probably have to take on supplies at Nuova Italia. We can get away from him once more, if we have to. But . . . he can catch us easily, and wherever we head, he can be there before us, with us only having a couple of days lead.

We'll jump off that bridge when we come to it, thought Captain Reed.

"Dr. Ching is aboard," came a voice from the communicator.

"Good," said Reed. "How soon can we break orbit?"

"Everything'll be secured in another three hours, Dad."

"Roger!"

"Sorry, sir."

"All right, Roger," said the old man. "Make ready to break orbit as soon as possible. And send Ching to the reception room. Have Olivera there, too. In fact, stall Ching a bit, and have Manny get there a few minutes earlier. Tell him I'll be right down."

"Yes, *sir.*"

"But, Peter," said Manuel Olivera, his dark eyes raised to the ceiling in supplication, "I am *not* a theoretical physicist. I am *not* a mathematician. I am a tinkerer, a librarian, a maker of stinks, a—"

"Manny! Manny! Please!" said the captain. "I know the whole song and dance by now. Nevertheless, you *are* the *Outward Bound's* chief scientist."

"Yes, yes," said the small dark-skinned man excitedly, "but you know as well as I do that all that means is that I'm a glorified librarian. We—"

"All right, all right. All I want you to do is *be* here, and pay attention. This Dr. Ching has something of value, I'm *sure* of it. And we may not have him very long. We've got to be quick, and—"

"Dr. Ching pen Yee to see you, captain," said an orderly.

"Send him in."

Dr. Ching was a small, though well-built man of about sixty. His straight black hair was parted neatly in the middle. Only his shifting eyes betrayed his nervousness.

"Thank you for accepting my passage, Captain Reed," he said.

"Not at all, Dr. Ching. Frankly, we hope you may be of value to us. As you know, the lifeblood of a tradeship is knowledge. We sell it, and we buy it. To be blunt, we have *bought* you from Maxwell. You get passage with us, for as long as you want, and in return, we expect you to share your knowledge."

"But, captain," said Ching nervously, "I am a mathematical physicist. You are engaged in the business of selling practical technological knowledge. We mathematical physicists are not noted for producing marketable knowledge."

Reed frowned. This Ching was cool, and he was scared. A tough combination to crack.

"Please let Mr. Olivera and myself be the judge of that. By the way, I believe I've forgotten to introduce you. This is Manuel Olivera, our chief scientist."

"How do you do, Mr. Olivera," said Ching smoothly. "Captain Reed, really you are wasting your time. I am purely a theorist."

Reed wondered if he should spring his knowledge of Admiral ben Ezra's pursuit. He decided it could wait.

"Suppose you just tell us what you're working on?" he said.

Ching fidgeted. "Mathematical theory," he said.

"Come now, Dr. Ching," snapped Olivera, "we are not complete scientific ignoramuses, you know. What sort of theory?"

"A development of a small corollary to the Special Theory of Relativity."

"Oh?" said Olivera. "Involving what?"

Ching's eyes flickered from focus to focus like a bird's. "Involving . . . some work with transfinite substitutions," he said vaguely.

Olivera continued his pursuit. "Transfinite substitutions? Where? For what?"

Ching laughed falsely. "Really, Mr. Olivera," he said. "It's all a complicated mathematical exercise. It amuses me to substitute infinite and transfinite numbers for some of the variables. As I said, nothing practical."

"Just why are you doing this?" snapped Olivera.

"Really," said Ching blandly, "that's an unanswerable question. Indeed. Why do men climb mountains? Because they are there. Really, gentlemen, I'm quite tired. May I be excused?"

Olivera was about to continue his sortie, but the captain waved him off.

"Of course," he said. "We will soon be leaving for Nuova Italia. In about two hours. We will have time to talk again, before we all go into Deep Sleep. By all means, rest up."

"Thank you, captain," said Ching. An orderly was called, and he led Ching off.

"Well, Manny?" asked the captain.

"Well, *what?* Am I a mind reader? Gibberish. Vagueness. Perhaps outright lies. I ask you, Peter, would Jacob ben Ezra travel fifty light-years after someone engaged in a complicated mathematical exercise?' Would Earth give a damn?"

"Of course not," said the captain.

"Then why in space didn't you tell him that you knew ben Ezra was after him?" snapped Olivera.

Peter Reed smiled thinly. "Time enough for that between now and Deep Sleep. That's a whole week. I think the strategic time to spring it is just before he goes into Deep Sleep. Impending Deep Sleep makes a man realize just how dependent he can be."

"You'd *better* loosen him up by then," said Olivera, "because it's just possible that when we wake up, we'll find ben Ezra right on our tails."

* * *

A three minute burst on the huge reaction rockets kicked
the *Outward Bound* out of orbit.

As she drifted slowly outward, the huge triangular photon sails were reeled out onto the mile-long spars, blotting
out whole sectors of stars.

The pale, almost invisible, blue stream of the ion drive
shot noiselessly, vibrationlessly out of the nozzles.

The *Outward Bound* was on her way to Nuova Italia.

During the next week, the ship would be secured, the
automatic systems checked, re-checked, and finally given
command of the ship. There would be a final course correction, and then the thousand men, women and children
who made up the crew of the *Outward Bound* would go
into Deep Sleep.

Deep Sleep was the technique that had given Man that
insignificant portion of the Galaxy which he possessed. A
starship could accelerate to nearly three-quarters the speed
of light, but this took over a year, and, although it had
been proven true that subjective time on a fast-moving
starship *did* contract, as Einstein had predicted, the factor
was still far too short. The spaces between the suns would
still eat up lifespans.

Deep Sleep had been developed to deal with this dilemma. Partly it was a technique developed from yoga,
partly it was simply a careful, controlled lowering of the
body temperature, till life slowed down to the barest
crawl. The elements of the technique had been known
even before rudimentary spaceflight. But it took the technical integration of all the factors to make Deep Sleep an
effective and relatively safe form of suspended animation,
and to give Man the stars.

Peter Reed was getting disgusted. It was now time to go
into Deep Sleep, and still no one had been able to get
anything out of Ching. Clearly, the man was scared silly.

Well, thought Reed, maybe I can shock him out of it
now.

He was standing in one of the Deep Sleep chambers.

he walls were lined with transparent plastic cubicles,
offin-sized, honey-combed with passages, through which
iquid oxygen was passed.

Another of the ship's economies, thought the captain.
he same oxygen that served as the ship's air supply was
ooled by the cold of space, and used to freeze the Deep
leep chambers. It took a lot of liquid oxygen, in fact, the
ntire ship's supply, but since no one would be needing it
vhile the crew was in Deep Sleep, and since it was
e-usable, it made a neat saving.

Most of the crew were already in Deep Sleep. The
ubicles were filled with frozen crewmembers, the Envi-
onment Masks snugly fitted over their faces. Only the
keleton Deep Sleep detail, the captain and Dr. Ching
emained unfrozen. Now, the captain and the passenger
vould take their places, and then the automatics would
iandle the Deep Sleep detail.

A crewman was escorting Ching to his cubicle. The
nathematician's face was pasty and pale. His eyes flick-
red furiously over the frozen figures in the plastic coffins.

Reed smiled, half in sympathy, half in satisfaction. He
iad spent a total time of nearly seven hundred years in
hose cubicles. Still, it always made him shudder a bit.
3ut Ching had only experienced Deep Sleep once, and
omehow, the second time was always the hardest.

"Well, Dr. Ching," he called out, "how do you feel?"

"A bit foolish, captain. I must admit that I am afraid,
nd yet there is really nothing to be afraid of."

For a moment, Reed's distaste for Ching was washed
way. The Grand Admiral of Earth's fleet had hounded
iim across fifty light-years, and now he was facing what
nust to him be a great irrational fear. And yet, he's so
alm.

"I don't see why a man like *you* should be afraid," said
he captain deliberately, hating what he was doing.

"Captain?"

"Well, it seems to me that a man who's being chased
cross the Galaxy by Jacob ben Ezra, and still refuses to
ell me *why*, must have a surplus of guts."

For a moment, Ching trembled. Then he smiled slowly. "I *thought* you knew," he said. "Why else would you be so interested in me?"

"Why don't you tell me what this is all about, Ching? What are you on to? Why is Earth so concerned? I don't expect you to believe that we're your *friends*, but surely you must realize that it's in our interest as traders to protect you if you're working on something important."

Ching sighed heavily. "Captain Reed," he said, "Earth is not after me because they *want* what I'm working on. I'm really not working on anything practical at all. Just mathematical and physical concept."

"And yet, they're chasing farther than they've ever chased a fugitive before."

"Yes," said Ching. "Captain, some day you may know why I must keep my secret. If Jacob ben Ezra catches up to us, you will be *glad* that I've remained silent."

"Why, man, why?"

"Because," said Ching, "I'm fairly certain that ben Ezra has orders to kill anyone who knows what I know."

The captain frowned. "Perhaps you will change your mind when we come out of Deep Sleep at Nuova Italia."

"Perhaps, captain, *you* will change *yours*."

Peter Reed shrugged irritably. "Let's get on with it," he said to the attendant.

He climbed into his cubicle, and settled himself on the foam-rubber mattress. The attendant secured him with clamps. The ship's spin would stop when the crew was in Deep Sleep. There would be no gravity.

The soft, lined mask was fitted over his face. He inhaled the soothing tranquilizer vapor. He was comfortable, content. He vaguely felt the prick of a needle, then his senses began to dull, first sight, then sound, then feel, then smell. The last sensation was a dry taste in his mouth, and then that was gone, and he was an entity within himself, in his own private universe . . . a mote swimming in the sea of himself . . . and then, even the sense of mind began to dull . . . to fade . . . to softly melt away, like a mouthful of cotton candy.

*   *   *

A blinding redness which pervaded the universe . . . a pins-and-needles feeling . . . then warmth, overwhelming, welcome warmth, motion, smell, sound.

Jacob ben Ezra sat up in his Deep Sleep cubicle, slowly, patiently teaching his old eyes to focus.

You never get really used to it, he thought. What year is this? Let's see . . . Maxwell to Nuova Italia means fourteen years in Deep Sleep, and when we left Maxwell, it was 3297 A.D., or '98? On Earth . . .

Ben Ezra gave a dry little laugh. Time! What is time? Does it matter? I am eighty years old, I am eight hundred years old, or maybe a thousand.

This life means giving up many things. A firm sense of time is one of them. The people who've sent me after Ching, back on Earth, are all dead. I'm a ghost, a shade, the expression of the will of a group of men, all of whom are dead—in a sense.

Man was not meant for this kind of life, thought Jacob ben Ezra sourly. This is a poor way to command the stars, a poor and pitiful way.

He laughed bitterly. This is a life fit only for Gypsies and Jews. Come to think of it, Gypsies don't have a sufficient sense of history, in the long run.

Maybe that's why so many in the Fleet are Jews. To a Jew, a thousand years is supposed to be a reasonable length of time. Or so the legends say. So they say.

But what is a Jew? There is no such thing as Judaism, anymore. There is hardly such a thing as race.

A Jew, thought Jacob ben Erza, nowadays is anyone who thinks of himself as one. *Homo interstellarus*.

Ben Ezra leaned on the shoulders of a waiting attendant, and climbed down from the cubicle. His legs were a bit rubbery, but he was used to it.

Homo interstellarus, he thought, as he made his way slowly to the conning globe, lousy Latin, but very good sense.

It was as if Jews had been training to man the Great Fleet for five thousand years. How long had they been a self-contained culture, independent of geography, living even, in their own time stream? In the pre-stellar past they had been feared for it, damned for it, but now, it had a purpose. Who else could isolate themselves on the twenty ships of the Great Fleet, but Jews? Knowing no planet, no time to call home?

"They, they," mumbled the admiral. Why not *we*, he thought. Heh! Peter Reed is as much a Jew as I am. What does it mean now? It means the exiles, the planetless ones, the timeless ones, defying the Universe, spitting in the face of Einstein himself.

The steps of Jacob ben Ezra became firm and sprightly. He lit a cigarette.

"Feels good!" he said to no one in particular.

Several men were already in the conning globe—Chief Navigator Richard Jacoby, several minor crewmen, and his aide, David Steen.

"They're there, sir," said Steen. "We've got a fix on 'em."

The admiral frowned. This job was getting more odious to him every minute.

"How far behind are we?" he asked.

"About six days."

"Then they haven't made orbit yet?"

"No, sir."

"Good. That means we can keep an eye on them. Jacoby, is it possible for them to get away?"

The tall, thin navigator frowned. "Depends on what you mean, admiral. Wherever they go, of course, we can track them. Do you mean will we catch up to them before they leave orbit? Then, I'd have to say no, not if they're trying to get away."

"Can we *stop* them?" said the admiral.

"You mean *destroy* them, sir?"

"I don't mean make love to 'em, Jacoby! I know we can destroy them, but can we get close enough to disable 'em, carefully, without killing?"

"Hard to say, at six days' distance."

"That's what I was afraid of. Well, tomorrow, we'll radio 'em to heave-to and wait for us."

"Do you think they will, sir?" asked Steen.

"That depends, David, that depends. If they know why we're after Ching, they'll do *anything* to keep him. But, then, they may not know. In which case, they won't take any silly chances."

"And if they try to get away?"

Grand Admiral ben Ezra frowned. "If they try to get away, we have two choices. We can blast 'em, or we can plot their next course, and be waiting for 'em. Six days, we can easily make up on the next hop. The thing is, if we *do* blast 'em, and can't confirm that Ching was aboard, then we'll have to backtrack to Maxwell, maybe even back to Earth, and we'll never really *know*."

"But, sir," said Steen, "do you really think Reed would risk his ship for Ching, *even if* he found out?"

Jacob ben Ezra laughed, and shook his head. "I'm not sure," he said, "but I am sure that Captain Reed is as clever as I am. Which means, if he *does* find out, he'll know that we can't blast him without *knowing* that Ching is aboard. If he finds out, he'll run all right. And you know something, David?"

"What, sir?"

The admiral lit another cigarette. "I'd do the same thing myself," he said.

Captain Peter Reed cursed loudly. "Just great, just wonderful! Six days away! Six days away, and that bloody sphinx of a Ching hasn't—I've a good mind to call it a business loss and turn him over to ben Ezra."

"Sir," said the radioman fearfully, "Admiral ben Ezra is still calling—"

"Put it through to this 'visor, but *don't* answer. And stop all communications with Nuova Italia. I want it to look like our radio's dead."

"Yes, sir."

"Roger!" said Reed into the communicator. "Prepare to

break orbit immediately, and stand by. And get Ching up to the conning globe on the double!"

"But, sir, Ching has never been in zero gravity before, he—"

"Drag him up here by the hair, if you have to!"

It was only three minutes later when Roger Reed hauled a green-looking Ching into the conning globe.

"Captain," said Ching, "is this *really* necessary? I—"

"I want you to hear something, my tight-lipped friend," said the scowling Peter Reed. "I want you to hear it directly."

He turned on the televisor. The tired, wizened face of Jacob ben Ezra filled the screen. Ching paled, even through his nausea.

". . . Calling the *Outward Bound* . . . Calling the *Outward Bound*. Calling Captain Peter Reed . . ."

The pale visage on the televisor paused to light a cigarette.

"Really, Peter," said Jacob ben Ezra, "this is ridiculous. I know you're reading me."

Peter Reed could not help smiling.

"Very well, Peter," said the voice of ben Ezra, "we'll play it your way. So *don't* answer me. *I'll* do the talking. You probably have a Dr. Ching pen Yee aboard. I want him. I've come all the way from Earth for him, and, by space, I'll have him, or I'll blow you to bits. You have five minutes, plus the time lag, to answer. If you don't answer *then*, I will take appropriate action."

Captain Reed turned the televisor off.

"Well, Dr. Ching," he said, "do I turn you over to ben Ezra, or do you talk?"

A new emotion crossed Ching's face. It did not seem to be fear; it was more of a manic defiance.

"You don't understand. I do not care about death, captain," he said. "I have not fled to save my life. Had I remained on Earth, my life would not have been endangered. But—"

"But *what*? You heard the admiral. You have five minutes to make up your mind."

Ching sighed. "It is my work that must go on. *That's*

what they want to stop. Very well, captain, I must take the chance."

"*So?*"

"There is no simple way of explaining it. I have told you that I am working on a corollary to the Special Theory of Relativity. It is the Special Theory of Relativity, as you must know, which limits all speed to the speed of light. Essentially, it means that at the speed of light, mass is infinite, therefore it would take an infinite thrust to accelerate to that limit, and exceeding it would be impossible. But, as I have said, I am working on transfinite substitutions. I hope to evolve an equation—"

"Come to the point, man, come to the point!"

"There is no simple point, captain. I am engaged in the preliminaries of a work that some day may lead to a theoretical means of exceeding the speed of light within the Einsteinian Universe—"

"*An Overdrive!*" shouted Captain Reed.

"Not for a long time," said Ching pedantically. "It—"

But the captain was no longer listening. *An Overdrive!* Countless others had tried before, but Earth thought *this* man was close enough to send ben Ezra sixty light-years to . . .

Reed's trader's brain analyzed the situation with the speed born of commercial instinct. An Overdrive would be the most valuable commodity any trader ever had to sell. The *Outward Bound* could sell it again and again, on each of the sixty-seven planets inhabited by Man, each time commanding a price undreamed of in all history!

And ben Ezra would not take the chance that Ching *wasn't* on the *Outward Bound*. He would have to *know*. He couldn't . . .

"Hang on to something," shouted Peter Reed.

He yelled into the communicator: "Break orbit! *Do it* now!"

"What course, sir?" came the tinny voice.

"Who cares?" roared Reed. "Just get us away from here. Raise the sails, activate the ion drive. Maximum thrust on the reaction rockets! Do it now! Now! *Now!* NOW!"

Jacob ben Ezra shook his head, with a Gallic shrug. Reed was running. What else could he do? But that means he *knows.* It must!

Ben Ezra lit a cigarette. "Change course," he said to his navigator. "Accelerate. Follow them."

"Are we going to attack?" asked Commander Dayan, floating alongside the admiral in the conning globe. His dark, mustachioed face was alight with an eagerness that ben Ezra found distasteful. But then, one could not really blame Dayan. Gunnery officers usually have nothing to do but sit around.

"Not now, at any rate," said the admiral. "Better strap in. Acceleration coming up."

Ben Ezra stared out the viewpoint at the stars.

My stars, he thought. *Our* stars. Mine and Peter Reed's. No wonder my stomach isn't in this. Reed and I have been in space longer than anyone else. In eight hundred years, we've met just five times, and yet . . .

And yet, I feel closer to him than to all the politicians on Earth. What do *they* know about the stars? All they're interested in is preserving their petty little planet's rule over Man. They wouldn't know what an Overdrive would mean. It would mean that Man would have the Galaxy, it would mean that one wouldn't have to be a pariah, a man without a planet or a time, to be a starman.

But is that what they think of? Huh! All they see is the end of Earth's control. Of course, they're right. The only thing that makes Earth undisputed master is *time.* Earth is always generations ahead of the planets. Its head start in technology will hold up forever—

But not if there should be an Overdrive—not if Man could go from Earth to the outer ring in months, not centuries.

He glanced at David Steen, strapped in beside him. Young but intelligent. Some day—

"It's a dirty business, David," he said, almost involuntarily.

"Sir?"

"I said it's a dirty business. I never thought I'd be a hired murderer."

"But, sir, we have orders. It's a military mission. You have no reason to blame—"

"Orders! The orders of men who are all dead by now. The orders of an Earth that doesn't even give a damn about the possibility of Man *really* having the stars. Orders to destroy, orders of a willful, selfish . . . ah!"

"Admiral ben Ezra, our orders are simply to make sure Dr. Ching doesn't escape. Not necessarily to kill anyone. Besides, we're— "

"Yes," said ben Ezra bitterly, "yes, I know. We're soldiers." A new and narrow look came into his large gray eyes.

"But you have a point, David," he said. "Our orders are simply to bring back Ching, and eliminate all knowledge of his work. They don't say anything about blowing up traders, do they? I've not been ordered to kill Peter Reed."

"No, sir."

"No, indeed," said the admiral slowly.

"By all space," he roared, "we're going to carry out our orders! But we're going to do it without killing Captain Reed!"

"Well," said Manuel Olivera, "where do we go from here?"

"Out to the outer ring, I suppose," said Peter Reed. "We are in a very peculiar position. I'm *sure* that ben Ezra won't blast us without boarding. He's got to make sure he gets Ching. But wherever we go, he can plot our course, and be there first. Whatever we do, we've got to do it between now and the next planetfall."

He leaned his face in both hands, propped upon his elbows on the mahogany desk top.

Ching sat nervously in front of him, and Olivera paced the room.

"I still don't see *why* Earth wants to stop you, Dr. Ching," said Olivera.

"In a way, I do," replied Ching. "Positively speaking, the Overdrive would mean the inevitable end of Earth's domination. Without the time differential, Earth would be just another planet."

He managed a small grin. "But on the other hand," he said, "scientifically speaking, they're being most foolish. I am perhaps twenty years from an equation from which an Overdrive could be developed. All I have, right now, is a new point of view. For a thousand years, men have been searching for an Overdrive, always trying to escape from the Einsteinian Universe. Sometimes they look for a mythical thing called hyperspace, or subspace, or the fourth dimension. What I have done, is simply to begin an inquiry, *within* Relativity Theory, modifying not the question, but the substitutions."

"What is all that about?" snapped Olivera.

"I'm not sure yet," said Ching abstractedly. "But basically, if you accept the Special Theory of Relativity, the reason that the speed of light cannot be exceeded is that mass is infinite at the speed of light, hence it would take an infinite force to accelerate it to that speed.

"*But*, if there were a drive whose thrust was a function of the mass it was accelerating, then, as mass increased, thrust would increase, and at the speed of light, theoretically, where mass was infinite, *thrust* would also be infinite. And if the thrust-mass equation involved a suitable exponential function—in theory, anyway—thrust could become *transfinite*."

"Making it possible to go faster than light!" said Olivera excitedly. "Yes, yes, Dr. Ching. If there ever is an Overdrive, it will have to be developed along those lines! Tell me, how close are you?"

Ching laughed bitterly. "As I said, perhaps as much as twenty years away. Who can tell? Right now, all I have is a point of view, a direction in which to proceed. I must experiment with substitutions, then I must develop the proper thrust-mass equation. And at that point, the real work only begins. I must then develop a theoretical basis for a drive that can utilize the thrust-mass equation, a drive, where, not only does thrust depend on mass, but in the precise proper function as well. It's a very long way off."

"But man, it would be an Overdrive!"

"Not even then," said Ching. "That would be the end of *my* work, and the beginning of someone else's. I am not a practical scientist. Someone else would have to take my equations and develop the actual Overdrive."

He sighed and shrugged. "That's why I can't understand why Earth won't let me be. All I want is to be free to develop my equations. It's my whole life! I could build no drive, I—"

"When you rule an empire of more than sixty planets, over a time differential of over two hundred years," said Captain Peter Reed, "you must plan and plot far ahead. You must take a very long view."

"Well, now that we know what we've got," said Olivera, "what are we going to do about it?"

Captain Reed drummed his fingers nervously on the desk top. "I'll be damned if I know," he said. "Fact: an Overdrive would be the greatest commercial coup in history. Fact: it would take about twenty years to develop one, from the start we have. And finally, fact: we will *have* to let ben Ezra aboard on our next planetfall. He'll be waiting for us, and there'll be no escaping. That's why he's let us get this far. This, gentlemen, is what is known as a bind."

"Time," said Ching absently, "why does it always come down to time? The Overdrive wouldn't even be necessary, if it weren't for the time factor. Then Earth would've let me continue my work unmolested. And now, it's a matter of time before ben Ezra gets me, too little time—"

"You're a mathematician," said Peter Reed. "You should know that time underlies the Universe, space . . . history—"

"Time," said Olivera. "Peter, we've just *got* to save the Overdrive! It's bigger than us; it's bigger even than the *Outward Bound*. It's bigger than Earth! We've just got to buy the time, *somehow*."

"Twenty years," said Peter Reed. "In twenty *days*, we'll

have to go into Deep Sleep, or we'll run the risk of depleting our oxygen, our food, our water. And when we come out, Jacob ben Ezra will be waiting for us."

A slow, grim smile parted Ching's tight lips. "Twenty years—" he said slowly. "Captain, where are we heading?"

"Out to the outer ring, maybe to Toehold."

"And how long will such a trip take?"

"About a hundred and twenty years."

"Captain," said Ching, "we don't *all* have to go into Deep Sleep, do we? There would be enough food and air for, say, one man to stay awake, for say, *twenty years?*"

Peter Reed suddenly became aware of the feverish glow of the abstract fanatic in Ching's eyes.

"You mean you would stay out of Deep Sleep? You would die in space, in the nothing between the stars? You would be alone, *utterly alone*, for twenty years."

"I am well aware of the consequences, captain. Nevertheless, it would enable me to complete my work. *That* is all that matters. Could it be done?"

Reed stared wonderingly at the small man. "Sure. There'd be plenty of food and air for one man to do it. By a factor of ten, at least."

"Well then, captain?"

"Are you sure, Dr. Ching? It's one thing to talk about it now, but when you've been alone for one, five, ten years—"

"I am willing to take that chance."

"Well . . . we could rig up a cubicle so that you could go into Deep Sleep any time it got to be too much for you—"

"Why, he might complete his work, and still make it to Toehold!" cried Olivera.

"He might," said Reed. "Of course, even then, we would still have the problem of dealing with ben Ezra—"

"Oh, space, Peter!" yelled Olivera. "One thing at a time. This is it! This is the *only* way!"

"I suppose you're right, Manny. Have your boys set up the necessary automatics. Let Dr. Ching get acquainted with our computer."

"Thank you, captain," said Ching. "We will beat them, after all."

"Perhaps," said Reed. Is your *we* the same as my *we*, he thought; is your *them* the same as my *them?*

Olivera had ceased his pacing. He appeared lost in thought.

"Manny," said the captain, reading his old friend's mood. "Manny, what is it?"

"Dr. Ching," said Olivera, "what will we have when our work is finished, I mean, what end result?"

"Why, I hope, an equation giving a principle upon which an Overdrive could be built," said Ching gravely.

"A *principle*," said Olivera slowly. "An *equation*. But not *plans*, not *blueprints*, not even a schematic diagram."

"What do you expect of me?" said Ching plaintively. "I'm a mathematician, not an engineer. Such a thing would take a pragmatic scientist, working hand in hand with—"

"Yes," said Manuel Olivera, "so it would."

"*Manny!*" shouted the captain. "You wouldn't—"

"I must, Peter, I must! Someone must. We've got to have more than an equation, when we run into ben Ezra. If we've got pragmatic plans, we can send out all six of our rigs to Toehold. It's an undeveloped planet, they'd never be able to do anything with an equation. But plans— And ben Ezra would have to destroy seven targets, instead of one. Someone would get through."

"It would not be as bad for him, captain, as it will be for me," said Ching. "He could stay in Deep Sleep until I was ready for him. It would only be a few years for him."

"All right, Manny," said Reed, "you win."

But even as he gave the orders for setting up the automatics, something was nagging at the back of his mind.

Disperse the plans indeed! Sacrifice the *Outward Bound!* There must be a better way. Perhaps, ben Ezra could be fooled—just this once. What if he *got* Ching? Might it not be possible to convince him that Ching had never talked? Perhaps, perhaps—

Even as the nothingness of Deep Sleep overtook him,

Peter Reed was still dreaming of the greatest commercia
coup in history.

Jacob ben Ezra was dissatisfied, and he didn't know
why. His ship was already orbiting Toehold, the *Outward
Bound* had been spotted, a week away, all was set, and
within eight days, he would have Ching.

But somehow, he felt dissatisfied.

"David," he said. "I feel *dirty*."

"But, sir, why?"

Ben Ezra lit a cigarette, the thirtieth of the twenty-fou
hour period. As far as he could remember, it was a recore
for him.

"We're men of space, David," he said. "We're no mor
emotionally bound to Earth than Reed is. *Homo Inter
stellarus*, I think of us as. An Overdrive is something w
should welcome, not suppress."

The young commander was silent. To him, ben Ezr
knew, orders were orders. He had been born aboard ship
the Fleet was all he knew or cared about. And the Flee
was an agent of Earth.

"Don't you see, David? Of course you don't! Our dut
as officers is clear—to obey orders. But we have a duty a
men, as well. And, by space, that duty is to preserve th
Overdrive!"

"You would disobey direct orders, sir?"

"No, dammit! I've been in this service all my adult life
Orders must be obeyed. If the Fleet decided to take th
law into its own hands, we'd be no better than pirates. No
David, orders must be obeyed. But that doesn't mean
have to like it. It won't help me sleep any better, o
enable me to smoke fewer of these infernal cigarettes."

"No, sir."

"I almost hope . . . I almost hope—"

"What, sir?"

Ben Ezra grinned humorlessly. "I almost hope Pete
Reed can figure out a good way to trick me. I'd almost lik
to see him get out of it."

*   *   *

Manuel Olivera held the sheaf of papers in front of him. "Seven years!" he said. "Seven awful, lonely years, the two of us working together. But here it is, here it is!"

Peter Reed looked in wonderment at Olivera. His hair was now flecked with gray. He had lost fifteen pounds. But the greatest change was in his eyes. There was a haunted fire, an emptiness. What those seven years must've been like, thought Reed.

"And now he's dead," said Olivera. "Dead of old age."

"But did he get into the cubicle?" asked Reed. It was essential to have Ching's body.

"Yes, he got in. But he was a broken old man. Even as I watched him go under, I knew he would never survive the thaw." Olivera sighed heavily. "It was hard for me, but what was it for him! Twelve years! Twelve years *alone!* It was a full twelve years before he thawed me out."

"But he did it," said Reed.

"Yes, he did it."

"And now we have ben Ezra to deal with. He's already orbiting Toehold. Six days—Manny?"

"What, Peter?"

"I don't suppose we could rig up an Overdrive? We have plans, blueprints—"

"Not a chance. There's a good three or four years' work, technical experimentation needed, and even if we had the time, we need things we couldn't possibly make ourselves."

Reed shrugged. "Just thought I'd ask. We're sitting on top of a mint—"

"A mint!" roared Olivera. "A mint! Is that all it means to you, a *commodity* to sell? Peter, I didn't think you were such a fool. Is that what Ching died for? To line our pockets?"

"Ching died for that mysterious thing called abstract knowledge, and you know it, Manny," said the captain. "He didn't care any more about giving the Overdrive to Man than he did about the profit!"

"Profit! You think you can make a profit out of this? Think, Peter, think. What will happen to the *Outward Bound* when Man has the Overdrive? We'll be finished.

All tradeships will be finished. We owe our existence
the time lag, as much as Earth's rule does. I thought y₀
realized that from the beginning. I thought you wer
willing to sacrifice it for Man. I . . . I was a bigger fo
than you are!"

It hit Reed like a piledriver. Manny was right. T
Overdrive meant the end of the tradeships. Selling th
Overdrive would ultimately be the end of the *Outwa*
Bound, of the way of life he had followed for close to
thousand objective years.

Peter Reed knew that if the Overdrive became know
he would be the last captain of the *Outward Bound*.

"You're right, Manny," he said. "I suppose that solv
our problem. We'll just give it all to ben Ezra."

"*Will we now*, captain?" sneered Olivera. "Even if y₀
don't care what this means to Man, think of your ow
hide. What do you think ben Ezra will do if he knows *u*
know?"

"Why, he'll—"

"Exactly. He'll kill every one of us. Or at least haul
back to Earth, where the best we can expect is to l
imprisoned for the rest of our lives. *Without trial*."

Reed cursed. It was true. The only thing to do, is
play it through. *At least, if we can fool ben Ezra, I c₀*
make my own decision.

"Well, captain?"

"Destroy those plans. But first, microengrave them ₀
some part of the ship, a wall, a toilet, anywhere. Dor
even tell me where. I don't want anyone but you to kno
till this is over. Then destroy our transmitters. Make
look like they've been out ever since Maxwell, but make
look like an accident."

"What about Ching? Should we destroy the body? May
we can convince ben Ezra that he was never aboard."

"Not a chance. I've got it! Rig his cubicle so that it lo₀
like the machinery failed, and he died of old age, *insi*
the cubicle. Can you do it?"

Olivera puckered his brows. "Won't be easy," he sai
"but I think so."

"Well, that's all we can do until ben Ezra boards."

"You're going to try and convince ben Ezra that Ching ever talked? You expect him to be so stupid as to swallow that?"

Peter Reed licked his lips.

"No," he said, "but I know Jacob ben Ezra. What I'm thinking on, is that he'll try and convince himself."

"To what do I owe this pleasure, Jacob?" said Peter Reed, sitting behind the big mahogany desk.

"To what— Peter, you *know* I've followed you all the way from Maxwell," said Admiral Jacob ben Ezra.

"All the way from Maxwell!" exclaimed Peter Reed. "Why in blazes didn't you give me a call on the . . . oh, al! I keep forgetting that the radio's out of commission. Then you *did* call me?"

Ben Ezra looked at his side, and then at the ceiling. "Yes, I did call you. Is your radio *really* out of order?"

"Freak accident," said Reed. "Meteor hit the radio shack. Small one, but enough to smash things up. Say, you wouldn't have a spare F-46E transmitter housing?"

"I'll see what I can do," said ben Ezra coolly.

"Roger, get us some drinks, will you?"

Roger Reed produced four of the hot-cold cocktails.

"These are most amusing, Jacob," said Captain Reed.

"I left Earth about the same time you did, this time, Peter," said ben Ezra. He lit a cigarette.

"Still smoking those filthy things, eh?" said Peter Reed conversationally.

"*Captain* Reed," said ben Ezra, "aren't you even interested in why I've followed you for a hundred light-years?"

Reed laughed. "Something sinister, Jacob? I assumed that when you hailed us at Maxwell, and we didn't answer, you thought we were in trouble, and—"

"Really, Peter!" said ben Ezra. "*I'll* come to the point, even if you won't. Do you have a passenger?"

Peter Reed frowned. "So that's it," he said. "Look,

Jacob, we're fully insured for this kind of thing. Milli
credit liability policy. It's a hefty premium, and the chanc
of it ever happening are so slight, but—"

"What in blazes are you talking about?"

"Why our passenger, of course," said Reed bland
"Isn't that what *you're* talking about? I sure as hell do
know how you found out, but I assure you it was a legi
mate accident, and we're fully covered."

"Covered? Accident?"

"Oh, come on, Jacob, stop playing cat and mouse w
me!" snapped Reed. "All right, all right, if that's the w
you want it, I'll tell you the whole thing as if you did
know what happened."

"I certainly wish you would," said ben Ezra.

"Well, we *did* have a passenger. Picked him up
Maxwell. Strange little fellow called Ching pen Yee. Th
Director, what was his name?"

"Lazlo Horvath," said David Steen.

"Yes, yes, Horvath. The dirty crook. Told me some ki
of fish story about how this Ching was some kind
important scientist. Well, ordinarily, you couldn't fool
with a thing like that, but as you know, we have the fo
field to sell this trip, and Horvath simply didn't ha
anything better to pay for it, so I took a chance on th
Ching. What a joke!"

"Joke?"

"Yes," said Reed. "Scientist? Why, the man was a ravi
lunatic! Classic case. Paranoid delusions. Thought the e
tire Terran hegemony was out to get him. Literally. N
only that, but delusions of grandeur as well. Why,
thought he was the greatest thing since Einstein! Secret
immortality, conversion bomb, all the usual mythi
nonsense."

"A madman?" said ben Ezra, his eyes narrowing to sli

"What a madman!" exclaimed the captain. "To top it
off . . . why, do you know what, Jacob? He thought he h
the secret of Overdrive as well!"

"*Really*," said ben Ezra, perhaps a shade too dryly.

"I swear, I expected him to pull the Philosopher's Stone self out of his pocket!" laughed Peter Reed.

"Indeed."

"Where is this Dr. Ching?" said David Steen.

Ben Ezra flashed him a dirty look.

"Ah, you know as well as I do, Jacob, don't you? A one in a million accident, but it *did* happen. The automatics in is Deep Sleep cubicle malfunctioned. He died of old age n the last hop."

"Died?" said ben Ezra slowly.

"I assure you, Jacob, there was no lapse in safety procedures, and we are fully covered."

"To be sure," said ben Ezra. "To be sure." His eyes vere even more unreadable than usual.

"Do you by any chance have the body?" he said.

"Yes," replied Reed. "It's still in the cubicle."

"Good. Mr. Ching had relations on Galdwin, which . . . r . . . is our next stop. We will take the body to them. David, get a detail."

"But, sir—"

"*David!*"

"Yes, sir."

"A most unfortunate accident, Peter," said ben Ezra.

"Yes."

"But you say the man was mad anyway," said ben Ezra, ringing his face close to Reed's.

Reed stared back. "Very mad," he said evenly.

"You are *quite* sure?" said ben Ezra.

Reed drummed his fingers nervously on the desk. Ben zra's glance fell to Reed's hand, for a short moment. eed's gaze followed. Then they were staring in each ther's eyes again.

"Quite sure," said Peter Reed.

"I see," said Jacob ben Ezra. The corners of his mouth urled upward in the slightest suggestion of a grin.

Reed's mouth went dry.

"Well, Peter," said ben Ezra, suddenly and unexpectdly convivial, "it's been nice meeting you again. Very ice. But I really must be going."

"Sorry to see you leave so soon," said Reed.

"I'll bet you are!" said ben Ezra with a little laugh.

He walked to the door and opened it.

"Good-by, Peter," he said.

"Good-by, Jacob."

As he stepped through the doorway, the admiral swiveled his neck to face Reed.

"Perhaps," he said dryly, *"I'll be seeing you a lot soone
than you think I think."* Then he was gone.

"What in space did he mean by that, Dad . . . sir?
asked Roger Reed.

The captain stared at the empty doorway.

"I think I know," he said, "but I'm sure I *want*
know."

Peter Reed floated by the viewport, watching ben Ezra
ship break orbit.

He's really going, Reed thought. But he did not feel lik
congratulating himself.

He *knew*. He *had* to know. Jacob would never hav
swallowed a cock-and-bull story like that unless he wante
to. Well, he's got Ching's body, and he'll take it back
Earth, and that'll be the end of it. The Overdrive is min

But what, he thought, am I going to do with it? The sa
thing would be to destroy the plans . . . or—

It'd take time and money to build it. The *Outwar
Bound* could never do it alone, but there are planets ou
here on the outer ring who'd do the work, and not ask to
many questions.

Or there's Maxwell. Horvath is dead, but there's never
dearth of his kind. The Overdrive would bring a fantast
price from someone like that. But what would he do wit
it? Rule the Galaxy?

The Galaxy . . . who can say anything about the Galaxy
Man has seen such a small piece of it. Naturally, th
chance of running into another intelligent race has bee
nil, as long as we were confined to such a small volume
space. But now— What exists in the center?

Without realizing it, Peter Reed had made his decisior

Ching had died for the Overdrive, thought Reed. Manny's given seven years of his life for it, seven lonely years.

And Jacob—Jacob took the biggest chance of his career to give Man the Galaxy.

Captain Reed sighed resignedly. One doesn't go in for this kind of life unless one is something of a romantic, he thought, no matter what I may say about profits.

What have all the profits been for? Just to keep the *Outward Bound* in space. Why stay in space? What logical answer is there?

Reed remembered a quotation from a man thousands of years dead, so long his name had been forgotten.

"Why climb mountains?" they had asked the mountaineer.

"Because they are there," he had said.

Why go to the stars? *Because they are there.* It was enough.

Manny understood that. In a way, perhaps Ching understood it, too.

And Jacob had risked a thousand-year career so that Man could have the Galaxy. *Because it was there.*

And can I do less, thought Peter Reed. A few hundred light years of space is no substitute for the Universe.

Roger may never be captain of the *Outward Bound*. The twilight of the tradeships has already begun—

Reed looked sadly out the 'port at ben Ezra's receding ship. Good-by, Jacob, he thought, good-by to a way of life a thousand years old.

But Man must have the Overdrive.

Jacob ben Ezra watched the green disk of Toehold slowly recede. Hidden on the outer side of the planet now, was the *Outward Bound*.

By now, he thought, Peter will have decided to build an Overdrive.

He laughed softly to himself. We old foxes understand each other. We both have our excuses—Peter his profits, me my duty.

But when it comes down to it, we're both in space for the same reason, and neither of us can put it into words.

So Earth will be satisfied. They'll have the body of poor Ching. Little will they know, little will they know, until it's too late.

There are planets out here that will ask few questions. Peter has the force field to sell, and for that, he can get his Overdrive built. And after that—

After that, in the short run, who knows? Ben Ezra shifted his gaze to the vast, multi-colored cloud of stars that is the center of the Galaxy.

In the short run, who knows, he thought. Who cares? But in the long run—

In the long run, Man will have the Galaxy, perhaps not to himself, *certainly* not to himself, but have it he will.

The admiral put out his half-finished cigarette. I've been in this business so long that I'm a legend, he thought. How ironic that the thing I can be most . proud of is something that, once the Overdrive is a reality, will be called a failure.

He looked at the cloud of stars. They seemed to be looking right back. Come on, they seemed to say, we've been waiting.

A failure— Maybe you could call it that—

He grinned at the far glow of the Center.

"Coming!" he said.

Editor's Introduction To:

IN the REALM OF THE HEART, IN THE WORLD OF THE KNIFE
Wayne Wightman

Robert Conquest's important book, *Harvest of Sorrow* (1986, Oxford University Press), tells how Lenin, and later Stalin, deliberately murdered more than ten million people by inducing an artificial famine in the Ukraine. Their cruelties knew no bounds: the Red Army even took the shovels, so that peasant children not only could not plant food, but could not bury their parents after they had starved.

Conquest opens this way: "Fifty years ago as I write these words, the Ukraine and the Ukrainian Cossack and other areas to its east—a great stretch of territory with some forty million inhabitants—was like one vast Belsen. A quarter of the rural population—men, women, and children—lay dead or dying, the rest in various stages of debilitation with no strength to bury their families or neighbors. At the same time (as at Belsen), well-fed squads of police or party officials supervised the victims."

Lenin probably believed he was helping mankind. It is doubtful whether Stalin believed in anything at all. Both were singularly effective not only at killing people, but at staying in power.

Acton tells us that all power tends to corrupt. Absolute power corrupts absolutely.

Others have not been so certain. Thomas Carlyle welcomes the hero as ruler, one whose "place is with the stars of heaven. To this man death is not a bugbear; to this man life is already as earnest and awful, and beautiful, and terrible, as death."

IN THE REALM OF THE HEART, IN THE WORLD OF THE KNIFE

Wayne Wightman

Obese and sweating, Errit Stattor strolled smiling through his outer office, reviewing those who served him. He tried to be humble. The archaic incandescent lighting made his aides look paper-yellow, hollow-eyed, and slack. When he entered those immense and weirdly anachronistic stained-glass doors, all voices ceased, all movement stopped, and in a single motion, everyone stood. They bowed, and as he passed by them, he smiled and nodded.

"Please," he said, "please sit—these formalities . . ."

But they remained standing and bowing. Stattor sighed. "Your devotion impresses me," he said, "but . . . please . . ."

No one sat, and he was impressed, but today, as he reviewed them, smiling, the fat of his cheeks pushed up in tight sweat-sheened balls beneath his eyes, he had more reason to appear pleased than they could know. Today, at 11:00 A.M., Usko Imani was going to be brought to him. She was the last woman who had voluntarily made love to him, and he had not seen her in twenty years, as of today. Seeing her, speaking to her, was to be a sort of anniversary gift to both of them. It was one of the several loose ends in his life that remained to be tied up.

As Stattor crossed through his office, sweat ran in crooked streams out of his scalp, and he smelled of deceased generations of sweat-loving bacteria. It was unfortunate, he knew; he did what he could about it, but nothing helped much. No one mentioned it.

With the yellow light hazing the air, Stattor's two dozen aides remained standing beside their desks, bowed and dead-faced, waiting for him to complete his passage among them.

Supervisor Stattor surveyed the nerve center of his domain, the place where he could order any action on any of twenty thousand worlds, and today he felt not only a peculiar sense of serenity beyond that which he normally experienced, but he also felt one of those increasingly frequent twinges of immortality. It seemed as though something grandly mysterious was about to happen to him. He suspected that it would not happen to him today—but then, it *would* happen, and it *would* be a surprise. . . . And it would be strange and wonderful, and this entire branch of humanity would know of it, because he was Errit Stattor, Supervisor of United Tarassis, and he had opened to mankind the treasures of alien technologies, and he was admired and respected on more worlds than he could comprehend. Without him, they knew and he knew that they would have become backward, a slave race, trashlife.

"Please," he said, "be comfortable. Treat me as anyone else."

No one moved, and Stattor appreciated their devotion.

He nodded and smiled at his personnel and left them in the yellow-aired room. The crystalline door of his private office sensed his presence, opened, and he passed grandly through it.

Alone, he folded forward and clasped his distended guts in his arms. His intestines felt like a tangle of fire, and waves of pain flowed up his legs and pooled in his thighs, reservoirs of agony. Being chain-whipped, he thought, would probably not hurt more. After so many organ replacements, so much reconstructive surgery, and with fifteen or twenty biomechs floating somewhere beneath his tides of fat, with all this, he could not walk far, or sleep well, or think as sharply as he once could. But he no longer needed to.

From a dozen light-years above the hub of the galaxy, in this space station that housed over 14,000 workers, he directed the ebb and flow of wealth and workers from world to world, eliminating obstacles and annoyances as this part of humanity moved in a swarming tide across the galaxy.

Stattor forced himself erect. The sight of his office usually soothed him. Standing just inside the doorway, on the carpeted area, where those who came to see him would stand, he relished the awesomeness of his design. The entry area was carpeted with the textured skin of some alien beast or other, but this was just a small part of his vast office, which was inside a transparent blister on one of the non-rotating rings of the station. To approach Stattor's gleaming desk, one had to step onto the thermoplast floor where underfoot, looking close enough to touch, stars and gasses defiled the purity of the void.

When one came to do business with Stattor, to ask his aid or intercession, one felt suspended in space, and Stattor would sit at his shining black desk, smiling, saying, "Please, allow me to help you. Ask what you need." And behind him, through the transparency, the frozen hub of the galaxy was smeared across half the sky. Just above his head and to the right was a globular cluster that looked too perfect to be real. Sitting there, like that, listening and smiling, Stattor listened and judged.

But now he hobbled to his specially designed chair, sank into it, and felt it adjust to him, caress him, comfort and hold him.

He rummaged through one of the desk drawers, pawing over his pharmaceuticals for help with his legs. They had been tingling since he had awakened. His right shoulder felt bruised for some unknown reason, and for three days now, his hands trembled. There were so many things in the drawer that he knocked it shut and leaned back and tried to breathe deeply. Phlegm rattled in his throat.

He thought of food. Sometimes that helped. He so

loved to eat, to chew, and churn his tongue through the flavors and then to feel them slide down his throat and enter his body. . . .

He had eaten with Usko Imani many times, long ago, in other days. Her fingers were long, delicate, and had wrapped like flower vines around . . .

He thought of food. He knew it was a weakness. Aside from opening up a new world of technology, Stattor loved nothing more than feeling thick sweet creams slicking the insides of his cheeks—or the oily spiciness of rare meat flooding across his tongue and through his mouth. In the privacy of his opulent living quarters, he would sometimes hold in his hand a cluster of some exotic fruit and slowly crush it and drink the cool juices from the cup of his palm. He adored these moments.

His stomach rumbled and burned. He wondered if Usko Imani was as close to death as he was. She had been imprisoned for seventeen years now at a labor camp. Most inmates lived only half that long. Something tickled in Stattor's throat. As he coughed it up and reswallowed it, needles of pain arced from his chest down to his arms. From his tunic he took a beta-blocker and swallowed it dry. When the pain subsided, he reached, without looking, to touch the call button on the autovox. He wanted to call Zallon, his chief aide, to ask about Usko, but his fingers missed the call button completely and fell through empty air.

The autovox had been moved.

Zallon had rearranged the position of the autovox without asking him.

Stattor remembered mentioning two days previously that it sometimes hurt his arm to reach across the desk to it. So Zallon had taken it upon himself to move it to the corner of the desk nearest Stattor's right hand. And he hadn't asked. And, Stattor noticed, in its current position, it blocked his view through the curved plastic bubble of a particularly attractive nebula, the Stattor Nebula. From the comfort of his chair, he could only see the upper right corner of it.

What had Zallon been thinking?

Stattor fumbled his numbed fingers over the face of the autovox and depressed the call button. "Zallon," he said, "come to me."

The door to the outer office instantly irised open and the chief of staff entered, his flat eyes shrouded in the shadows of his eye-ridges. His eyelids were very thick, as though he had some exotic disease. "Yes sir?"

"The autovox . . ." Stattor said, raising his eyebrows and putting an apologetic smile on his face. "I reached for it, and . . . it had been moved. I know you must have gone to some trouble." He imagined that he looked like anyone's uncle.

Zallon's throat convulsed as he swallowed. "If it caused you any inconvenience, Supervisor, I deeply regret—"

"Is Usko Imani going to be here by eleven?"

"Yes, Supervisor." His shrouded eyes glittered with fear. "She's on the station now. They're cleaning her up."

"Fine." Stattor smiled pleasantly at Zallon. "Bring me the dispersal list. I'll look at that before she gets here."

"Yes, Supervisor." Zallon nodded and quickly departed. The crystalline door irised shut behind him.

Again, Stattor glanced at the repositioned autovox. It completely blocked the lower left corner of his nebula. He deeply regretted that, and something would have to be done. There were few pleasures left in his life, and the view from his desk was one of them. Zallon should have consulted him. Something should be done.

He leaned back in his chair and it adjusted to him. Lately he had felt more comfortable alone, much unlike the old days. In his thoughts he saw the face of Usko Imani, twenty years ago, when he had last seen her, several years before he had ordered her arrest and imprisonment at an outer world mining camp where alien lowlife and criminal humans worked side by side, clawing chromium ore out of subterranean dirt. Now, today, he would see her again and have the chat he had planned for two decades.

Ghostly silent, Zallon returned and moved across the

carpeted entryway onto the transparent floor. He laid the list precisely in front of Stattor.

"If my actions have displeased you, Supervisor—"

At the slightest motion of Stattor's head, Zallon left the office, silent as air, the door closing behind him.

Usko Imani had been beautiful. Once they had made love, and he remembered those moments more clearly than he remembered the day he made himself Supervisor of United Tarassis. He remembered her hands and her lips—he remembered the way she laughed and the way, that one time, her hands had touched him.

He fingered the dispersal list, not looking at it, and let his thoughts drift over the early years when she and Stattor and a handful of others had struggled in the corporate courts, suing for the right to borrow technology from alien cultures, and then maneuvering to set up United Tarassis. She had been undeviating in her loyalty and purpose and as idealistic as she had been beautiful. And, in the end, after the tired degenerate government had granted their petition, United Tarassis moved on hundreds of alien worlds, taking what was useful and selling the rest. Finally, United Tarassis had become the government.

He remembered the day of the court's final decision in their favor . . . they had celebrated, he and Usko alone, and without expecting it or knowing what it would lead to, they had made love—for the first and only time. He had been different then. The world had been new and wide and various, and in the unknown he saw beauty and richness and joy.

His eyes stopped on the repositioned autovox. He wondered what other action Zallon might be capable of without telling him.

He gazed at the list lying on the desk before him . . . the dispersal list . . . it consisted of the names of those who no longer functioned effectively in the workings of the corporation. It was a grim task, looking over the names—but he did it, sparing some nameless underling the guilt of passing the names on to the Action Committee. But Stattor was used to it. These were the names of the unreliable and

the potentially unreliable who would be sedated and shot
into the core of the space station where their component
molecules would separate and give up their energies to
power the station's lights for several evenings, provide
heat and comfort and enable the work of probing distant
worlds to go on. Here, nothing was wasted.

He usually gave the lists only a cursory glance and then
forwarded them to the Action Committee. It was his pre-
rogative, of course, to put a checkmark beside the name of
any person he decided to exempt from execution.

Most of the names were unfamiliar. Blisson, E., . . .
Lanyon, R., . . . Blodian, A.

Aros Blodian was on the list? Stattor remembered him
from twenty or more years ago. He and Usko and a dozen
others had worked for the same goals, for the advancement of humankind through the use of alien resources.
But then . . . Stattor vaguely remembered ordering Blodian
to be confined for some reason or other—but the recollec-
tion was unclear. And now one of the Division heads was
asking for Blodian's dispersal.

Stattor turned his chair to face the galaxy-smeared void.
Those old days always seemed warm and fragrant when
Stattor thought of them, and for a few moments, the
constriction in his chest loosened and he could breathe
easier. Blodian had been one of the inner members of the
movement until . . . until what?

Stattor gazed above the glow of the galaxy's hub into the
emptiness and remembered one evening in particular,
sitting with Aros beside a rippled lake, the purple sky
paling to a cream color over the rounded mountains. They
had been discussing the construction of probe stations like
the one in which Stattor now sat and meditated on the
loose ends of his life.

He and Aros were on a planet that had evolved only
vegetation, and there, amid the tree-ferns and thick-leafed
shrubs, beside the warm water of the lake, they had felt
comfortable to sit without much talking and to listen to the
water lap at the pebbled shore. The air had been rich with

the smells of earth, and for the moment, everything was beauty, quiet, and pleasure.

And Usko had been there, he remembered suddenly. Yes, Usko had been there, and he remembered her laughing—she had come up from the shore, laughing and carrying a thick bouquet of colorful weeds. How strange that he should remember such details now, from so long ago and so far away, from such an ancient evening.

Stattor took up a pen and started to place a checkmark next to Blodian's name. For old times' sake. He had been a friend. And now he was probably old and gnarled and with none of the fire he had had in former days when he would take on the most dangerous of schemes, and through courage alone, force them to success.

The autovox chirped.

Stattor reached for it, without looking, and his hand dropped through the air, touching nothing. He glared at the machine.

"What," he said, barely parting his teeth when he spoke.

Zallon's voice was restrained. "Usko Imani has arrived, Supervisor."

Stattor inhaled deeply. His stomach rumbled and his back ached. What would she think of him? Would she recoil at his fatness? He wanted her to like him. Would she be gray and old and unrecognizable?

Stattor tried to calm himself by gazing again into space.

The churning hub of the galaxy lay frozen before him. It seemed as though it had paused for the period of his lifetime so he could look upon it, become familiar with it, and use it for humankind. Years ago, he could stare at those trailing billows of stars for hours, but, now, in truth, the part he most liked to look upon was the area above the galaxy, beyond the sprinkle of globular clusters, higher up, where there was darkness, emptiness, and only the occasional blemish of a distant smear of stars. The smoothness of the black, the absence of matter, of life, those were the things that now appealed to him. Something grand approached.

Stattor turned his chair back to face the door from the

waiting room, positioned his feet beneath his weight, braced his hands on his desk, and stood.

In the instant before he spoke to the autovox, he thought of her lips and hands, of how once she had looked at him and how once she had touched him. . . .

"Send her in," he said.

In the several seconds before the door irised open, he started to feel oppressed by the heaviness of his body, and he felt the rolls of fat pressing against each other around his neck and around his stomach. A dozen pains sparkled in his ankles, and it was no wonder, he thought, that his body was trying so desperately to die.

The door opened.

Usko Imani had been a square-shouldered, strong-bodied woman with long, tight-curled blond hair, a woman whose footing on the earth had been as solid as her belief in Stattor and the blending of alien and human technologies. As long as Stattor had known her, all those years, he had never suspected that she ever felt any doubt about what she was doing or her purpose in the world. When it came to her belief in utilizing alien ways, she never hesitated, whatever it cost her.

But now she hesitated. She stood in the doorway, stooped and gray-skinned, her hair a thinning shag of frizz across parts of her scalp. Inside the person who stood on the carpeted entryway, staring at the transparent floor before her, Stattor could detect only the faintest ghost of who she had been.

She glanced to either side of the doorway, then across to Stattor, and then behind him at the shimmering hub of the galaxy.

"Come in," he said, gesturing at one of the chairs. "Please."

Tentatively, she moved into the room, placing her feet on the transparent floor, as though she might disturb the universe with her passage. She sat down very slowly, her black prison garb pulling tight at her bony joints. She allowed her gaze to meet his.

Stattor smiled. "It's been a long time," he said. "How many years?"

"Twenty, I guess," she said unsurely. Her voice was gravelly and low and the right side of her mouth drooped when she spoke. She folded her knobby hands on her lap. "A long time."

Stattor lowered his mass into his chair. The pain in his ankles was replaced by a tight compressed feeling in his spine. "A long time," he repeated. "Twenty years, exactly, as of today."

"I didn't know that," she said. "I didn't think I'd see you again."

"Life is mysterious, isn't it? I've been feeling the need to tie up some loose ends," he said. He paused and nodded his head backward at the stars. "Up here, apart from any world, it's easy to forget one's past. By the way, do you remember Aros Blodian? I was thinking of him today."

Her old face looked vaguely surprised. "Of course I remember him. Where is he? Is he here?"

"I was thinking of a time when the three of us were at a lake, it was evening, and you were coming up from the shore. You were laughing. It's kind of a mental snapshot."

She looked at him blankly. "I can't remember."

Stattor shifted in his chair. His stomach burned a little on one side. His hands ached again too. "You probably wonder why I sent you to prison. You hadn't done anything disloyal to United Tarassis."

She nodded. "I wondered," she said slowly, the one side of her mouth dead and unmoving, "but I always understood."

"You understood?"

"Sometimes things have to be done that seem unfair. The individual sometimes has to sacrifice himself in that way, for the benefit of others."

"You never grew bitter? You never cursed me for your years in prison?"

She glanced at the floor, seemed uncomfortable, and moved in her chair with a tired nervousness. "It's because of you that our race has advanced to its position. You led us in the exploration of alien cultures. If my imprisonment helped humankind—and it did, or you wouldn't have put me there—then I have lived my life just as I always wanted."

With one finger, Stattor wiped the sweat out of the fold of skin beside his mouth. "I had forgotten how devoted you were. Tell me what life in prison was like."

"In camp, we got news every week," she said, "so I know what you've accomplished in all these years." She cleared her throat and ran the back of one hand across her temple, as though she were pushing back her short bristly hair. "I was in a support camp on Perda, 37th Sector. It's a cold place." She held out her left hand for him to see the missing fingertips. "We had aliens working in the chromium mines nearby. In my camp, we sewed shirts and pants for them, and in the last six years, we made shoes once every two months. Since we got heaters in a year ago, I could cut out ninety-six pairs of soles a day." She reversed her folded hands. "I have friends there. . . . I haven't been lonely. But it is cold. The ground is frozen most of the year." Her face brightened momentarily. "There're birds there." She shook her head as though chastising herself. "They were insects, but they were so big we thought of them as birds. Two weeks a year, in the warm season, they migrate south, and they sing." She looked weakened, haggard and old, but she did not look unhappy. "In ways I don't understand, my imprisonment served the higher destiny of mankind. I'm not bitter."

"You suffered," Stattor said.

"Everyone suffers."

"Have I suffered?" Stattor said, spreading his arms at the stars.

"You guided us." Her voice was firm. "Without you, we would still be in our provincial human backwater, weak and struggling for any step of progress."

Stattor leaned forward on his desk. He was smiling. The desk creaked under his weight. "You no longer have to suffer, Usko. I've set up a physical rehabilitation program for you, and when you've recovered, you'll be given living quarters on the world of your choosing, transportation privileges wherever you want to go, and an allotment of 500,000 credits a year."

She stared at him, and it seemed that for a full half minute she did not register what he had said.

"How much did they pay you on Perda?" he asked.

She swallowed heavily, her chin dipping as she did so. "They put 200 a year into an account for each of us."

"And how much have you earned so far?"

She shook her head helplessly. "I can't figure like that anymore."

"You may not know," Stattor said, "there's a severance tax of 28 percent. A prisoner who completes his sentence is required to pay for the food he has eaten." He smiled. "The severance tax was my idea."

"If it hadn't been necessary for our cause, you wouldn't have done it."

Stattor shook his head. This was the Usko Imani of his memories. When he had doubts, he had only to speak to her; her vision was intensely single-minded, sincere, and idealistic. She was unique. In part, that was why he had sent her to Perda.

"Would you like a drink?" Stattor asked suddenly.

"I haven't had a drink in—"

He pressed the call button and said to Zallon, "Bring Ms. Imani a gin and lemon." Stattor turned back to Usko and said, "That was your favorite drink. I remember. Perhaps you'll still have a taste for it." He leaned back in his chair. "No one was ever more dedicated to our cause than you. I admired you. I envied you for that. I remember a justice named Kudensa, a skinny, reactionary low-grade. . . . Do you remember him?"

She shook her head.

"You volunteered to bed him, to get information, although we all knew what he would put you through."

Still, she was shaking her head.

"I remember it took eight weeks for you to recover."

She looked blank. "Did I get the information?"

Stattor nodded. "You did." He thought he saw her face start to relax.

Zallon entered with a tray, from which he took the cloudy yellow drink and placed it in Usko's hands with a linen napkin. Without a sound, the aide left the office.

"It was very loyal of you to do that," Stattor said.

"I don't remember it. It couldn't have hurt me badly. The good of humankind is important. I've served that."

"You're the only person who could say that that I would believe. That's why I put you in prison."

She had her drink halfway to her lips—her gnarled hands stopped there.

"Because of your idealism," Stattor explained. "That's why you spent twenty years in prison."

"I don't understand."

Stattor shrugged and sipped his drink. "Let's talk about the old days for a minute. Do you remember the Setback? When we lost nearly all of our secret council?"

Her face went suddenly grim. "I remember. On Perda, every year, we have half a day off to remember and study the works of those we lost. And to read the story of Kenda Dean, the informer."

"You knew Kenda well, didn't you?"

"I never suspected he could do such a thing—or that the government had been paying him the whole time. I accept it now, but I never understood it."

"You never understood it because he didn't do it. *I* did it. *I* informed."

She looked at him as though he were still speaking. Then, suddenly, she laughed, and he remembered how, long ago, she had laughed. He remembered her lips as she had come up from the lakeside. He remembered her hands and he remembered the morning they had awakened in each other's arms.

"It's true," he said. "I informed on them all."

"You didn't. You couldn't have."

"The government police had been paying me for almost a year prior to that. I used the police to eliminate opposition to my chairmanship of the movement."

"You couldn't—"

"I did it for myself. I have always done everything for myself."

"This is some kind of test," she said. "You're testing me in some clever way. You could never do such a thing. You've led the human race to dominance in the galaxy. You've devoted your life to—"

"To the acquisition of power," he said. "I did it for myself."

"I won't believe this."

"Believe it. I did it because I wanted everything, and everything is mine now." He grinned. "Everything. You're mine."

"That isn't true. It's a lie, a test."

"It isn't wise, Usko, to tell Supervisor Stattor that he is lying. Normally, those who accuse me of lying are thrown into the core of the station." He smiled a bit more fiercely. "Then we can turn our thermostats up a few degrees."

"You couldn't have done that."

"If you don't tell me that you believe me, Usko, you'll be back cutting out your ninety-six pieces of shoe leather before the day is over. You'll do it till you die." He paused. "By the way, do you know where your 'leather' comes from?"

"Animals," she said tentatively.

"If you think your supervisor is incapable of betrayal and cruelty, I'll tell you where your shoe leather comes from." He waited for her response, but she said nothing. He leaned forward and the desk creaked under his weight. "Do you believe me?"

"Whatever you did, you did for the advancement of knowledge and for the security of the human race."

"I did it because I don't like competition, either from humans or trashlife. I had your friends butchered because they were in my way."

"You can't make me believe this," she said firmly. She sat up straighter and reached forward to put her drink on the edge of his desk. "We all sacrificed for our people, not for ourselves. I knew you well."

"You never knew me," he said. He leaned back and laced his fingers over his rolled stomach. For a moment, he seemed to be chewing something. "You're overburdened with misinformation. Let me clarify your situation. You have a choice. You can tell me that you believe me—that I informed on your friends and as a result they were sliced. Then you can walk out of here, have a warm place to live, and 500,000 credits a year. Or you can believe that this is a test, that Supervisor Stattor is lying to you, and *that*, Usko, is treason. For treason, you will spend the rest of your life dying on Perda, cutting shoe soles out of 'leather'."

Whatever small thing Stattor had sucked out of his teeth, he swallowed.

"Well?" he asked.

Her age, her fear, and her dread pushed her deeper into her chair. She had lowered her head and Stattor could see the dry frizzy hair that grew there in erratic patches.

She looked up. Above the mouth that was twisted by paralysis, her eyes sparkled as though they were filled with chips of silver. "You brought me here to offer me comfort and disgrace or a slow death for a wasted life. Why?"

"I'm an insecure man. I sleep better when I know that others operate from self-interest. Your idealism makes me . . . uneasy." Stattor smiled. "When you accept my offer of generosity, you'll be as corrupt as the rest of us. There's no reason for you to go back to prison now, because the ideal you sacrificed for was an illusion."

"You're taking the one thing . . ."

Stattor smiled even harder. "And we used to think human nature was so damned mysterious." He pressed the call button on the autovox and Zallon entered immediately. "See that Ms. Imani has priority transportation to the rehabilitation center. Her welfare is of special importance to me."

"I understand."

"That's gratifying," Stattor said.

As Zallon helped her out of her chair, she said, "If I were strong enough to use these hands—"

"We mustn't let our lives be spoiled with regrets," Stattor said pleasantly.

As Zallon helped Usko through the door, she looked back once, it was just a glimpse, and Stattor was reminded of the other reason he had sent her to prison. It happened so many years ago, when they had awakened in each other's arms. She had slept so beautifully, her smooth, translucent eyelids closed over her quiet eyes—and then she had awakened and her eyes had opened suddenly and she had looked at him. There, wrapped in the sheets, with the morning sun streaming across the room, she had looked at him with that same expression—a kind of horrified surprise.

The door irised shut behind them, and Stattor nodded to himself. Yes, it was probably at that moment, with the sun filling the room—and he remembered there was a bowl of oranges on a table, radiant with sunlight—it was at that moment that he decided that some way, somehow, he would do this to her, and not long after that he began giving information to the government police.

So now it had all worked out. The loose end was tied to everything else.

He swept his hand across the lower part of his stomach. He did not feel so bad now. Neither his arms nor his legs ached, and his stomach did not seem filled with bile.

Stattor turned in his chair and gazed out the transparent bubble at the churning hub of the galaxy and then at his globular cluster. But beyond those stars, in the textureless black, there was what drew his eyes. When he looked into it, he almost felt his soul drawn out of his bloated and diseased body and sent into a place where there was neither light nor matter nor decay nor care.

The autovox chirped.

"Supervisor," Zallon's voice said gently, "there is the matter of the dispersal list."

Stattor grunted and spun his chair to face the desk again. The list lay there, face up, awaiting his final decision whether or not to exempt any of the condemned. He thought of Aros waiting in some detention cell, old, haggard, half dead, and then he thought of himself and Usko, there beside the lake, so long ago. She had brought a bouquet of colored weeds up from the shoreline, and Aros had stood up, laughing, his arms wide to receive her—

His eyes stopped on the autovox.

Zallon had overstepped his limits. Stattor could barely see the green blossom of his nebula behind it. His emotionless aide, that sunken-eyed reptile, never revealed his feelings about anything, so how could he be trusted? He was an unknown.

Excepting no one from execution, Stattor pushed the list away from him. He had never liked Aros. Nor Zallon. With his fatted hand, Stattor retrieved the list and entered Zallon's name at the bottom. One way or another, so many people tried to stand in his way, to annoy him, or to prevent the grand and mysterious thing that was about to happen to him. It was very close. He could feel it come nearer every hour.

For a moment, his stomach did not burn and the betablocker made his life easier. He leaned back in his chair and again turned to face the absorbing blackness beyond the galaxy, and he was content to know that soon, so very soon, his flesh would turn to myth.

Editor's Introduction To:

LITANY FOR DICTATORSHIPS
Stephen Vincent Benet

Whitaker Chambers says of his education at Columbia:
"Nothing that I can remember was said about the Russian Revolution. No one in Contemporary Civilization parted the curtain of falling snow to show me Petrograd with a cold rain blowing in from the Gulf of Finland on a day in November 1917. The tottering republican government of Russia had ordered the drawbridges over the Neva River to be raised."

Of course, Chambers had this advantage over our generation: at least he knew there had been a Republican government of Russia. Nowadays, everyone is taught that the Bolsheviks overthrew the czars, and no one remembers Alexander Kerensky and the Social Democrats who, for a few months, gave Russia the only republican rule it has ever had.

Chambers continues his story.
"The great spans tilted slowly through the air. The Red Guards and the Communist Party resolutes had begun to execute that careful plan, the brainchild of Comrades Trotsky, Podvoisky, and Antonov-Avseenko, which proved to be a master technique for the revolutionary seizure of a mod-

ern city. The Communists were occupying the public buildings, the ministries, the police stations, the post office,
newspaper and telegraph offices, the telephone exchange,
banks, powerhouses, the railroad stations. To cut off the
working-class Viborg quarter from the other bank of the
Neva, and to prevent its masses from re-enforcing the
insurgent Communists, the falling republican government
had raised the bridges.

"In from the Gulf of Finland steamed the armored cruisers of the Baltic fleet, whose crews had already gone over
to the Bolsheviks. The cruisers nosed into the Neva within
point-blank range of the bridges. Their slender guns rose
with mechanical deliberateness, and, as they rose, the
spans of the bridges slowly dropped again. The masses
streamed across into the central city. This was the crisis of
the uprising and one of the decisive moments of history.

"The upraised guns of the cruisers—one hopefully renamed *The Dawn of Freedom*—did not lower. They swung
and lobbed their shells into the Winter Palace, which
stood next to the Admiralty on the river bank. Inside, the
rump of the government was in its final, dying session.
Outside, fierce fighting was going on. Directing it was one
of history's most grotesque figures, Antonov-Avseenko—
the Communist mathematician and tactician, the co-contriver
of the *coup d'etat*, the man with the scarecrow face and
shoulder-long hair under the shapeless felt. Antonov rushed
toward the guns at the head of the steps. His armed rabble
followed him. They stormed the doors. The Winter Palace
fell. With it, in that vast, snow-afflicted sixth of the earth's
surface, fell the absolute control of the destinies of 160
million people."

—Whitaker Chambers, *Cold Friday*

The odd part is that after the Bolsheviks took over, it
became fashionable in the West to act as if they were the
true republicans. Lincoln Stefans, "America's Philosopher,"
visited the Soviet Union and returned to say, "I have been
over into the future, and it works." American labor union
leaders visited terrible places in the Gulag and came home

praising the Soviet's "rehabilitation programs." And everywhere, Western intellectuals proclaimed "there is no enemy to the left."

Republics were in danger only from the right; this despite the news from the Soviet Union.

Make no mistake: as Robert Conquest shows in *Harvest of Sorrow*, the truth about the artificial famine in the Ukraine was widely available in the west. The *Manchester Guardian* and *Daily Telegraph*, *Le Figaro*, *Neue Zuricher Zeitung*, and the *Christian Science Monitor* and *New York Herald Tribune* gave broad coverage. Most of this was ignored by Western intellectuals. Some didn't believe it. Others said you can't make omelets without breaking eggs, as if that trite phrase excused turning the breadbasket of Europe into a death camp of starving people.

George Bernard Shaw said, "I did not see a single undernourished person in Russia, young or old. Were they padded? Were their hollow cheeks distended by pieces of foam rubber inside?" Of course, Shaw went where he was told, accompanied by official guides, unlike Malcolm Muggeridge, who went to the Ukraine in secret, and found the people starving.

Then there were Beatrice and Sydney Webb, champions of English Socialism, who said, "The cost of collectivization was driving out the universally hated kulaks and the recalcitrant Don Cossacks by tens or even hundreds of thousands of families," and conclude that dekulakization was planned from the start to summarily eject from their homes "something like a million families. Strong must have been the faith and resolute the will of the men who, in the interest of what seemed to them the public good, could make so momentous a decision."

Robert Conquest observes that these words might equally be applied to Hitler and the Final Solution.

Steven Vincent Benet was one of our better poets, and a man who believed in freedom and the Republic, but even he did not see that between Red Fascism and Black Fascism there was only this difference: the Red variety was much more efficient and racked up a much higher score of victims.

Benet's "Litany" was dedicated to the victims of Black Fascism, but it can serve for all, including, of our charity, Trotsky and Antonov, who were themselves murdered by the regime they created.

LITANY FOR DICTATORSHIPS
Stephen Vincent Benet

For all those beaten, for the broken heads,
The fosterless, the simple, the oppressed,
The ghosts in the burning city of our time . . .

For those taken in rapid cars to the house and beaten
By the skillful boys, the boys with the rubber fists,
—Held down and beaten, the table cutting their loins,
Or kicked in the groin and left, with the muscles jerking
Like a headless hen's on the floor of the slaughter-house
While they brought the next man in with his white eyes
    staring.
For those who still "Red Front!" or "God Save the Crown!"
And for those who are not courageous
But were beaten nevertheless.
For those who spit out the bloody stumps of their teeth
    Quietly in the hall,
Sleep well on stone or iron, watch for the time
And kill the guard in the privy before they die,
Those with the deep-socketed eyes and the lamp burning.

For those who carry the scars, who walk lame—for those
Whose nameless graves are made in the prison-yard
And the earth smoothed back before morning and the lime
    scattered.

*For those slain at once. For those living through months
    and years
Enduring, watching, hoping, going each day
To the work or the queue for meat or the secret club,
Living meanwhile, begetting children, smuggling guns,
And found and killed at the end like rats in a drain.*

*For those escaping
Incredibly into exile and wandering there.
For those who live in the small rooms of foreign cities
And who yet think of the country, the long green grass,
The childhood voices, the language, the way wind smelt
    then,
The shape of rooms, the coffee drunk at the table,
The talk with friends, the loved city, the waiter's face,
The gravestones, with the name, where they will not lie
Nor in any of that earth. Their children are strangers.*

*For those who planned and were leaders and were beaten
And for those, humble and stupid, who had no plan
But were denounced, but grew angry, but told a joke,
But could not explain, but were sent away to the camp,
But had their bodies shipped back in the sealed coffins,
"Died of pneumonia." "Died trying to escape."*

*For those growers of wheat who were shot by their own
    wheat-stacks,
For those growers of bread who were sent to the ice-
    locked wastes,
And their flesh remembers their fields.*

*For those denounced by their smug, horrible children
For a peppermint-star and the praise of the Perfect State,
For all those strangled or gelded or merely starved
To make perfect states; for the priest hanged in his cassock,
The Jew with his chest crushed in and his eyes dying,
The revolutionist lynched by the private guards
To make perfect states, in the names of the perfect states.*

*For those betrayed by the neighbours they shook hands
    with
And for the traitors, sitting in the hard chair
With the loose sweat crawling their hair and their fingers
    restless
As they tell the street and the house and the man's name.*

*And for those sitting at table in the house
With the lamp lit and the plates and the smell of food,
Talking so quietly; when they hear the cars
And the knock at the door, and they look at each other
    quickly
And the woman goes to the door with a stiff face,
    Smoothing her dress.*
                    *"We are all good citizens here.
We believe in the Perfect State."*
                            *And that was the last
Time Tony or Karl or Shorty came to the house
And the family was liquidated later.
It was the last time.*
                *We heard the shots in the night
But nobody knew next day what the trouble was
And a man must go to his work. So I didn't see him
For three days, then, and me near out of my mind
And all the patrols on the streets with their dirty guns
And when he came back, he looked drunk, and the blood
    was on him.*

*For the women who mourn their dead in the secret night,
For the children taught to keep quiet, the old children,
The children spat-on at school.*
                        *For the wrecked laboratory,
The gutted house, the dunged picture, the pissed-in well,
The naked corpse of Knowledge flung in the square
And no man lifting a hand and no man speaking.*

*For the cold of the pistol-butt and the bullet's heat,
For the rope that chokes, the manacles that bind,*

The huge voice, metal, that lies from a thousand tubes
And the stuttering machine-gun that answers all.

For the man crucified on the crossed machine-guns
Without name, without resurrection, without stars,
His dark head heavy with death and his flesh long sour
With the smell of his many prisons—John Smith, John
    Doe,
John Nobody—oh, crack your mind for his name!
Faceless as water, naked as the dust,
Dishonored as the earth the gas-shells poison
And barbarous with portent.
                This is he.
This is the man they ate at the green table.
Putting their gloves on ere they touched the meat.
This is the fruit of war, the fruit of peace,
This ripeness of invention, the new lamb,
The answer to the wisdom of the wise.
And still he hangs, and still he will not die,
And still, on the steel city of our years
The light fails and the terrible blood streams down.

We thought we were done with these things but we were
    wrong.
We thought, because we had power, we had wisdom.
We thought the long train would run to the end of Time.
We thought the light would increase.
Now the long train stands derailed and the bandits loot
    it.
Now the boar and the asp have power in our time.
Now the night rolls back on the West and the night is
    solid.
Our fathers and ourselves sowed dragon's teeth.
Our children know and suffer the armed men.

Editor's Introduction To:

DOING WELL WHILE DOING GOOD
Hayford Pierce

In Volume One of this series, we learned how Chap
Foey Rider, Anglo-Chinese chairman of Rider Factoring,
discovered the Galactic Postal Union through observation
of the simple fact that the farther a letter had to travel, the
faster it arrived.

As a result, the Postal Union has sent an ambassador,
and Chap Foey Rider must think fast.

DOING WELL WHILE DOING GOOD
Hayford Pierce

From the unassuming Lexington Avenue offices of Rider
Factoring, Ltd., Chap Foey Rider managed, in his spare
time, his family's investment portfolio. In late November
he called his broker with orders to sell all transportation
securities: General Motors, Exxon, United Aircraft, Braniff
Airlines, Norfolk & Western Railways, the proceeds going
into 90-day Treasury Bills. Calling a second broker, he

gave instructions to sell short a broad range of transportation stocks.

So. In for a penny, in for a pound, he reflected. He then sat back and waited, a plump, middle-aged, Anglo-Chinese merchant of nondescript features. If he was apprehensive, he gave little sign of it, beguiling the time by smoking an occasional cigarette.

At 3:14 the intercom buzzed.

"Mailroom, Mr. Rider. A large package just arrived. The return address says Sagittarius. Official Service of the Mandator?" The voice trailed off in a rising note of hysteria.

"Splendid," said Chap Foey Rider, making a note to overhaul the mailroom personnel, "I shall be there directly."

He gathered his four sons, John, Chong, Chan, and Wong, graduates respectively of Cal Tech, MIT, Stanford Engineering, and Harvard College, and proceeded sedately to the mailroom.

"This is ridiculous, as well as being impossible," sniffed the son from Harvard. "A vulgar hoax."

Chap Foey Rider did not reply.

A parcel some four feet around sat on the floor. His sons unwrapped the paper and twine. Chap Foey Rider was unsurprised to find that the transparent crating revealed a living being sprawled at ease in a comfortable-looking easy chair. The alien, humanoid save for light golden down on the unclothed portions of his body, nodded tolerantly and waited patiently for the crate to be dismantled.

He stood up and stepped forward. There was a slight, pleasant odor, as of cinnamon. Chap Foey Rider inclined his head a measured two inches. It was a moment of high emotion: the stars had come to mankind.

"I am Xanthil, Ambassador Plenipotentiary," said the alien benignly. "You, sir, are the Mr. Rider who has been in communication with the Mandator of the Galactic Confederation?"

"Yes, Excellency. On behalf of Rider Factoring, Ltd., may I welcome you to Earth, Ambassador Xanthil."

"It is most kind of you." The Ambassador coughed delicately. "Your air," he murmured apologetically. "Its level of pollutants is somewhat higher than on my native planet. No, no, do not concern yourself. This capsule is a quite efficient internal filter." He swallowed, then inhaled deeply. "Ah. Splendid."

Chan and Wong, the two younger sons, failed to keep their eyebrows from rising slightly.

"If his Excellency would care to step this way," suggested Chap Foey Rider, "he might deign to join us in a cup of tea, that is, an herbal infusion of mildly stimulating but non-hallucinatory and non-toxic nature."

"I should be delighted."

"And may I apologize for the foulness of—"

"Not a word, my dear sir. Indeed, 27,000 members of the Galactic Postal Union stand ready to serve you. Air-scrubbing equipment of worldwide capacity is readily available." His spaniel-like eyes glanced keenly at Chap Foey Rider.

"One could expect no less," replied the factor politely, absorbed in directing the Ceremony of the Teapot. "A matter of mere financial detail, one would suppose. Sugar, Excellency?"

"A sweetener? Two, please. As you say, a matter of minor but tiresome details of finance. But no doubt your world has experts in the matter of commodity exchange?"

"Oh, no doubt," said Chap Foey Rider. "No doubt at all."

The second cup of tea was interrupted by the intrusion of four Treasury Department agents. An imperturbable Chap Foey Rider heard them out, bade his farewells to Ambassador Xanthil, and accompanied them to the elevator. "You'll be hearing more from us, pal," muttered one of the Secret Servicemen under his breath. "Trying to keep a deal like this under the table, for Chrissakes, is like practically treason."

Chap Foey Rider inclined his head a quarter-inch in curt dismissal and marched back to his office.

"Let me call the lawyers, sir," said the Harvard son excitedly. "Illegal entry, unauthorized—"

"A moment, Wong," said Chap Foey Rider, raising a palm. "A moment's reflection first. Surely an obvious corollary suggests itself?"

"Huh? You mean they've got lawyers too?"

Chap Foey Rider sighed. "I advise you to leave such twaddle to the ACLU. Rider Factoring is a business concern. Ah, Miss Zielonka, step right in. A letter, please."

He rubbed his chin thoughtfully, then leaned back in his chair.

"Galactic Chamber of Commerce," he dictated, "Galactic Center, Sagittarius. Attention: Department of Comparative Ecology and Biochemistry. Gentlemen: I have been referred to you by Ambassador Xanthil, who assures me that—"

"Ah-*hah!*" ejaculated the Stanford Engineering son.

"I *see*," hissed the MIT son.

"Cunning old devil," muttered the Cal Tech son.

"See *what?*" cried the Harvard son plaintively. "What's there to—"

Chap Foey Rider waved them to silence. "John, if you would be so good as to finish this letter for me. Chong, kindly advise the newspapers of our visitor's arrival, not neglecting the *Wall Street Journal*. Chan, you might find it worthwhile to begin spreading rumors around the market. There is much to do and little time to do it in. Oh, and Wong," he added kindly, "you might . . . well, you might bring us another cup of tea."

The news of an intragalactic Postal Union comprising 27,000 member worlds, utilizing faster-than-light delivery equipment was received on Earth with mixed emotions. From that segment of the population which actually believed the news (14.6 percent), praise and opprobrium were heaped on Chap Foey Rider in equal amount.

"This great innovator," began the Hong Kong *South China Morning Post*.

"This further proof of Chinese-American collusion," roared *Tass*.

"This is a disturbing example of the abuses of unregenerate and unregulated entrepreneurialism at its worst," chided the *Washington Post*. "Although Mr. Rider is clearly to be commended for the initial astuteness by which (apparently) he alone has given Mankind the universe, the furtive, almost criminal, fashion in which Mr. Rider allegedly attempted to sequestrate the Galactic Ambassador for motives which surely can only be construed as furthering his own selfish . . ."

Chap Foey Rider snorted, tossed the newspapers into the wastepaper basket, and returned to his desk. An initial reply had been received from the Chamber of Commerce and this time there was no officious mailroom meddler to tip off the government busybodies. Work was already under way.

John was in Atlanta, talking with officers of the Coca-Cola Bottling Company.

Chong was in Los Angeles, negotiating with hotel and apartment house owners and managers.

Chan was in Tokyo, dickering with city officials.

Wong was in the mailroom, drawing up a mailing list and brewing tea.

And he himself was waiting for the New York Stock Exchange to reopen after a three-day suspension in trading. He was genuinely curious as to whether American Airlines, previously at 62, would open at a nominal ⅛ or if it would be as high as ¼. Not that it was a purely intellectual curiosity, of course: his forthcoming expenses would be enormous. Every additional dollar that could be milked from his farsighted move of selling the market short would be welcome. That 360 computer promised for installation tomorrow, for instance—even leasing it took a substantial amount of money. What would his branch managers in Bangkok and Calcutta think of such profligacy: they, who still ran their offices with abaci?

He shook his head. One must simply move with the times. This mailing list, for example. Without the computer it would be impossible. And as for his projected activities . . . which reminded him. He made a neat note. Somewhere among 27,000 worlds there must exist a more compact, a more efficent, a *cheaper* computer. A useful agency to pick up. He smiled infinitesimally: how fortunate his subconscious had urged him to lease the 360 for a single month only. And, all things considered, this might be the best time to sell the portfolio's 1,000 shares of IBM.

After calling his broker, he turned on the radio for the noontime news. It was much as he expected.

Ambassador Xanthil had been welcomed in Moscow by tumultuous applause and a medal: Hero of the Soviet Union, First Class.

There was consternation in Washington, whence the alien had managed to extricate himself for a worldwide tour without having made a single commitment to the furtherance of the economic or military well-being of the United States. A Democratic President and Republican Congress, recently each so eager to claim total credit for the diplomatic coup of the century, were now engaged in acerbic partisan bickering.

"Who lost us the universe?" cried the Democrats.

"Who sold us down the starstream?" riposted the Republicans.

From there the dialogue degenerated to shrill cries of Yalta and Watergate.

The single common ground was the unanimous decision to reactivate the House Un-American Activities Committee for the purpose of investigating Chap Foey Rider.

"But why you, sir?" asked Wong, setting a cup of tea at his father's elbow. "You'd think they'd be grateful to you."

"Hell hath no fury like an industrialist scorned," replied Chap Foey Rider drily.

"So?"

"Ambassador Xanthil has made it abundantly clear that whereas the Galactic Confederation has nothing but the highest esteem for Earth and its aspirations, it is, nevertheless, an association bound together exclusively by trade and commerce. It is not interested in theological discussions of the free-enterprise system versus godless communism, nor does it indulge in Marshall Plans or foreign aid for undeveloped or emerging planets. Its 27,000 mem-

bers are eager to provide us with unlimited amounts of
goods and services, philosophies and technologies, but—
and this is the key point, Wong—but only through the
intermediary of the Postal Union and in exchange for
equivalent value of goods or services rendered. In other
words, they expect us to pay for what we order."

"Well, gee," said Wong, frowning deeply, "that *sounds*
OK, I guess, but golly, is that really the way things are
run these days? I mean, you can't expect undeveloped and
disadvantaged nations or worlds to pay for *every*thing, can
you? Why," he exclaimed, making a broad gesture, "just
look at our entire government policy!"

"Exactly," said Chap Foey Rider. "Your argument is
most cogent, and will have certainly been brought force-
fully to the attention of Ambassador Xanthil. Unfortunately, he professes to reflect a universal ennui at the
prospect of trading Edsels, the Penn Central, F-111's, or
Lockheed overruns for controlled fusion plants, death rays,
or transmutation machines.

"Nor, on a higher plane, does he believe that the galactic demand for the philosophic thoughts of Billy Graham
or Jonathan Livingston Seagull will generate sufficient rev-
enues to maintain even a fourth-class postal service between here and Alpha-Centauri."

"But that's Robber Baronism," protested Wong hotly.
"Like that *Post* editorial said, that's unregenerate and
unregulated—"

"Kindly spare me," said Chap Foey Rider wearily.

"Well, anyway, whatever happened to Good Old American Can-Do?"

"Can-Do, I am afraid, appears to have sailed off with his
pal Know-How in a beautiful pea-green boat," sighed Chap
Foey Rider. "They were last sighted approaching Japan."

"Why, that's the most cynical thing I've ever heard,"
snapped the Secretary of State. "You mean to say that *you*
alone—out of all the billions of the world—appear to have
exclusive intercourse with the unspeakable rulers of this
preposterous Galactic Confederation?"

Chap Foey Rider spread his hands in protest. "It is not I who imposed the circumstance, sir. Nor do I know to my own knowledge that the situation is as you describe it. I merely mentioned that my own correspondence with various galactic contacts remains uninterrupted. A question of prepaid postage on the other end, perhaps? Have you yourself," he inquired ingeniously, "tried addressing a letter and slipping it into a mailbox?"

"Of course I have, you fool!" roared the Secretary of State, his face a fiery red. "I and 200 million other people. And it comes back from the post office marked unpaid postage."

"Interesting," mused Chap Foey Rider. "But you did hear Ambassador Xanthil's speech in Paris, didn't you? The one in which he said a temporary embargo had been placed on postal service to this world while he studies the mutual benefits and feasibility of actually establishing permanent relations."

"I heard it, all right," grumped the Secretary. "Damned impertinence, if you ask me: saying that on second thought it appears that Terra has nothing at all worth exchanging with the rest of the universe."

"He was not impressed, I take it, by the Russian offer of 2,000 Marxist-Leninist dialecticians and a ten-year supply of Siberian timber against assistance in establishing worldwide Soviet hegemony?"

The Secretary of State's jowls quivered. "No," he snapped, "nor by the joint Chinese-Indian offer of 500 million field hands, nor by the English offer of the Royal Family and Sten guns, nor the Danish offer of unlimited Greenland icecap, the Chilean offer of unlimited Pacific Ocean, the Australian offer of unlimited sand and rabbits, or the French proposal of Algerian wine and left-over maxis."

He pounded the table. "I tell you frankly, these shortsighted chauvinists have gummed up the works! If only they'd had the decency, the common sense, the . . . the *fairmindedness*, to let a single party, such as the United States, represent mankind . . ."

His voice trailed off for a moment. "And you, Rider," he

gritted between clenched teeth, "*you*, you continue your treasonable, seditious—"

"Oh, come, sir. Has an Iron Curtain suddenly been rung down? I must review my copies of the Congressional Record. In the meanwhile, I am certain my legal counselor will find your remarks to be of interest." Chap Foey Rider rose to his dignified height of five and a half feet.

"For heaven's sake, Rider, don't play the fool. If it weren't for your new-found notoriety you'd have been locked up long ago. You've virtual immunity and you know it. Even your letters—"

"Ah. I wondered about that. Have you found the agents from the Galactic Postal Union who are so obviously working somewhere within our own postal services? No? I *am* rather curious about them, you know. Are there vast numbers of agents infiltrated throughout the Earth, rather as a Peace Corps, happily speeding the mail on its appointed rounds, or are there just a few of them to speed up an occasional item in the hope that some Earthling would draw the correct conclusion and apply for Galactic membership? An interesting speculation, don't you think?"

"Don't rub it in, Rider, your immunity won't last forever. In the meantime, every Secret Service in the world is following your business career with fascination. Your real estate acquisitions in Los Angeles and Tokyo are proceeding smoothly, I hope?"

"*Cosi-cosa.*"

"And your takeover of American Bottled Gas?"

"The last stockholders gave their approval this morning."

"Your killing on the market?"

"Reinvested, Mr. Secretary, reinvested. Consolidated Aerosol, Inc."

"And your negotiations with Coca-Cola, hmmm?"

Chap Foey Rider waggled a finger. "One perceives that to you my life is an open book, from you there is nothing hidden." Smiling, he stood up a second time. "If I may be of further assistance at any future time, sir . . ."

*   *   *

Throughout December and January Rider Factoring's 360 hummed busily. Stacks of print-outs piled up, were scanned, hidden away in strongrooms guarded by armed Pinkerton operatives.

Chap Foey Rider paid personal visits to Phoenix, Gary, Pittsburgh, Tokyo, the Ruhr, Djakarta, and São Paulo. The worldwide legal expenses of Rider Factoring rose sharply.

The stock market also began to rise as the likelihood increased that the Ambassador from the Galactic Confederation would recommend against diplomatic and commercial ties with Earth. The specter of instantaneous displacement booths replacing the automobile and the 747 began to fade. On the big board Boeing jumped from 3⅞ to 17¼. Lobbyists in Washington and Bonn grew cheerful.

Already glutted with American dollars, the Arab oil producers made a half-hearted attempt to sell crude oil to the stars, then reverted to their long-range goal of purchasing controlling interests in Ford and General Motors.

France withdrew its offer of Algerian red and proposed the establishment in Paris of Galactic Postal Union and diplomatic headquarters in return for 74 million liters of unsaleable '76 Bordeaux wine (a rainy spring, followed by an August drought).

Peking aired a violent attack, on Galactic Adam-Smithism and Running-Dog Laissez-Faireism; and made a final, take-it-or-leave-it offer: a six-month lecture tour by the Chairman himself in return for exclusive distribution rights to matter transmitters, anti-gravity devices, and purely-self-defensive war materiel.

More pragmatic, Moscow proposed a cultural exchange: the Bolshoi Ballet (supplemented by an additional 4,000 blonde standby ballerinas) in return for 4,000 scientists and technologists. It being well-known that the Soviet postal service was the most efficient on Earth, it was only logical that in addition the USSR be granted sole rights to administer all postal commerce between the stars and Earth.

Jack Anderson reported from Washington that Ambassador Xanthil planned a speech to the General Assembly on

February 1. He would regretfully report that as there appeared to be no mutually beneficial articles of exchange between Earth and the rest of the Galaxy, he would have to recommend that postal service to the third planet be postponed for the indefinite future. Someday, perhaps, when global unity was achieved and priorities ordered, business relations would prove worthwhile. In the meantime, the enormous costs of instantaneously transmitting matter to a postal branch of a galactic backwater could not be seriously contemplated. The final decision, naturally, must be that of the Mandator himself, but . . .

Chap Foey Rider pursed his lips. Even in middle age he retained his youthful capacity for astonishment at the antics of trained statesmen and diplomats. The prospect of world government he found dismaying: any state larger than Andorra was intrinsically incapable of—

"Pop! Sir!" It was Wong, rushing into the office. "Turn on the TV! Xanthil's been kidnapped, being held as hostage!"

Scarcely surprised, Chap Foey Rider clicked on the small portable discreetly hidden away in a filing cabinet.

It was true. For reasons best known to himself, Xanthil had elected to swing through Central Africa. The newly-emerged nation of Xenophobia was locked in the throes of civil war: supported by the West were the Arab Blacks; supported by the East were the Black Arabs. They had joined sides long enough to mount a joint commando operation to Chad, where the commandos had gunned down the Ambassador's entourage and taken refuge with their hostage in the American Embassy. The Arab Blacks demanded 100 million dollars and the release of seven commandos convicted in Johannesburg of exploding a DC-10 in full flight; the Black Arabs demanded 100 million dollars and the release of three commandos convicted in Teheran of firebombing a hospital.

The images relayed by satellite were sharp and clear: the dust-colored American Embassy; the broken windows; the tanks and milling soldiers surrounding the building. A figure stumbled through a window and onto a second-story balcony: Xanthil, grasped by three of his captors. Moments later he was pulled back into the building.

The hours dragged by. An ultimatum by the commandos was released. They were not barbarians; mere footsoldiers in the fight for freedom. Xanthil was unharmed and comfortable in the code room. If, on the other hand, their most reasonable requests were not acceded to within the next three hours . . .

The world was informed by CBS that the finest military minds of sixteen nations were working on the problem of securing Ambassador Xanthil's safe release.

Chap Foey Rider's lips tightened, and his gaze fell upon his four sons. They were young, well-coordinated, husky; all had fought in various of his country's wars. He sighed.

Four unregistered pistols were found in the filing drawer marked Miscellaneous. Chap Foey Rider led the way to the mailroom. The transparent carton from the stars was still there. It was a tight fit, but John, Chong, Chan, and Wong were crushed in and the lid replaced.

Using a red Magic-Marker, Chap Foey Rider carefully addressed the package on its transparent surface: Code Room, American Embassy, Chad. Fragile, Emergency Routing Via Mandator's Office, Sagittarius. Official Service of the Mandator, Prepaid.

As he drew the final "d" there was a soft implosion and the package vanished. So. His reasoning *had* been correct. Displacement equipment *was* focused on the mailroom. Psionically activated? Possibly. Who cared?

Chap Foey Rider paced the mailroom nervously, lighting and stubbing out cigarettes in rapid succession.

Forty-seven minutes later the package reappeared. His four sons emerged.

"Xanthil?" snapped Chap Foey Rider.

"No sweat, sir," said John. "He's fine. There was a guard in the code room we had to take care of, which alerted the others. It took twenty minutes to mop them up, by which time the army had broken in. Xanthil's diplomatic skills were needed to dissuade them from shoot-

ing us on the spot. Eventually he quite kindly readdressed
the package for us, and here we are. The Ambassador
expresses his most sincere thanks and will tender them
personally before returning to Sagittarius. In the meantime, *noblesse oblige* requires him to carry on with his
sightseeing tour of Central Africa."

Chap Foey Rider mopped his brow with a silken ban-
danna pulled from his right sleeve. "Excellent. Well done.
And now, if you will straighten your garb, there is a
gentleman from Caracas . . ."

". . . and so," said Ambassador Xanthil to the General
Assembly, "I must confess that second thoughts are frequently wrong; that one's initial impression is the most
trustworthy and reliable . . .

"The unfortunate Xenophobian incident is, of course,
irrelevant. Personal feelings must not be allowed to intrude into the smooth workings of commerce and trade, of
course . . .

"It is my pleasure to inform you that I shall shortly be
recommending to His Excellency the Mandator that a
permanent postal branch be established on Earth, one
which will promote . . .

"You may find it odd, perhaps, that the initial contracts
are not with any of the great sovereign members of this
splendid body . . .

"I am sure, however, that as trading skills are honed,
worldwide participation in intragalactic commerce will
shortly follow and . . ."

"Well, Rider," rasped the Secretary of Commerce, "are
you quite content?" State merely glared, too choked with
emotion to utter.

"Content?" said Chap Foey Rider, his brow furrowed.
"Of course I'm content. I have achieved a lifelong ambition."

"Grrrr," said Transportation, inarticulately but force-
fully. Boeing had fallen back to 2¼.

"A lifelong ambition, I say. Everybody talks about the
weather, and now I've done something about it."

"The weather!" cried State. "What are you raving about?"

Chap Foey Rider blinked. "You haven't heard the details of the small trade I've worked out? Why, it's simplicity itself. Not only does it provide for the cost of installing the Postal Union, it generates sufficient foreign exchange to permit the purchase of goods and services—"

"Kindly get on with it," sighed Treasury. "You can crow later."

"Since you insist. You may have noticed that Ambassador Xanthil initially found our air unpleasantly full of pollutants? No? Ah. In any case, worldwide air-scrubbing machinery was mentioned, which implied that our own smog is by no means a phenomenon confined to Earth. A corollary immediately suggested itself: surely, out of 27,000 galactic members, some worlds have solved their problem of air pollution not by scrubbing, but by evolution. The air-cleansers came too late: the inhabitants *enjoy* breathing smog."

"What!" cried Environment. "That's ridiculous!"

"Not at all," disclaimed Chap Foey Rider. "The Galactic Chamber of Commerce was kind enough to place me in contact with reputable businessmen and financiers on 2,600 such worlds. With the help of my computer, we have mailed out some 89,000 aerosol cans and bottled samples of choice *grand cru* smogs from Los Angeles, Tokyo, São Paulo, and dozens of others of our magnificently polluted cities. Mostly to travel agencies and purveyors of gourmet foods and choice wines, of course. The response has been overwhelming, if I may say so. The first tours to hotels and resorts will be starting shortly. The revenue derived will—"

"Hotels and resorts and apartment houses which *you* own, Rider!" shouted CIA. "All over the world you've been—"

"Well, certainly," said Chap Foey Rider, puzzled. "How else could I generate capital to—"

"Battening on the miseries of the world," hissed State. "*Hyena* is the word generally—"

"—generate capital to purchase the anti-pollution controls and devices which within the decade will enable the world to scrub its air and keep it forever clean?" concluded Chap Foey Rider blandly. "The equipment *is* expensive, you know. And, no doubt, I've been sadly overcharged by unscrupulous traders. Ah, well, a businessman's plaint: I won't pass my own commercial shortcomings along to the rest of the world. No, a modest one percent service charge is all that Rider Factoring will add to the landed CIF price. Look upon it as a gift, gentlemen, to the world."

"A gift! One percent of how many billions comes to what? And what about the millions you'll make with your guided tours and your bottles of"—Treasury shuddered—"of canned smog for the fine food trade?"

Chap Foey Rider sniffed delicately at an aerosol can. "Ah, Bangkok, City Hall Plaza, 3:30 P.M., February 13. A vintage day, gentlemen, a vintage day. A choice connoisseur's item, would you care for a sniff. No? To answer your questions. It is not obvious that my small, temporary windfall is self-liquidating in nature? Modest to start with, as the air-cleansing machinery is put into operation it will become ever more modest. Two or three years from now the skies of Los Angeles will be so clear that only the most undiscriminating lover of smog will be visiting. In ten years the trade will be gone forever. Likewise the bottled and canned exports of smog. No more raw material."

Chap Foey Rider spread wide his hands. "Frankly, gentlemen, your opprobrium oppresses me. I, a small, insignificant trader, a benefactor of mankind even, some might say, in an unassuming and humble—"

"Oh, very well," sighed the President of the United States, waving Chap Foey Rider toward the door. "What's done is done. I can see you plainly lack the makings of a statesman."

That was true, Chap Foey Rider reflected, as he left the White House by the East Entrance. A statesman he would never be. Fortunate it was that in his old age he would be able to fall back upon his carefully laid-down cellars of millions and millions of bottles and cans of the choicest *grands crus* of fine smog and pollution. And as the winds of Earth were remorselessly cleansed, surely their value on the galactic market, ten or fifteen years from now, would be well (he smiled apologetically), astronomical.

Editor's Introduction To:

THE LAST DEPARTMENT
Rudyard Kipling

It is said that after the Revolution of 1848, when Metternich was leaving the Schoenbrun Palace of Vienna for
the last time, one of his aides looked at the acres and acres
of clerks still seated at their desks.

"My Prince, what will they do?"

Metternich smiled. "You and I go. Perhaps His Majesty
will go. But these—*Das Buros* are eternal."

Kipling wouldn't have been much surprised to find that
the Galactic Confederation was a bureaucracy.

THE LAST DEPARTMENT
Rudyard Kipling

Twelve hundred million men are spread
About this Earth, and I and You
Wonder, when You and I are dead,
"What will those luckless millions do?"

90

"None whole or clean," we cry, "or free from stain
Of favour." Wait awhile, till we attain
   The Last Department where nor fraud nor fools,
Nor grade nor greed, shall trouble us again.

Fear, Favour, or Affection—what are these
To the grim Head who claims our services?
   I never knew a wife or interest yet
Delay that pukka step, miscalled "decease";

When leave, long overdue, none can deny;
When idleness of all Eternity
   Becomes our furlough, and the marigold
Our thriftless, bullion-minting Treasury

Transferred to the Eternal Settlement,
Each in his strait, wood-scantled office pent,
   No longer Brown reverses Smith's appeals,
Or Jones records his Minute of Dissent.

And One, long since a pillar of the Court,
As mud between the beams thereof is wrought;
   And One who wrote on phosphates for the crops
Is subject-matter of his own Report.

These be the glorious ends whereto we pass—
Let Him who Is, go call on Him who Was;
   And He shall see the mallie[1] steals the slab
For currie-grinder, and for goats the grass.

A breath of wind, a Border bullet's flight,
A draught of water, or a horse's fright—
   The droning of the fat Sheristadar[2]
Ceases, the punkah stops, and falls the night

For you or Me. Do those who live decline
The step that offers, or their work resign?
   Trust me, To-day's Most Indispensables,
Five hundred men can take your place or mine.

[1] The cemetery gardener.
[2] Clerk of the Court.

Editor's Introduction To:

CONSTITUTION FOR UTOPIA
John W. Campbell, Jr.

The late John W. Campbell, Jr. dominated science fiction for thirty years. More: he influenced the thinking of a generation of readers and writers both through his story selections and editorials. Trained largely as an engineer, Campbell had boundless faith in rational thought and the ability of the human race to act rationally.

He also believed that his editorials spoke to the potential leadership of the world. He was right, of course: many of the best and brightest did read *Astounding Science Fiction*. Most of them were technically oriented, and went to engineering schools rather than liberal arts, but that wouldn't have disturbed Campbell a bit. As far as he was concerned, the engineers were the truly important people of the West, and if they would only organize, something might come of that.

Mankind has been drawing up pictures of The Good Society for five thousand years. Plato's *Republic* attempts to define the harmonious state, and Plato wasn't the first to try it. Since him there have been literally thousands of others: intellectuals such as Michael Harrington and

Marseglio of Padua; dried-out old lizards sunning themselves in Santa Barbara as they rewrite the Constitution of the United States; poets such as Dante; experienced statesmen such as Machiavelli and Sir Thomas More; irresponsible literary gadflies such as Jean Jacques Rousseau.

Given all that talent focused on the question, one might think there is little new to say, but that never daunted Campbell, who rejects most of what has been written before, then turns Acton's dictum about power on its head.

In effect, Campbell says that the form of government doesn't matter: monarchy, aristocracy, empire, republic, democracy—all will work if the rulers are wise and benevolent; none will if they are not.

The key, according to Campbell, is that whoever governs must be *responsible*. It is not absolute power that corrupts, it is absolute immunity from the consequences of abusing that power that turns one into a Kurtz or a Stalin.

CONSTITUTION
John W. Campbell, Jr.

The standard operating procedure for the Utopia-inventor is to describe his Utopia in terms of how he *wants* it to work. That is, he describes what he considers the goal-ideal of a society should be, and how he thinks that goal-ideal will be achieved, in terms of how happy, healthy and wise citizens of Utopia co-operate beautifully to produce wonderful music together. Usually, there's no crime, because, says the author, in so perfect and happy a state no one wants for anything.

There is, however, an astonishing lack of discussion of the legal code on which these Utopias are based—the machinery of the social system is always happily hidden out of sight, and we don't need to look at it, because it works so nicely.

I've seen—and in a college textbook, at that!—a definition of the Socialistic System that read, in essence, "Socialism is a system assuring maximum distribution of the wealth of the society to the productive citizens . . ." That makes things real nice for Socialists; if that is the definition, then, by definition, they're bound to be right! If a system doesn't "assure maximum distribution of the wealth" then, it isn't Socialism, and any system that does achieve that obviously desirable goal is, by definition, a version of Socialism, and see, doesn't that prove Socialism is the ideal system?

It's been standard operating procedure to define Utopias in just such terms—and consider the legal code required to achieve them "a mere detail." Something gross-materialists, anti-idealist, conservative—or whatever opprobrious term happens to be current—people throw up as a deliberate effort to becloud the real, important issues.

Now Utopias always have been in the legitimate field of interest of science fiction; let's try, in leadership assembled, rather than in congress assembled, to see what the whole group of some 100,000 readers can come up with in the way of designing a mechanism for a Utopian culture! This editorial is not intended as an Answer to the Question; it's intended to start the ball rolling; Brass Tacks can be the forum. What we're seeking is to pound out a Constitution for Utopia, defining a system that will generate the cultural system we want—*not* a eulogistic rhapsody about how glorious it will be when we get it done.

As a locale, let's consider that the Utopian culture is to be started among the people living in, on, and among the asteroids, about seventy-five years hence. (The locale is not critical, of course; the machinery of government is designed for human beings; what devices they use, where they live, is of secondary consequence.)

To begin with, recognize that we are NOT going to get a culture that is the perfect heart's-desire system of every inhabitant. This is called Heaven.

What we'll have to do is seek an *optimum* culture. It's

an engineering problem, and should be approached as such. Many a time an engineer would *like* a material as transparent as glass, as strong and tough as steel, capable of resisting an oxidizing atmosphere at 2500°C., as light as foam plastic, and as cheap as cast iron. *And* as conductive as copper.

The useless engineer is the one who says, "See! They won't give me what I need! It's impossible to solve the problem!" The engineer who *is* an engineer starts figuring the optimum balance of characteristics that will yield not a perfect-ideal, but a thing that will work, and work with a reliability level high enough to be useful for the task at hand.

Now one of the first and broadest questions usually raised is, of course, "What form of government should it be?" Monarchy? Democracy? Oligarchy? Communism?

That question, I suggest, is of no importance whatsoever! Utopia can be a Communism, an Anarchy, or an Absolute Tyranny; the matter is of no real consequence.

My evidence is quite simple: Traditionally, benevolent tyranny is the optimum form of government . . . if you can just assure that the tyrant is, and remains, benevolent. Also, traditionally, both Heaven and Hell are absolute monarchies.

Wise, benevolent, and competent rulers can make *any* form of government utopian—and fools who are benevolent, kind, and gentle, can turn any form of government into Hell. Scoundrels need not apply; scoundrels normally have a reasonable degree of competence, and will, for their own benefit, maintain a higher standard of efficient government than will benevolent fools. Witness the incomparable mare's-nest of the Congo, which has resulted far more from the blundering of fools than machinations of villains. Villains wouldn't have loused things up so completely; nobody can make anything out of the idealistic shemozzle the Congo's become.

Anarchy is government-that-is-no-government. In other words, each individual citizen is his own ruler. Given that all the citizens are wise, benevolent, and competent, anarchy will produce a Utopia. Unfortunately, this requires that each citizen *be in fact*, not simply in his own perfect sincere convictions, actually wise, benevolent, and competent. The observable norm of human experience is that the incompetent fool will show the highest certainty of his own wise competence, the strongest conviction that his answers can be doubted, questioned, even discussed, only by black-hearted, evil-minded villains who seek to oppose his good, wise intentions.

Given that all the rulers are in fact wise, benevolent and competent, Communism works just dandy. The Catholic Church has certainly not opposed the *concept* of Communism—they had it centuries ago in various monastic orders. It's just that the Church objects to the actuality—the legalistic mechanisms—of Russian and Chinese style Communism.

Since it can be pretty fairly shown that *any* form of government—from pure anarchy through absolute tyranny, with every possible shading in between—will yield Utopia *provided the rulers are wise, benevolent, and competent*, the place to start engineering our Utopia is with the method of selecting rulers.

I suggest, in fact, that the only constitution Utopia needs is the method of selecting rulers. England has gotten along rather well for quite a period of time without a formal constitution; if they had a better system of selecting their rulers, no need for a constitution would arise. Wise rulers will change traditional methods of governmental operation when, but only when, the change is warranted. We need not bind future centuries with a code that *now* seems optimum; conditions can change rather drastically. Let us set up a method of selecting wise rulers—and then let their wisdom be fully free to operate. If they choose Tyranny—then it can be assumed that Tyranny is, for that time and situation, the optimum governmental system. With a wise tyrant, it is optimum in war, for instance.

The problem is, was, and continues to be—"How to select the rulers?" Plato talked of "philosopher-kings" . . .

but had a little difficulty defining them. The genetic system, based on the unfortunately false proposition "like father, like son" has been tried very widely. Of course, it's heresy to say so in a democracy, but we're members of the Constitutional Convention of the Minor Planetoids, assembled on Ceres, in 1035 A.D., and we can observe that, as a matter of fact, despite the inaccuracy of that father-son idea, the system worked about as well as any other that's been tried. For one thing, it gave England some three hundred years of highly successful government. It's still not good enough—but it's not completely worthless. It must be recognized as having a very real degree of merit. Aristocracy as a system has worked quite well indeed.

Plato's philosopher-king idea runs into the difficulty that, even today, we haven't any battery of tests that can be applied to small children that will, with useful reliability, distinguish the deviant-and-criminal from the deviant-and-genius. Plato's system depended on spotting the youthful philosopher-kings and educating them to the tasks of government; the system won't work, because we can't spot the wise-benevolent.

It gets into further serious difficulty; the way to pass any test is to give the answers the examiner expects. It has nothing whatever to do with giving the *right* answers. Consider a question like "Is the government of the German Third Reich a democracy?" In Germany, in 1941, the answer was, of course, "Ja!" In the rest of the world the answer was different. Incidentally, can anyone give me a standard dictionary definition of "democracy" that does *not*, actually, apply to Hitler's Reich? The *forms* of democracy were there, you know . . . it was just that the rulers operating under those forms were not "wise, benevolent, and competent."

Any formal technique of testing applicants for rulership will have, underlying it, some formal theory of what constitutes "wise, benevolent and competent" . . . which theory rather inevitably turns out to mean "like me."

That's perfectly understandable; the men drawing up the constitution are, of course, playing the role of rulers, temporarily. They feel themselves to be wise, benevolent, and competent . . . or they wouldn't be trying. And, of course, basically everyone feels himself "wise, benevolent, and competent," with the exception of rare moments when, in defense of justice, he has been forced to be malevolent and punish some wrong-doer who unjustly attacked his basic rights. Be it clearly recognized that a homicidal paranoic psychotic, who has just murdered fourteen people, feels deeply that he is wise, benevolent, and competent, and has courageously acted in defense of justice against great odds. They were all persecuting him, and he has simply rebelled against their tyrannies.

Any method of testing, any formal, logical, reasonably worked out and rationally structured technique of selecting those fit to rule . . . will be structured according to the examiners' theories of what "wise, benevolent and competent" means. The use of *any* rationally designed test simply means that the rationality of the test-builders is clamped on the examinees. They pass if they agree with the test-builders.

I suggest, therefore, that the selection of rulers must be based on some nonrational method! Some method which, because it does not involve any formal—or even hidden-postulate!—theory, will not allow any special philosophy of "wise, benevolent and competent" to be clamped on the future rulers.

One possible irrational method would, of course, be selection by random chance. I think it's not necessary to go into details as to the unsuitability of that particular non-rational method.

The method I propose is a non-rational method which, however, practically every logician will immediately claim is the very essence of rationality. It is, of course . . . in an *ex post facto* sense. I suggest a pure, nontheoretical pragmatic test.

Of course, since the ultimate goal of rationality and logic is the mapping of pragmatic reality, there's a strong tendency for logicians to claim that any real, pragmatic test is logical. That's not a valid statement; while it is true that a chain of reasoning is valid if, and only if, it correlates with reality, it is not true that a thing is real only if it correlates with logic.

A pragmatic test is, therefore, a non-rational test. It may be said that "It is rational to use a pragmatic test," but that doesn't make a pragmatic test a rational test. It does not depend on theory—and any rationality does.

The only way we can maintain flexibility of viewpoint in our rulers is to make their selection immune to theoretical determination.

Aristocracy operates on the theory that wise men have wise sons. The theory has value . . . but it isn't sound enough for reliable, long-term use. It gets into trouble because, *theoretically*, the son of the benevolent monarch will be benevolent, but practice turns up a not-quite-drooling idiot every now and then—and the theory of aristocracy can't acknowledge that.

The Communists hold the reasonable sounding proposition that only the politically educated should be allowed to vote. Therefore only Party members, who have been given a thorough education in political theory and practice, are permitted to vote. There's certainly a lot of sound value in that idea; it's not unlike Plato's carefully educated philosopher-kings as rulers. And suffers the same serious flaw; the way to pass an examination is to give the answers the examiner expects. The idea sounds good, but has the intrinsic difficulty that it rigidly perpetuates the political theories of the originators.

A theocracy accepts that only the dedicated priest is fit to rule, because his dedication to things above and beyond this world, and his communion with God, make him uniquely qualified. That system's worked fairly well, now and then.

Robert Heinlein, in his recent novel *Starship Trooper*, proposed that only those who accepted the responsibility of defending the nation in the armed forces should have the right to vote. There are very few systems of selecting rulers that have not been tried somewhere, some when;

that military-responsibility test for rulers has been tried. It works very well . . . so long as the military is run by wise, benevolent and competent instructors. That, however, as I've said, is true of any system of government whatever. In actual practice, the Roman Legions became the effective rulers of Rome during the Empire period—and the results were horrible. Anyone wishing to be Emperor need only bid for it, and if he offered the Legions enough money, they'd murder the current emperor, and install him. One Emperor lasted four days, as I remember it, before someone outbid him.

This, again, is based on the theory that the Legions *should* feel responsible.

Finally, the theory of popular democracy says "Let everyone vote; do no selecting of rulers, and there will be no unjust rulers in power."

That theory is fundamentally false, by ancient and repeated pragmatic test. Maybe it *should* be true, but it isn't. The most deadly dangerous, destructive and degrading of all possible rulers is installed in power when true Popular Democracy gets into power.

The difficulty is this; the old saw that "Power corrupts; absolute power corrupts absolutely," is not quite correct. Power does not corrupt; no matter how great the power a man may hold, he will not become corrupt . . . *if he is not also immune*. It is immunity that corrupts; absolute immunity corrupts absolutely. I need very little powers to be a force for unlimited destruction—if I am absolutely immune.

Therein lies the key to that horrible mass-entity known as the Mob. A mob has no organization that can be punished; it *is* immune.

The members of the mob are immune through anonymity. It has huge physical mass-power; it is immune to the resistance of its victims, and to the opposition of any normal police force. Only an army can disrupt a mob; even so, the mob cannot be punished—called to account and its immunity broken—because it simply disperses, and no one of the ordinary citizens who composed it is the mob, or "belongs to" the mob.

The immunity of the mob can produce a corrupting and degrading effect that utterly appalls those who were swept up in it, afterward. No viciously sadistic affair in the Roman Arena exceeds in corruption and degradation what a modern mob, anywhere in any nation today, including the United States, will do. The mob will do things that not one member of that mob will consider doing.

Immunity, and the sense of immunity, is the deadliest of corrupting influences. It is, in essence, simply the result of cutting off the normal negative feedback, the pain-messages that warn of excesses. Imagine yourself not only blinded, but deprived of all kinesthetic sense, so you could not tell where your limbs were, how hard your muscles were pulling, or whether you were touching anything; you would then be totally immune to external messages. You would certainly tear yourself to pieces in a matter of minutes.

The record of history seems to indicate one fundamental law of civilizations: *The Rulers must always be a minority group*, or the culture will be destroyed.

Note this: under the exact and literal interpretation of democracy, it is perfectly legitimate democracy for a ninety per cent majority to vote that the ten per cent minority be executed by public torture, in a Roman Arena style spectacle.

The advantage of having the Rulers a minority group is that, under those conditions, no group has the deadly feeling of immunity. The Rulers are a minority, and know it, and must rule circumspectly; like the *mahout* driving an elephant, they must rule always with the realization that they rule by sufferance only—not by inalienable right.

The majority, then, knows it is ruled—that it is not immune to punishment, that it is not free to become a mob.

True popular democracy—true rule by the majority—establishes the government of the mob. It was the growing influence of the people of Rome, under the venal and

practically inoperative rule of the Legions—the Legions
wanted money, not political responsibility; they were fools,
rather than villains—that built up to the demand of "Corn
and Games!" and the consequences that followed.

A minority group, aware that it is a minority group, is
also aware of the problems of other minority groups through
direct, personal experience.

Long ago, Machiavelli pointed out that the Prince cannot rule in the face of the active opposition of his people;
the Prince must rule circumspectly, for he is a minority.

So whatever system of choosing Rulers we may select
for our Utopia—it must be a system that never allows any
groups to achieve the position that, inevitably, every group
wants to achieve—a position of security! The concept of
"security" is, in essence, the same as "immunity"; I am
secure if I am immune to all attack, or efforts to punish or
compel me. The Rulers must never be secure; since they
are to have the power of rule, they must not be a majority,
so that there will be the ever-present insecurity of the
potential threat of the great mass of people. The majority,
on the other hand, must never have security from the
power of their rulers—or they become a self-destructive
mob.

This boils down to the proposition that we want a non-
theoretical-rational test for selecting a minority group of
people who will be, with high reliability, relatively wise,
benevolent, and competent.

The simplest test for this, that does not depend on the
rationale and prejudgment of the examiners, is the one the
founders of the United States proposed—and which we
have rejected. It's quite nontheoretical, and hence has a
tendency to be exceedingly irritating to our sense of justice—
sense of "what ought to be." The test is simply whether or
not a man is competent to manage his own affairs in the
real world about him; is he a successful man in the pragmatic terms of economic achievement?

The difference between a crackpot and a genius *is* that a
genius makes a profit—that his idea is economically useful,

that it returns more in product than it consumes in raw material.

Now it is perfectly true that competence does not guarantee benevolence. But it's also true we have, for this argument, agreed that we're not designing a constitution for Heaven, but for Utopia—an optimum engineering system, not a perfect system. Inasmuch as no one can define "benevolent," we're stuck on that one. But we can say this with pretty fair assurance: a man who consistently injures his associates will not have a successful business for long. A man may *hurt* his associates quite commonly, and be highly successful—provided his hurts are, however painful, essentially beneficial. The good dentist is a simple example. But the man who injures will not be successful for long; the "painless" dentist who is incompetent, and uses lavish anesthesia to cover up his butchery, for instance, doesn't *hurt* his patients, but won't remain in business long.

The founders of this nation proposed that a voter must have five thousand dollars worth of property—a simple economic test, perfectly pragmatic tied with no theoretical strings about how he garnered his five thousand dollars. The equivalent today would be somewhat nearer one hundred thousand dollars.

That particular form of the test is not quite optimum, I think; instead of a capital-owned test, an earned-income test would be wiser, probably. A man can inherit property without inheriting the good sense of the father who garnered it. But earned-income is a test of *his* competence.

It violates our rational-theoretical sense of justice, because not all men have equal opportunities for education, a start in business, et cetera.

But we're seeking a non-theoretical, non- "just", purely pragmatic test, so that alone would not be an argument against the economic-success test.

Also—to use the dental analogy in another context—if a certain man wants to be a dentist, and has never had the opportunity to study the subject, but sets himself up as a dentist, and wants to work on your teeth . . . why shouldn't he? Is it his fault he never had an opportunity to go to dental school? Why shouldn't he start trying out his own original ideas on your teeth . . . ?

Are you being unfair to him if you refuse to allow him to practice on you?

And are you being unfair when you refuse to allow a man who never had an opportunity for an adequate education to practice on your nation's affairs? Look, friend—this business of running a nation isn't a game of patty-cake; it's for blood, sweat and tears, you know. It's sad that the guy didn't have all the opportunities he might have . . . but the pragmatic fact is that he didn't, and the fact that he can't make a success of his own private affairs is excellent reason for taking the purely pragmatic, nontheoretical position that that is, in itself, reason for rejecting his vote on national affairs.

There's another side to this pragmatic test, however; neither Abraham Lincoln, George Washington Carver, nor Thomas Edison ever had an adequate opportunity for education. The guy who bellyaches that his failure in life is due to lack of opportunity has to explain away such successful people as those three before he has any right to blame all his misfortunes on the hard, cruel world around. Those three individuals all get the vote, aristocrats, and formal intellectualists to the contrary notwithstanding. One un (formally) educated frontiersman, one Negro born a slave, and one nobody who never got beyond grammar school; three properly qualified Rulers. They made a success of their private affairs; let them have a hand in the nation's affairs. We do not care who their parents were; we need not concern ourselves with their children, for the children will vote if they, themselves make a success of their own private affairs.

Let's make the Test for Rulers simply that the individual's earned annual income must be in the highest twenty per cent of the population. This automatically makes them a minority group, selected by a pragmatic test. It bars no one, on any theoretical or rationalized grounds whatever;

any man who demonstrates that he can handle his private affairs with more than ordinary success is a Voter, a Ruler.

The earned-annual-income figure might be determined by averaging the individual's actual income over the preceding ten per cent of his life, taken to the nearest year. Thus if someone eighteen years old has, for two years, been averaging in the top twenty per cent—he votes. He may be young, but he's obviously abnormally competent. The system also lops off those who are falling into senility. It automatically adjusts to inflation and/or recession.

It isn't perfect; remember we're designing Utopia, not Heaven. We *must not* specify how the income is earned; to do so would put theory-rationalizations back in control. If a man makes fifty thousand dollars a year as a professional gambler—he votes. Anybody who guesses right that consistently has a talent the nation needs.

There may be many teachers, ministers, and the like, who by reason of their dedication to their profession do not make the required income level. If they're competent teachers and ministers, however, they'll have many votes—through their influence on their students or parishioners. If they're incompetent, they will have small influence, and deserve no vote.

The economic test does not guarantee benevolence; it does guarantee more-than-average competence, when so large a number as twenty per cent of the population is included. And while it doesn't guarantee benevolence—it provides a very high probability, for each successful man is being judged-in-action by his neighbors and associates. They would not trade with him, or consult him, if his work were consistently injurious.

There are exceptions, those eternally-puzzling areas of human disagreement between sincerely professed theory, and actual practice. Prostitution is perhaps the clearest example; for all the years of civilized history, prostitution has been condemned. It's been legislated against, and its practitioners scorned . . . by the same population that, through all the years of civilized history, have continued to support in action that ancient and dishonored institution.

The people who voted to keep Prohibition on the books were also those who contributed to the high income of bootleggers.

There are many such areas of human ambivalence; no theoretical or rational solution appears to be in sight. The simple fact remains that, by popular vote-in-action, not in theory, prostitution, illegal gambling, and various other socially-denounced institutions continue to win wide popular support.

So . . . Utopia still won't be Heaven. But maybe we can say it will never be a Blue Nose Hell, either!

O.K., friends—now it's your turn!

Editor's Introduction To:

MINOR INGREDIENT
Eric Frank Russell

The anarchist writer Max Stirner said, "If slaves ceased to submit it would be all over with masters." True enough. But if the key to good government is wise and benevolent public officials, how does one go about training them?

MINOR INGREDIENT
Eric Frank Russell

He dragged his bags and cases out of the car, dumped them on the concrete, paid off the driver. Then he turned and looked at the doors that were going to swallow him for four long years.

Big doors, huge ones of solid oak. They could have been the doors of a penitentiary save for what was hand-carved in the center of a great panel. Just a circle containing a four-pointed star. And underneath in small, neat letters the words: "God bless you."

Such a motto in such a place looked incongruous; in fact,

somewhat silly. A star was all right for a badge, yes. Or an engraved, stylized rocketship, yes. But underneath should have been "Onward, Ever Onward" or "Excelsior" or something like that.

He rang the doorbell. A porter appeared, took the bags and cases into a huge ornate hall, asked him to wait a moment. Dwarfed by the immensity of the place he fidgeted around uneasily, refrained from reading the long roll of names embossed upon one wall. Four men in uniform came out of a corridor, marched across the hall in dead-straight line with even step, glanced at him wordlessly and expressionlessly, went out the front. He wondered whether they despised his civilian clothes.

The porter reappeared, conducted him to a small room in which a wizened, bald-headed man sat behind a desk. Baldhead gazed at him myopically through old-fashioned and slightly lopsided spectacles.

"May I have your entry papers, please." He took them, sought through them, muttering to himself in an undertone. "Umph, umph! Warner McShane for pilot-navigator course and leader commission." He stood up, offered a thin, soft hand. "Glad to meet you, Mr. McShane. Welcome to Space Training College."

"Thank you," said McShane, blank-faced.

"God bless you," said Baldhead. He turned to the waiting porter. "Mr. McShane has been assigned Room Twenty, Mercer's House."

They traipsed across a five-acre square of neatly trimmed grass around which stood a dozen blocks of apartments. Behind them, low and far, could be seen an array of laboratories, engineering shops, test-pits, lecture halls, classrooms and places of yet unknown purpose. Farther still, a mile or more behind those, a model spaceport holding four Earthbound ships cemented down for keeps.

Entering a building whose big lintel was inscribed "Mercer's," they took an elevator to the first floor, reached Room 20. It was compact, modestly furnished but comfortable. A small bedroom led off it to one side, a bathroom on the other.

Stacking the luggage against a wall, the porter informed, "Commodore Mercer commands this house, sir, and Mr. Billings is your man. Mr. Billings will be along shortly."

"Thank you," said McShane.

When the porter had gone he sat on the arm of a chair and pondered his arrival. This wasn't quite as he'd expected. The place had a reputation equaled by no other in a hundred solar systems. Its fame rang far among the stars, all the way from here to the steadily expanding frontiers. The man fully trained by S.T.C. was somebody, really somebody. The man accepted for training was lucky, the one who got through it was much to be envied.

Grand Admiral Kennedy, supreme commander of all space forces, was a graduate of S.T.C. So were a hundred more now of formidable rank and importance. Things must have changed a lot since their day. The system must have been plenty tough long, long ago, but had softened up considerably since. Perhaps the entire staff had been here too long and were suffering from senile decay.

A discreet knock sounded on the door and he snapped, "Come in."

The one who entered looked like visible confirmation of his theory. A bent-backed oldster with a thousand wrinkles at the corners of his eyes and white muttonchop whiskers sticking grotesquely from his cheeks.

"I am Billings, sir. I shall be attending to your needs while you are here." His aged eyes turned toward the luggage. "Do you mind if I unpack now, sir?"

"I can manage quite well for myself, thank you." McShane stifled a grim smile. By the looks of it the other stood in more need of helpful service.

"If you will permit me to assist—"

"The day I can't do my own unpacking will be the day I'm paralyzed or dead," said McShane. "Don't trouble yourself for me."

"As you wish, sir, but—"

"Beat it, Billings."

"Permit me to point out, sir, that—"

"No, Billings, you may not point out," declared McShane, very firmly.

"Very well." Billings withdrew quietly and with dignity.

Old fusspot, thought McShane. Heaving a case toward the window, he unlocked it, commenced rummaging among its contents. Another knock sounded.

"Come in."

The newcomer was tall, stern-featured, wore the full uniform of a commodore. McShane instinctively came erect, feet together, hands stiffly at sides.

"Ah, Mr. McShane. Very glad to know you. I am Mercer, your housemaster." His sharp eyes went over the other from head to feet. "I am sure that we shall get along together very well."

"I hope so, sir," said McShane respectfully.

"All that is required of you is to pay full attention to your tutors, work hard, study hard, be obedient to the house rules and loyal to the college."

"Yes, sir."

"Billings is your man, is he not?"

"Yes, sir."

"He should be unpacking for you."

"I told him not to bother, sir."

"Ah, so he has been here already." The eyes studied McShane again, hardening slightly. "And you told him not to bother. Did he accept that?"

"Well, sir, he tried to argue but I chased him out."

"I see." Commodore Mercer firmed his lips, crossed the room, jerked open a top drawer. "You have brought your full kit, I presume. It includes three uniforms as well as working dress. The ceremonial uniforms first and second will be suspended on the right- and left-hand sides of the wardrobe, jackets over pants, buttons outward."

He glanced at McShane, who said nothing.

"The drill uniform will be placed in this drawer and no other, pants at bottom folded twice only, jacket on top with sleeves doubled across breast, buttons uppermost, collar to the left." He slammed the drawer shut. "Did you know all that? And where everything else goes?"

"No, sir," admitted McShane, flushing.

"Then why did you dismiss your man?"

"I thought—"

"Mr. McShane, I would advise you to postpone thinking until you have accumulated sufficient facts to form a useful basis. That is the intelligent thing to do, is it not?"

"Yes, sir."

Commodore Mercer went out, closing the door gently. McShane aimed a hearty kick at the wall, muttered something under his breath. Another knock sounded on the door.

"Come in."

"May I help you now, sir?"

"Yes, Billings, I'd appreciate it if you'd unpack for me."

"With pleasure, sir."

He started on the job, putting things away with trained precision. His motions were slow but careful and exact. Two pairs of boots, one of slippers, one of gym shoes aligned on the small shoe rack in the officially approved order. One crimson lined uniform cloak placed on a hanger, buttons to the front, in center of the wardrobe.

"Billings," said McShane, after a while, "just what would happen to me if I dumped my boots on the window ledge and chucked my cloak across the bed?"

"Nothing, sir."

"Nothing?" He raised his eyebrows.

"No, sir. But I would receive a severe reprimand."

"I see."

He flopped into a chair, watched Billings and stewed the matter in his mind. They were a cunning bunch in this place. They had things nicely worked out. A tough customer feeling his oats could run wild and take his punishment like a man. But only a louse would do it at the expense of an aged servant.

They don't make officers of lice if they can help it. So they'd got things nicely organized in such a manner that bad material would reveal itself as bad, the good would show up as good. That meant he'd have to walk warily and watch his step. For four years. Four years at the time of life when blood runs hot and surplus energies need an aggressive outlet.

"Billings, when does one eat here?"

"Lunch is at twelve-thirty, sir. You will be able to hear the gong sound from the dining hall. If I may say so, sir, you would do well to attend with the minimum of delay."

"Why? Will the rats get at the food if it has to wait a while?"

"It is considered courteous to be prompt, sir. An officer and a gentleman is always courteous."

"Thank you, Billings." He lifted a quizzical eyebrow. "And just how long have *you* been an officer?"

"It has never been my good fortune, sir."

McShane studied him carefully, said, "If that isn't a rebuke it ought to be."

"Indeed, sir, I would not dream of—"

"When I am rude," interrupted McShane, still watching him, "it is because I am raw. Newcomers usually are more than somewhat raw. At such moments, Billings, I would like you to ignore me."

"I can't do that, sir. It is my job to look after you. Besides, I am accustomed to jocularity from young gentlemen." He dipped into a case, took out a twelve by eight pin-up of Sylvia Lafontaine attired in one small ostrich feather. Holding it at arm's length, he surveyed it expressionlessly, without twitching a facial muscle.

"Like it?" asked McShane.

"Most charming, sir. However, it would be unwise to display this picture upon the wall."

"Why not? This is my room, isn't it?"

"Definitely, sir. I fear me the commodore would not approve."

"What has it got to do with him? My taste in females is my own business."

"Without a doubt, sir. But this is an officer's room. An officer must be a gentleman. A gentleman consorts only with ladies."

"Are you asserting that Sylvia is no lady?"

"A lady," declared Billings, very, very firmly, "would never expose her bosom to public exhibition."

"Oh, hell!" said McShane, holding his head.

"If I replace it in your case, sir, I would advise you to keep it locked. Or would you prefer me to dispose of it in the furnace room?"

"Take it home and gloat over it yourself."

"That would be most indecent, sir. I am more than old enough to be this person's father."

"Sorry, Billings." He mooched self-consciously around the room, stopped by the window, gazed down upon the campus. "I've a heck of a lot to learn."

"You'll get through all right, sir. All the best ones get through. I know. I have been here many years. I have seen them come and watched them go and once in a while I've seen them come back."

"Come back?"

"Yes, sir. Occasionally one of them is kind enough to visit us. We had such a one about two months ago. He used to be in this very house, Room 32 on the floor above. A real young scamp but we kept his nose to the grindstone and got him through very successfully." The muttonchop whiskers bristled as his face became suffused with pride. "Today, sir, he is Grand Admiral Kennedy."

The first lectures commenced the following morning and were not listed in the printed curriculum. They were given in the guise of introductory talks. Commodore Mercer made the start in person. Impeccably attired, he stood on a small platform with his authoritative gaze stabbing the forty members of the new intake with such expertness that each one felt himself the subject of individual attention.

"You've come here for a purpose—see that it is achieved . . . The trier who fails is a far better man than the failure who has not tried . . . We hate to send a man down, but will not hesitate if he lets the college down . . . Get it fixed firmly in your minds that space-navy leadership is not a pleasant game; it is a tough, responsible job and you're here to learn it."

In that strain he carried on, a speech evidently made many times before to many previous intakes. It included plenty of gunk about keep right on to the end of the road, what shall we do with a drunken sailor, the honor of the Space Service, the prestige of the College, the lights in the sky are stars, glory, glory, hallelujah, and so forth.

After an hour of this he finished with, "Technical knowledge is essential. Don't make the mistake of thinking it enough to get top marks in technical examinations. Officers are required to handle men as well as instruments and machines. We have our own way of checking on your fitness in that respect." He paused, said, "That is all from me, gentlemen. You will now proceed in orderly manner to the main lecture room where Captain Saunders will deal with you."

Captain Saunders proved to be a powerfully built individual with a leathery face, a flattened nose, and an artificial left hand permanently hidden in a glove. He studied the forty newcomers as though weighing them against their predecessors, emitted a noncommittal grunt.

He devoted himself an hour to saying most of the things Mercer had said, but in blunter manner. Then, "I'll take you on a tour to familiarize you with the layout. You'll be given a book of rules, regulations and conventions; if you don't read them and observe them, you've only yourselves to blame. Tuition proper will commence at nine-thirty tomorrow morning. Parade in working dress immediately outside your house. Any questions?"

Nobody ventured to put any questions. Saunders led them forth on the tour which occupied the rest of the day. Conscious of their newness and junior status, they absorbed various items of information in complete silence, grinned apologetically at some six hundred second-, third- and fourth-year men hard at work in laboratories and lecture rooms.

Receiving their books of rules and regulations, they attended the evening meal, returned to Mercer's House. By this time McShane had formed a tentative friendship with two fellow sufferers named Simcox and Fane.

"It says here," announced Simcox, mooching along the corridor with his book open in his hands, "that we are confined to college for the first month, after which we are permitted to go to town three evenings per week."

"That means we start off with one month's imprisonment," growled Fane. "Just at the very time when we need a splurge to break the ice."

McShane lowered his voice to a whisper. "You two come to my room. At least we can have a good gab and a few gripes. I've a full bottle of whiskey in the cupboard."

"It's a deal," enthused Fane, his face brightening.

They slipped into Room 20, unobserved by other students. Simcox rubbed his hands together and Fane licked anticipatory lips while McShane went to the cupboard.

"What're we going to use for glasses?" asked Fane, staring around.

"What're we going to use for whiskey?" retorted McShane, straightening up and backing away from the cupboard. He looked at them, his face thunderous. "It's not here."

"Maybe you moved it and forgot," suggested Simcox. "Or perhaps your man has stashed it some place where Mercer can't see it."

"Why should he?" demanded Fane, waving his book of rules. "It says nothing about bottles being forbidden."

"I'd better search the place before I blow my top," said McShane, still grim. He did just that and did it thoroughly. "It's gone. Some dirty scout swiped it."

"That means we've a thief in the house," commented Simcox unhappily. "The staff ought to be told."

Fane consulted his book again. "According to this, complaints and requests must be taken to the House Proctor, a fourth-year man residing in Room 1."

"All right, watch me dump this in his lap." McShane bolted out, down the stairs, hammered on the door of Room 1.

"Come in."

He entered. The proctor, a tall, dark-haired fellow in the mid-twenties, was reclining in a chair, legs crossed, a heavy book before him. His dark eyes coldly viewed the visitor."

"Your name?"

"Warner McShane."

"Mr. McShane, you will go outside, close the door, knock in a way that credits me with normal hearing, and re-enter in proper manner."

McShane went red. "I regret to say I am not aware of what you consider the proper manner."

"You will march in at regulation pace, halt smartly, and stand at attention while addressing me."

Going out, McShane did exactly as instructed, blank-faced but inwardly seething. He halted, hands stiffly at sides, shoulders squared.

"That's better," said the proctor. His gaze was shrewd as he surveyed the other. "Possibly you think I got malicious satisfaction out of that?"

No reply.

"If so, you're wrong. You're learning exactly as I learned—the hard way. An officer must command obedience by example as well as by authority. He must be willing to give to have the right to receive." Another pause inviting comment that did not come. "Well, what's your trouble?"

"A bottle of whiskey has been stolen from my room."

"How do you know that it was stolen?"

"It was there this morning. It isn't there now. Whoever took it did so without my knowledge and permission. That is theft."

"Not necessarily. Your man may have removed it."

"It's still theft."

"Very well. It will be treated as such if you insist." His bearing lent peculiar significance to his final question. "Do you insist?"

McShane's mind whirled around at a superfast pace. The darned place was a trap. The entire college was carpeted with traps. This very question was a trap. Evade it! Get out of it while the going is good!

"If you don't mind, I'll first ask my man whether he took it and why."

The change in the proctor was remarkable. He beamed at the other as he said, "I am very glad to hear you say that."

McShane departed with the weird but gratifying feeling that in some inexplicable way he had gained a small victory, a positive mark on his record-sheet that might cancel out an unwittingly-earned negative mark. Going upstairs, he reached his door, bawled down the corridor, "Billings! Billings!" then went into his room.

Two minutes passed before Billings appeared. "You called me, sir?"

"Yes, I did. I had a bottle of whiskey in the cupboard. It has disappeared. Do you know anything about it?"

"Yes, sir. I removed it myself."

"Removed it?" McShane threw Simcox and Fane a look of half-suppressed exasperation. "What on earth for?"

"I have obtained your first issue of technical books and placed them on the rack in readiness, sir. It would be advisable to commence your studies at once, if I may say so."

"Why the rush?"

"The examination at the end of the first month is designed to check on the qualifications that new entrants are alleged to possess. Occasionally they prove not to the complete satisfaction of the college. In such a case, the person concerned is sent home as unsuitable." The old eye acquired a touch of desperation. "You will have to pass, sir. It is extremely important. You will pardon me for saying that an officer can manage without drink when it is expedient to do so."

Taking a deep breath, McShane asked, "Exactly what have you done with the bottle?"

"I have concealed it, sir, in a place reserved by the staff for that purpose."

"And don't I ever get it back?"

Billings was shocked. "Please understand, sir, that the whiskey has been removed and not confiscated. I will be most happy to return it in time for you to celebrate your success in the examination."

"Get out of my sight," said McShane.

"Very well, sir."

When he had gone, McShane told the others, "See what I've got? It's worse than living with a maiden aunt."

"Mine's no better," said Fane gloomily.

"Mine neither," endorsed Simcox.

"Well, what are we going to do about it, if anything?" McShane invited.

They thought it over and after a while Simcox said, "I'm taking the line of least resistance." He raised his tone to passable imitation of a childish treble. "I am going to go home and do my sums because my Nanny will think I'm naughty if I don't."

"Me, too," Fane decided. "An officer and a gentleman, sir, never blows his nose with a ferocious blast. Sometimes the specimen I've got scares hell out of me. One spit on the floor and you're expelled with ignominy."

They ambled out, moody-faced. McShane flung himself into a chair, spent twenty minutes scowling at the wall. Then, becoming bored with that, he reached for the top book in the stack. It was thrillingly titled "*Astromathematical Foundations of Space Navigation.*" It looked ten times drier than a bone. For lack of anything else to do, he stayed with it. He became engrossed despite himself. He was still with it at midnight, mentally bulleting through the star-whorls and faraway mists of light.

Billings tapped on the door-panels, looked in, murmured apologetically, "I realized that you are not yet in bed, sir, and wondered whether you had failed to notice the time. It is twelve o'clock. If I may make so bold—"

He ducked out fast as McShane hurled the book at him.

Question Eleven: The motto of the Space Training College is "*God Bless You.*" As briefly as possible explain its origin and purpose.

McShane scribbled rapidly. "The motto is based upon three incontrovertible points. Firstly, a theory need not be correct or even visibly sensible; it is sufficient for it to be workable. Secondly, any life form definable as intelligent must have imagination and curiosity. Thirdly, any life form possessed of imagination and curiosity cannot help but speculate about prime causes."

He sharpened his thoughts a bit, went on, "Four hundred years ago a certain Captain Anderson, taking a brief vacation on Earth, stopped to listen to a religious orator who was being heckled by several members of the audience. He noticed that the orator answered every witticism and insult with the words, 'God bless you, brother!' and that the critics lacked an effective reply. He also noted that in a short time the interrupters gave up their efforts one by one, eventually leaving the orator to continue unhampered."

What next? He chewed his pen, then, "Captain Anderson, an eccentric but shrewd character, was sufficiently impressed to try the same tactic on alien races encountered in the comos. He found that it worked nine times out of ten. Since then it has been generally adopted as a condensed, easily employed and easily understood form of space-diplomacy."

He looked it over. Seemed all right but not quite enough. The question insisted upon brevity but it had to be answered in full, if at all. "The tactic has not resolved all differences or averted all space wars but it is workable in that it has reduced both to about ten per cent of the potential number. The words 'God bless you' are neither voiced nor interpreted in conventional Earth-terms. From the cosmic viewpoint they may be said to mean, 'May the prime cause of everything be beneficial to you!' "

Yes, that looked all right. He read it right through, felt satisfied, was about to pass on to the next question when a tiny bubble of suspicion lurking deep in his subconscious suddenly rose to the surface and burst with a mentally hearable pop.

The preceding ten questions and the following ones all inquired about subjects on which he was supposed to be informed. Question Eleven did not. Nobody at any time had seen fit to explain the college motto. The examiners had no right to assume that any examinee could answer it.

So why had they asked it? It now became obvious—they were still trapping.

Impelled by curiosity he, McShane, had looked up the answer in the college library, this Holy Joe aspect of space travel being too much to let pass unsolved. But for that he'd have been stuck.

The implication was that anyone unable to deal with Question Eleven would be recognized as lacking in curiosity and disinterested. Or, if interested, too lazy and devoid of initiative to do anything about it.

He glanced surreptitiously around the room in which forty bothered figures were seated at forty widely separated desks. About a dozen examinees were writing or pretending to do so. One was busily training his left ear to droop to shoulder level. Four were masticating their digits. Most of the others were feeling around their own skulls as if seeking confirmation of the presence or absence of brains.

The discovery of one trap slowed him up considerably. He reconsidered all the questions already answered, treating each one as a potential pitfall. The unanswered questions got the same treatment.

Number Thirty-four looked mighty suspicious. It was planted amid a series of technical queries from which it stuck out like a Sirian's prehensile nose. It was much too artless for comfort. All it said was: In not more than six words define courage.

Well, for better or for worse, here goes. "Courage is fear faced with resolution."

He wiped off the fiftieth question with vast relief, handed in his papers, left the room, wandered thoughtfully around the campus.

Simcox joined him in short time, asked, "How did it go with you?"

"Could have been worse."

"Yes, that's how I felt about it. If you don't hit the

minimum of seventy-five per cent, you're out on your neck. I think I've made it all right."

They waited until Fane arrived. He came half an hour later and wore the sad expression of a frustrated spaniel.

"I got jammed on four stinkers. Every time there's an exam I go loaded with knowledge that evaporates the moment I sit down."

Two days afterward the results went up on the board. McShane muscled through the crowd and took a look.

McShane, Warner. 91%. Pass with credit.

He sprinted headlong for Mercer's House, reached his room with Simcox and Fane panting at his heels.

"Billings! Hey, Billings!"

"You want me, sir?"

"We got through. All three of us." He performed a brief fandango. "Now's the time. The bottle, man. Come on, give with that bottle."

"I am most pleased to learn of your success, sir," said Billings, openly tickled pink.

"Thank you, Billings. And now's the time to celebrate. Get us the bottle and some glasses."

"At eight-thirty, sir."

McShane glanced at his watch. "Hey, that's in one hour's time. What's the idea?"

"I have readied paper and envelopes on your desk, sir. Naturally, you will wish to inform your parents of the result. Your mother especially will be happy to learn of your progress."

"My mother especially?" McShane stared at him. "Why not my father?"

"Your father will be most pleased, also," assured Billings. "But generally speaking, sir, mothers tend to be less confident and more anxious."

"That comes straight from one who knows," commented McShane for the benefit of the others. He returned attention to Billings. "How long have you been a mother?"

"For forty years, sir."

The three went silent. McShane's features softened and his voice became unusually gentle.

"I know what you mean, Billings. We'll have our little party just when you say."

"At eight-thirty to the minute, sir," said Billings. "I will bring glasses and soda."

He departed, Simcox and Fane following. McShane brooded out the window for a while, then went to his desk, reached for pen and paper.

"Dear Mother,—"

The long, vast, incredibly complicated whirl of four years sufficiently jam-packed to simulate a lifetime. Lectures, advice, the din of machine shops, the deafening roar of testpits, banks of instructions with winking lights and flickering needles, starfields on the cinema screen, equations six pages long, ball games, ceremonial parades with bands playing and banners flying, medical check-ups, bloodcounts, blackouts in the centrifuge, snap questions, examinations.

More examinations, more stinkers, more traps. More lectures each deeper than its predecessor. More advice from all quarters high and low.

"You've got to be saturated with a powerful and potent education to handle space and all its problems. We're giving you a long, strong dose of it here. It's a very complex medicine of which every number of the staff is a part. Even your personal servant is a minor ingredient."

"The moment you take up active service as an officer every virtue and every fault is enlarged ten diameters by those under you. A little conceit then gets magnified into insufferable arrogance."

"The latter half of the fourth year is always extremely wearing, sir. May I venture to suggest that a little less relaxation in the noisiest quarter of town and a little more in bed—"

"You fellows must get it into your heads that it doesn't matter a hoot whether you've practiced it fifty or five hundred times. You aren't good enough until you've reduced it to an instinctive reaction. A ship and a couple of hundred men can go to hell while you're seeking time for thought."

"Even your personal servant is a minor ingredient."

"If I may be permitted the remark, sir, an officer is only as strong as the men who support him."

For the last six months McShane functioned as House Proctor of Mercer's, a dignified and learned figure to be viewed with becoming reverence by young and brash first-year men. Simcox and Fane were still with him but the original forty were down to twenty-six.

The final examination was an iron-cased, red-hot heller. It took eight days.

McShane, Warner. 82%. Pass with credit.

After that, a week of wild confusion dominated by a sense of an impending break, of something about to snap loose. Documents, speeches, the last parade with thudding feet and *oompah-oompah*, relatives crowding around, mothers, brothers, sisters in their Sunday best, bags, cases and boxes packed, cheers, handshakes, a blur of faces saying things not heard. And then an aching silence broken only by the purr of the departing car.

He spent a nervy, restless fortnight at home, kissed farewells with a hidden mixture of sadness and relief, reported on the assigned date to the survey-frigate *Mamasea*. Lieutenant McShane, fourth officer, with three men above him, thirty below.

The *Mamasea* soared skyward, became an unseeable dot amid the mighty concourse of stars. Compared with the great battleships and heavy cruisers roaming the far reaches she was a tiny vessel—but well capable of putting Earth beyond communicative distance and almost beyond memory.

It was a long, imposing, official-looking car with two men sitting erect in the front, its sole passenger in the back. With a low hum it came up the drive and stopped. One of the men in front got out, opened the rear door, posed stiffly at attention.

Dismounting, the passenger walked toward the great

doors which bore a circled star on one panel. He was a big man, wise-eyed, gray-haired. The silver joint under his right kneecap made him move with a slight limp.

Finding the doors ajar, he pushed one open, entered a big hall. Momentarily it was empty. For some minutes he studied the long roster of names embossed upon one wall.

Six uniformed men entered from a corridor, marching with even step in two ranks of three. They registered a touch of awe and their arms snapped up in a sixfold salute to which he responded automatically.

Limping through the hall, he found his way out back, across the campus to what once had been Mercer's House. A different name, Lysaght's, was engraved upon its lintel now. Going inside, he reached the first floor, stopped undecided in the corridor.

A middle-aged civilian came into the corridor from the other end, observed him with surprise, hastened up.

"I am Jackson, sir. May I help you?"

The other hesitated, said, "I have a sentimental desire to look out the window of Room Twenty."

Jackson's features showed immediate understanding as he felt in his pocket and produced a master key. "Room Twenty is Mr. Cain's, sir. I know he would be only too glad to have you look around. I take it that it was once your own room, sir?"

"Yes, Jackson, about thirty years ago."

The door clicked open and he walked in. For five minutes he absorbed the old familiar scene.

"Thirty years ago," said Jackson, standing in the doorway. "That would be in Commodore Mercer's time."

"That's right. Did you know him?"

"Oh yes, sir." He smiled deprecatingly. "I was just a boy message-runner then. It's unlikely that you ever encountered me."

"Probably you remember Billings, too?"

"Yes, indeed." Jackson's face lit up. "A most estimable person, sir. He has been dead these many years." He saw the other's expression, added, "I am very sorry, sir."

"So am I." A pause. "I never said good-bye to him."

"Really, sir, you need have no regrets about that. When a young gentleman passes his final and leaves us we expect great excitement and a little forgetfulness. It is quite natural and we are accustomed to it." He smiled reassurance. "Besides, sir, soon after one goes another one comes. We have plenty to keep us busy."

"I'm sure you have."

"If you've sufficient time to spare, sir," continued Jackson, "would you care to visit the staff quarters?"

"Aren't they out of bounds?"

"Not to you, sir. We have a modest collection of photographs going back many years. Some of them are certain to interest you."

"I would much like to see them."

They walked downstairs, across to staff headquarters, entered a lounge. Carefully Jackson positioned a chair, placed a large album on a table.

"While you are looking through this, sir, may I prepare you some coffee?"

"Thank you, Jackson. It is very kind of you."

He opened the album as the other went to the kitchen. First page: a big photo of six hundred men marching in a column of platoons. The saluting-base in the mid-background, the band playing on the left.

The next twenty pages depicted nobody he had known. Then came one of a group of house-masters among whom was Commodore Mercer. Then several clusters of staff members, service and tutorial, among which were a few familiar faces.

Then came a campus shot. One of the figures strolling across the grass was Fane. The last he'd seen of Fane had been twelve years back, out beyond Aldebaran. Fane had been lying in hospital, his skin pale green, his body bloated, but cheerful and on the road to recovery. He'd seen nothing of Fane since that day. He'd seen nothing of Simcox for thirty years and had heard of him only twice.

The middle of the book held an old face with a thousand wrinkles at the corners of its steady, understanding eyes, with muttonchop whiskers on its cheeks. He looked at that one a long time while it seemed to come at him out of the mists of the past.

"If I may say so, sir, an officer and a gentleman is never willfully unkind."

He was still meditating over the face when the sound of distant footsteps and a rattling coffee tray brought him back to the present.

Squaring his gold-braided shoulders, Fleet Commander McShane said in soft, low tones, "God bless you!"

And turned the page.

Editor's Introduction To:

THE TURNING WHEEL

Philip K. Dick

I was, I think, the first science fiction author to write a novel using a microcomputer as a word processor. Now, of course, few are written any other way. One wonders whether the late Philip K. Dick would have used a computer, and if so, would he have used it for more than writing?

There are those who argue that Phil Dick was the best writer science fiction ever produced. Certainly he was one of the most unusual.

His stories include a number of utopian and dystopian themes. Often the two are combined in strange ways. *The Man in the High Castle*, which won the Hugo in 1962, describes a world in which the Axis won World War II. The *I Ching*, that curiously fascinating book of Chinese meditations which many use as an oracle, figures heavily in the story, and according to Dick was used to direct the plot. Now that the *I Ching* is available on microcomputers— Jim Baen, the publisher of this series, not only publishes an electronic version, but was instrumental in creating it—one wonders what else Dick might have done with it.

I only met Phil twice. The most important meeting was

at an academic affair in Fullerton, California. I was president of the Science Fiction Writers of America, and was there to help bless some award or other. It wasn't a good time for SF writers. I was barely making a living, but I was doing better than Phil Dick. According to his autobiography, that was the year he and his wife were eating dog food to stay alive.

In later years Phil experienced considerable success. His *Do Androids Dream of Electric Sleep?* was made into the film *Blade Runner*, with considerable profit to Dick, and his other works began to sell. Then Phil died suddenly, of a cerebral hemorrhage. From what I knew of him, he wouldn't have been much surprised.

The economist Joseph A. Schumpeter thought capitalism was doomed. He didn't much enjoy the prospect, and his analysis was quite different from Marx's, but he was certain that capitalist society would "progress" to the point of collapse.

The key element of his analysis was that he believed, in total contrast to Aristotle, that the bourgeoisie couldn't rule. The destruction of feudalism "meant for the bourgeoisie the breaking of so many fetters and the removal of so many barriers. Politically it meant the replacement of an order in which the bourgeois was a humble subject by another that was more congenial to his rationalist mind and to his immediate interests. But, surveying that process from the standpoint of today, the observer might well wonder whether in the end such complete emancipation was good for the bourgeois and his world. For those fetters not only hampered, they also sheltered." (*Capitalism, Socialism, and Democracy* 3rd ed. Harper, 1950)

What Schumpeter foresaw was a breakdown in the ability to rule, and a focusing of the rationalism of the bourgeoisie not only on the older institutions, but also on the basis of capitalism itself. The problem is that humans are not rational; there needs to be an element of mysticism in government; and there is none of that about the bourgeois. Schumpeter notes, "the stock exchange is a poor substitute for the Holy Grail. We have seen that the industrialist and merchant, as far as they are entrepreneurs, also fill a function of leadership. But economic leadership of this type does not readily expand, like the medieval lord's military leadership, into the leadership of nations. On the contrary, the ledger and the cost calculation absorb and confine."

C. Northcote Parkinson, like Schumpeter, sees that democratic capitalism will probably lead inevitably to socialism. Democracies survive until the citizens discover they can vote themselves largess from the public treasury. Then they begin the inexorable process of transferring wealth from the productive to the numerous. What happens next depends in large part on how much wealth there is. Given enough money, the situation can last for a long time, provided there are no powerful external enemies. Eventually, though, the need for economic production, coupled with the disincentive of the productive to do any more work than they have to, often leads to an authoritarian society.

There could be another form of social collapse: religion is often more powerful than economics.

At the time Phil Dick wrote this, California's political economy was greatly influenced by a man who put naturalism and environmentalism ahead of everything else, and who boasted that "the only physics I ever took was Ex Lax." At the same time another former Californian, then resident in the Mediterranean, had started what was first billed as a major advance in scientific psychology, then a secular movement, and finally a mystical church that taught an extreme form of reincarnation. That church looked very much like it would grow exponentially.

Mix hatred of technology, environmentalism, and naturalism; add the notion that science is a bore, while poets and bards are the most important creatures ever born; and you get a religion that certainly will make the world a place different from what it is now.

THE TURNING WHEEL
Philip K. Dick

Bard Chai said thoughtfully, "Cults." He examined a tape-report grinding from the receptor. The receptor was rusty and unoiled; it whined piercingly and sent up an acrid wisp of smoke. Chai shut it off as its pitted surface began to heat ugly red. Presently he finished with the tape and tossed it with a heap of refuse jamming the mouth of a disposal slot.

"What about cults?" Bard Sung-wu asked faintly. He brought himself back with an effort, and forced a smile of interest on his plump olive-yellow face. "You were saying?"

"Any stable society is menaced by cults; our society is no exception." Chai rubbed his finely-tapered fingers together reflectively. "Certain lower strata are axiomatically dissatisfied. Their hearts burn with envy of those the wheel has placed above them; in secret they form fanatic, rebellious bands. They meet in the dark of the night; they insidiously express inversions of accepted norms; they delight in flaunting basic mores and customs."

"Ugh," Sung-wu agreed. "I mean," he explained quickly, "it seems incredible people could practice such fanatic and disgusting rites." He got nervously to his feet. "I must go, if it's permitted."

"Wait," snapped Chai. "You are familiar with the Detroit area?"

Uneasily, Sung-wu nodded. "Very slightly."

With characteristic vigour, Chai made his decision. "I'm sending you; investigate and make a blue-slip report. If this group is dangerous, the Holy Arm should know. It's of the worst elements—the Techno class." He made a wry face. "Caucasians, hulking, hairy things. We'll give you six months in Spain, on your return; you can poke over ruins of abandoned cities."

"Caucasians!" Sung-wu exclaimed, his face turning green. "But I haven't been well; please, if somebody else could go—"

"You, perhaps, hold to the Broken Feather theory?" Chai raised an eyebrow. "An amazing philologist, Broken Feather; I took partial instruction from him. He held, you know, the Caucasian to be descended of Neanderthal stock. Their extreme size, thick body hair, their general brutish cast, reveal an innate inability to comprehend anything but a purely animalistic horizontal; proselytism is a waste of time."

He affixed the younger man with a stern eye. "I wouldn't send you, if I didn't have unusual faith in your devotion."

Sung-wu fingered his beads miserably. "Elron be praised," he muttered; "you are too kind."

Sung-wu slid into a lift and was raised, amid great groans and whirrings and false stops, to the top level of the Central Chamber building. He hurried down a corridor dimly lit by occasional yellow bulbs. A moment later he approached the doors of the scanning offices and flashed his identification at the robot guard. "Is Bard Fei-p'ang within?" he inquired.

"Verily," the robot answered, stepping aside.

Sung-wu entered the offices, bypassed the rows of rusted, discarded machines, and entered the still-functioning wing. He located his brother-in-law, hunched over some graphs at one of the desks, laboriously copying material by hand. "Clearness be with you," Sung-wu murmured.

Fei-p'ang glanced up in annoyance. "I told you not to come again; if the Arm finds out I'm letting you use the scanner for a personal plot, they'll stretch me on the rack."

"Gently," Sung-wu murmured, his hand on his relation's shoulder. "This is the last time. I'm going away; one more look, a final look." His olive face took on a pleading, piteous cast. "The turn comes for me very soon; this will be our last conversation."

Sung-wu's piteous look hardened into cunning. "You wouldn't want it on your soul; no restitution will be possible at this late date."

Fei-p'ang snorted. "All right; but for Elron's sake, do it quickly."

Sung-wu hurried to the mother-scanner and seated himself in the rickety basket. He snapped on the controls, clamped his forehead to the viewpiece, inserted his identity tab, and set the space-time finger into motion. Slowly, reluctantly, the ancient mechanism coughed into life and began tracing his personal tab along the future track.

Sung-wu's hands shook; his body trembled; sweat dripped from his neck, as he saw himself scampering in miniature. *Poor Sung-wu*, he thought wretchedly. The mite of a thing hurried about its duties; this was but eight months hence. Harried and beset, it performed its tasks—and then, in a subsequent continuum, fell down and died.

Sung-wu removed his eyes from the viewpiece and waited for his pulse to slow. He could stand that part, watching the moment of death; it was what came next that was too jangling for him.

He breathed a silent prayer. Had he fasted enough? In the four-day purge and self-flagellation, he had used the whip with metal points, the heaviest possible. He had given away all his money; he had smashed a lovely vase his mother had left him, a treasured heirloom; he had rolled in the filth and mud in the centre of town. Hundreds had seen him. Now, surely, all this was enough. But time was so short!

Faint courage stirring, he sat up and again put his eyes to the viewpiece. He was shaking with terror. What if it hadn't changed? What if his mortification weren't enough? He spun the controls, sending the finger tracing his time-track past the moment of death.

Sung-wu shrieked and scrambled back in horror. His future was the same, exactly the same; there had been no change at all. His guilt had been too great to be washed away in such short a time; it would take ages—and he didn't have ages.

He left the scanner and passed by his brother-in-law. "Thanks," he muttered shakily.

For once, a measure of compassion touched Fei-p'ang's

efficient brown features. "Bad news? The next turn brings an unfortunate manifestation?"

"Bad scarcely describes it."

Fei-p'ang's pity turned to righteous rebuke. "Who do you have to blame but yourself?" he demanded sternly. "You know your conduct in this manifestation determines the next; if you look forward to a future life as a lower animal, it should make you glance over your behaviour and repent your wrongs. The cosmic law that governs us is impartial. It is true justice: cause and effect; what you do determines what you next become—there can be no blame and no sorrow. There can be only understanding and repentance." His curiosity overcame him. "What is it? A snake? A squirrel?"

"It's no affair of yours," Sung-wu said, as he moved unhappily toward the exit doors.

"I'll look myself."

"Go ahead." Sung-wu pushed moodily out into the hall. He was dazed with despair: it hadn't changed; it was still the same.

In eight months he would die, stricken by one of the numerous plagues that swept over the inhabited parts of the world. He would become feverish, break out with red spots, turn and twist in an anguish of delirium. His bowels would drop out; his flesh would waste away; his eyes would roll up; and after an interminable time of suffering, he would die. His body would lie in a mass heap, with hundreds of others—a whole streetful of dead, to be carted away by one of the robot sweepers, happily immune. His mortal remains would be burned in a common rubbish incinerator at the outskirts of the city.

Meanwhile, the eternal spark, Sung-wu's divine soul, would hurry from this space-time manifestation to the next in order. But it would not rise; it would sink; he had watched its descent on the scanner many times. There was always the same hideous picture—a sight beyond endurance—of his soul, as it plummeted down like a stone, into one of the lowest continua, a sinkhole of a manifestation at the very bottom of the ladder.

He had sinned. In his youth, Sung-wu had got mixed up with a black-eyed wench with long flowing hair, a glittering waterfall down her back and shoulders. Inviting red lips, plump breasts, hips that undulated and beckoned unmistakably. She was the wife of a friend, from the Warrior class, but he had taken her as his mistress; he had been *certain* time remained to rectify his venality.

But he was wrong: the wheel was soon to turn for him. The plague—not enough time to fast and pray and do good works. He was determined to go down, straight down to a wallowing, foul-aired planet in a stinking red-sun system, an ancient pit of filth and decay and unending slime—a jungle world of the lowest type.

In it, he would be a shiny-winged fly, a great blue-bottomed, buzzing carrion-eater that hummed and guzzled and crawled through the rotting carcasses of great lizards, slain in combat.

From this swamp, this pest-ridden planet in a diseased, contaminated system, he would have to rise painfully up the endless rungs of the cosmic ladder he had already climbed. It had taken eons to climb this far, to the level of a human being on the planet Earth, in the bright yellow Sol system; now he would have to do it all over again.

Chai beamed, "Elron be with you," as the corroded observation ship was checked by the robot crew, and finally okayed for limited flight. Sung-wu slowly entered the ship and seated himself at what remained of the controls. He waved listlessly, then slammed the lock and bolted it by hand.

As the ship limped into the late afternoon sky, he reluctantly consulted the reports and records Chai had transferred to him.

The Tinkerists were a small cult; they claimed only a few hundred members, all drawn from the Techno class, which was the most despised of the social castes. The Bards, of course, were at the top; they were the teachers of society, the holy men who guided man to clearness. Then the Poets; they turned into saga the great legends of

Elron Hu, who lived (according to legend) in the hideous days of the Time of Madness. Below the Poets were the Artists; then the Musicians; then the Workers, who supervised the robot crews. After them the Businessmen, the Warriors, the Farmers, and finally, at the bottom, the Technos.

Most of the Technos were Caucasians—immense white-kinned things, incredibly hairy, like apes; their resemblance to the great apes was striking. Perhaps Broken Feather was right; perhaps they did have Neanderthal blood and were outside the possibility of clearness. Sung-wu had always considered himself an anti-racist; he disliked those who maintained the Caucasians were a race apart. Extremists believed eternal damage would result to the species if the Caucasians were allowed to intermarry.

In any case, the problem was academic; no decent, self-respecting woman of the higher classes—of Indian or Mongolian, or Bantu stock—would allow herself to be approached by a *Cauc*.

Below his ship, the barren countryside spread out, ugly and bleak. Great red spots that hadn't yet been overgrown, and slag surfaces were still visible—but by this time most ruins were covered by soil and crabgrass. He could see men and robots farming; villages, countless tiny brown circles in the green fields; occasional ruins of ancient cities—gaping sores like blind mouths, eternally open to the sky. They would never close, not now.

Ahead was the Detroit area, named, so it ran, for some now-forgotten spiritual leader. There were more villages, here. Off to his left, the leaden surface of a body of water, a lake of some kind. Beyond that—only Elron knew. No one went that far; there was no human life there, only wild animals and deformed things spawned from radiation infestation still lying heavy in the north.

He dropped his ship down. An open field lay to his right; a robot farmer was plowing with a metal hook welded to its waist, a section torn off some discarded machine. It stopped dragging the hook and gazed up in amazement, as Sung-wu landed the ship awkwardly and bumped to a halt.

"Clearness be with you," the robot rasped obediently, as Sung-wu climbed out.

Sung-wu gathered up his bundle of reports and papers and stuffed them in a briefcase. He snapped the ship's lock and hurried off toward the ruins of the city. The robot went back to dragging the rusty metal hook through the hard ground, its pitted body bent double with the strain, working slowly, silently, uncomplaining.

The little boy piped, "Whither, Bard?" as Sung-wu pushed wearily through the tangled debris and slag. He was a little black-faced Bantu, in red rags sewed and patched together. He ran alongside Sung-wu like a puppy, leaping and bounding and grinning white-teethed.

Sung-wu became immediately crafty; his intrigue with the black-haired girl had taught him elemental dodges and evasions. "My ship broke down," he answered cautiously; it was certainly common enough. "It was the last ship still in operation at our field."

The boy skipped and laughed and broke off bits of green weeds that grew along the trail. "I know somebody who can fix it," he cried carelessly.

Sung-wu's pulse-rate changed. "Oh?" he murmured, as if uninterested. "There are those around here who practise the questionable art of repairing."

The boy nodded solemnly.

"Technos?" Sung-wu pursued. "Are there many of them here, around these old ruins?"

More black-faced boys, and some little dark-eyed Bantu girls, came scampering through the slag and ruins. "What's the matter with your ship?" one hollered at Sung-wu. "Won't it run?"

They all ran and shouted around him, as he advanced slowly—an unusually wild bunch, completely undisciplined. They rolled and fought and tumbled and chased each other around madly.

"How many of you," Sung-wu demanded, "have taken your first instruction?"

There was a sudden uneasy silence. The children looked at each other guiltily; none of them answered.

"Good Elron!" Sung-wu exclaimed in horror. "Are you all untaught?"

Heads hung guiltily.

"How do you expect to phase yourselves with the cosmic will? How can you expect to know the divine plan? This is really too much!"

He pointed a plump finger at one of the boys. "Are you constantly preparing yourself for the life to come? Are you constantly purging and purifying yourself? Do you deny yourself meat, sex, entertainment, financial gain, education, leisure?"

But it was obvious; their unrestrained laughter and play proved they were still jangled, far from clear— And clearness is the only road by which a person can gain understanding of the eternal plan, the cosmic wheel which turns endlessly, for all living things.

"Butterflies!" Sung-wu snorted with disgust. "You are no better than the beasts and birds of the field, who take no heed of the morrow. You play and game for today, thinking tomorrow won't come. Like insects—"

But the thought of insects reminded him of the shiny-winged blue-rumped fly, creeping over a rotting lizard carcass, and Sung-wu's stomach did a flip-flop; he forced it back in place and strode on, toward the line of villages emerging ahead.

Farmers were working the barren fields on all sides. A thin layer of soil over slag; a few limp wheat stalks waved, thin and emaciated. The ground was terrible, the worst he had seen. He could feel the metal under his feet; it was almost to the surface. Bent men and women watered their sickly crops with tin cans, old metal containers picked from the ruins. An ox was pulling a crude cart.

In another field, women were weeding by hand; all moved slowly, stupidly, victims of hookworm, from the soil. They were all barefoot. The children hadn't picked it up yet, but they soon would.

Sung-wu gazed up at the sky and gave thanks to Elron; here, suffering was unusually severe; trials of exceptional vividness lay on every hand. These men and women were being tempered in a hot crucible; their souls were probably purified to an astonishing degree. A baby lay in the shade, beside a half-dozing mother. Flies crawled over its eyes; its mother breathed heavily, hoarsely, her mouth open. An unhealthy flush discolored her brown cheeks. Her belly bulged; she was already pregnant again. Another eternal soul to be raised from a lower level. Her great breasts sagged and wobbled as she stirred in her sleep, spilling out over her dirty wraparound.

"Come here," Sung-wu called sharply to the gang of black-faced children who followed along after him. "I'm going to talk to you."

The children approached, eyes on the ground, and assembled in a silent circle around him. Sung-wu sat down, placed his briefcase beside him and folded his legs expertly under him in the traditional posture outlined by Elron in his seventh book of teaching.

"I will ask and you will answer," Sung-wu stated. "You know the basic catechisms?" He peered sharply around. "Who knows the basic catechisms?"

One or two hands went up. Most of the children looked away unhappily.

"First!" snapped Sung-wu. *"Who are you?* You are a minute fragment of the cosmic plan.

"Second! *What are you?* A mere speck in a system so vast as to be beyond comprehension.

"Third! *What is the way of life?* To fulfill what is required by the cosmic forces.

"Fourth! *Where are you?* On one step of the cosmic ladder.

"Fifth! *Where have you been?* Through endless steps; each turn of the wheel advances or depresses you.

"Sixth! *What determines your direction at the next turn?* Your conduct in this manifestation.

"Seventh! *What is right conduct?* Submitting yourself to the eternal forces, the cosmic elements that make up the divine plan.

"Eighth! *What is the significance of suffering?* To purify the soul.

"Ninth. *What is the significance of death?* To release he person from this manifestation, so he may rise to a ew rung of the ladder.

"Tenth—"

But at that moment Sung-wu broke off. Two quasi-uman shapes were approaching him. Immense white-kinned figures striding across the baked fields, between he sickly rows of wheat.

Technos—coming to meet him; his flesh crawled. Caucs. 'heir skins glittered pale and unhealthy, like nocturnal nsects, dug from under rocks.

He rose to his feet, conquered his disgust, and prepared o greet them.

Sung-wu said, "Clearness!" He could smell them, a nusky sheep smell, as they came to a halt in front of him. 'wo bucks, two immense sweating males, skin damp and ticky, with beards, and long disorderly hair. They wore ailcloth trousers and boots. With horror Sung-wu per-eived a thick body-hair, on their chests, like woven mats—ufts in their armpits, on their arms, wrists, even the backs f their hands. Maybe Broken Feather was right; perhaps, n these great lumbering blond-haired beasts, the archaic Jeanderthal stock—the false men—still survived. He could lmost see the ape, peering from behind their blue eyes.

"Hi," the first Cauc said. After a moment he added eflectively, "My name's Jamison."

"Pete Ferris," the other grunted. Neither of them ob-erved the customary deferences; Sung-wu winced but nanaged not to show it. Was it deliberate, a veiled insult, r perhaps mere ignorance? This was hard to tell; in lower classes there was, as Chai said, an ugly undercurrent of esentment and envy, and hostility.

"I'm making a routine survey," Sung-wu explained, "on irth and death rates in rural areas. I'll be here a few days. s there some place I can stay? Some public inn or hostel?"

The two Cauc bucks were silent. "Why?" one of them lemanded bluntly.

Sung-wu blinked. "Why? Why what?"

"Why are you making a survey? If you want any information we'll supply it."

Sung-wu was incredulous. "Do you know to whom you're talking? I'm a Bard! Why, you're ten classes down; how dare you—" He choked with rage. In these rural areas the Technos had utterly forgotten their place. What was ailing the local Bards? Were they letting the system break apart?

He shuddered violently at the thought of what it would mean if Technos and Farmers and Businessmen were allowed to intermingle—even intermarry, and eat, and drink, in the same places. The whole structure of society would collapse. If all were to ride the same carts, use the same outhouses; it passed belief. A sudden nightmare picture loomed up before Sung-wu, of Technos living and mating with women of the Bard and Poet classes. He visioned a horizontally-oriented society, all persons on the same level, with horror. It went against the very grain of the cosmos, against the divine plan; it was the Time of Madness all over again. He shuddered.

"Where is the Manager of this area?" he demanded. "Take me to him; I'll deal directly with him."

The two Caucs turned and headed back the way they had come, without a word. After a moment of fury, Sung-wu followed behind them.

They led him through withered fields and over barren, eroded hills on which nothing grew; the ruins increased. At the edge of the city, a line of meagre villages had been set up; he saw leaning, rickety wood huts, and mud streets. From the villages a thick stench rose, the smell of offal and death.

Dogs lay sleeping under the huts; children poked and played in the filth and rotting debris. A few old people sat on porches, vacant-faced, eyes glazed and dull. Chickens pecked around, and he saw pigs and skinny cats—and the eternal rusting piles of metal, sometimes thirty feet high. Great towers of red slag were heaped up everywhere.

Beyond the villages were the ruins proper—endless miles of abandoned wreckage; skeletons of buildings; concrete walls; bathtubs and pipe; overturned wrecks that had been ars. All these were from the Time of Madness, the decade that had finally rung the curtain down on the sorriest interval in man's history. The five centuries of madness and jangledness were now known as the Age of Heresy, when man had gone against the divine plan and taken his destiny in his own hands.

They came to a larger hut, a two-story wood structure. The Caucs climbed a decaying flight of steps; boards creaked and gave ominously under their heavy boots. Sung-wu followed them nervously; they came out on a porch, a kind of open balcony.

On the balcony sat a man, an obese copper-skinned official in unbuttoned breeches, his shiny black hair pulled back and tied with a bone against his bulging red neck. His nose was large and prominent, his face, flat and wide, with many chins. He was drinking lime juice from a tin cup and gazing down at the mud street below. As the two Caucs appeared he rose slightly, a prodigious effort.

"This man," the Cauc named Jamison said, indicating Sung-wu, "wants to see you."

Sung-wu pushed angrily forward. "I am a Bard, from the Central Chamber; do you people recognize *this*?" He tore open his robe and flashed the symbol of the Holy Arm, gold worked to form a swath of flaming red. "I insist you accord me proper treatment! I'm not here to be pushed around by any—"

He had said too much; Sung-wu forced his anger down and gripped his briefcase. The fat Indian was studying him calmly; the two Caucs had wandered to the far end of the balcony and were squatting down in the shade. They lit crude cigarettes and turned their backs.

"Do you permit this?" Sung-wu demanded, incredulous. "This—mingling?"

The Indian shrugged and sagged down even more in his chair. "Clearness be with you," he murmured; "will you join me?" His calm expression remained unchanged; he seemed not to have noticed. "Some lime juice? Or perhaps coffee? Lime juice is good for these." He tapped his mouth; his soft gums were lined with caked sores.

"Nothing for me," Sung-wu muttered grumpily, as he took a seat opposite the Indian; "I'm here on an official survey."

The Indian nodded faintly. "Oh?"

"Birth and death rates." Sung-wu hesitated, then leaned toward the Indian. "I insist you send those two Caucs away; what I have to say to you is private."

The Indian showed no change of expression; his broad face was utterly impassive. After a time he turned slightly. "Please go down to the street level," he ordered. "As you will."

The two Caucs got to their feet, grumbling, and pushed past the table, scowling and darting resentful glances at Sung-wu. One of them hawked and elaborately spat over the railing, an obvious insult.

"Insolence!" Sung-wu choked. "How can you allow it? Did you see them? By Elron, it's beyond belief!"

The Indian shrugged indifferently—and belched. "All men are brothers on the wheel. Didn't Elron Himself teach that, when He was on Earth?"

"Of course. But—"

"Are not even these men our brothers?"

"Naturally," Sung-wu answered haughtily, "but they must know their place; they're an insignificant class. In the rare event some object wants fixing, they are called; but in the last year I do not recall a single incident when it was deemed advisable to repair anything. The need of such a class diminishes yearly; eventually such a class and the elements composing it—"

"You perhaps advocate sterilization?" the Indian inquired, heavy-lidded and sly.

"I advocate *something*. The lower classes reproduce like rabbits; spawning all the time—much faster than we Bards. I always see some swollen-up Cauc woman, but hardly a single Bard is born these days; the lower classes must fornicate constantly."

"That's about all that's left them," the Indian murmured mildly. He sipped a little lime juice. "You should try to be more tolerant."

"Tolerant? I have nothing against them, as long as they—"

"It is said," the Indian continued softly, "that Elron Hu, Himself, was a Cauc."

Sung-wu spluttered indignantly and started to rejoin, but the hot words stuck fast in his mouth; down the mud street something was coming.

Sung-wu demanded, "What is it?" He leaped up excitedly and hurried to the railing.

A slow procession was advancing with solemn step. As if at a signal, men and women poured from their rickety huts and excitedly lined the street to watch. Sung-wu was transfixed, as the procession neared; his senses reeled. More and more men and women were collecting each moment; there seemed to be hundreds of them. They were a dense, murmuring mob, packed tight, swaying back and forth, faces avid. An hysterical moan passed through them, a great wind that stirred them like leaves of a tree. They were a single collective whole, a vast primitive organism, held ecstatic and hypnotized by the approaching column.

The marchers wore a strange costume: white shirts, with the sleeves rolled up; dark gray trousers of an incredibly archaic design, and black shoes. All were dressed exactly alike. They formed a dazzling double line of white shirts, gray trousers, marching calmly and solemnly, faces up, nostrils flared, jaws stern. A glazed fanaticism stamped each man and woman, such a ruthless expression that Sung-wu shrank back in terror. On and on they came, figures of grim stone in their primordial white shirts and gray trousers, a frightening breath from the past. Their heels struck the ground in a dull, harsh beat that reverberated among the rickety huts. The dogs woke; the children began to wail. The chickens flew squawking.

"Elron!" Sung-wu cried. "What's happening?"

The marchers carried strange symbolic implements, ritualistic images with esoteric meaning that of necessity escaped Sung-wu. There were tubes and poles, and shiny webs of what looked like metal. *Metal!* But it was not rusty; it was shiny and bright. He was stunned; they looked—new.

The procession passed directly below. After the marchers came a huge rumbling cart. On it was mounted an obvious fertility symbol, a corkscrew-bore as long as a tree; it jutted from a square cube of gleaming steel; as the cart moved forward the bore lifted and fell.

After the cart came more marchers, also grim-faced, eyes glassy, loaded down with pipes and tubes and armfuls of glittering equipment. They passed on, and then the street was filled by surging throngs of awed men and women, who followed after them, utterly dazed. And then came children and barking dogs.

The last marcher carried a pennant that fluttered above her as she strode along, a tall pole, hugged tight to her chest. At the top, the bright pennant fluttered boldly. Sung-wu made its marking out, and for a moment consciousness left him. There it was, directly below; it had passed under his very nose, out in the open for all to see—unconcealed. The pennant had a great T emblazoned on it.

"They—" he began, but the obese Indian cut him off.

"The Tinkerists," he rumbled, and sipped his lime juice.

Sung-wu grabbed up his briefcase and scrambled toward the stairs. At the bottom, the two hulking Caucs were already moving into action. The Indian signalled quickly to them. "Here!" They started grimly up, little blue eyes mean, red-rimmed and cold as stone; under their pelts their bulging muscles rippled.

Sung-wu fumbled in his cloak. His shiver-gun came out; he squeezed the release and directed it toward the two Caucs. But nothing happened; the gun had stopped functioning. He shook it wildly; flakes of rust and dried insulation fluttered from it. It was useless, worn out; he tossed it away and then, with the resolve of desperation, jumped through the railing.

He, and a torrent of rotten wood, cascaded to the street. He hit, rolled, struck his head against the corner of a hut, and shakily pulled himself to his feet.

He ran. Behind him, the two Caucs pushed after him through the throngs of men and women milling aimlessly along. Occasionally he glimpsed their white, perspiring faces. He turned a corner, raced between shabby huts, leaped over a sewage ditch, climbed heaps of sagging debris, slipping and rolling and at last lay gasping behind a tree, his briefcase still clutched.

The Caucs were nowhere in sight. He had evaded them; for the moment, he was safe.

He peered around. Which way was his ship? He shielded his eyes against the late-afternoon sun until he managed to make out its bent, tubular outline. It was far off to his right, barely visible in the dying glare that hung gloomily across the sky. Sung-wu got unsteadily to his feet and began walking cautiously in that direction.

He was in a terrible spot; the whole region was pro-Tinkerist—even the Chamber-appointed Manager. And it wasn't along class lines; the cult had knifed to the top level. And it wasn't just Caucs, anymore; he couldn't count on Bantu or Mongolian or Indian, not in this area. An entire countryside was hostile, and lying in wait for him.

Elron, it was worse than the Arm had thought! No wonder they wanted a report. A whole area had swung over to a fanatic cult, a violent extremist group of heretics, teaching a most diabolical doctrine. He shuddered—and kept on, avoiding contact with the farmers in their fields, both human and robot. He increased his pace, as alarm and horror pushed him suddenly faster.

If the thing were to spread, if it were to hit a sizable portion of mankind, it might bring back the Time of Madness.

The ship was taken. Three or four immense Caucs stood lounging around it, cigarettes dangling from their slack mouths, white-faced and hairy. Stunned, Sung-wu moved back down the hillside, prickles of despair numbing him. The ship was lost; they had got there ahead of him. What was he supposed to do now?

It was almost evening. He'd have to walk fifty miles through the darkness, over unfamiliar, hostile ground, to reach the next inhabited area. The sun was already beginning to set, the air turning cool; and in addition, he was sopping wet with filth and slimy water. He had slipped in the gloom and fallen in a sewage ditch.

He retraced his steps, mind blank. What could he do? He was helpless; his shiver-gun had been useless. He was alone, and there was no contact with the Arm. Tinkerists swarming on all sides; they'd probably gut him and sprinkle his blood over the crops—or worse.

He skirted a farm. In the fading twilight, a dim figure was working, a young woman. He eyed her cautiously, as he passed; she had her back to him. She was bending over, between rows of corn. What was she doing? Was she—good Elron!

He stumbled blindly across the field toward her, caution forgotten. "Young woman! *Stop!* In the name of Elron, stop at once!"

The girl straightened up. "Who are you?"

Breathless, Sung-wu arrived in front of her, gripping his battered briefcase and gasping. "Those are our *brothers!* How can you destroy them? They may be close relatives, recently deceased." He struck out and knocked the jar from her hand; it hit the ground and the imprisoned beetles scurried off in all directions.

The girl's cheeks flushed with anger. "It took me an hour to collect those!"

"You were killing them! Crushing them!" He was speechless with horror. "I saw you!"

"Of course." The girl raised her black eyebrows. "They gnaw the corn."

"They're our brothers!" Sung-wu repeated wildly. "Of course they gnaw the corn; because of certain sins committed, the cosmic forces have—" He broke off, appalled. "Don't you *know*? You've never been told?"

The girl was perhaps sixteen. In the fading light she was a small, slender figure, the empty jar in one hand, a rock in the other. A tide of black hair tumbled down her neck. Her eyes were large and luminous; her lips full and deep red; her skin a smooth copper-brown—Polynesian, probably. He caught a glimpse of firm brown breasts as she bent to grab a beetle that had landed on its back. The sight made his pulse race; in a flash he was back three years.

"What's your name?" he asked, more kindly.

"Frija."

"How old are you?"

"Seventeen."

"I am a Bard; have you ever spoken to a Bard before?"

"No," the girl murmured. "I don't think so."

She was almost invisible in the darkness. Sung-wu could scarcely see her, but what he saw sent his heart into an agony of paroxysms; the same cloud of black hair, the same deep red lips. This girl was younger, of course—a mere child, and from the Farmer class, at that. But she had Liu's figure, and in time she'd ripen—probably in a matter of months.

Ageless, honeyed craft worked his vocal cords. "I have landed in this area to make a survey. Something has gone wrong with my ship and I must remain the night. I know no one here, however. My plight is such that—"

"Oh," Frija said, immediately sympathetic. "Why don't you stay with us, tonight? We have an extra room, now that my brother's away."

"Delighted," Sung-wu answered instantly. "Will you lead the way? I'll gladly repay you for your kindness." The girl moved off toward a vague shape looming up in the darkness. Sung-wu hurried quickly after her. "I find it incredible you haven't been instructed. This whole area has deteriorated beyond belief. What ways have you fallen in? We'll have to spend much time together; I can see that already. Not one of you even approaches clearness—you're jangled, every one of you."

"What does that mean?" Frija asked, as she stepped up on the porch and opened the door.

"Jangled?" Sung-wu blinked in amazement. "We *will*

have to study much together." In his eagerness, he tripped on the top step, and barely managed to catch himself. "Perhaps you need complete instruction; it may be necessary to start from the very bottom. I can arrange a stay at the Holy Arm for you—under my protection, of course. Jangled means out of harmony with the cosmic elements. How can you live this way? My dear, you'll have to be brought back in line with the divine plan!"

"What plan is that?" She led him into a warm living room; a crackling fire burned in the grate. Three men sat around a rough wood table; an old man with long white hair and two younger men. A frail, withered old woman sat dozing in a rocker in the corner. In the kitchen, a buxom young woman was fixing the evening meal.

"Why, *the* plan!" Sung-wu answered, astounded. His eyes darted around. Suddenly his briefcase fell to the floor. "Caucs," he said.

They were all Caucasians, even Frija. She was deeply tanned; her skin was almost black; but she was a Cauc, nonetheless. He recalled: Caucs, in the sun, turned dark, sometimes even darker than Mongolians. The girl had tossed her work robe over a door hook; in her household shorts her thighs were as white as milk. And the old man and woman—

"This is my grandfather," Frija said, indicating the old man. "Benjamin Tinker."

Under the watchful eyes of the two younger Tinkers, Sung-wu was washed and scrubbed, given clean clothes, and then fed. He ate only a little; he didn't feel very well.

"I can't understand it," he muttered, as he listlessly pushed his plate away. "The scanner at the Central Chamber said I had eight months left. The plague will—" He considered. "But it can always change. The scanner goes on prediction, not certainty; multiple possibilities; free will. . . . Any overt act of sufficient significance—"

Ben Tinker laughed. "You want to stay alive?"

"Of course!" Sung-wu muttered indignantly.

They all laughed—even Frija, and the old woman in her shawl, snow-white hair and mild blue eyes. They were the first Cauc women he had ever seen. They weren't big and lumbering like the male Caucs; they didn't seem to have the same bestial characteristics. The two young Cauc bucks looked plenty tough, though; they and their father were poring over an elaborate series of papers and reports, spread out on the dinner table, among the empty plates.

"This area," Ben Tinker murmured. "Pipes should go here. And here. Water's the main need. Before the next crop goes in, we'll dump a few hundred pounds of artificial fertilizers and plough it in. The power plough should be ready then."

"After that?" one of the tow-headed sons asked.

"Then spraying. If we don't have the nicotine sprays, we'll have to try the copper dusting again. I prefer the spray, but we're still behind on production. The bore has dug us up some good storage caverns, though. It ought to start picking up."

"And here," a son said, "there's going to be need of draining. A lot of mosquito breeding going on. We can try the oil, as we did over here. But I suggest the whole thing be filled in. We can use the dredge and scoop, if they're not tied up."

Sung-wu had taken this all in. Now he rose unsteadily to his feet, trembling with wrath. He pointed a shaking finger at the elder Tinker.

"You're—meddling!" he gasped.

They looked up. "Meddling?"

"With the plan! With the cosmic plan! Good Elron—you're interfering with the divine processes. Why—" He was staggered by a realization so alien it convulsed the very core of his being. "You're actually going to set back turns of the wheel."

"That," said old Ben Tinker, "is right."

Sung-wu sat down again, stunned. His mind refused to take it all in. "I don't understand; what'll happen? If you slow the wheel, if you disrupt the divine plan—"

"He's going to be a problem," Ben Tinker murmured thoughtfully. "If we kill him, the Arm will merely send another; they have hundreds like him. And if we don't kill him, if we send him back, he'll raise a hue and cry that'll bring the whole Chamber down here. It's too soon for this to happen. We're gaining support fast, but we need another few months."

Sweat stood out on Sung-wu's plump forehead. He wiped it away shakily. "If you kill me," he muttered, "you will sink down many rungs of the cosmic ladder. You have risen this far; why undo the work accomplished in endless ages past?"

Ben Tinker fixed one powerful blue eye on him. "My friend," he said slowly, "isn't it true one's next manifestation is determined by one's moral conduct in this?"

Sung-wu nodded. "Such is well known."

"And what is right conduct?"

"Fulfilling the divine plan," Sung-wu responded immediately.

"Maybe our whole Movement is part of the plan," Ben Tinker said thoughtfully. "Maybe the cosmic forces *want* us to drain the swamps and kill the grasshoppers and inoculate the children; after all, the cosmic forces put us all here."

"If you kill me," Sung-wu wailed, "I'll be a carrion-eating fly. I *saw* it, a shiny-winged, blue-rumped fly crawling over the carcass of a dead lizard— In a rotting, steaming jungle in a filthy cesspool of a planet." Tears came; he dabbed at them futilely. "In an out-of-the-way system, at the bottom of the ladder!"

Tinker was amused. "Why this?"

"I've sinned." Sung-wu sniffed and flushed. "I committed adultery."

"Can't you purge yourself?"

"There's no time!" His misery rose to wild despair. "My mind is *still* impure!" He indicated Frija, standing in the bedroom doorway, a supple white and tan shape in her household shorts. "I continue to think carnal thoughts; I can't rid myself. In eight months the plague will turn the wheel on me—and it'll be done! If I lived to be an old man, withered and toothless—no more appetite—" His plump body quivered in a frenzied convulsion. "There's no *time* to purge and atone. According to the scanner, I'm going to die a young man!"

After this torrent of words, Tinker was silent, deep in thought. "The plague," he said at last. "What, exactly, are the symptoms?"

Sung-wu described them, his olive face turning to a sickly green. When he had finished, the three men looked significantly at each other.

Ben Tinker got to his feet. "Come along," he commanded briskly, taking the Bard by the arm. "I have something to show you. It is left from the old days. Sooner or later we'll advance enough to turn out our own, but right now we have only these remaining few. We have to keep them guarded and sealed."

"This is for a good cause," one of the sons said. "It's worth it." He caught his brother's eye and grinned.

Bard Chai finished reading Sung-wu's blue-slip report; he tossed it suspiciously down and eyed the younger Bard. "You're sure? There's no further need of investigation?"

"The cult will wither away," Sung-wu murmured indifferently. "It lacks any real support; it's merely an escape valve, without intrinsic validity."

Chai wasn't convinced. He reread parts of the report again. "I suppose you're right; but we've heard so many—"

"Lies," Sung-wu said vaguely. "Rumours. Gossip. May I go?" He moved toward the door.

"Eager for your vacation?" Chai smiled understandingly. "I know how you feel. This report must have exhausted you. Rural areas, stagnant backwaters. We must prepare a better programme of rural education. I'm convinced whole regions are in a jangled state. We've got to bring clearness to these people. It's our historic role; our class function."

"Verily," Sung-wu murmured, as he bowed his way out of the office and down the hall.

As he walked he fingered his beads thankfully. He breathed a silent prayer as his fingers moved over the surface of the little red pellets, shiny spheres that glowed freshly in place of the faded old—the gift of the Tinkerists. The beads would come in handy; he kept his hand on them tightly. Nothing must happen to them, in the next eight months. He had to watch them carefully, while he poked around the ruined cities of Spain—and finally came down with the plague.

He was the first Bard to wear a rosary of penicillin capsules.

Editor's Introduction To:

REACTIONARY UTOPIAS
Gregory Benford

It is sometimes said that Professor Gregory Benford is the only person alive who may win both a Hugo and a Nobel Prize.

He already has his Hugo, and as a professor of physics at the University of California at Irvine, he has at least a shot at the Nobel.

If he ever wanted to give up both science fiction and physics, he could make a good living at literary criticism. Most critical essays have little to say. This one says a lot.

Fair warning: Ursula K. LeGuin's *The Dispossessed* won a Hugo; second place was *The Mote in God's Eye* by Larry Niven and Jerry Pournelle.

REACTIONARY UTOPIAS
Gregory Benford

One of the striking facets of fictional utopias is that nobody really wants to live there. Perhaps the author, or a

few friends, will profess some eagerness. But seldom do
utopian fictions awaken a real longing to take part.

I suspect this is because most visions of supposedly
better societies have features which violate our innate
sense of human progress—they don't *look* like the future.
They may even resemble a warped, malignant form of the
past.

Time and again, utopists envision worlds where one
aspect of human character is enhanced, and much else is
suppressed. Plato's Republic was the first and most easily
understandable of these; he thought the artists and similar
unreliable sorts should be expelled. Too disruptive, y'know.

Should we be uncomfortable with this fact? If we value
western European ideals, yes.

Utopian fictions stress ideas, so we need a way to advance the background assumption while suppressing the
foreground of plot and character.

Nearly all utopias have one or more characteristics which
I'll call *reactionary*, in the sense that they recall the past,
often in its worst aspects. Here "reactionary" means an
aesthetic analogy, no more. It may apply to works which
are to the "left" in the usual political spectrum. (I think
this one-dimensional spectrum is so misleading that the
customary use of "reactionary" means little.) "Regressive"
might be an alternate term, meaning that a utopia seeks to
turn back the tide of western thought.

Looking over the vast range of utopian literature, I
sense five dominant reactionary characteristics:

1. *Lack of diversity.* Culture is everywhere the same,
with few ethnic or other divergences.

2. *Static in time.* Like diversity, change in time would
imply that either the past or the present of the utopia was
less than perfect, i.e., not utopian.

3. *Nostalgic and technophobic.* Usually this takes the
form of isolation in a rural environment, organization
harkening back to the village or even the farm, and only
the simplest technology. Many writers here reveal their
fondness for medieval society. The few pieces of technology superior to today's usually exist only to speed the plot

or provide metaphorical substance; they seldom spring from the society itself. (Only those utopias which include some notion of scientific advancement qualify as SF. Otherwise they are usually simple rural fantasies. This point also calls into question classifying any utopia as SF if it is drastically technophobic. Simply setting it in the future isn't enough.)

4. *Presence of an authority figure.* In real utopian communities, frequently patriarchal, this is an actual person. Historically, nearly all utopian experiments in the west have quickly molded themselves around patriarchal figures. In literary utopias, the authority is the prophet who set up the utopia. Often the prophet is invoked in conversations as a guide to proper, right-thinking behavior.

5. *Social regulation through guilt.* Social responsibility is exalted as *the* standard of behavior. Frequently the authority figure is the focus of guilt-inducing rules. Once the authority figure dies, he or she becomes a virtual saint-like figure. Guilt is used to the extreme of controlling people's actions *in detail*, serving as the constant standard and overseer of the citizen's actions.

These five points outline a constellation of values which utopists often unconsciously assume.

Before backing up these points with specifics, consider some utopias which *don't* share all or most of them. Samuel Delany's *Triton* seems to have none of these features; indeed, it proclaims itself a "heterotopia," stressing its disagreement with the first point. Often Delany depicts societies which express his delight in the freakish. Franz Werfel's *Star of the Unborn* (1946) depicts a heavily technological future with many desirable aspects, while accepting the inevitability of war, rebellion, and unsavory aspects. Advanced technology is carefully weighed for its moral implications in Norman Spinrad's *Songs from the Stars*.

Nonreactionary, or genuinely progressive utopias, often reject regulation through guilt. This divides utopias roughly along the axis of European vs. American, with the Europeans typically favoring "social conscience"—a term that often just means guilt.

Consider Edward Bellamy's *Looking Backward* (the most prominent Amerian utopia of the 19th century) and William Morris's reply to it, *News from Nowhere*. Both stabilize society more through gratification of individual needs than through guilt. Indeed, one of the keys to American politics is just this idea. Huxley's *Island* (written after his move to California) sides more with gratification, though of course his *Brave New World* (written in England) depicts the horrific side of a state devoted to gratification without our "sentimental" humanist principles.

LeGuin as Reactionary

Utopists often thought to be forward-looking, chic, and left-wing may be in fact reactionary. Consider, for example, Ursula LeGuin. Arguably her *The Dispossessed* is the finest American utopian novel of our time, and much of her work touches on these issues.

A first clue comes from the strangely 19th-century middle-European "feel" of her background society in *The Dispossessed*. This gives a curious static flavor, and of course recalls her reverence for the European tradition of utopian thought.

Her utopian experiment on the world Anarres is strikingly technophobic. Except for minor intrusions of a faster-than-light communicator and interplanetary travel (old SF staples), there is little which suggests the future at all. The vague middle-European feel to the architecture, organization of work, etc. is clearly nostalgic; rural Europe itself isn't even like that anymore. Plainly the author disapproves of the techno-flash and dazzle of the opposite world, Urras.

There, Shevek can't connect with the womanly embodiment of Urras's temptation, and he symbolically spills his seed on the ground before her. Indeed, after this novel LeGuin saw space travel as "a bunch of crap flying around the world, just garbage in the sky."[1] NASA's planetary missions, or Shevek's science, can be clean, serene. Technology, though, is practical, dirty, and liable to fall into the wrong hands.

We learn that the Hainish, who began the colony worlds, are burdened and driven by some strange guilt. Considering their superiority in so many fields, it is difficult not to conclude that LeGuin feels we should regard their guilt as admirable, too. This book is the culmination of her utopian thinking, a path which leads through the short story, "The Ones Who Walk Away from Omelas." (This parable might be titled "The Ones Who Walk Away from Omelettes," because we know what it takes to make one—you must break some eggs.)

The Dispossessed reeks with Old-Testament themes and images, using guilt as the principal social control. The founder, Odo, is the central saint of a communal society. Her pain and suffering during nine years' imprisonment *make possible* the virtue of the later Anarres society. Citizens remind each other of the events and connect her suffering with their dedication.

The implied lesson is that utopia will not arrive until man comes to grips with his own inner nature, which means in turn that a citizen is *born guilty*. This is central. Citizens must repay Odo's pain with their submission to the general will and society's precepts. Living on Anarres has an uncanny resemblance to being nagged by your mother.

The marriage vows in Castro's Cuba explicitly require a couple to raise all children according to "socialist morality." On Anarres a child is not a true citizen, psychically, until he has undergone a guilt-inducing experience—an unconscious, implicit rite.[2] Both processes seek to induce early control. The crucial scene in the protagonist Shevek's childhood is the boy's imprisonment game, described in careful detail. (This incident is clearly central, an act of juvenile delinquency taking up more space than Shevek's entire courtship of his wife!)

Odo is clearly the guilt-inducing authority figure which appears so often in reactionary utopias, though she is not the customary type: male, dynamic, assertive. Odo dies just before her utopia begins (see the short story "The Day Before the Revolution") and has some resemblance to

LeGuin herself. It is interesting, then, that Odo avoided the problems of building a real utopia, for LeGuin does this too.

Reading the Silences

There is a further method of investigating utopian writings, after first applying the litmus test of the above characteristics: reading the author's silences.

Plausibly, the yearning which motivates a writer to construct a utopia, devoting narrative energy to it, will in turn lead the author to neglect certain disturbing problems. The novel then reflects the author's avoidance of crucial questions that arise naturally from the imagined world. Conscious avoidance (or, more importantly, unconscious neglect) of these tells us what the writer fears and feels uncomfortable with. We might then expect the inhabitants of a utopia also never to think of the blind areas in their own society.

The principal ignored problem of Anarres is the problem of evil and thus violence; to LeGuin they are often synonymous. Guilt ("social conscience") simply overcomes such discordant elements. In the middle of a drought in which people starve no matter how evenly food is shared, somehow no one thinks of taking up arms with some friends and seizing, say, the grain reserves. Similarly, there is no on-stage evidence in *The Dispossessed* of hardened criminals, insane people, or naturally violent types (indeed, violence is "unnatural," and an impulse toward it is the principal offense which calls up guilt). There *is* a "prison camp" for "undesirables," evidence for the ambiguity of this utopia. But people seem to go there for offenses such as writing unpopular plays or, perhaps, voting Republican.

LeGuin's silence is conspicuous. This arouses the suspicion that the shying away from violence of any sort is part and parcel of the emotional posture of which *The Dispossessed* is only one reflection.

Tolstoy is the obvious father of many of LeGuin's ideas, techniques, and even literary mannerisms. As Samuel R.

Delany has remarked in "To Read *The Dispossessed*,"[3] whenever LeGuin begins to discuss politics (a common occasion) or show it (quite rare), she uses a language which ". . . sentence by sentence is pompous, ponderous, and leaden." He surmises that her style owes much to the Victorian translations of the great European novels, and that when she attempts depth she unconsciously lapses into this voice. These are "signs of a 'European' or 'Russian' profundity that the (translated) texts do not have." (This brilliant essay stresses the micro-text and ignores the book's principal strength, its beautiful structuring. As Delany deftly shows, hidden assumptions or avoided problems often show up best at the sentence or even phrase level. He also misses some of the lovely passages which her style achieves.)

Why Tolstoy? He, as well as the Russian anarchist Prince Kropotkin, took an absolutist position—no cooperation with any state control which used force. It is worth noting that the home of much idealist anarchist thinking, Russia, is now the largest prison state in history. One suspects that this comes in part from the inability of the 19th-century socialist thinkers there to confront the problem of violence in any moderate way.

One would then expect LeGuin's Anarres to evolve, if it ever slipped free of the authorial hand, in the direction of 19th-century Russia—without, of course, the apparatus of the Czar, etc. These are the roots of modern totalitarianism.

Failing to confront the problem of evil and violence gives these forces more power, not less. A quite plausible outcome, then, would see the reduction of Anarres to warring camps, each promising to restore order and ideological purity, perhaps even concluding with a Bolshevik-style victory.

LeGuin attempts to finesse this entire problem. It doesn't work. Her ignoring of a remarkable historical parallel (the demise of Russian socialist idealism at the hands of Lenin) marks *The Dispossessed* as a deeply reactionary work, concerned more with repealing history than with understanding it to make a better future.

This came up recently when I was discussing Soviet SF with one of the principal SF critics there. Appropriately enough, it was a cold day in 1984 and we were crossing Red Square beneath a leaden sky threatening snow. He remarked that *The Dispossessed* was not translated into Russian, in part because it referred to ideas the regime didn't like. Then he said rather wistfully, "For us, you know, it is terribly nostalgic. And irrelevant. That's the way some thought it could be, back in the beginning."

LeGuin seems to have tentatively approached the problem of real-world violence in the cartoon version of real politics depicted in *The Eye of the Heron*. There, descendants of the Mafia confront nonviolent anarchists in highly implausible fashion, leading to retreat of the anarchists into the wilderness—a note oddly reminiscent of many American escape-adventures. One must conclude that LeGuin can hardly bear to confront this crucial issue, and when she does sees no solution.

But there seems to me a deeper reason for LeGuin's silence about the realities of the world: fundamentally, the real world does not matter.

As the British critic Roz Kaveny has remarked in a review of *Malafrena*, "Throughout there is the sense that fills all of LeGuin's work: that politics is important less for what it can do for other people than as a way of achieving personal moral self-realization. Altruism is seen as good for its own sake and not because it may be useful to the under-privileged, although the altruist is supposed to be too busy to ever think in precisely those terms."

A utopia of hard-scrabbling scarcity solves so many problems quite cheaply. No worries of distribution of wealth, no leverage for power relationships. And it casts all in a superior light: poor people can have few sins. Throughout, no one questions a system which produces poverty, because, after all, it provides lovely opportunities for sacrifice.

A genuine revolutionary in such a place would be he who puts productivity over political theory. No such figure appears—another author's silence. But reality, after all, is not the principal concern of such narratives.

So the crucial scene in *The Eye of the Heron*, in which anarchist confronts Mafia thug and the protagonist dies, is *skipped*. We learn of it obliquely, via dialogue, in flashback. Partly this comes no doubt from her aversion for violence, but I suspect we are meant to see the moral grandeur of the survivors as the central fact. Even death is another way to strike a moral posture—or rather, to *be seen* doing so.

Similarly, the street confrontations on Urras in *The Dispossessed* rang false to many reviewers, and for good reason: they are the only example of real-world political confrontation in the book, and LeGuin knows very little of such things.

So her anarchists, confronting theory rather than facts, come over as nice, reasonable, and fairly boring. They behave like middle-class middle-brows, except that they are scrupulously horrified at the idea of property. (One of the book's assets lies in reassuring the middle-brow reader that revolutions will let him feel moral and yet comfortable. Everyone, after all, believes himself capable of overcoming his own greed and being a nice guy.) The conspicuous villains of the book are a physicist who steals Shevek's work, and of course lots of pseudo-American capitalists on Urras.

But not quite. As Delany pointed out in his essay, she treats the homosexual Bedap with an unconscious condescension. It is clear that Bedap should reform himself—stop being gay—because it does not fit in with the utopia she is constructing in her head. Which in turn intersects with the reactionary utopist's dislike of cultural diversity. Homosexuals cannot be eliminated from human society (without genetic engineering at least); they are a fact impossible to ignore, but clearly their presence troubles LeGuin's blueprints.

In her world, a quiet talk over herbal tea will surely fix matters up. A romantic, she ignores the problem of evil. In LeGuin's land, crowds watching a potential suicide on a window ledge never shout "Jump!" Averting her gaze from the 20th century, she sees evil people as those unfortunates who have not been given sufficient chance to be good.

The real question here is not the use of violence—which is, in LeGuin's work, an invariable sign of Wrongness—but rather, is moral order compatible with human diversity? Her answer is clear: her societies should opt for the age-old solution known to the Pharaohs—moral authoritarianism. Even in the dystopian future America of her novelette, "The New Atlantis," dissidents retreat into classical music and romantic humanism as a counter to the oppressive state. Old world values can, perhaps, redeem us.

Active thwarting of violence is not allowed, though. LeGuin labels her utopia as ambiguous, clearly knows something is wrong, but does not confront the deep problems. Rather than think through the hidden assumptions of Anarres, Shevek returns to pursue his own moral self-realization. Perhaps he, too, will become a martyr, like Odo—and thus engender more guilt, more attendant control.

Looking Backward

But *why* are utopists so often reactionary? Obviously, some underlying aspects of LeGuin's thought come from the failures of European utopian theory. But there's more to it than that.

While there is much in reactionary utopias we should scorn, I think we should properly look at *The Dispossessed* and some more obviously feminist utopias as responses to earlier, more mechanistic and masculine utopias. (As examples of novels which clearly are such reactions, see Suzy McKee Charnas's *Motherlines*, Marge Piercy's *Woman on the Edge of Time*, and Joanna Russ's *The Female Man*.) They depict communal societies with pleasant characteristics: relative lack of government, ecologically virtuous, with diffusion of parenting, freedom of movement, sexual freedom, and no crime.

Women's utopias often use the family as a model for

social structure, but it's "the unowned, non-patriarchal family, headed by nobody."[4] This, with their classlessness, makes them seem like fantasies about how families ought to be (and seldom are).

If masculine utopias fret over the means of production, feminist ones are bothered by the means of reproduction. They uncouple sex from power. But this is not enough to provide social ordering.

Perhaps it is natural for women to extend the family as a model, since they have not so often experienced society as a focus of conflicting forces. When dreaming of the future, we all tend to take the most pleasant areas of our lives and puff them up into metaphors for better societies.

It isn't surprising, then, that the problem of control doesn't rear its vexing head in such utopias, and the principal problem seems to be work assignments (who's going to do the dishes?). I recall Lenin's famous remark as he took over the government, little anticipating how hard it would be. He said, "A baker can run the state," and proceeded with a lot of half-baked approaches. In the end, Stalin came along to crack heads and force-march Russia into the future.

In most feminist utopias, no trace remains of general competitiveness and the desire to be better than others. Somehow, they have been laundered from the human psyche. (Interestingly, few support this by asserting that women are inherently better—that is, uncompetitive. The idea seems to be that men have merely taken a wrong turn lately.)

There is no doubt which authority figure is to set the house rules, as Joanna Russ's choice of words signifies: "Careful inspection of the manless societies usually reveals the intention (or wish) to allow men in . . . if only they can be trusted to behave."[5] If you don't, presumably you are sent to your room, i.e., exiled—unless it's James Tiptree's (Raccoona Sheldon's) utopia in "Houston, Houston, Do you Read?", where you'll be killed with minimal regrets. In no case should divisive ideas or surging hormones be allowed to thwart the communal good. Unsurprisingly, the authority figure is the only fallback enforcer in such worlds. The problem of control is simply neglected.

These feminist utopias are primarily reactive, responding to perceived masculine evils. The qualities they long for—stronger communal feeling, harmony with the natural world, violence only if it expresses anger in limited ways or in self-defense, good country vs. bad city (where the streets are unsafe)—reflect current needs. But by concentrating on these concerns they run the risk of forsaking the gains of the present, and becoming reactionary because they cannot imagine *new* ways to organize a community.

Freedom to do as we please, so long as we all agree with each other and remain in a state of harmony with the cosmos, is no freedom at all. It is little better than a religion in which faith in a deity has been replaced by faith in some supposed truths of the human spirit. It is a single-party system that is as superficially benign, yet as subtly authoritarian, as Disneyland.

Why does much utopian thought tend in this direction? The central difficulty confronting social planners is just that contained in the name—they must *plan*, and so must fear the wild card, the diverse, the self-regulating. History provides methods for governing errant wild spirits, so a planner looks longingly backward for models. Few peer ahead to landscapes where men and women have more freedom, can interact swiftly and chaotically yet with good result.

Some SF authors have seen this. Norman Spinrad's depictions of electronic democracy, from *Bug Jack Barron* onward, are deliberately saturated with lust for power and sharp contradictions. Frederik Pohl has meditated throughout a long career on these problems, notably in the recent *The Years of the City*, which abounds in utopian visions threaded with practical lore.

And what about looking at such older (more apparently "right-wing") utopian novels such as Heinlein's *Beyond This Horizon* and Niven and Pournelle's *Oath of Fealty*? I suspect they'll prove to be rather more enlightened than some recent chic visions.

It seems to me that reactionary facets spring in part from lack of imagination. Feminists, searching for ways to revise our society, fall upon analogies with the family, even if these do not provide solutions to the genuine problems of a diverse, urban, cantankerous world.

Instead, utopists long for sweeping simplicities. The supremacy of communal values, the need to suppress the individual, the fear of diversity or of science, the longing for a respite from change—these find many echoes in socialist thinking, in Third World societies, in all those who look hopefully forward to a restful era when we could, thank God, sleep off the binge known as modern times.

References

1. "In a World of Her Own," *Mother Jones*, January 1984.

2. Sheila Finch, *Science Fiction Review*, December, 1985.

3. Samuel R. Delany, "To Read *The Dispossessed*," *The Jewel-Hinged Jaw*, Berkley, New York, 1977.

4. Joanna Russ, "Recent Feminist Fictions," in *Future Females*, Bowling Popular Press, 1981.

5. Ibid.

Editor's Introduction To:

THESE SHALL NOT BE LOST
E. B. Cole

John W. Campbell, Jr. had his own notions of utopia: a world in which social science worked. He had no doubt that we would some day have scientific penology and sociology.

Campbell paid lip service to cultural relativism, but in fact, he was pretty sure what the Good Society would look like. The original Campbell blurb to this story was:

"No one man—no one race—no one culture—can think up all the ideas that might be possible. So, for the Philosophical Corps, no culture should be wholly lost . . ."

Which was all very well, but just as Indiana Jones's blatant pot-hunting horrifies genuine archaeologists, real anthropologists aren't likely to approve of the Philosophical Corps, which has no compunctions about *changing* cultures it doesn't like.

It's a real dilemma, of course. A society that really believes that everything is relative is a society that won't have any defenders. People don't get killed for a standard of living. If you can't tell why your culture is better than your enemy's, you won't last long.

The relativistic dilemma haunts *Nomenklatura* who own

the Soviet Union. Of course, they don't want the average Soviet citizen to think that the U.S.S.R. and the U.S.A. are in any way moral equals, which is why all the propaganda, and why World War II is to this day known in Russia as the Great Patriotic War. For that matter, it's why the Red Army's name got changed to "Army of the Soviet Union."

If you don't think you're right, you have little to fight for. On the other hand, a society that can't admit it's wrong will soon turn to persecutions of another kind. It's a moot point which is worse—to fall into the hands of the True Believer or the cynical Nomenklatura. Neither one believes in the Rule of Law, and without law, neither republic nor empire is endurable.

THESE SHALL NOT BE LOST
E. B. COLE

Exploratory Cruiser *Calimunda*, No. 4735
107-463-578
From: Commanding Officer
To: Office of the Chief Explorer
Subject: Preliminary Report, Planet No. 5, Sun G3-4/572 GSC

1. The subject planet is one of fourteen in a system with a rather large G3 sun. Reports will be submitted at a later date on two other inhabited planets in this system.

2. Enclosures include Chemical, Geophysical, Biological and Ethnic reports in accordance with SGR 45-938.

A brief summary follows:

a. *Chemical:* Subject planet has an oxygen-nitrogen envelope, with traces of other gases. Water vapor varies in its partial pressure over a medium range, with local exceptions. Presence in varying quantity of all natural elements was noted in the planetary crust and in the seas. No trace was found of artificial elements, their resultants or products.

b. *Geophysical:* Two major land masses were noted. These form large polar caps, extending well toward the equator, but are so broken up by seas as to form several subdivisions. Some islands exist in the equatorial seas, but none of these can be considered as important land masses. The planet has both rotation and revolution, with a slight axial perturbation. No satellite exists. The seas are tideless. The land temperatures range from approximately 230° to 395° absolute. Atmospheric pressure is 0.9 bars, mean, at sea level and gravitation is 960. Atmospheric turbulence is moderate. Precipitation is light over most of the planet. Some comparatively large areas ashore appear to have virtually none.

c. *Biological:* All life forms noted were on the carbon-hydrogen-oxygen cycle.

Vegetable life was found to be reasonably prolific, stationary in type, and relatively uncomplicated in structure, though taking numerous forms. Life cycles were variable, being virtually ephemeral in some cases and of medium duration in some of the larger vegetation observed.

Animal life proved to be varied, running from simple to complex in structure. Both warm and cold-blooded forms were observed in virtually all areas investigated, existing both at sea and shore. All animal life cycles, including that of the dominant species, were of short or extremely short duration.

d. *Ethnic:* The dominant form of life is humanoid, type 6.4151. Skin pigmentation is variable. Some inter-mixing of pigmentation groups was noted, but in the main, each group has its own area.

Civilization groups were observed in four areas. Civilization level was quite primitive, being on the imperial threshold. Centers of civilization were in the planetary semitropical bands in both hemispheres, with territorial extensions well into the temperate areas.

In general, the civilizations observed are in the first

stages of development. No mechanical means are used for power sources. Slave or animal labor is used in all phases of activity. Media of exchange are in existence, but no co-ordinated system of banking was discovered. Among the ruling classes, knowledge of mechanics or computational mathematics is unfashionable. Chief avocations appear to be literature, music, martial exercises and a sort of philosophy unsupported by research.

3. Recommendations:

It is believed that this planet is presently in a stasis, or approaching a stasis which may prevent further progress for several periods, and even cause lost ground unless assistance is given. Recommendation is therefore made that this planet be referred to the Philosophical Corps for further action.

Hel Guran
Comdr., ExpC
Commanding

3 Enclosures:
1. Chemical Survey, Form EC-107
2. Geophysical Survey, Form EC-232
3. Ethnic Survey, Form EC-296

Informal Report

From: OIC, Team 6
To: Commanding Officer, 7342 Philosophical Group
Subject: Initial check, Planet 5, Sun G3-4/572 GSC

1. Team six has set up a base on an island at co-ordinates 220.4070-302.0050. Pursuant to orders, observers have been sent to the four civilizations noted. Transcripts of observer reports are enclosed herewith.

2. As can be seen from the observer reports, the civilization centered at 523.4060-220.0060 is the probable dominant. Of the rest, one is so completely in stasis as to require long attention; the other two are so thoroughly lacking in desirable factors and so tainted with inherent weakness as to be inconsiderable.

The dominant is presently subject to powerful stresses, both external and internal. Complete collapse is probable within a period or less, and it is believed that this collapse would be impractical to forestall, due to the large number of unassimilated savage and semisavage tribes in close proximity to the Imperial borders, as well as to the serious internal faults. In any event, desirability of complete preservation is open to question. Among the internal stresses will be noted a strong trend toward insensate cruelty, sufficient to destroy most cultures. A long history of corruption in government and trade is also noted. On the other hand, governmental and legal structure are excellent, cultural level is good, and the arts and sciences are satisfactorily advanced. These should not be lost.

3. It is recommended that operators be sent in with a view to isolation and retention of worthwhile institutions and knowledge during the period of extreme uncertainty which will follow the collapse of the Empire. Provision should be made for possible deposit of further knowledge useful to the planet's future.

> Jon Dall
> Capt. PhC
> OIC, Team 6

4 Enclosures
Observer Reports

7342 Philosophical Group
Office of the Commanding Officer

579.0352

From: Commanding Officer, 7342 Philosophical Group
To: OIC, Team 6
Subject: Operation No. 705

1. Informal report received and noted. The reports have been reviewed and forwarded. Recommendation is hereby

approved and operation is designated as number seven hundred five.

2. Operation will be organized to conform with SGR 10-351 and Handbook PH-205. Control observers without recall will be sent in advance. These will act as foci in case modification of standard procedure is necessary, and may be used as operation assistants. Discretion is granted.

Coatl Myxlr
Col. PhC
Commanding

Gradually, the reddish tinge of the setting sun faded. A chill came into the air as the stars appeared and cast their feeble light over the village. A guard closed the gate, then returned to his game in the guardroom.

In town, a man walked by the houses. Unobtrusively, he opened a door and entered. Soon, another came to the same door. Another came, then others.

Inside, Master Operations Technician Marc D'lun glanced around at the group.

"Well, gentlemen," he greeted them, "I see you have all arrived. Are your integrations complete?"

One of the men nodded.

"Yes, they are," he announced. "I am now the tent-maker, Kono Meru. The records indicate that I am thirty years old. I was born in a nomad camp out in the hills, and am now an orphan." He pointed at another man. "Xler, there, is an itinerant woodcutter, named Kloru Mino. He's twenty-six. Both parents were pretty old. They died a couple of years ago. The rest of the section are nomads, herders, artisans, and so on. Records are all straight. We all have a number of acquaintances, but no close friends or relatives."

"Very good, sergeant. The team's been setting us up in the meantime. Our operations center is in a cliff out in the hills." D'lun looked around the group of men. "Of course, you all know of Marko Dalu, the healer. Otherwise you wouldn't have found me. Records did an excellent job for all of us, but that's normal. Now, let's get to business.

"In the first place, the observers have given us a lot on this civilization. Zlet, you're Intelligence. Suppose you give us a rundown."

Zlet, now renamed Kara Fero, nodded.

"The Empire has been in existence now for about fourteen centuries. It started with a rather small province, Daltur, which had a definitely democratic government and a definitely independent population. All inhabitants voted for every leader in their government. There was no such thing as an appointive or a hereditary job. In every decision of policy, majority ruled. They were surrounded by petty kingdoms, tyrannies, and the usual conglomeration of city states. The small seaport of Baratea became their capital, and as time went on, their trade excited the envy and very often the anger of their neighbors. Periodically, the Dalturans found themselves embroiled in wars, and they developed a system of military service. Many of their citizens devoted themselves to the study of tactics and military science, and it wasn't long before they started annexing other areas and cities. Pretty soon, they were too bulky for their old democracy. For a while, they fumbled around in their efforts to find a workable government, and it looked as though the Dalturan Empire was going to fall apart from sheer unwieldiness." Fero paused, glancing about. Someone held out a cup of wine. Fero nodded his thanks, and took a sip.

"Some of their leaders, however, were pretty sharp on civic theory," he continued. "They worked out a rather good system and put it into effect. Actually, it's a simple idea, but it has resulted in an imposing governmental structure. The basic idea was that of a governing panel of selected persons, the 'Eligible Ones,' from whom leaders were chosen. By means of competitive examinations and contests, they selected the best of their youth. These were placed in training as potential leaders, and when deemed ready, were proposed for official posts. Only members of this panel were eligible for such posts. When not in office, or when training, they lived in simple surroundings, supported by the state. Popular vote placed them in office, and a system of electors was worked out to simplify the gathering of that vote.

"Nominally, this system is still in effect," added Fero. "The only trouble is that it's showing signs of weathering. Here and there, along the line, certain electors took matters into their own hands. Some of the Eligibles played along, for value received, of course. Appointive officials started appearing. A priesthood sprang up among the 'Eligible Ones.' Next thing, sons of the 'Eligible Ones' started taking their places among the governing group without benefit of the traditional selection. A few centuries ago, a hereditary dynasty was set up, supported by the priesthood, and the inevitable happened. The Emperor became divine."

Fero reached for the wine cup, took another sip, then continued.

"As it stands now," he concluded, "we have a sick Empire. The divine ruler is totally unfit to make the decisions required of him. A group of advisors have taken over the reins of government, and are running things strictly for their own profit and that of their friends. The average citizen has no more choice in government or even in his own fate than his cattle. Of course, he can still vote, but the results of the ballot invariably swing into line with the wishes of the ruling group. Our common citizen is becoming aware of the situation and dissatisfaction is spreading throughout the Empire. The governors and priests know it, but they are incapable of quelling the feeling. They can't return to the old uncomplicated days of the democracy and still hold their positions, so they depend more and more upon force and terrorism for their authority. Meanwhile, the outer fringes of the Empire are under pressure from a number of unassimilated tribes, who have no desire to deal with Daltur in any way. The Empire will probably stagger along under its own inertia for a few more centuries, but the final collapse is already on the tape."

*   *   *

Marko Dalu nodded as Fero sat down. "That's the general picture," he commented. "Not particularly original, of course, but it's not pretty, and it's up to us to take action. Naturally, you have all studied the handbooks and a number of case histories, so I don't think I'll have to go into basic details." Dalu looked around the group. "We have about a hundred thousand people in this area," he added, "and about two sun cycles to work on them. We might get three. Sergeant Miller, suppose you go into individual assignments. I'll listen."

As Miller talked, Dalu sat listening and checking off points. Finally, he leaned back, satisfied. Yes, they should be able to collect at least a hundred and fifty useful recruits from this population. Properly guided, their influence should make quite an impact upon the millions within and without the Empire. Yes, he decided, between a hundred and fifty and two hundred should be a great sufficiency for the initial phases. Now, the only question would be to gather the right people, instruct them properly, equip them and put them to work.

"Of course," Sergeant Miller was saying, "these agents will have to have some sort of publicly known basic philosophy. Their mission depends to a great extent upon popular reaction and recognition. We can't simply tell them, 'Go out and reform the Empire,' and turn them loose." He paused, turning slightly. "That is Sergeant D'lun's department."

Marko Dalu smiled to himself. Yes, there would have to be considerable publicity, some of it pretty dramatic. Actions would have to be taken and words spoken whose echoes would ring through history for centuries to come. He remembered some of the melodrama that had been played out for similar purposes. "Hope we can play this one straight," he muttered to himself.

Miller finished his talk and sat down. Marko Dalu looked up. "Any questions?" he asked.

No one spoke.

"There's one other thing," added Dalu, "the legal system of the Empire. Fundamentally, it's good. Simple, to be sure, but good. The underlying theory is equity, which is correct. Laws are quite easy to understand, reasonably definite, yet they admit of equitable decisions. The system of elected judges, public hearings and scant ceremony is worth saving. We can't say so much for the ecclesiastical courts. They are overburdened with ceremony. Bribery is altogether too easy and too common, and the closed hearings and drastic punishments are definitely undesirable. The same equity should be used in criminal cases as is at least nominally shown in civil affairs." He looked around again. "If there are no questions, I think we can call this meeting over. You can go ahead and start evaluating your acquaintances and making more. Shoot them into me as fast as you are sure of their potentialities. I'll screen 'em and pass them on to Base."

One by one, the men took their leave, and melted away into the shadowy streets.

Slowly, the galley picked its way through the crowded harbor, edging through the narrow channel to the Baratea dockside. Already, the merchants were on deck, watching the sweating slaves hoist bales of goods from the hold. An overseer called time; an unimaginative man, he called with a monotonous, annoying chant. Below, the slow drumbeat of the oarmaster competed with him for rhythm.

Philar, master of the ship's guard, leaned against the low rail, aloof from the activity. He was bored. He was also mildly irritated. Why, he wasn't sure. He was just bored and irritated. Nothing had happened this voyage to cause annoyance. In fact, nothing had happened this voyage. The normal, dull routine of life had droned on day by day, just as it had during most of a long career. There had been no attempts at uprising by the galley slaves; no pirate attacks; no adventures with marine monsters; nothing. Philar yawned. Looking across the harbor, he could see his favorite wine shop. There, stories would be circulating of sea monsters; of mutinies successfully coped with; of pirate attacks skillfully repelled by bravery at arms. Old comrades would be coming in, their purses heavy with rewards, their armor renewed; some, perhaps, with new insignia of rank. He, Philar dar Burta, senior guardmaster, would merely sit. He would listen to the talk, and when questioned, all he could say would be:

"We went to Bynara. The merchants haggled. Some got richer; some got poorer. We came back. Have some wine."

Everyone in the room would shake their heads. Some-one would say, "Good old Philar. Nothing ever happens. Nothing ever goes wrong. Now, the last time I went to Bynara—"

At a sharp command from the oarmaster, the port oars were shipped. Slowly, the galley swung into the dock, to be secured by the shouting dockhands. A gangway was being rigged aft. Philar shifted his attention to the dock-ers. Good man, that dockmaster. His handling of men and materials spoke plainly of long years of experience.

Oh, well, thought the guardmaster. He had long experi-ence, too. It was honorable service he had behind him, though uneventful. For forty-five years, he had perfected himself and others in the arts and in the ancient sciences of war and defense. From one assignment to another, he had gone his uneventful way, covering every corner of the sprawled Empire. Always, however, he had arrived at a new assignment just after the excitement was over, or he had received orders and left just before the trouble started. He shook his head. Funny, how battle had passed him by. Many of his comrades and pupils in the training fields and guardrooms had gone on to promotion and rewards. Oth-ers had simply gone. Here, though, was good, solid, old Philar; a dependable guardmaster, but somehow one who never wet his sword or did anything very remarkable. Even in his youth, during the war with Maelos, he had been assigned to the reserve which, due to the proficiency of the commanders, had never been called up.

As he gazed at the practiced movements of the steve-dores, they faded from view, to be replaced by other images. Again, he was an awkward new recruit. Daltur was at war. They were on the training field. The old fieldmaster who had instructed was long since gone, but

Philar could still hear his voice; cautioning, criticizing, advising.

"You, there, Philar," he had cried. "Hold up that point. Hold it up, I say! This is no corn you're mowing now. That's a man before you. Were Holan there of Maelos, he'd be drinking your blood by now. Here, let me show you." Indignantly, the elder had snatched Holan's sword, turning quickly. A swift pass ensued. Philar's blade was brushed aside and a heavy blow on his helmet made him stagger.

"See, now," the instructor had growled, throwing the sword back to its owner, "that was the flat. The edge would've made you dog meat." He turned away. "Go to it again."

The shouting from the dock filtered through the guardsman's reverie, scattering the picture. He shook his head.

"Guess I'm getting old," he muttered. "Better retire to a farm before I get feeble-minded."

Truthfully, he didn't feel any older than he had when he came into the service. Men said, however, that one can only live so long. He knew he was approaching that age. Most of his allotted time had gone. Shrugging, he gazed over the crowded wharf. A courier was approaching.

The man drew his car to the gangway, tossed the reins to a dockhand, and came striding up to the deck. As he approached, he performed a quick salute.

"You are the guardmaster, Philar dar Burta?"

Philar nodded. "I am," he announced. "What have you?"

The courier extended a sealed tablet. "Orders, sir. I await your pleasure."

The old guardsman's eyebrows contracted as he took the package. "What have we here?" he muttered. Turning, he broke the seal with a few quick taps against the rail, and scanned the characters impressed on the tablets within.

The first was the standard company master's commission.

"By the grace of Halfazor, Emperor of Daltur, First Prince of the Seas, Defender of Truth and Divine Lord of all Things living, know all men that, placing great faith in

the loyalty, ability and wisdom of Philar dar Burta, I
present him as Kalidar of Guardsmen. All men and all
other Things living beneath the heavens as ordained by
the Divine Halfazor will then render him such aid as is
necessary to complete his ordered course. All men under
his command, or of inferior rank will unquestioningly obey
his orders henceforth—"

It was signed by the Master of the Palace Guard, Milbar.

Philar looked over the tablet again. Yes, he had read
correctly the first time. After forty-five years, promotion
had come. Now, Philar was one of those who grandly
crooked a finger for a car to pick him up. No longer did he
have to walk the streets to his barrack. Rather, he would
ride to his lodging. No more would he sit in the wine shop
of an evening, listening to the boasts of those younger than
himself. Rather, he would drink with a few of his own
chosen friends in his own room. He shook his head, then
looked at the other tablet. Here was an assignment.

"By the grace . . . Proceed to Kleedra . . . Deal with
rebellious elements . . . Bring offenders to swift justice—"

It was also signed by old Milbar.

Philar dropped the two tablets into his pouch, then
leaned against the rail again. He looked toward the courier. His courier, now. By Halfazor! Rebellion in the Empire! Of course, merely a minor affair, but rebellion none
the less. Most peculiar. Why, the Kleedrans had been a
minor tribe in a little backwater corner of the Empire for
years, even lifetimes. He could remember back thirty or
more years, when he was on duty in the sleepy little
walled village—fifty men, under a senior guardmaster.
Even at that, it had been a soft assignment. He shook his
head again, then turned sharply.

"Mylan. Mylan, come here, I say," he shouted.

His senior watchmaster came out of a hatch, blinked,
then stood before him.

Philar put his hand on the man's shoulder. "Take over,
friend," he said. "I'm giving you the ship."

Mylan frowned. "What happened?"

His senior grinned. "I just got promoted and reassigned," he announced.

Mylan's smile was slightly forced. "Congratulations," he said. Then, formally, "I hope I may serve under you later, sir." He gave a salute.

Philar nodded, returning the salute. "Possibly we may serve together," he gave the formal reply. He turned, and went down the gangway.

Mylan watched him as he climbed into the car. The courier snapped his reins and they were off. The new guardmaster leaned against the rail, frowning.

Why, he wondered, should they promote that soft, easy-going old fool when real men were around for the asking. He glanced down at his own trim armor, with its fine inlaid design. How much, he wondered, had he spent in bribes to the aides? How many times had he sent the Kalidar choice bottles? And then they promoted an idiot who wouldn't unsheath his sword. Why, the poor old poltroon wouldn't even strike an erring guard. Had to talk softly to them.

He spat over the side, then turned, fingering his sword hilt. Well, anyway, things on this ship would be far different now, with a man in charge. He raised his voice.

"Turn out the guard," he shouted. "Get moving there. We haven't all day to clear this ship." Unsheathing his sword, he smacked with the flat at the legs of the guards as they passed. "Come on, come on," he urged. "On the double, there."

Plono Baltur shook his head as he looked at his tent. There was no question about it, long and hard use was showing. The tent had patches upon its patches. Yes, this man was right. He must do something about it, but there was the cost. He turned again. Kono Meru stood watching him.

"I am not a rich man," began Baltur. "My needs are simple."

Meru waved a hand airily. "No matter," he declared, "my tents are good. They last for years, yet the cost is low." Turning to one of his animals, he started unpacking a bale. "You will see," he said, "how strong material can be, and yet how light in weight." He spread the contents of the bale on the ground, whipping the expanse of cloth open with practiced gestures, and talking as he worked.

Without realizing just how it happened, Baltur found himself bargaining over the tent first, then talking of his personal affairs. Soon, they were talking of the affairs of the province, then of Imperial policy. With a start, Baltur realized that he had bared some of his innermost thoughts. Dangerous thoughts, some of them, and these to a man he had just met. He swallowed hard, then looked straight at the tentmaker. What if this man were an Imperial spy?

His companion smiled gently. "No, Plono Baltur, I am far from being an agent of the Emperor." He nodded toward the herdsman's tent. "Shall we go inside?"

Baltur shrugged, held the tent flap aside, then entered after his visitor.

Inside, Kono Meru swept his elaborate headdress off, revealing a crop of black hair, surmounted by a golden circlet.

"First," he said, "let me introduce myself. I am known on this world as the tentmaker, Kono Meru. On other worlds, I have had different names."

He held up a hand. "No, make no mistake about me. I am a man like yourself. Neither I nor any of my companions are supernatural. We merely come from worlds other than this one. Older worlds. We have certain tools unknown to your world, like this 'mentacom' here." He pointed to the circlet. "The device has a long, technical name, but we usually just call it a mentacom. It allows us to make direct contact with the mind of another being, making words unnecessary." Kono paused.

"We also have knowledge unheard of by your world as yet," he continued. "Possession of that knowledge has brought with it obligations and duties. My duty and that of my companions is to make worlds we are assigned to into better places for their inhabitants to live in, that the universe of worlds may prosper."

"There are, then, other worlds than this?" Baltur stared at him.

"Worlds beyond number," Meru assured him. "Many of them inhabited by men such as you and I."

"Why do you tell me these things?" queried the herder. "I am but a simple man. It is not for me to make great decisions." He spread his hands. "Rather, should you go to those who rule."

Kono Meru smiled. He had been right. The man had both mental flexibility and analytical ability. "It is our opinion," he stated, "that those who now rule this Empire are failing to do a good job. You have agreed with us on that."

Baltur started. "I . . . I merely—"

His companion held up a hand, then pointed to the golden circlet. "You had the thought," he said positively. "Also," he added, "you said that men are not to be treated as cattle, thinking as you said it that in many ways, you and your people are being so treated."

Baltur paled. "I admit it," he muttered. "I had the thought."

Meru smiled. "How, then, can I go to rulers who consider men as cattle, and ask them to give those cattle a voice in the government?"

"I see." Baltur walked across the tent, seated himself, and leaned back against some cushions. "What, then, can I do? I am a herdsman. I have no great wealth, no power."

"Do you want to do something?"

"Yes, yes, I think so."

"You are willing to accept hardship and danger?"

Baltur shrugged. "If it will do good."

"Good. You will go, then, to the healer, Marko Dalu. Until you see him, you will forget all that we have spoken about." As he spoke, the tentmaker removed a small instrument from his clothing, pointing it toward the herdsman. "When you see Marko Dalu, you will remember your talk with me, and will ask him for further information and instruction." Kono Meru stood, walking to the tent entrance. "Now, I will help you set up your new tent, then we will part company."

The following morning, Baltur woke, feeling weak and nauseated. He stirred about the new tent, preparing his breakfast, then looked at the result with distaste. Finally, he tried some. It tasted terrible. He spat it out. Now, he realized that he had a headache. He thought back to the night before. No, he hadn't touched any wine.

"Something else is wrong," he muttered. "What was the name of that healer?"

He went outside, looking over his herd, then started making preparations for the trip into the village.

Nodan, aide to the Master of the Palace Guard, was a puzzled man. He looked after the retreating figure of Company Master Philar, his brows contracted in thought. Finally, he spoke to his superior.

"Why, sir? Why promote that man and send him on this assignment? Surely, there are others better fitted for command."

Milbar smiled thoughtfully. "For instance?" he inquired.

The smile made Nodan bold. "For instance, the senior watchmaster, Mylan dar Byklor, sir," he said. "Surely, there's a man who could take over a mission and make it successful."

Milbar's smile grew broader. "Ah, yes, Mylan. Makes up a nice bribe, doesn't he?"

Nodan flushed. His mouth opened, but his superior held up a hand.

"No, no. Don't worry. Of course I'm not blind, but I know that one must live. Why not a little on the side now and then." The older man dropped his hand, then played with his fingers for a moment.

"No," he continued, "this promotion and assignment is not exactly a reward. You see, the situation in Kleedra is most peculiar." He shook his head. "Most peculiar," he repeated. "Really, it isn't a genuine rebellion. No arms have shown. None have flouted authority. It seems rather a change in attitude. Many of the townspeople and more of the countryfolk seem to regard the Empire with a sort of tolerance, rather than with the normal respect. It is nothing we can put our fingers on. We can't declare a state of emergency, since there is none.

"It seems, however, that there is a man. A physician named Marko—Marko Dalu. He appears to be the central figure. People come to him from quite considerable distances, not so much for medical care as for something else. He goes out quite a bit, too. We've noticed that whenever he does, he gathers quite a crowd. Always makes speeches. Not much to them, but they seem to result in a very unsatisfactory attitude toward the Empire."

"But," Nodan suggested, "can't he be put in constraint on a treason or a heresy charge?"

"Oh, easily." His superior nodded. "Of course he can. We can arrest anyone for that, and in this case, we could make it stick." He paused, a smile creeping over his face. "But we want to do it in such a way as to be profitable." He paused again. "We must sacrifice troops to an unlawful mob." He beat softly on the table. "Our overlordship will be challenged." His voice lowered again, and he faced Nodan squarely. "Then, of course, Kleedra will be reconquered. It will resume its rightful place as a subject village, and all will be well again."

Nodan's smile was admiring. "A truly clever plan," he applauded. "And, of course, our Philar, the bluff old warrior, is just the man to make the plan work?"

"Naturally," nodded Milbar, "he will swagger in at the head of his reinforced company, full of righteousness and patriotic vim. He'll seize his prisoner and start out of town. Then, the trap will spring. He has never been in combat on the battlefield, nor have the men we are giving him. A determined mob will make dog meat of them; with some encouragement, of course, and at a price. After that, I'll send in experienced troops and take over the district."

Milbar leaned back in his chair, contemplating the future with considerable satisfaction.

*   *   *

It was a warm day. Back in the hills, a faint blue haze obscured details of trees and ground. On one of the hillsides, before a cliff, a large group of people had gathered. They faced a single man expectantly. He held up his hands for silence.

"Peace, my friends," he said. He spoke in almost a normal tone, yet those most distant heard him clearly.

Back in the crowd, among a small group of his friends, Plono Baltur nodded to himself. Yes, the mental communicator was a remarkable device. In this age, a public address system would be supernatural. It would be a strange device to be regarded with superstitious fear, yet the far more advanced mentacom merely gave a feeling of ease. It operated unobtrusively, without causing any comment, or revealing itself in any way. He looked about the group. Yes, a lot of people were listening.

"Men have spoken words of violence," Marko was continuing. "This cannot be. Those who resort to violence will perish uselessly. It is only for those who abstain, who pass their days in peace who, with their sons, will inherit the future."

A murmur passed through the crowd: This was not exactly what many of them had come to hear. To a great many men in this audience, the stories of Marko Dalu and his strange abilities, coupled with his remarkable deeds, had come as a cry to action. Now, they felt let down.

"The rule of fear, of force and violence, cannot last," declared Dalu. "It must and will come to an end, since force creates counterforce. It is not up to us to dash ourselves senselessly at overwhelming odds, but rather to practice and teach those virtues that have been handed to us from the ancient days, in anticipation of the days to come, when many men will also practice them. Thus will all benefit."

Gradually, as he spoke, most of his hearers nodded in agreement. Not all he said was understood, nor was it meant to be. Only a few men still felt a vague dissatisfaction. As the crowd broke up, scattering to various pursuits, a few of these approached the philosopher.

"You preach against violence," said one of them. "Then you say in effect that the Empire is bound to be destroyed. Who, then, is going to do this?"

Marko smiled. "That is not a matter for you or for me, my friend," he said. "The teachers say, I believe, that the Empire is ruled by the Divine Emperor?"

The man nodded. "That is true."

"Then," argued Dalu, "cannot the Divine Halfazor take care of the purging of his own Empire?"

The man was obviously not satisfied, but he felt compelled to agree. He cast about for some way to pursue his questioning without venturing into the dangerous grounds of heresy. Back in the shadows, a small instrument was leveled his way. Suddenly, he felt that he was wasting his time. Here was no opportunity to build up a case against this Dalu. He turned and walked away. The instrument scanned the group. Several others decided that further discussion would be profitless. They left, to report another failure to their various superiors. Marko smiled at their retreating backs.

"Do you who remain have any further questions?" he asked.

One man stepped forward. "We do," he announced. "At least, I do." He glanced around at the three men with him. "I feel that there must be something to be done other than just passive waiting."

Marko looked at the four men. "Do all of you have that feeling?"

They all nodded. "I do," they chorused.

"Then," Marko added, "are you willing to risk torture and death for your beliefs?"

The men looked uncertain. "I mean it," Marko assured them. "If you join me, you will never gain riches. You may suffer hunger, thirst, torture, death. Danger will be your constant companion. You will be censured, with no chance of retaliation."

One man shook his head. "This is a dismal outlook," he announced.

"Yes, but one which must be faced," Marko told him.

The man looked at the philosopher for a moment, then turned. Slowly, he walked away. The others stood fast.

"I am a fool," announced one of them. "My better judgment tells me to leave, but I am still here. What must we do?"

The other two simply nodded.

"Follow me," ordered Marko. He turned, walking into the shadow of the cliff. He walked up to the cliff, then melted into it. The three men looked at each other, then shrugged. They, too, walked into the cliff.

Inside, they looked around in bewilderment. It was a cave, but the lighting was brilliant. Around the walls were arranged masses of unfamiliar equipment. Several men in strange clothing stood about the room. Marko Dalu was stripping off his robes. Now, he turned toward them, the light gleaming from his insignia.

"Gentlemen," he greeted them, "allow me to introduce myself. I am a member of a service which will remain unknown to your planet for many centuries. You have been chosen for that same service, provided you can prove yourselves fit during the next few hours. I think you can." He waved a hand and one of the uniformed men pulled a lever.

Instantly, the lights went out. Images started forming in the minds of the three men. Rapidly, they saw the early days of a planet. They saw the gradual appearance of man, then his development to a civilization comparable to their own. Empires arose—and fell. Once, civilization was wiped out, only to start anew from the very beginnings. Machines were developed—machines which the men somehow understood, though they had never seen their like before. Wars were fought. New weapons were devised. Defenses were developed, then, new weapons. Lands were devastated. Finally, an entire continent was laid bare of life, but its final, despairing effort was decisive. As they watched, the immense forces interacted. Gravitic stresses, far beyond the wildest dreams of the weapon designers, developed. Then came complete catastrophe. At first slowly, then with vicious rapidity, the planet ripped itself to bits. As the images faded, a few rocks started their endless circling of the sun which had once given life to a great planet.

"That," said Dalu's voice, "was a drastic case. Now, a different picture."

Again, the images formed. This planet, too, had its wars, but after the fall of one civilization, international and interracial understanding developed. The wars lessened in severity, then ceased. Scientific devices, once developed as weapons, took their places in a peaceful, planetwide economy. The population grew, and, as life spans lengthened, the race spread to other planets, then to other suns. The images faded upon a peaceful and prosperous vista.

"The other side of the picture," remarked Dalu. "Now for the mechanics of the thing."

Hours passed. Finally, the three men walked out of the cliff again. Coming out into the blackness of the night, they looked toward each other wordlessly. Then, each engaged with his own thoughts, they went their separate ways.

Inside the cave, D'lun spoke to Communications Technician Elkins.

"Well, what do you think of 'em?"

"Looked like a good bunch to me, sergeant." Elkins turned from his instruments. "When do they come in for their basic training?"

"We've got a flight to Base scheduled in two more nights. These three bring it up to twenty." D'lun stretched. "I'm going to send them back for the full thirty days, of course, then I think that'll be the last class. We've got more than we have to have, really." He looked at the communicator. "Besides," he added, "that last message you got doesn't give us a lot more time anyway. This group may report back after we've left."

"Leaves it up to Baltur to break 'em in?"

"Baltur's a good man," remarked D'lun. "He soaked up instruction like a sponge. He can break these people in and run the operation nicely. 'Course, he'll have help and close support from Base and Sector for the next twenty years, anyway. After that, it'll settle to routine."

"Yes, Kalidar, we have a certain amount of unrest here. There's no open rebellion, though." The district governor frowned. "No question about it, this man Marko is a disturbing influence, but he's never preached revolt or sedition; on the contrary, he speaks of peace."

Philar leaned back, folding his arms. "Although my orders, governor, are not too clear, they do make definite mention of rebellious elements. Mention is also made of offenders. Surely some reports must have reached the Imperial Halls."

The governor nodded. "Of course. We have naturally reported the trend of public thinking. In answer, you are sent. Now, we suppose the Imperial Guard will eliminate the cause of the disturbance. We will take care of other matters as they arise. Immediate action is in your hands, Kalidar."

"I see. You may be assured we will take action. Now, about quarters. I have a hundred thirty-seven men."

The governor arose. "Oh, that is quite simple. The old camp is still in very good condition. The village guard is using only a small part of it, so you may move your men in whenever you see fit. There is an excellent inn across the square where you may easily find accommodation for yourself."

As Philar rejoined his troops, he was doing a lot of thinking. One of those little hunches that had visited him so often during his years of service was gnawing feebly. No question about it, something was wrong here. Something more than a simple case of sedition, but what was it? He took possession of the Casern, absorbed the village guard into his own company, then called in his guardmasters. One by one, they filed in. Their commander greeted each by name, then:

"Gentlemen," he commenced, "we have a little investigation to make here before we can take action. I want your men to mingle with the townspeople much more than is usual."

Five sets of eyebrows raised, but there was a low chorus of acquiescence.

"Of course, any unusual comments heard, or any strange attitudes will be immediately reported." Philar hesitated. "Now, to my part. I want to interview a man, but I'm not about to just pull him in for questioning."

Dielo, previously the guardmaster-in-charge of the village, stepped forward. "Why not, sir," he queried. "We have nearly two hundred men now. Any insurrection could be put down easily."

"Possibly," agreed his superior. "Quite possibly, but why decimate the village unnecessarily?" He raised his hand as the other was about to speak. "No, I think I'll do it my way. Are any of our guardsmen feeling ill, or possibly suffering from the strain of our march?"

The master of the third guard smiled. "There's always Gorlan, sir," he remarked. "I never knew him to miss a chance to make sick quarters."

The commander's answering smile was understanding. "Good. Then let him take to his pallet, and call in the physician Marko. Obviously, this is a case for one with knowledge beyond simple camp surgery." He looked the group over for a moment, then, "You may go now," he added.

As the guardmasters filed out, Dielo muttered to himself, "Cautious old fool! Someone should make up his mind for him."

"Halt!" The command was sharp. "Guardmaster Dielo, I heard that." Philar's hand fell to his sword. "Were you one of my regular men, I'd merely break you and give you a few days without water, but you have been a Guardmaster-in-Charge." He paused, a crooked smile growing on his lips. "By the Emperor's sandals, I wanted a sick man. Now, I'll get one. Draw your sword."

Dielo's sword left its sheath. "Now, here's quick promotion," he exulted. "I'm a real swordsman, not a windy old failure."

The clang of swords echoed down the lanes of the old camp, bringing guardsmen at the run. The two men circled about. Slash, parry; slash, parry, slash. Stroke and counterstroke. Now a retreat, now an advance. No blood drawn yet. It was an exhibition of practiced and formal arms play. No question remained in the minds of the observers. Here were masters at work.

Philar was becoming annoyed. This man's boast had been partially correct. Surely, here was no beginner. In fact, this man was very nearly as good as that old fieldmaster who had taught recruits so many years before. Echoes of long gone lessons ran through Philar's mind.

"You, there, keep that point up. He'll drink your blood."

An idea came into his head. He had often wondered about it, he remembered now. Most unconventional, but it should work. What's to lose, besides a head? On guard again, he disobeyed that first of all maxims. Casually, he allowed his point to lower below the permissible area. Instantly, Dielo seized his advantage. With a quick lunge, he beat down at the lowered sword, prepared to make the devastating swing to the head on the rebound. It was an easy stroke, and one which always worked, but this time, something went wrong. The lowered sword moved aside. As Dielo's blade continued its downward path, he felt something sharp slide under his kilt. A quick slash, and his leg became useless. He dropped to the ground with a grunt of surprise. Somehow, that blade which had come from nowhere swung over again, striking his sword hand. He lay weaponless.

The victor stepped back. "So," he thought, "the old, tried swordplay does have its weaknesses." He looked down at the victim of his strategy. The initial shock had passed. Pain was now coursing through the man.

"Please, sir," gasped Dielo. "Please, no sword art." He groaned. "Please make an end."

"No," denied Philar gently, "you are one of my men, and it is my duty to take care of you. You are badly hurt."

He looked up. "Quick, Zerjo," he called to a guardmaster, "get the physician Marko. This is a case for his skill alone." He pointed to a couple of guardsmen. "Staunch me this man's wounds quickly, then carry him to a pallet. We will await the physician there."

Marko Dalu sat relaxed. Wine cup in hand, he was engaged in talking to a group of friends. Out in the hills, others were listening on their small communicators.

"Gentlemen," he was saying, "we have completed the first phase. It has become increasingly apparent that the only method of encysting the principles of government, art and science already attained is within a cloak of mysticism. You, therefore, will probably have to become the founders of a new religion. We will arrange a spectacular martyr-dom of Marko Dalu, which may be used as you gentlemen see fit.

"Naturally, you and your successors will be visited peri-odically by members of the Corps, who will give you assistance and advice, but to a large extent, you will be on your own. Again, I have to tell you, gentlemen, that this service you have chosen is a dangerous one. You are powerfully armed and protected, but there are restrictions as to your use of your arms. Some of you may suffer torture. Some may die. I don't believe, however, that I have to point out to you the importance of your work, or the fact that your comrades will do all they can to get you out of any danger.

"I may add one thing. If any of you wish to withdraw, the way is still open." He sipped from his cup, waiting. The communicator was silent. None in the group before him spoke. Finally, one man stood up.

"I don't believe anyone wants to quit," he remarked, "so I would like to ask one question." He paused, looking about the room. "We have been given equipment and knowledge that is far in advance of this world of ours. Are we to retain this and yet keep it secret?"

Marko nodded. "You have the knowledge of your world on the one hand, and the knowledge of other worlds on the other. These must be kept separate for many centuries. Advanced knowledge may be hinted at under certain circumstances, but the hints must be very vague, and the source must never be given. The equipment must be safeguarded at all costs. You all have demolition instructions which must be carried out at any hint of danger or compromise of your equipment. Does that answer the question?"

The man nodded. "Perfectly," he said. "I was sure of the answer, but I wanted it clearly stated." As he sat down, Marko's apprentice ran in, closely followed by a guardmaster of the Empire, in full uniform. The boy was nervous.

"Sir," he started, "a guardsman—"

Zerjo thrust the boy aside. "No need for anxiety," he announced. "It is urgent, though. One of my comrades is seriously hurt. We would have you attend him."

Marko arose, smiling. "You know, of course," he remarked, "I am not regarded with too great favor by the governor."

"No matter," Zerjo was impatient. "Men say you are the best healer in Kleedra. Tonight, we have need of such."

"Very well, then." Marko bowed. "Let us go." He reached to an alcove, securing cloak and bag.

As they approached the camp, a crowd gathered. An angry murmur arose. Marko stopped.

"Easy, my friends," he cautioned. "Here is no cause for disturbance. I merely go to practice my profession."

From the rear of the crowd, a voice called out, "He better come out soon, guardsman." Zerjo looked around angrily, hand going to sword, but Marko placed a hand on his arm, urging him forward.

"Pay no attention," he reasoned. "They mean no harm. It is just that they do not wish to see harm done."

"Yes," growled Zerjo, "or they want to start a rebellion tonight."

Marko urged him on. "There will be no rebellion," he said firmly, "tonight, or ever." They walked into the camp.

As they entered the barrack, Philar looked up. "The

man's pretty badly hurt," he informed Marko. "See what you can do for him."

The physician knelt beside the pallet, his fingers exploring the wound in the man's leg. He shook his head. "It'll be hard to make that limb usable again," he said. "How did it happen?"

Philar looked sharply at him. "He talked," he announced, "when he should have listened."

"I shall take care, then, to guard my own tongue," commented the physician. He bent again to his work.

Philar stood watching for a moment, then, "I would have words with you when your work is done." He strode away, thoughtfully. Something was strange about this healer. Surely, somewhere, sometime, he had seen the man before. He cast back into his long and excellent memory. No, it was impossible, he decided. The man was no more than thirty-five years of age. That meant he was barely born when Philar was last in this district. Besides, he was said to be from the countryside, rather than the town or hills. Still, somehow, the man was familiar. He seemed like an old companion.

Finally, Marko stood up. "At least," he remarked, "the pain is eased. The man will sleep now, and perhaps his leg will heal with time." He turned toward Philar. "You wished to speak to me?"

Philar nodded. "Yes. Come in here." He pointed to a small guardroom. "There are many things I want to ask you, and for the present, I'd rather speak in private."

He closed the curtains at the portal, then turned. "Now, then," he began.

Marko held up his hand in a peculiar gesture. "Awaken," he ordered.

"Now, by the sacred robes—" Philar's voice trailed off. "What did you say?"

Marko grinned at him. "I said, 'wake up,' " he repeated. "We've got work to do, pal."

Philar brushed a hand over his forehead. "Yeah," he

agreed. "Yeah. We have, haven't we?" He pulled off his helmet, holding out a hand. "Gimme."

From somewhere in his robes, Marko produced a thin, brilliantly yellow circlet with a single ornamented bulge. Philar put it on his head, cocked it to one side, then slammed the helmet back on.

"C'mon, chum, let's take a walk," he growled.

A guard snapped to attention outside the portal. Absently, his commander returned his salute, and the two men strode out of the camp. As they left, Zerjo stepped up to his guard.

"What did they say?" he queried.

The guard shook his head. "Honest, master, I don't know. They spoke in some foreign language."

"Foreign language?" queried Zerjo. He looked at the guard questioningly. "Was it one of the local dialects?"

The guard shook his head again; emphatically, this time. "No, sir."

"Wish I'd been here," grumbled the guardmaster.

The morning was clear and hot. Philar stepped gratefully into the shaded door of the temple. Glancing about, he strode rapidly back toward the altar. A priest came toward him, hands outstretched.

"The benediction of our Divine Emperor be upon you, my son," he intoned, "but this part of the temple is only for the priesthood."

Philar looked at the man sternly. "You are the head priest here?" he demanded.

"No, I am but an assistant, but—"

"Take me to the head priest," ordered the guardsman.

The priest turned. "This way," he said.

As they entered his sanctum, the head of Kleedra's priesthood turned angrily. "I told you I was not to be disturbed," he said imperiously.

The company master stepped forward. "I," he announced, "am the Kalidar, Philar dar Burta. I have come here to inquire as to why you have allowed a heretic and traitor to run at large for so long in your district."

The priest glared angrily. "You, a mere soldier, dare to question me in this manner?" he stormed.

Philar met his eyes with a level stare. "I asked," he said firmly, "why you allow freedom to a heretic and traitor?"

The priest faltered. Somehow, the presence of this old soldier put a fog on his normally keen, calculating mind.

"Why do you allow the heretic and traitor Marko Dalu to walk the streets of Kleedra?" Philar demanded.

"But, the man is a civil offender," the priest protested.

Philar snorted. "Has he not scoffed at the Divinity of the Glorious Emperor? Has he not hinted at higher powers than those of our temple? Has he not criticized the conduct of the temple and of the priests? And, has he not done all these things in public? His are certainly more heretical than civil offenses. It is up to you, and you alone. What are you going to do?"

The priest spread his hands. He knew there was something wrong with this conversation. He knew that there were other plans, but he couldn't think straight; not with this furious soldier standing over him.

"What can we do?" he inquired.

"First, send your priests out among the people and have them denounce Marko as a dangerous heretic, an evil man, who would cause the destruction of the entire village. Go to the governor and demand a temple trial for this man. Have the priests hint to the people that if Marko is not delivered to the temple, pestilence, fire and the sword will surely visit them." He paused. "I can assure you that fire and the sword are awaiting any open disobedience," he added.

The priest lifted his head. "These things, I will do," he said decisively.

Philar, Kalidar of the Imperial Guard of the Dalturan Empire, leaned back at his ease in his own quarters. At last, this assignment was nearly accomplished. Soon, he'd be able to go back and relax for a while. In the privacy of his room, he had removed his helmet, and the golden circlet glowed against his dark hair.

"Well, Marc," he was thinking, "I'm coming after you tomorrow. How do you feel?"

"Swell," came the answering thought.

"By the way, did you run to completion on this one?" Philar asked.

Marc was disdainful. "Think I'm a snail? Great Space, they gave me almost four years. I had the job done in three. I beat it all through their heads, then clinched it on the other side. Picked up more recruits than we actually need for the job, too."

Philar started ticking off points on his fingers. "Philosophy, Ethics—"

"Yeah, yeah," he was interrupted. "Philosophy, Behaviorism, Organization, Techniques, Ethics, the works. I even got time to throw in a lot of extra hints that'll take two or three periods to decipher. They've got physical and biological science, up to and including longevity. They've got Galactic Ethics. I even slipped them a short course in Higher Psychology. 'Course, they'll have to do all the groundwork for themselves, but my recruits understand a good share of the stuff. When they're able to release their knowledge, this planet'll be on the team."

"Nice going, pal," Philar chuckled. "Well, as I said, I'm coming after you tomorrow, complete with a whole bunch of nice, tough Dalturan guardsmen. Hope your body shield's in good shape."

"You space worm," stormed Marko. "If you let those primeval monkeys get rough with me, so help me, I'll—"

"Ah, ah," Philar shook his finger, "naughty thoughts."

"Master Intelligence Technician Philar!" A third thought broke in sternly.

Philar groaned. "Oooh, I've done it again. Yes, sir."

"Attention to orders. After completion of your assignment tomorrow, you will march to the seaport, Dalyra. There, you will embark for the capital, Baratea. During the voyage, you will fall over the side and be lost." An impression of amusement intruded. "I'll be at the controls, sergeant, and for your sins, I'm going to bring you in wet.

My friend, you will be so waterlogged that you'll be able to go without water for at least half a period."

"Yes, captain." Philar was doleful. He took the circlet off, holding it at arm's length and looking at it sourly.

"Thought control," he snorted aloud. "Thought control, that's what it is." He clapped the mentacom back on and composed himself to sleep.

Kloru Noile, High Priest of Kleedra, sat at his worktable. As he read, he nodded his head. Finally, he looked up. "Well, Plana," he remarked to his assistant, "looks as though the last of the despots has called it a day." He held out the paper. The man took it and read.

Informal Report

From: Barcu Lores, Security Technician Second Class
To: NCOIC, Philosophical Section 5/G3-4/572
Subject: Duke Klonda Bal Kithrel

1. Psychological work on the subject is nearing completion. Bal Kithrel has decided to allow elections of all magistrates, as well as three members of the advisory council. He is also considering a revision of the property laws. It is believed that this is the beginning of constitutional rule in this area. Work is continuing—

Plana handed the paper back. "I believe, sergeant," he remarked, "that we'll get a good inspection report this time."

Editor's Introduction To:

DATA vs. EVIDENCE IN THE VOODOO SCIENCES

Jerry E. Pournelle, Ph.D

Contact! is an annual convention combining anthropologists and science fiction writers. The first one was held in the spring of 1983 in Santa Cruz, California.

I was invited to attend and present a paper. That sounded like fun, but it wasn't easy. As it happened, the previous week I was supposed to go to Houston, Texas for the L-5 Society Convention on Space Development, and from there to Ithaca, New York, where I delivered the annual C. P. Snow Memorial Lecture. I went directly from Ithaca to Santa Cruz. Since I hadn't been home for over a week, my paper was mostly written on airplanes.

That, incidentally, is much easier to do than it used to be, thanks to my NEC PC-8201 portable lap computer.

The first Contact! conference proved to be as interesting as I'd hoped, and the second was in many ways better. The conventions tend to be equally divided between fairly serious analysis and pure fun, with a kind of space-age Dungeons and Dragons game thrown in for free.

Since I wrote this essay, Charles Murray has published *Losing Ground*, a book that proves, or purports to prove, that most of the welfare policies of the U.S. are having precisely the opposite effect that the social scientists thought they would have. He cites the great Negative Income Tax experiment, which was apparently done quite well, and which seems to show beyond all doubt that if you give people free money, they don't work as much as they do when you don't. Naturally, the book has been either ignored or savagely attacked.

This was written some years ago, in haste, on an airplane, but I see no reason to revise a word of it.

DATA VS. EVIDENCE IN THE VOODOO SCIENCES
Jerry Pournelle

"Literary intellectuals at one pole—at the other scientists . . . Between the two a gulf of mutual incomprehension."

Lord C. P. Snow: *The Two Cultures on the Scientific Revolution* [1959]

The late C. P. Snow was concerned that we were developing two powerful cultures, neither of which understood the other. He thought this very dangerous. Science, with its power over the physical world, is terrifying if not humanely controlled; humanists without science are helpless.

Examples of the consequences of this gap are not hard to find. Consider the following, which seems particularly relevant to science fiction readers.

From *Aviation Technical News* Volume IX, No. 5, published by Kerr Industrial Applications Center, Southeastern Oklahoma State University, for NASA's Technology Utilization Division. I give an EXACT quote:

LONG TIME PARKING

(From *Goddard News* Jan. 15, 1983, article by Charles Recknagel)

"The international Sun-Earth Explorer space craft has been parked 1.6 million km from the earth since 1978.

During these approximately five years the space craft has been suspended at the point where the Earth's and the Sun's gravitational pull are equal. The point is called the 'Liberation point.' After monitoring the charged particles emanating from the sun these many years, NASA decided in Oct. of 82 that they would crank up the satellite and use it for another purpose. The vehicle will swing within 100 km. of the moon's surface Dec. 23 of '83."

Note "Liberation Point," and the ludicrous orbital mechanics. One might almost excuse John Holt. Holt, a well-known educator and popular lecturer, author of *Why Children Fail; How Children Learn; What Do I Do Monday?*, chose to attack the concept of space colonies in a special issue of *CoEvolution Quarterly* (1977) devoted to the subject.

In a section entitled *Technical Debate* Holt says, "It seems that if L-5 is a point where the gravitational fields of earth and moon cancel each other out, any movement toward either earth or moon would lead to a further movement in that direction, there being no correcting or opposing force. The effect of these forces might be very slight, so that we could say of a 64 million ton cylinder that it would take many thousands or tens of thousands of years before it finally reached the earth. Still, it would be rather hard for those on earth."

Holt's argument against space colonies *sounds* scientific, and he probably believes he is being scientific. He also objects on "moral" grounds. When Tom Heppenheimer (certainly no soft-spoken advocate) says that Holt's arguments are "largely theological, reflecting bias or intuitive dislike, rather than any semblance of reasoned assessment," Holt replies:

"Again 'theological.' My objections to this project are variously ethical, moral, philosophical, political, and economic. (I might add that, according to Gerald Piel, publisher of *Scientific American*, many scientists themselves oppose this project on moral grounds.) To call such objections 'theological' is imprecise, and has in it more than a whiff of Dr. Strangelove, or hard-nosed talk about 'megadeaths' or 'credible first strike capability' or 'acceptable risks.' And this may be the point to note that in all of O'Neill's and Heppenheimer's talk about space colonies there is no mention of risks. The risks would in fact be enormous. We have already lost three lives in space, and almost three more; the Russians have lost at least three. This is a death rate of something over 6%. But our ventures into space have been very modest, and surrounded by the most elaborate and expensive precautions. It seems altogether reasonable to assume that if we begin complicated mining and industrial operations on the moon, our casualty rate will be higher, perhaps much higher."

When Heppenheimer says that "It cannot be denied that large numbers of people will freely volunteer to live in space, even under austere conditions, when this becomes possible," Holt, in footnote #51 (of 56; his annotations are at least as long as Heppenheimer's text; Heppenheimer's text was itself a reply to an unannotated essay by Holt; this is known as the fairness doctrine) says:

"I do deny it—unless, of course, they have been told terrible lies about what life and work in space is really like. I expect that this will happen, and in fact is happening, and it is one of my ethical and moral reasons for opposing this project."

The interesting part is that we are listening to scientific-sounding nonsense from a man who does not know high school physics, and seems to know little of probability. He is, however, a "humanist," and thus should know human behavior. Yet I wonder, and call to evidence Shackleton's experience:

Ernest Shackleton was adjutant to the 1901 South Polar expedition. In 1900 he placed the following advertisement:

"MEN WANTED for Hazardous Journey. Small wages, bitter cold, long months of complete darkness, safe return doubtful. Honor and recognition in case of success." When he later reported on the advertisement's success, he said, "It seemed as though all the men in Great Britain were determined to accompany me, the response was so overwhelming."

I suspect I would have little difficulty recruiting qualified people for L-5 colonies, or indeed for an early lunar colony. Perhaps I'm wrong, but unlike Holt I have some evidence, and a smattering of data.

One may believe, as I do, that communications between scientists and non-scientists are in a sad state, and that this is a dangerous situation, without accepting C. P. Snow's picture as accurate. In my judgment the critical gap is not between "scientists" and "humanists," or between the sciences and the arts; the critical gap is between the so-called "social sciences" and everyone else.

This gap is exacerbated to the extent that neither scientists nor humanists believe there is scientific value in the "social sciences." In my judgment there is very little science in the "social sciences" and the use of the word "science" to describe these disciplines is generally either mendacious or farcical. Alas, it may also be tragic.

The real difference between arts and sciences is the difference between data and evidence; and the "social sciences" don't know the one from the other.

Imagine a spectrum. On one end you have science fiction. On the other end, you have hard science. What connects them is the nature of their subject matter.

The scientist requires hard facts. He needs data, ideally in the from of repeatable experiments. Data, to a scientist, is best generated in controlled experiments which can be described, published, and repeated.

ART FORM	LEGAL	SCIENCE
Verisimilitude	Evidence	Data
Plausibility	Selection	All of the data
Argumentative	"Proof"	Validation

Figure One: From Verisimilitude to Data

The science fiction writer doesn't need any data. Certainly he must use some hard facts, because if *everything* is contrary to the reader's expectations, the work isn't going to be taken seriously: therefore, the science fiction writer makes use of "facts" not as data, but for verisimilitude and plausibility.

However, science fiction can't "prove" anything about the universe. We can speculate about it, we can try to expand people's horizons and stretch their imaginations; but we cannot, as science fiction writers, add to scientific knowledge, and this goes for "insights into the human condition" every whit as much as for contributions to nuclear physics.

Science fiction can't prove anything, because science fiction makes up its data. You can prove anything if you can make up your data.

Example: An earlier paper given at this very panel (at the Contact! symposium) uses the speech by the Army major in the film *Close Encounters* as an example of how the military thinks. This is patently absurd; it is at best evidence of Steve Spielberg's theory of how the military thinks, and it's probably not even useful for inferring that. Once again we have confusion of data, evidence, and plausibility.

The social scientist vaguely understands this fundamental principle, but doesn't really distinguish between data and evidence. Thus when Margaret Mead studied adolescence in Samoa, she was seeking evidence for a theory. Later writers, wishing to challenge the biggest name in the field, have done precisely the same thing. None of them seem interested in gathering data.

When this was put to Dr. Paul Bohanan, dean of the School of Social Sciences at the University of Southern California, he replied that Mead's value didn't lie in her data-gathering. She stretched imaginations and made people think larger thoughts.

Granted this may be true, but it seems more the job of a science fiction writer than a scientist.

As art forms, the social sciences may or may not be useful; but they are not content as art forms. Whenever anything of social significance happens—a riot, for example—

the TV screens are filled with learned social scientists giving us both explanations and advice.

On their advice, for example, the police have been withdrawn from riot areas. The results have been uniformly disastrous, but this doesn't prevent the social scientists from advising the same remedy the next time.

You can prove anything if you make up your data. You can prove nearly anything if you are allowed to select your evidence and forget embarrassing facts.

The social sciences have made an art of forgetting embarrassing facts.

If a fact doesn't fit the theory, leave the fact for another discipline. Sociology has nothing to learn from anthropology which has nothing to learn from social psychology. None of these has anything to learn from the mathematics, physics, or chemistry departments.

The solution to C. P. Snow's dilemma seems clear. Scientists must learn something of the humanities. That, I think, is done rather more often than not. Scientists do read books. I have met the maniac scientist bent on discovery no matter the harm far more often in literature than in the laboratory.

Secondly, the humanists must learn something of science. This is less common, but it does happen. It isn't necessary that the humanist become a scientist, or even learn how to do science; it is necessary that he learn the principles of scientific reasoning.

I would be far more willing to believe that the two cultures could coexist, however, were it not for the contamination of the "social sciences," which pose as sciences to the humanists, and humanities to the scientists, but which are not in fact much good as either. The poet who believes he knows something of science having taken "Sosh 103" and "Ed Stat" is far more dangerous than ever he would have been if he had remained ignorant.

Meanwhile, novelists have as much right to be called "experts" on human behavior as any social scientist, which is to say we can learn as much about our fellow humans from a good novel as from a sociology treatise; and I know which I would rather read. Similarly, the poet may find beauty in the theory of probability, and will learn something of the difference between data and evidence while studying it; "Stat for Social Scientists" teaches nothing, and is dull in the bargain.

When the social scientists are challenged as unscientific, their usual plea is that their subject matter is very complex and thus the methodology of physical science won't work. This is an interesting argument, but it would carry more weight if students of social science knew something of physical science's methodologies. Granted that the "social sciences" have an intrinsically more difficult job; is this any reason to abandon the tools of science?

Editor's Introduction To:

NICARAGUA: A SPEECH TO MY FORMER COMRADES ON THE LEFT

David Horowitz

Western diplomats seem to have forgotten long ago that the objective of negotiation is to wring concessions from their opponents.

It may seem too casually cruel to lampoon intelligent, patriotic men whose only fault was a shortage of ideas they needed to understand what was, to them at least, a new political phenomenon: totalitarianism. Precisely because they were intelligent, we see their errors not so much as personal lapses, but as reflections of a fundamental lack of an interpretative framework. More serious is the fact that after the war, we still lacked this framework for understanding Communist totalitarianism, despite the price paid by the West for those "pioneers of detente" who considered Munich a response to Nazi totalitarianism.

Misunderstanding of communism stamped all postwar Western statesmen. They could not grasp its particularity, the laws by which it functions. They persisted in explaining it by its leaders' psychology. Or they likened it to the forms of political power with which they were familiar: czarism, the French Revolution, "socialism minus freedom." Some simply thought of it as a preliminary to freedom. "Roosevelt never understood communism," Averill Harriman said. "He viewed it as a sort of extension of the New Deal." Perhaps the veteran diplomat should have noticed this when he was in a position to do something about it.

—Jean-Francois Revel
How Democracies Perish, Doubleday, 1983

The lessons learned so painfully about Hitler in the '30s were not applied to Stalin in the '40s and '50s. When I was an undergraduate in the '50s, it was fashionable for the professors to say that "Whereas the Nazis were purely criminals, Communism, for all its faults, is within the Western progressive tradition." In other words, all that was needed was reform: there wasn't anything fundamentally wrong with the communist system.

It is remarkable how few political leaders are influenced by evidence. During the '30s there was plenty of evidence for the famines in the Ukraine, but as George Orwell observed, "Huge events like the Ukraine famine of 1933, involving the deaths of millions of people, have actually escaped the attention of the majority of the English russophiles." Those events escaped most of the American left as well.

So, apparently, has the slaughter in Cambodia, the pitiable condition of the Boat People, and Yellow Rain. To a great many tenured professors on U.S. campuses, there is still no enemy to the left, nor can there be.

You can prove anything if you can make up your data; the corollary is that you can prove almost anything if you can ignore the data that won't fit.

David Horowitz was a founder of the Vietnam Solidarity Campaign, and editor of *Ramparts* magazine. He was solidly for Castro after the Cuban Revolution.

NICARAGUA: A SPEECH TO MY FORMER COMRADES ON THE LEFT

David Horowitz

Twenty-five years ago I was one of the founders of the New Left. I was one of the organizers of the first political demonstrations on the Berkeley campus—and indeed on any campus—to protest our government's anti-Communist policies in Cuba and Vietnam. Tonight I come before you as the kind of man I used to tell myself I would never be: a supporter of President Reagan, a committed opponent of Communist rule in Nicaragua.

I offer no apologies for my present position. It was what I thought was the humanity of the Marxist *idea* that made me what I was then; it is the inhumanity of what I have seen to be the Marxist *reality* that has made me what I am now. If my former comrades who support the Sandinistas were to pause for a moment and then plunge their busy political minds into the human legacies of their activist pasts, they would instantly drown in an ocean of blood.

The issue before us is not whether it is morally right for the United States to arm the *contras*, or whether there are unpleasant men among them. Nor is it whether the United States should defer to the wisdom of the Contadora powers— more than thirty years ago the United States tried to overthrow Somoza, and it was the Contadora powers of the time who bailed him out.

The issue before us and before all people who cherish freedom is how to oppose a Soviet imperialism so vicious and so vast as to dwarf any previously known. An "ocean of blood" is no metaphor. As we speak here tonight, this empire—whose axis runs through Havana and now Managua—is killing hundreds of thousands of Ethiopians to consolidate a dictatorship whose policies against its black citizens make the South African government look civilized and humane.

A second issue, especially important to me, is the credibility and commitment of the American Left.

In his speech on Nicaragua, President Reagan invoked the Truman Doctrine, the first attempt to oppose Soviet expansion through revolutionary surrogates. I marched against the Truman Doctrine in 1948, and defended, with the Left, the revolutions in Russia and China, in Eastern Europe and Cuba, in Cambodia and Vietnam—just as the Left defends the Sandinistas today.

And I remember the arguments and "facts" with which we made our case and what the other side said, too—the Presidents who came and went, and the anti-Communists on the Right, the William Buckleys and the Ronald Reagans. And in every case, without exception, time has proved the Left wrong. Wrong in its views of the revolutionaries' intentions, and wrong about the facts of their revolutionary rule. And just as consistently the anti-Communists were proved right.

Today the Left dismisses Reagan's warnings about Soviet expansion as anti-Communist paranoia, a threat to the peace, and a mask for American imperialism. We said the same things about Truman when he warned us then. Russia's control of Eastern Europe, we said, was only a defensive buffer, a temporary response to American power—first, because Russia had no nuclear weapons; and then, because it lacked the missiles to deliver them.

Today, the Soviet Union is a nuclear superpower, missiles and all, but it has not given up an inch of the empire which it gained during World War II—not Eastern Europe, not the Baltic states which Hitler delivered to Stalin and whose nationhood Stalin erased and which are now all but forgotten, not even the Kurile Islands which were once part of Japan.

Not only have the Soviets failed to relinquish their conquests in all these years—years of dramatic, total decolonization in the West—but their growing strength and the wounds of Vietnam have encouraged them to reach for more. South Vietnam, Cambodia, Laos, Ethiopia, Yemen, Mozambique, and Angola are among the dominoes which have recently fallen into the Soviet orbit.

To expand its territorial core—which apologists still refer to as a "defensive perimeter"—Moscow has already slaughtered a million peasants in Afghanistan, an atrocity warmly endorsed by the Sandinista government.

Minister of Defense Humberto Ortega describes the army of the conquerors—whose scorched-earth policy has driven half the Afghan population from its homes—as the "pillar of peace" in the world today. To any self-respecting socialist, praise for such barbarism would be an inconceivable outrage—as it was to the former Sandinista, now *contra*, Eden Pastora. But praise for the barbarians is sincere tribute coming from the Sandinista rulers, because they see themselves as an integral part of the Soviet empire itself.

"The struggle of man against power is the struggle of memory against forgetting." So writes the Czech novelist Milan Kundera, whose name and work no longer exist in his homeland.

In all the Americas, Fidel Castro was the only head of state to cheer the Soviet tanks as they rolled over the brave people of Prague. And cheering right along with Fidel were Carlos Fonseca, Tomas Borge, Humberto Ortega, and the other creators of the present Nicaraguan regime.

One way to assess what has happened in Nicaragua is to realize that wherever Soviet tanks crush freedom from now on, there will be two governments in the Americas supporting them all the way.

About its own crimes and for its own criminals, the Left has no memory at all.

To the Left I grew up in, along with the Sandinista founders, Stalin's Russia was a socialist paradise, the model of the liberated future. Literacy to the uneducated, power to the weak, justice to the forgotten—we praised the Soviet Union then, just as the Left praises the Sandinistas now.

And just as they ignore warnings like the one that has come from Violetta Chamorro, the publisher of *La Prensa*, the paper which led the fight against Somoza, and a member of the original Sandinista junta—"With all my heart, I tell you it is worse here now than it was in the times of the Somoza dictatorship"—so we dismissed the anti-Soviet "lies" about Stalinist repression.

In the society we hailed as a new human dawn, 100 million people were put in slave-labor camps, in conditions rivaling Auschwitz and Buchenwald. Between 30 and 40 million people were killed—in peacetime, in the daily routine of socialist rule. While leftists applauded their progressive policies and guarded their frontiers, Soviet Marxists killed more peasants, more workers, and even more Communists than all the capitalist governments together since the beginning of time.

And for the entire duration of this nightmare, the William Buckleys and Ronald Reagans and the other anti-Communists went on telling the world exactly what was happening. And all that time the pro-Soviet Left and its fellow-travelers went on denouncing them as reactionaries and liars, using the same contemptuous terms with which the Left attacks the President and his supporters today.

The Left would *still* be denying the Soviet atrocities if the perpetrators themselves had not finally acknowledged their crimes. In 1956, in a secret speech to the party elite, Khrushchev made the crimes a Communist fact; but it was only the CIA that actually made the fact public, allowing radicals to come to terms with what they had done.

Khrushchev and his cohorts could not have cared less about the misplaced faith and misspent lives of their naive supporters on the Left. The Soviet rulers were concerned about themselves: Stalin's mania had spread the slaughter into his henchmen's ranks; they wanted to make totalitarianism safe for its rulers. In place of a dictator whose paranoia could not be controlled, they instituted a dictatorship by directorate—which (not coincidentally) is the

form of rule in Nicaragua today. Repression would work
one way only: from the privileged top of society to the
powerless bottom.

The year of Khrushchev's speech—which is also the
year Soviet tanks flattened the freedom fighters of Buda
pest—is the year that tells us who the Sandinistas really
are.

Because the truth had to be admitted at last, the Left all
over the world was forced to redefine itself in relation to
the Soviet facts. China's Communist leader Mao liked
Stalin's way better. Twenty-five million people died in the
"great leaps" and "cultural revolutions" he then launched
In Europe and America, however, a new anti-Stalinist Left
was born. This New Left, of which I was one of the
founders, was repelled by the evils it was now forced to
see, and embarrassed by the tarnish the Soviet totalitari
ans had brought to the socialist cause. It turned its back on
the Soviet model of Stalin and his heirs.

But the Sandinista vanguard was neither embarrassed
nor repelled. In 1957, Carlos Fonseca, the founding father
of the Sandinista Front, visited the Soviet Union with its
newly efficient totalitarian state. To Fonseca, as to Borge
and his other comrades, the Soviet monstrosity was their
revolutionary dream come true. In his pamphlet, *A Nica
raguan in Moscow*, Fonseca proclaimed Soviet Commu
nism his model for Latin America's revolutionary future.

This vision of a Soviet America is now being realized in
Nicaragua. The *comandante* directorate, the army, and the
secret police are already mirrors of the Soviet state—not
only structurally but in their personnel, trained and often
manned by agents of the Soviet axis.

But the most important figure in this transformation is
not a Nicaraguan at all. For twenty years, from the time
the Sandinistas first arrived in Havana, they were disciples
of Fidel Castro. With his blessings they went on to Mos
cow, where Stalin's henchman completed their revolution
ary course. Fidel is the image in which the Sandinista
leadership has created itself and the author of its strategy.

ts politburo, the *comandante* directorate, was personally created by Fidel in Havana on the eve of the final struggle, sealed with a pledge of millions in military aid. It was Fidel who supplied the arms with which the Sandinistas waged their battles, just as he supplied the Cuban general—Zenen Casals—who directed their victorious campaign (just as the Soviets supplied the general who directed Fidel's own victory at the Bay of Pigs). *Without Castro's intervention, Arturo Cruz and the other anti-Somoza and prodemocratic* contras *would be the government of Nicaragua today*.

And it was Fidel who showed the Sandinistas how to steal the revolution after the victory, and how to secure their theft by manipulating their most important allies: the American Left and its liberal sympathizers.

Twenty-five years ago Fidel was also a revolutionary hero to us on the New Left. Like today's campus radicals, we became "coffee-pickers" and passengers on the revolutionary tour, and we hailed the literacy campaigns, health clinics, and other wonders of the people's state.

When Fidel spoke, his words were revolutionary music to our ears: "Freedom with bread. Bread without terror." "A revolution neither red nor black, but Cuban olive-green." And so in Managua today: "Not [Soviet] Communism but Nicaraguan *Sandinismo*" is the formula Fidel's imitators proclaim.

Fidel's political poems put radicals all over the world under his spell. Jean-Paul Sartre wrote one of the first and most influential books of praise: "If this man asked me for the moon," he said, "I would give it to him. Because he would have a need for it."

When I listen to the enthusiasts for the Sandinista redeemers, the fate of a hero of the Cuban revolution comes to my mind. For in the year that Jean-Paul Sartre came to Havana and fell in love with the humanitarian Fidel, Huber Matos embarked on a long windowless night of the soul.

The fate of Huber Matos begins with the second revolution that Fidel launched.

All the fine gestures and words with which Fidel seduced us and won our support—the open Marxism, the socialist humanism, the independent path—turned out to be calculated lies. Even as he proclaimed his color to be olive-green, he was planning to make his revolution Moscow red.

So cynical was Fidel's strategy that at the time it was difficult for many to comprehend. One by one Fidel began removing his own comrades from the revolutionary regime and replacing them with Cuban Communists.

Cuba's Communists were then a party in disgrace. They had opposed the revolution; they had even served in the cabinet of the tyrant Batista while the revolution was taking place!

But this was all incidental to Fidel. Fidel knew how to use people. And Fidel was planning a *new* revolution he could trust the Communists to support: he had decided to turn Cuba into a Soviet state. And Fidel also knew that he could no longer trust his own comrades, because they had made a revolution they thought was going to be Cuban olive-green.

Although Fidel removed socialists and the Sandinistas removed democrats, the pattern of betrayal has been the same.

To gain power the Sandinistas concealed their true intention (*a Soviet state*) behind a revolutionary lie (*a pluralist democracy*). To consolidate power they fashioned a second lie (*democracy, but only within the revolution*) and those who believed in the first lie were removed. At the end of the process there will be no democracy in Nicaragua at all, which is exactly what Fonseca and the Sandinistas intended when they began.

When Huber Matos saw Fidel's strategy unfolding in Cuba, he got on the telephone with other Fidelistas to discuss what they should do. This was a mistake. In the first year of Cuba's liberation, the phones of revolutionary legends like Huber Matos were already tapped by Fidel's secret police. Huber Matos was arrested.

In the bad old days of Batista oppression, Fidel had been arrested himself. His crime was not words on a telephone, but leading an attack on a military barracks to overthrow the Batista regime. Twelve people were killed. For this Fidel spent a total of eighteen months in the tyrant's jail before being released.

Huber Matos was not so lucky. Fidel was no Batista, and the revolution that had overthrown Batista was no two-bit dictatorship. For his phone call, Huber Matos was tried in such secrecy that not even members of the government were privy to the proceeding. When it was over, he was sentenced to solitary confinement, in a cell without sunlight, for *twenty-two years*. And even as Fidel buried his former friend and comrade alive, he went on singing his songs of revolutionary humanism and justice.

Milan Kundera reveals the meaning of this revolutionary parable of Huber Matos and Fidel. Recalling a French Communist who wrote poems for brotherhood while his friend was being murdered by the poet's comrades in Prague, Kundera says: "The hangman killed while the poet sang."

Kundera explains: "People like to say revolution is beautiful; it is only the terror arising from it which is evil. But this is not true. The evil is already present in the beautiful; hell is already contained in the dream of paradise. . . . To condemn Gulags is easy, but to reject the poetry which leads to the Gulag by way of paradise is as difficult as ever." Words to bear in mind today as we consider Nicaragua and its revolution of poets.

To believe in the revolutionary dream is the tragedy of its supporters; to exploit the dream is the talent of its dictators. Revolutionary cynicism, the source of this talent, is Fidel's most important teaching to his Sandinista disciples. This is the faculty that allows the *comandantes* to emulate Fidel himself: to be poets and hangmen at the same time. To promise democracy and organize repression, to attack imperialism and join an empire, to talk peace and plan war, to champion justice and deliver Nicaragua to a fraternity of inhumane, repressive, militarized, and economically crippled states.

"We used to have one main prison, now we have many," begins the lament of Carlos Franqui, a former Fidelista, for the paradise that Nicaragua has now gained. "We used to have a few barracks; now we have many. We used to have many plantations; now we have only one, and it belongs to Fidel. Who enjoys the fruits of the revolution, the houses of the rich, the luxuries of the rich? The *comandante* and his court."

To this grim accounting must be added the economic ruin that Fidel's Marxism has wrought. Among the proven failures of the Marxist promise, this is the most fateful of all. The failure of Marxist economies to satisfy basic needs, let alone compete with the productive capitalisms of the West, has produced the military-industrial police states which call themselves socialist today. Nicaragua, with its Sandinista-created economic crisis and its massive military build-up, is the latest example of this pattern.

Twenty-five years ago we on the Left applauded when Fidel denounced Cuba's one-crop economy and claimed that U.S. imperialism was the cause of the nation's economic plight. It seemed so self-evident. Cuba was a fertile island with a favorable climate, but U.S. sugar plantations had monopolized its arable land, and the sugar produced was a product for export, not a food for Cubans. The poor of Cuba had been sacrificed on the altar of imperialist profit. Whenever we were confronted by the political costs Castro's revolution might entail, we were confident that this gain alone—Cuba's freedom to grow food for Cubans—would make any sacrifice worthwhile. The same illusion—that the revolution will mean better lives for Nicaragua's poor—underlies every defense of the Sandinistas today.

It is nearly three decades since Cuba's liberation, and Cuba is still a one-crop economy. But the primary market for its sugar is now the Soviet Union instead of the United States. Along with this have come other economic differences as well. Cuba's external debt is now *200 times* what it was when Fidel took power. And it would be far greater if the Communist *caudillo* had not mortgaged his country to his Soviet patron. So bankrupt is the economy Castro has created that it requires a Soviet subsidy of over $4 billion a year, one-quarter of the entire national income, to keep it afloat. Before the revolution, Cubans enjoyed the highest per-capita income in Latin America. Now they are economic prisoners of permanent rationing and chronic shortages in even the most basic necessities. The allotted rations tell a story in themselves: two pounds of meat per citizen per month; 20 percent less clothing than the allotment a decade earlier; and in rice, a basic staple of Cuba's poor, *half* the yearly consumption under the old Batista regime.

The idea that Marxist revolution will mean economic benefit for the poor has proved to be the most deadly illusion of all. It is *because* Marxist economies *cannot* satisfy economic needs—not even at the levels of the miserably corrupt capitalisms of Batista and Somoza—that Marxist states require permanent repression to stifle unrest and permanent enemies to saddle with the blame.

This is also why Castro has found a new national product to supply to the Soviet market (a product his Sandinista disciples are in the process of developing in their turn). The product is the Cuban nation itself, as a military base for Soviet expansion.

The event that sealed the contract for this development was the moment of America's defeat in Vietnam in April 1975. This defeat resulted in America's effective withdrawal from the crucial role it had played since 1945, as the guardian of the international status quo and the keeper of its peace.

To the Soviet imperialists, America's loss was an opportunity gained. In 1975 the Kremlin began what would soon be a tenfold increase in the aid it had been providing to Cuba. Most of the aid was of military intent. Toward the end of the year, 36,000 Cuban troops surfaced in Africa, as an interventionary force in Angola's civil war. Soviet aid to Cuba tripled and then quintupled as Castro sent another 12,000 Cuban troops to provide a palace guard for Ethiopia's new dictator, Mengistu Haile Mariam, who had thrown himself into the Soviet embrace with a campaign which he officially called his "Red Terror." A year after his henchmen had murdered virtually the entire graduating class of the high schools of Addis Ababa—just the most poignant of Mengistu's 100,000 victims—Fidel presented him with a Bay of Pigs medal, Cuban socialism's highest award.

Ethiopia's dictator is only one of the international heroes who regularly pass through the Cuban base to be celebrated, trained, and integrated into a network of subversion and terror that has come to span every continent of the globe. And in the Sandinista revolution Fidel's colonial plantation has produced its most profitable return: an opportunity for Moscow to expand its investment to the American land mass itself.

Nicaragua is now in the grip of utterly cynical and utterly ruthless men, exceeding even their sponsors in aggressive hostility to the United States. The Soviets may be the covert patrons of the world's terrorist plague, but not even they have had the temerity to embrace publicly the assassin Qaddafi as a "brother" the way the Sandinistas have. The aim of the Sandinista revolution is to crush its society from top to bottom, to institute totalitarian rule, and to use the country as a base to spread Communist terror and Communist regimes throughout the hemisphere.

The Sandinista anthem which proclaims the Yankee to be the "enemy of mankind" expresses precisely the revolutionaries' sentiment and goal. That goal is hardly to create a more just society—the sordid record would dissuade any reformer from choosing the Communist path—but to destroy the societies still outside the totalitarian perimeter, and their chief protector, the United States.

Support for the *contras* is a first line of defense. For Nicaraguans, a *contra* victory would mean the restoration of the democratic leadership from whom the Sandinistas stole the revolution in the first place, the government that Nicaragua would have had if Cuba had not intervened. For the countries of the Americas, it would mean a halt in the Communist march that threatens their freedoms and their peace.

In conclusion, I would like to say this to my former comrades and successors on the Left: you are self-righteous and blind in your belief that you are part of a movement to advance human progress and liberate mankind. You are in fact in league with the darkest and most reactionary forces of the modern world, whose legacies—as the record attests— are atrocities and oppressions on a scale unknown in the human past. It is no accident that radicals in power have slaughtered so many of their own people. Hatred of self, and by extension one's country, is the root of the radical cause.

As American radicals, the most egregious sin you commit is to betray the privileges and freedoms ordinary people from all over the world have created in this country— privileges and freedoms that ordinary people all over the world would feel blessed to have themselves. But the worst of it is this: you betray all this tangible good that you can see around you for a socialist pie-in-the-sky that has meant horrible deaths and miserable lives for the hundreds of millions who have so far fallen under its sway.

Editor's Introduction To:

THE GODS OF THE COPYBOOK HEADINGS

Rudyard Kipling

I had to memorize this poem in high school. I suppose I resented that at the time, but I've not regretted it since.

American education goes through many fads. More than forty years ago when I was in the Capleville, Tennessee, public school, with two grades to a room and some 25 pupils per grade, *everyone* in the school not only could read, but did read. I still have the reader. In fifth grade we were assigned Macauley's "Horatius," and were required to memorize at least this verse:

> *Then up spake brave Horatius,*
> *The captain of the gate,*
> *'To every man upon this earth,*
> *Death cometh soon or late.*
> *And how can man die better,*
> *Than facing fearful odds,*
> *For the ashes of his fathers,*
> *And the temples of his gods?'*

In those days we had no Federal aid to education, and

thus couldn't afford fancy books about Dick and Jane and
their running dog Spot. We had to read Hiawatha, James
Fenimore Cooper, Washington Irving, Huck Finn and
Evangeline and the King of the Golden River, Edgar Lee
Masters and Stephen Vincent Benet. Of course today's
schools have more money, and can buy the improved
reading materials written by professors of education. Every pupil gets a textbook. It's probably fortunate for the
textbook writers, since few of them publish anywhere else.

Textbooks weren't so common in my time—at least in
the less affluent districts. Instead we used the copybook:
literally a bound notebook into which one copied materials
the teachers thought you ought to learn. The notion was
that you'd learn penmanship as well as what you'd copied.

In some cases the material itself wasn't assigned: you'd
be given headings, and told to go to the library and copy
out something about them. The copybook headings might
include history, or poetry, or Proverbs; and sometimes
they would include more terrible things. As for instance:

Some say that Darkness was first, and from Darkness
sprang Chaos. From a union between Darkness and Chaos
sprang Night, Day, Erebrus, and the Air.

From a union between Night and Erebrus sprang
Doom, Old Age, Death, Murder, Continence, Sleep,
Dreams, Discord, Misery, Vexation, Nemesis, Joy, Friend-
ship, Pity, the Three Fates, and the Three Hesperides.

From a union between Air and Day sprang Mother
Earth, Sky, and Sea.

From a union between Air and Mother Earth sprang
Terror, Craft, Anger, Strife, Lies, Oaths, Vengeance, In-
temperance, Altercation, Treaty, Oblivion, Fear, Pride,
Battle; also Oceanus, Metis, and other Titans, Tartarus,
and the Three Erinnyes, or Furies . . .

—Hesiod (translated by Robert Graves)

We were supposed to take each of those as a heading.
Doubtless it did much for my vocabulary. And to this day

I remember that it was the particular task of Nemesis to punish hubris, or overweening pride, by visiting her victim with catastrophe.

THE GODS OF THE COPYBOOK HEADINGS
Rudyard Kipling

As I pass through my incarnations in every age and race,
I make my proper prostrations to the Gods of the Market-Place.
Peering through reverent fingers I watch them flourish and fall,
And the Gods of the Copybook Headings, I notice, outlast them all.

We were living in trees when they met us. They showed us each in turn
That Water would certainly wet us, as Fire would certainly burn:
But we found them lacking in Uplift, Vision and Breadth of Mind,
So we left them to teach the Gorillas while we followed the March of Mankind.

We moved as the Spirit listed. They never altered their pace,
Being neither cloud nor wind-borne like the Gods of the Market-Place;
But they always caught up with our progress, and presently word would come
That a tribe had been wiped off its icefield, or the lights had gone out in Rome.

With the Hopes that our World is built on they were utterly out of touch.

*They denied that the Moon was Stilton; they denied she
was even Dutch.*

*They denied that Wishes were Horses; they denied that a
Pig had Wings.*

*So we worshipped the Gods of the Market Who promised
these beautiful things.*

*When the Cambrian measures were forming, They prom-
ised perpetual peace.*

*They swore, if we gave them our weapons, that the wars of
the tribes would cease.*

*But when we disarmed They sold us and delivered us
bound to our foe,*

*And the Gods of the Copybook Headings said: "Stick to
the Devil you know."*

*On the first Feminian Sandstones we were promised the
Fuller Life*

*(Which started by loving our neighbour and ended by
loving his wife)*

*Till our women had no more children and the men lost
reason and faith,*

*And the Gods of the Copybook Headings said: "The Wages
of Sin is Death."*

*In the Carboniferous Epoch we were promised abundance
for all,*

By robbing selected Peter to pay for collective Paul;

*But, though we had plenty of money, there was nothing
our money could buy,*

*And the Gods of the Copybook Headings said: "If you
don't work you die."*

*Then the Gods of the Market tumbled, and their smooth-
tongued wizards withdrew,*

*And the hearts of the meanest were humbled and began to
believe it was true.*

*That All is not Gold that Glitters, and Two and Two
make Four—*

*And the Gods of the Copybook Headings limped up to
    explain it once more.*

*As it will be in the future, it was at the birth of Man—
There are only four things certain since Social Progress
    began:—
That the Dog returns to his Vomit and the Sow returns to
    her Mire,
And the burnt Fool's bandaged finger goes wabbling back
    to the Fire;
And that after this is accomplished, and the brave new
    world begins,
When all men are paid for existing and no man must pay
    for his sins,
As surely as Water will wet us, as surely as Fire will burn,
The Gods of the Copybook Headings with terror and
    slaughter return!*

Editor's Introduction To:

CUSTOM FITTING
James White

I first met James White at the World Science Fiction Convention held in Brighton. A group of us that included Larry Niven and Alfred Bester had drinks in the delightful club bar of the Old Ship, a hotel that predates the English Regency.

Jim White stands about six foot five. Within minutes of meeting me he had given me a badge that read "S.O.P. O.A.H.W.G.," and asked me to join. I had to confess that I had no clue as to what this meant.

"Society of Persons of Average Height with Glasses."

I stand about six two. I looked up at Jim's bifocal spectacles through mine. "Average height?"

"I am prepared to prove that eighty percent of the human race consists of dwarves."

Of course I'd known Jim White's work for years. His most famous series takes place on Sector General, a huge space colony hospital for humans and aliens alike. White also created strange and fascinating aliens in *All Judgment Fled*, a novel about some of the perils of an interstellar biological survey expedition.

Another member of our party at the Old Ship was Jack

Cohen, possibly the world's leading expert on reproductive biology. Jack often creates aliens, and since he doesn't write science fiction, gives them to the first writer who will listen. One of his chance remarks led to the novel, *The Legacy of Heorot*, by Larry Niven, Jerry Pournelle, and Steve Barnes.

Herewith a story by Jim White, a Person of Average Height with Glasses. It was originally written for Judy-Lynn del Rey, who was a giant.

CUSTOM FITTING
James White

For many years Hewlitt had been in the habit of spending half an hour sunning himself at the entrance to his shop when the sunlight was available in sufficient strength. The period was determined by the length of time it took for the sun to clear the eaves of the buildings on his side of the street and to move far enough out to necessitate his pulling out the shop's awning so that the cloth on display would not fade. He spent the time watching the passersby—hoping that some of them wouldn't—and anything else of interest. Usually there was nothing interesting to see, but today was an exception.

A large, plain furniture van, preceded by a police car and followed closely by an Electricity Department truck, turned into his street from the main road. The presence of the police vehicle was explained by the fact that the convoy was moving in the wrong direction along a one-way street. When the procession finally halted, the removals van was directly facing him.

For perhaps a minute there was nothing to see except the reflection of himself and his doorway in the dark, glossy flanks of the van. It was the slightly distorted picture of a thin and rather ridiculous figure wearing a black jacket and waistcoat with striped trousers, a small flower in the lapel, and a tape measure—the outward sign of his profession—hanging loosely from his neck. The lettering on the door behind the figure was executed in gold leaf in a bold italic script and said, in reverse:

GEORGE L. HEWLITT,
TAILOR

Suddenly—as if some hypothetical film director had shouted "Action!"—everything happened at once.

Two senior police officers carrying traffic-diversion signs left their vehicle and moved in opposite directions to seal off each end of the street. The Electricity Department truck disgorged a gang of neatly overalled workmen, who quickly began unloading collapsible screening, a night-watchman's hut, and a man wearing a well-tailored suit of dark gray worsted and a tie which was strictly establishment. He also wore a very worried expression as he glanced up and down the street and at the windows overlooking it.

"Good morning, Mr. Hewlitt," the man said, coming forward. "My name is Fox. I'm with the Foreign Office. I, ah, would like to consult you professionally. May I come inside?"

Hewlitt inclined his head politely and followed him into the shop.

For a few minutes nothing else was said because Fox was pacing nervously about the interior, staring at the shelves of neatly rolled cloth lengths, fingering the pattern books which were placed strategically on the polished wooden counters, and examining the paneling and crystal-clear mirrors in the big fitting room. While the Foreign Office official was looking over the premises, Hewlitt was studying Fox with equal attention.

Fox was of medium height, slimly built, with a head-forward tendency and prominent shoulder blades. From the small but noticeable lateral crease behind the jacket collar, it was obvious that he tried to correct the HF and PSB tendency by carrying himself unnaturally erect. Plainly

Fox's tailor had had problems, and Hewlitt wondered if he was about to inherit them.

"How may I help you, sir?" Hewlitt said when his visitor had finally come to rest. He used a tone which was friendly but one with that touch of condescension which very plainly said that it would be Hewlitt's decision whether or not he would build a jacket around Fox's prominent shoulder blades.

"I am not the client, Mr. Hewlitt," Fox said impatiently. "*He* is waiting outside. However, this matter must be treated in the strictest confidence—kept absolutely secret, in fact, for the next two weeks. After that you may discuss it with whom you please."

"From our thorough if necessarily hasty inquiries," the Foreign Office official went on, "we know that you live above these premises with your wife, who is also your seamstress and a partial cripple. We also know that your work is competent, if a little old-fashioned as regards styling, and that your stock is remarkably lacking in materials using man-made fibers. For many years your financial position has not been good, and I should say at this juncture that your silence as well as your workmanship will be very highly paid.

"The garment itself should present no difficulty," Fox ended, "since all that is required is a fairly well-fitting horse blanket."

Coldly, Hewlitt said, "I am completely lacking in experience where horse blankets are concerned, Mr. Fox."

"You are being proud and unnecessarily stubborn, Mr. Hewlitt. This is a very important client, and may I remind you that across the street there is a branch of a well-known multiple tailoring company which is also capable of doing the job."

"I agree," said Hewlitt dryly. "That company could do a pretty good job—on a horse blanket."

Fox smiled faintly, but before he could reply one of the workmen entered and said, "The screens are in position, sir, and the van is blocking the view from the other side of the street. Now we need the pole to pull out the sun awning. That will hide the shop front from upper-story windows on the other side of the street."

Hewlitt pointed toward the recess behind the display window where the awning pole was kept.

"Thank you, sir," said the workman in the tones of a senior public servant who is addressing a lowly member of the public he serves, then he turned away.

"Wait," said Fox, visibly coming to a decision. "When you've done that, ask His Excellency if he would be good enough to come in, please."

The strict secrecy being observed, the Foreign Office involvement, and the type of garment required had led Hewlitt to expect some highly controversial political figure: an overweight person from an underfed nation who was intent on expressing his individuality and independence by wearing an English-tailored native garment. Such a person might well be frightened of an assassin's bullet and feel it necessary to take these elaborate precautions; but that, after all, was not any of Hewlitt's business. But when he *saw* the client . . .

I'm dreaming, he told himself firmly.

The creature resembled a centaur, complete with hooves and a long, streaming tail. At first glance the torso from the waist up resembled that of a human being; but the musculature of the arms, shoulders, and chest was subtly different, and the hands were five-digited, each comprised of three fingers and two opposable thumbs. The head, carried erect above a very thick neck, was made to seem disproportionately small. The face was dominated by two large, soft, brown eyes that somehow made the slits, protuberances, and fleshy petals which comprised the other features visually acceptable.

Apart from a large medallion suspended around its neck, the being wore no clothing. Its skin was a mottled pinkish-brown color, and the creature twitched continually as if to dislodge invisible flies. It was obviously male.

"Your Excellency," said Fox smoothly, "may I present Mr. George Hewlitt. He is a tailor, or maker of clothing, who will produce for you garments suitable for your stay on Earth."

Instinctively Hewlitt put out his hand. He discovered that his client's grip was firm, the digits warm and bony, and the way the lower thumb curled upward into his palm was indescribable but not unpleasant. For some odd reason he could no longer think of the being as an "it."

"The initial requirement," Fox said briskly, "is for a garment which will be comfortable and will keep His Excellency warm during the presentation ceremonies and socializing that will follow. The garment should be black, edged with gold or silver braid, perhaps, and should carry pseudo-heraldic decorations. No existing family crests can be used, obviously. He will also require a second garment, less formal, for use during sightseeing tours out-of-doors."

"A braided and decorated horse blanket, then," said Hewlitt, "and a plain one for walking out. But if you could tell me the kind of function His Excellency is to attend, I would be in a better position to produce something suitable."

Fox shook his head. "Security."

"I can, if necessary, work blindfolded and with one arm tied behind my back," Hewlitt said, "but I do not produce my best work under those conditions. However, if His Excellency would kindly follow me into the fitting room?"

With a soft, irregular thumping of hooves the client, accompanied by Fox, followed into the fitting room and stood looking at himself in the angled mirrors. Rarely had Hewlitt seen a customer more ill at ease. The other's hide was twitching and tightening along his back and flanks before Hewlitt had even laid the tape on him.

Without being obtrusive about it, Hewlitt studied the twitching hide, looking for insects or other evidence of parasitic presences. Relieved at not finding any, he thought for a moment, then switched on the wall heaters, which were never used during the summer months. Within a few minutes the room was uncomfortably warm and the twitching had stopped.

While Hewlitt went to work with his tape measure and

pad, he asked, "I assume that my client's home planet is warmer than Earth?"

"Yes," said Fox. "Our weather at present would approximate to one of their sunny days in late autumn."

From small of back to root of tail, 63 inches, Hewlitt wrote carefully. He said, "In cool weather they wear clothing, then?"

"Yes, a form of toga wrapped around their bodies in a loose spiral, with— Oh, now I see why you switched on the heaters. I should have thought of that; it was very remiss of me. But His Excellency does not want to wear his native clothing for very good reasons, so he thought it better to suffer a little discomfort rather than to take the risk of your being influenced, even unconsciously, by his native dress. It is most important that he wear clothing which is made and styled on Earth."

From center line back to foreleg knee joint, 42 inches, Hewlitt wrote. To Fox he said, "The requirement is for a blanket-like garment, but surely my client will require additional clothing if he is to feel—"

"Just the blanket, Mr. Hewlitt."

"If the positions were reversed," said Hewlitt patiently, "you would no doubt feel much more *comfortable* if you were wearing shorts as well."

Irritably, Fox said, "Please follow instructions, Hewlitt. Your fee will be generous, regardless of how many or how few garments you make for His Excellency. Your attempts to drum up extra business is a waste of your time and ours."

"The majority of civilized people on Earth wear undergarments," said Hewlitt, "and unless climatic conditions, religious beliefs, or the dictates of local fashion rule otherwise, I should think that the same applies on other worlds."

"You are being argumentative, uncooperative, and you are introducing unnecessary complications into what is a very simple set of instructions," said Fox angrily. "Let me remind you that we can still go across the street!"

"Please do so," said Hewlitt.

Fox and Hewlitt glared at each other for several seconds

while the alien, his features unreadable by virtue of their complete alienness, turned his outsize brown eyes on each of them in turn.

Suddenly a soft, gobbling noise issued from one of the fleshy slits in his face and, simultaneously and much louder, a pleasant baritone voice spoke from the ornament suspended from the alien's neck. It said, "Perhaps I can resolve this difficulty, gentlemen. It seems to me that Mr. Hewlitt has displayed qualities of observation, good sense, and concern for the comfort of his customer, myself. Therefore, I would prefer him to continue to act as my tailor providing he is willing to do so."

Fox swallowed, then said weakly, "Security, Your Excellency. We agreed that you would not speak to any member of the public until . . . the day."

"My apologies, Mr. Fox," the alien replied through his translation device, "but on my world a specialist like Mr. Hewlitt is considered something more than a member of the public."

Turning to Hewlitt, he went on, "I would be most grateful if you could give the matter of my underwear your attention. However, for reasons which Mr. Fox would prefer to remain secret for the present, this garment must also be of Earth material and styling. Is this possible?"

Hewlitt bowed slightly and said, "Of course, sir."

"Not *sir!*" said Fox, obviously angered because his instructions had been ignored by the alien. "This is His Excellency the Lord Scrennagle of Dutha—"

Scrennagle held up one double-thumbed hand as he said politely, "Pardon the interruption. That is only an approximation of my rank and title. 'Sir' is sufficiently respectful and conversationally much less cumbersome."

"Yes, Your Excellency," said Fox.

Hewlitt produced a swatch of patterns and a style book from which Scrennagle chose a soft lambswool in pale cream which would not, the tailor assured them, react in any fashion with his skin. The style plates fascinated him, and when Hewlitt began to sketch similar designs modified to fit his centaur-like body, the alien was practically breathing down the tailor's neck.

Polite questioning had elicited the facts that Scrennagle insisted on dressing himself and that the area of skin covering the spine between waist and tail was the part of his body most susceptible to cold.

"If you wouldn't mind, sir," said Hewlitt at that point, "I would like you to advise me regarding the positioning of fastenings, openings for the elimination of body wastes, and so on . . ."

Scrennagle could twist the upper part of his body so that his hands could reach either flank as far back as the tail, although he could only see the lower end of his back. The undergarment which Hewlitt had to devise would have to be stepped into and pulled up on to the fore and hind legs in turn. It would be double-backed and buttoned through, with one wide flap of cloth going over the back to the opposite flank and fastening there, while the other flap passed over the back in the opposite direction to button on the other flank—rather like a double-breasted suit worn back-to-front. Scrennagle said that the double thickness of cloth at the back would be very comfortable, the local temperature being what it was; and he found no fault in the more complicated flap and fastening arrangements for the fly and rear.

He was politely insistent, however, that his tail should not be even partially concealed. There were strong psychological reasons for this, apparently.

"I quite understand, sir," said Hewlitt. "And now if you will stand quite still I shall measure you. The dimensions and contour descriptions required will be much more complex than those needed for the blankets. Once I have drafted a properly fitting pattern for the garment, however, making additional ones will present no problems. Initially a set of four undergarments should be sufficient to—"

"Hewlitt—!" Fox began.

"No gentleman," Hewlitt said very quietly, "no matter

how high or low his station, would undertake a major journey with just one set of underwear."

There was, of course, no reply to that; and Hewlitt resumed measuring his client. While he worked he told Scrennagle exactly what he was doing and why. He even went so far as to discuss the weather in his attempts to make his client relax bodily so that he would not shape the garment to a figure that was being held in an unnatural pose through tension.

"I intend making the leg sections reach less than half-way between the hip joints and knees, sir," he said at one point. "This will give the maximum comfort and warmth commensurate with the length of the over-garment. However, it would assist me greatly if I knew something more about the purpose of this blanket—what movements you would be making in it, whether or not you are expecting to be photographed, the geographical or architectural surroundings—so that the garment will not look out of place."

"You're fishing for information," said Fox sharply. "Please desist."

Hewlitt ignored him and said to Scrennagle, "You can rely on my discretion, sir."

"I know that," said Scrennagle. Turning so that he could see Fox in the fitting-room mirror, he went on: "A certain amount of curiosity is natural in these circumstances, and if Mr. Hewlitt has been entrusted with the secret of my presence in this city, surely the reason for my being here is a minor additional confidence which should not overstrain his capacity for—"

"With respect, Your Excellency," said Fox, "these matters must not be made public until all the necessary preparations have been made."

Hewlitt wrote *Girth at forelegs, 46 inches*. Controlling his exasperation, he said, "If the material, finish, and decoration of these garments are to fit the occasion—an important occasion no doubt—I really should be told something about it."

There was silence for a moment, then Scrennagle and

his translation device made noises which were possibly the equivalent of clearing an alien throat. His head went up and he stood very still as he said, "As the accredited representative of Dutha and of the Galactic Federation on Earth, I shall be presenting my credentials at the Court of St. James with the usual attendant ceremonies. In the evening of the same day there will be a reception at which the Sovereign will also be present. Although I am officially only an ambassador, the honors will be similar to those accorded a visiting head of state. The reception will be covered by the media, and interviews will be given following the official . . ."

Hewlitt was no longer listening to him. His sense of outrage was so great that no word could filter through to his mind with any meaning in it. Quietly he excused himself to Scrennagle; then to Fox he said, "Could I have a private word with you, outside?"

Without waiting for a reply he stalked out of the fitting room and across to the door, which he held open so that Fox could precede him into the hallway. Then he closed the door firmly, so firmly that the glass shattered and tinkled onto the porch tiling.

"And for this," he whispered fiercely, "you want me to make a—a *horse blanket?*"

Just as fiercely, Fox replied, "Believe it or not, I sympathize with your feelings. But this could be the most important event in human history and *it must go well!* Not just for Scrennagle's sake. What we do here will be the yardstick, the example, for embassies all over the world; and they must have no room for criticism. Some of them will feel that they should have had the first visit, and would welcome the chance to criticize. They must not be given that chance."

One of the Special Branch men in the too-clean overalls came onto the porch, attracted by the sound of breaking glass. Fox waved him away, then went on, "Of course he should wear more than a horse blanket. I know that as well as you do. But I didn't want you to know how important this is. Apart from the danger of a leak, a very small risk in your case, I didn't want you to worry about the job so much that you would go to pieces."

"At the same time," he went on harshly, "we cannot afford to have him appear ridiculous, to look like a cross between a dressed-up horse and a tail-coated chimpanzee from a circus. He is far too important an individual, and this is much too important an occasion for our planet and our race, for us to risk anything going wrong."

More quietly he went on, "Scrennagle wants to make a good first impression, naturally; but we as a species must also make a good impression on him. So it is probably safer in many respects to let him wear a blanket, even though it lacks both imagination and dignity. But, Hewlitt, if you *want* to tailor something more elaborate for the first ambassador from the stars, it must be exactly right for the occasion. Do you want to take on such a heavy responsibility?"

Hewlitt's vocal equipment seemed to be completely paralyzed by a combination of extreme anxiety and sheer joy at what was the ultimate challenge not only to an individual, but to a member of one of the oldest crafts known to mankind. He nodded.

Fox's relief was obvious. He said, very seriously, "You are assuming a large part of the responsibility which is properly mine. I'm grateful, and if you have any suggestions which might help . . ."

"Even if they are none of my business?" Hewlitt asked; then he added, "My *tailoring* business, that is."

"Go on," Fox said warily.

"We were discussing dressed-up horses just now," Hewlitt went on. "My client resembles a horse much more than he does a human being. He is too much of a diplomat to complain; but put yourself in his place for a moment and think of the effect on you of the pomp and pageantry, the transport arrangements and—"

"Scrennagle has already studied and adapted himself to the more personal aspects of our civilization," said Fox. "At meals he lies with legs folded underneath his body, allowing his erect torso to rise to a comfortable height for eating and conversation. Since he has no lap, the napkin remains folded by his plate. Where toilet facilities are concerned—"

"I was thinking," said Hewlitt, "of how he might feel about horses pulling him or their being ridden by human beings. I would suggest that a state limousine rather than a coach be used, and that the escort and guards be chosen from regiments other than the Household Cavalry or Horse Guards. There are several physiological similarities between Scrennagle and terrestrial horses. Not as many as those between an ape and a human being; but it might be better not to have too many animals around which closely resemble the visiting ambassador, wouldn't you say?"

"I *would* say," Fox said, and swore quietly. "Somebody should have thought of that."

"Somebody just did," Hewlitt said, opening the door and motioning Fox to precede him over the broken glass and back to the fitting room, where the most important client an Earth tailor had ever had was waiting and gently stamping all four of his feet.

"My apologies for the delay, sir," said Hewlitt politely, "but I now have a clearer idea of what is expected of me and of *you*, sir. Before I resume measuring, do you have any allergies toward certain materials, or any particularly sensitive areas, which might cause you discomfort?"

Scrennagle looked at Fox, who said, "We have investigated this matter in great detail; and there is a long list of items which could cause trouble—some of them serious trouble—if they were allowed to remain in contact with His Excellency's skin for long periods.

"The situation is this," he continued. "Extraterrestrial pathogens cannot live in human bodies, and vice versa. This means that we cannot possibly contract a disease from Scrennagle and he is likewise impervious to our germs. However, purely chemical reactions are a different matter. One of the things likely to cause His Excellency to break out in a rash or worse is the synthetic fibers used in clothing, virtually all kinds of synthetics. You see the problem?"

Hewlitt nodded. The ambassador's underwear, shirts, ties, and socks would have to be made from pure wool, cotton, or real silk; the suiting materials would have to be woolen worsted and, for the casuals, Harris or Irish Thornproof tweed. Bone buttons would be required and zip fasteners made from metal rather than nylon. Trimmings, the canvas stiffening, the wadding for shaping and softening the outlines would also have to be non-synthetic; and the thread used to hold everything together would have to be the old-style sewing cotton rather than nylon thread. He could see the problem, all right, and like most big problems this one was composed of a lot of little ones.

"One of the reasons why you were chosen for this job," said Fox, "was that you were old-fashioned enough in your ideas to keep such things in stock. But frankly, I was worried in case you would be too old-fashioned to react properly toward an . . . unusual . . . client. As it happened, you showed no sign of xenophobia whatsoever."

"I used to read a lot of science fiction, before it became too soft-centered," Hewlitt said dryly. Then he turned to Scrennagle. "I shall require additional measurements, sir, since I shall be building something a little more ambitious than a blanket. And it will be necessary to draft patterns for the garments as I go along. Making up, fitting, and finishing will take time if the work is to be done properly. I shall therefore board up the broken pane and attach a notice saying that I am closed for alterations . . ." He looked along Scrennagle's extraterrestrial body contours and thought, *There will probably be a lot of alterations.* "And I shall, of course, work on this order exclusively. But I cannot see it being complete in less than ten days."

"You have twelve days," said Fox, looking relieved. "I shall have the broken pane replaced as soon as possible. During our investigation your shop front was photographed, so we shall be able to reproduce the gold lettering. After all, the breakage was indirectly my fault."

"I venture to disagree," Scrennagle broke in. "As the prime cause of the trouble, I would be obliged, Mr. Hewlitt, if you would allow me to replace the glass from material in my ship as a memento of my visit. The material is transparent and proof against both meteorite collisions and minor emotional disturbances."

"You are very kind, sir," said Hewlitt, laughing. "I accept." He wrote on the measurement pad, *From center back to wrist, 35 inches*.

It took nearly three hours to complete the job to his satisfaction, including a half-hour's discussion regarding the musculature and jointing of the limbs and torso and the provision needed to give comfort as well as style to the garments, particularly in the areas of the neck, chest, armpits, and crotch.

When Scrennagle and Fox left, Hewlitt locked the door and climbed the stairs past his first-floor stockrooms to the flat above to break the news to his wife.

Mrs. Hewlitt had been a virtual cripple since a street accident eighteen years earlier. She could walk about the flat for three hours a day without too much discomfort, and these hours she saved for the evening meal and for talking to her husband afterwards. The rest of the time she spent rolling about the flat in her wheelchair, tidying, cooking, sewing if there was work for her to do, or sleeping, which she did not do very well even at night.

He told her about his extraterrestrial client, and of the necessity for keeping the matter a close secret for the time being. She studied his sketches and measurements with interest, working out the yardages of material and trimmings needed for the job. Hewlitt should be ashamed of himself, she said, for trying to make her believe such a tall story. She reminded him that in her youth she once had to make a costume for a stage horse. The reason for the number of costumes required, particularly the sets of underwear, was unclear, she said; but no doubt they were being used in a sophisticated pantomime or farce in which the stage horse was expected to partially disrobe. The detail required in the fly fastenings, she added disapprovingly, probably meant that it was a very sophisticated and *naughty* show.

"Not at all, dear," said Hewlitt with a perfectly straight

face. "It will be more in the nature of a spectacular, and you'll be able to see the highlights, and our costumes, on TV."

Hewlitt, who had always held moral cowardice to be the better part of valor, noted her pleased and excited expression and said nothing more.

During the three days and for most of the intervening nights before Scrennagle was due for his first fitting, the pleasure and the sense of excitement remained with Mrs. Hewlitt, even though on one occasion she said that there had been a time when they would have refused such a gimmicky commission. Hewlitt replied by saying that the work required the highest standards of tailoring and finish, regardless of its ultimate destination, and that the work was the most professionally challenging as well as the most remunerative he had ever been given. But secretly he was becoming prey to self-doubts.

His problem was to design, cut, and build a suit which would not make a horse look like a man but like a very well-dressed and dignified horse. The whole idea was ridiculous, yet Scrennagle was much too important a personage to be left open to the slightest suggestion of ridicule.

As Hewlitt had expected, the first fitting was visually a disaster. The fore and hind trouser legs were unpressed, shapeless, and held together temporarily with tacking stitches, while the embryo morning coat looked even worse with just one sleeve attached and tacking cotton holding together the lapel canvas, fronts, and shoulder wadding. While he plied his needle, chalk, and pins, Hewlitt transmitted confidence and reassurance for all he was worth; but it was obvious that neither Scrennagle nor Fox was receiving.

The Foreign Office official looked desperately worried and unhappy, and the pattern of wrinkling and puckering on the ambassador's features was almost certainly the extraterrestrial equivalent of these emotions.

Hewlitt kept his own doubts to himself and did his best to retrieve something from the situation by producing the first two sets of underwear, both of which fitted perfectly.

He explained that these were relatively simple garments made from material which stretched and clung. He ignored the hints dropped by both Scrennagle and Fox that it might, after all, be better to settle for the horse blanket over underwear idea, and he requested a second fitting in four days' time.

Scrennagle's jacket was a large and structurally complex garment which covered not only the forward torso but the body back to the hind quarters. It was cut away sharply at the front, after which the skirt maintained a level line two inches below the point where the legs joined the body. But the jacket, because of the length and area of material used, made the trouser-clad legs look disproportionately thin.

Hewlitt apparently had been able to reduce the area of the jacket by introducing a set of false pleats running along the spine and dividing at the tail opening; and he had used a series of strategically placed darts to shape the garment at awkward body contours. But he had had to scrap and recut the original trousers, making them nearly twice as wide but with a neat taper to approximately double the hoof diameter at the bottoms. This meant redesigning the method of suspension across the back and modifying the crotch, but the over-all effect looked much better balanced.

During the second fitting Hewlitt was pleased to find that he had been able to cure a troublesome tendency to crease where the foreleg muscles periodically distorted the waistcoat while Scrennagle was walking. But the garments, to Scrennagle's and Fox's untutored eyes, still looked like the proverbial pound of tripe. It was obvious that they were both coming to a decision—almost certainly the wrong one—and Hewlitt tried desperately to head them off.

"We are extremely lucky," he said, smiling, "in that a size 16 neckband shirt is a perfect fit on you, sir, as is a size 8 hat. The hat will be carried rather than worn for the most part, likewise the gloves, which don't quite fit—"

"Don't you think," said Fox suddenly, "that you may be trying for the impossible, Mr. Hewlitt?"

More quietly, Scrennagle joined in. "This is by no means

a criticism of your professional ability, and you may well produce the garments required; but wouldn't you agree that something in the nature of the blanket already discussed would serve as a useful standby? It would also relieve you of a heavy responsibility."

"I did not ask to be relieved of the responsibility," said Hewlitt. The responsibility was beginning to scare him sick. He really should take this easy way out—but he had too much confidence, or perhaps over-confidence, in his ability. He went on, "I have undertaken to clothe you suitably for the forthcoming social and formal occasions, sir, and you can trust me to fullfil my obligations.

"However," Hewlitt continued quickly, "I have a minor problem regarding foot coverings. The black woolen socks can be adapted and cut to fit, but Earth-type shoes would look out of place and would be difficult for you to wear with confidence. Would it be possible to use a non-toxic paint to color the osseous material of your hooves—glossy black for the formal occasion and brown for the walkabouts? They should also be padded, since hoof sounds might also be considered out of place." *It would make you sound too much like a horse*, Hewlitt said silently. Aloud: "And there is the matter of displaying the tail, sir. It is a long, luxuriant, and remarkably handsome tail—"

"Thank you," said Scrennagle.

"—but it is constantly in motion and likely to be a distraction to people holding a conversation with you. Mr. Fox tells me that these movements are involuntary. However, as I see it, your tail is analogous to the cranial and/or facial hair in an Earth-person. Those who have such hair frequently display it to the best advantage on formal occasions. It can be pleated, braided, decorated in various fashions, and combed or oiled to give it a richer texture. If you have no objections, sir, we might plait your tail, adding, say, a few lengths of white or silver cord, then coil it neatly and secure it with a retaining strap which I can add to the center seam?"

"I have no objections, Mr. Hewlitt," said Scrennagle. "We do something similar on Dutha."

"These are details, Hewlitt," said Fox. "Important details, I admit, which will apply to whatever type of garment is worn. But—"

"There is also the matter of decorations, sir," Hewlitt continued. "These are colored ribbons and pieces of engraved metal which indicate that the person wearing them has achieved some great feat, or that an ancestor has done so. The evening reception will include many people wearing dress uniforms and full evening wear to which are added the kind of decorations I have been describing. I would like you to wear some kind of decoration or award," he went on seriously, "but preferably one that has not simply been invented for the occasion. Can you suggest something which might be suitable, sir?"

Scrennagle was silent for a moment, then he said, "My race has no equivalent for these awards, except possibly the translator which is necessary to the performance of my work. There is a somewhat larger version, decorated with the Federation symbol, which is worn when more than one translation has to be handled at the same time. But these, also, are merely the tools of our profession."

"But it is not a common profession, surely?"

"It is not," said Scrennagle. The expression which twisted the alien features might have been one of pride.

"Would you have any objections to displaying this device on a colored ribbon?"

"No objections."

"Thank you, sir," Hewlitt said. He went on briskly, "The morning wear will be ready for collection before breakfast time on the day required, and the evening wear in the afternoon of the same day. Your walking-out suits and accessories, which will not be required until your list of formal visits is complete, will be much easier to make as a result of experience gained with the first garments—"

"Which will be," said Fox very firmly, "a well-cut and tastefully decorated blanket."

Hewlitt pretended to ignore him as he said, "You may trust me, sir."

"I am trusting you, Mr. Hewlitt, more than any other person on this planet . . ."

Long after they had gone, Hewlitt thought about Scrennagle's parting remark. While his wife and he worked on the recutting and finishing of the first outfit, he worried. Was he being a stupid, self-opinionated, sartorial snob or did he really have the right to dictate to Scrennagle as he had been doing?

The ambassador was an extremely important being who was, in the way of all representatives of other governments, anxious to make a good impression. But he would also be receiving impressions, favorable or otherwise, from the people he was meeting. Being realistic about it, the latter impressions were the more important as far as the human race was concerned. In all probability Scrennagle was important enough to make the decision whether his world and the rest of the Federation maintained contact with Earth or left it strictly alone.

And this was the being that he, a conceited and impoverished little tailor, was going to dress for the most important occasion in human history. He was, of course, going to dress him to the best of his ability; but the media were fond of poking fun at VIP's. Given half a chance, they would tear Scrennagle apart; and the ambassador would go away and neither he nor his friends would ever return to the place where the people lacked manners and where the Federation representative had been made to look a fool.

Many times while he was reopening a seam to remove an unsightly fullness or while giving the pockets the swelled edges that were his own particular signature on a suit, he thought about putting aside the work for the few hours necessary for him to make a blanket. He thought about it long and seriously, but he kept working on the job in hand while he was making up his mind. When he and his wife went to bed in the early hours of the following morning, and arose to resume work a short time later, he still had not made up his mind.

Producing a glorified horse blanket would be insurance against the dress wear turning out to be a sartorial disaster. But if he made the blanket he would simply be obeying orders and shifting the responsibility back to Fox. He would also be allowing a man who knew less than he did to tell him what to do.

Then suddenly the morning coat and trousers were finished, pressed, and hanging with their accessories on the form which Hewlitt had adapted from the limbs and torsos of one and a half window-display models; and there was no longer enough time to make a blanket because it was the morning of *The* Day and Scrennagle was due at any moment.

The ambassador said little while Hewlitt was showing him how to fasten the shirt, knot the tie, and fit, among other items, the footless dark socks over his black-painted hooves. While fitting the trousers, waistcoat, and jacket the tailor talked about the desirability of moving slowly— sudden movements lacked dignity and looked bad on TV. He was aware that he was talking too much and that he was making himself sound ridiculous by punctuating every few words with a yawn.

Perhaps Scrennagle would not realize how nervous and unsure of himself Hewlitt felt because the over-all ensemble did not look exactly as he had envisaged it—and in his present physical and mental state of fatigue he did not know what it looked like.

During the proceedings Fox maintained the tightest-lipped silence he had ever experienced; but he tossed Hewlitt a copy of the morning paper and nodded worriedly as they left.

The news about Scrennagle was published as a Court Circular:

> His Excellency the Lord Scrennagle of Dutha will be received in audience by the Queen this morning, and will present his Letters of Credence as Ambassador Extraordinary and Plenipotentiary from the Galactic Federation to the Court of St. James. A State Reception will be held in his honor at the Palace, during which sound and vision broadcast facilities will be available.

Hewlitt moved the TV into his workroom so that he could watch without disturbing his wife, who was still asleep, while he worked on the evening suit.

But the TV coverage was unsatisfactory. Apparently the Court Circular had been treated by the press as some kind of hoax. A tourist had been able to film Scrennagle's arrival at St. James', and he would probably receive a fortune for a few feet of badly focused film which did not give any indication of how well or otherwise the ambassador's suit fitted him.

Hewlitt waited for a couple of hours, then switched on his transistor radio to hear an excited voice saying that news had just been received from the Palace to the effect that Dutha was an inhabited planet circling a sun some two thousand light-years from Earth and that the Duthan, Scrennagle, was being accorded the honors of a visiting head of state as well as those of an ambassador. Whether the whole thing was a hoax or not, the voice went on, tonight's reception would be covered to the same extent as the early moon landings.

His wife heard the same news item. She looked dreadfully tired but happier than he had seen her for a great many years. But she was not talking to him for the time being because he had told her the truth and had deliberately made it sound like a lie.

Hewlitt's mind and fingers were so stiff and tired that he was almost an hour late in completing the suit. But that did not matter: Scrennagle did not call for it. Just two hours before the reception was due to begin, a uniformed inspector arrived to say that there had been unforeseen delays and that he would collect the outfit and take it to Scrennagle's ship. A few minutes later, a more senior police officer arrived to say that since there was no longer any need for secrecy they were removing the screens from his shop front and that a couple of glaziers had also arrived to replace his door window.

"Can't it wait until morning?" Hewlitt asked, clenching his teeth to fight back a yawn.

"You look very tired, sir," the policeman said. "I would

be happy to stay here until they've finished, and lock the door as I leave. I'll put your key in the letterbox."

"That is very considerate of you," said Hewlitt warmly. "I do need rest. Thank you."

"My pleasure, sir," said the officer, so respectfully that he seemed to be ready to salute.

The warm feeling left by the unusually friendly policeman faded as Hewlitt mounted the stairs. He thought about the probable reasons why Scrennagle sent for his suit rather than collect it himself. The outfit he had worn this morning had probably been a mess, and this evening he would be wearing a horse blanket tailored on short notice by someone else. Being a diplomat and a considerate being as well, Scrennagle would not want to complain in person to Hewlitt, or to pass on the criticisms which had doubtless been made about his appearance. He would simply take delivery of the second outfit and say nothing.

But Hewlitt's misery was short-lived. As he slumped into his chair before the TV screen, a panel of experts were discussing the implications of contact with an extrasolar race, and pundits always put him to sleep.

The first few bars of the fanfare which opened the late-night newscast, especially extended to cover the visit of the extraterrestrial, jerked Hewlitt awake. Quickly he wheeled his wife in from the kitchen, then settled back to see how Scrennagle had comported himself.

Unlike the amateur film taken at St. James', Scrennagle's arrival for the reception was covered in close-up, middle distance, and from every angle.

The ambassador was *not* wearing a horse blanket.

His jacket was a good fit at the collar and shoulders, but showed a tendency to wrinkle across the back when Scrennagle straightened after making a bow—something he had to do every few minutes. The trousers hung well, making the legs look neither too blocky nor too thin, and the black socks and dully polished hooves were elegantly inconspicuous. The tail was coiled and tied forward like that of some heraldic beast, and its occasional twitchings were barely noticeable.

The only touch of color was the wide silk ribbon that diagonally bisected the white shirt front and waistcoat. It was pale blue with a thin edging of red and gold on which was centered the intricately decorated translation device which bore the symbol of the Federation. Although not the most impressive decoration there, it still managed to hold its own among all the Baths and Garters.

Scrennagle of Dutha, Hewlitt realized suddenly, looked *well* . . .

Then the Duthan was making his speech, outlining briefly the purpose of his visit and touching on some of the advantages which membership in the Galactic Federation would confer in both directions.

It had been just over one hundred and fifty years earlier that one of the Federation's unmanned searchships found intelligent life and a rapidly developing technology on Earth. The long delay in responding to the situation, Scrennagle explained, was due to the fact that the searchships—which rarely found anything—were not fitted with power-hungry, ultimate drive because machinery, unlike Duthans, Earth-humans, and members of other intelligent species, did not age or become bored. The searchship had spent many years in orbit photographing, analyzing, evaluating specimens of flora and fauna, the written and spoken languages—the last being particularly difficult for its soft-landed probes to obtain because radio and television had not then been invented.

When the data had been returned to Dutha for study, several difficult decisions had had to be taken. There was, of course, no question that contact should not be attempted with the rich and varied cultures on Earth. But at the time the material had been gathered, many sociopolitical groupings were showing signs of imminent collapse while others were rapidly growing in power and influence.

At that time the British Empire, with its center of power and commerce in London, was the most important and influential grouping, but it, too, was showing signs of collapse. It had grown slowly, however, and its traditions and laws were deeply rooted. The indications were that it would collapse not catastrophically, but wane slowly and disintegrate in a stable fashion. It was also thought that the manners and practices observed a century and a half earlier would not significantly alter in such a long-lived grouping . . .

"That is why I landed quietly in this country rather than in one of the others," Scrennagle continued. "I now know that the decision was the correct one. But we, too, have certain rules of behavior in these circumstances. You might think that for a highly advanced Galactic culture we are surprisingly old-fashioned. But an acceptable code of behavior plays a vital part in dealings between species so widely varied as the members of our Federation.

"One of our strictest rules," he added, wrinkling his facial openings in what was undoubtedly a smile, "is that visitors such as myself conform to all of the social practices and customs of the host planet, even to the extent of wearing its clothing . . ."

He concluded by saying that his intention was to make a round of official visits to heads of state on Earth. Then, later, he would return to take a leisurely sightseeing tour of the planet which would enable him to meet people in more relaxed conditions. He added that Earth had been the first new world to be offered membership in something over four centuries, and he would be happy to answer questions on every subject under this or any other sun.

The next item was the TV interview, during which, at long last, the subject of Scrennagle's clothing came up.

". . . we will need much more time to consider the wider aspects of your visit," the interviewer was saying, "but right now, Your Excellency, I would like to ask a question, and also compliment you, on your clothing. Or perhaps I should compliment your extraterrestrial tailor?"

"You should compliment my terrestrial tailor," Scrennagle said, then went on: "On many worlds clothing is simply a means of giving protection from extremes of weather, while on others the fabrication, styling, and wearing of clothing has been raised to the level of a major art form. Earth is in the latter category and possesses at least one tailor who is capable of making an extraterrestrial . . . presentable."

The interviewer laughed and asked, "Who is he, Your Excellency?"

"I would rather not say at present," Scrennagle replied. "He and his wife have worked long and hard, and they deserve at least one night's sleep before fame descends on them. Suffice it to say that my tailor is relatively unknown but a craftsman of the highest order. He is also something of a tyrant in sartorial matters, a characteristic common to tailors throughout the Galaxy. He is not afraid to accept a professional challenge, as you can see."

"Yes, indeed," said the interviewer.

"No doubt there will be other challenges," Scrennagle went on, turning his face directly into the camera, but Hewlitt knew that he was not speaking solely to the interviewer. "My race was chosen to make first contact with Earth-humans simply because my people most closely resembled yours—despite what you must think are major physiological differences. Other races in the Federation have much more varied and interestingly arranged limbs and appendages; and to the uninitiated they may even appear to be quite horrendous. But ambassadors from all these species in time will visit Earth to present their credentials and their good wishes. And they will all require to be suitably attired for the occasion. They will be very pleased and reassured to know," he ended, "that there is an Earth-human tailor in whom they can place their complete trust . . ."

The intense feelings of pride and excitement which should have kept him awake that night, but did not, were with him in undiminished intensity when he opened the shop next morning. His reflection in the store window opposite looked the same as always, but something different about the reflected picture made him turn around quickly.

The new door pane was not quite the same as the old one. It now read GEORGE L. HEWLITT, TAILOR, centered above a beautifully executed copy of the design which appeared on Scrennagle's translator—the symbol which represented all the worlds of the Galactic Federation—followed by the words BY APPOINTMENT.

Editor's Introduction To:

CONQUEST BY DEFAULT
Vernor Vinge

Basing government on reason alone is giving it a shaky foundation. They say that virtue is the love of order. But should and can this love dominate over the love of my own well-being? Let them give me a clear and sufficient reason to prefer it. At bottom their supposed principle is a pure play of words; because I can in turn state that vice is the love of order taken in a different sense. The difference is that the good man refers himself to the order of the whole and the bad man sees the whole in relation to himself: he makes himself the center of all things, while the good man sees himself at the circumference and looks to the center of the whole.

—Jean Jacques Rousseau, *Emile*

At this point in his personal copy of *Emile*, Voltaire wrote, "These horrors should never be discovered to the public."

The notion of government is embedded in human history. Although we have many theories of anarchy, there

have in practical terms been no lasting anarchic systems at
all.

Government is supposed to promote "the general good."
Even the anarchists suppose that the enforcement of contracts is good for everyone (although by definition a contract that needs enforcement is not good for the party who
wishes to terminate the contract.)

Some libertarians postulate a social order in which contracts are enforced through a "private" mechanism that has
no powers other than the enforcement of contracts. No
one has ever seen such an institution in operation; we do
not know what will keep the enforcers from expanding
their powers. We do know that power seeks to extend
itself.

Suppose that it does not: suppose a society in which
there is no law but contract law; a society in which anything goes; a society so free, and thus so diverse, that no
notion of "general good" is possible. Can such a society
hang together? Who would want it to?

CONQUEST BY DEFAULT
Vernor Vinge

This all happened a long time ago, and almost twenty
light-years from where we're standing now. You honor me
here tonight as a humanitarian, as a man who has done
something to bring a temporary light to the eternal darkness that is our universe. But you deceive yourselves. I
made the situation just civilized enough so that its true
brutality, shed of bloody drapery, can be seen.

I see you don't believe what I say. In this whole audience I suspect that only a Melmwn truly understands—
and she better than I. Not one of you has ever been kicked
in the teeth by these particular facts of life. Perhaps if I
told you the story as it happened to me—I could make you
feel the horror you hear me describe.

Two centuries ago, the Pwrlyg Spice & Trading Company completed the first interstellar flight. They were thirty years ahead of their nearest competitors. They had a whole planet at their disposal, except for one minor complication . . .

The natives were restless.

My attention was unevenly divided between the beautiful girl who had just introduced herself, and the ancient city that shimmered in the hot air behind her.

Mary Dahlmann. That was a hard name to pronounce, but I had studied Australian for almost two years, and I was damned if I couldn't say a name. I clumsily worked my way through a response. "Yes, ah, Miss, ah, Dahlmann, I am Ron Melmwn, and I am the new Company anthropologist. But I thought the Vice President for Aboriginal Affairs was going to meet me."

Ngagn Chev dug me in the ribs, "Say, you really can speak that gabble, can't you, Melmwn?" he whispered in Mikin. Chev was vice president for violence—an O.K. guy, but an incurable bigot.

Mary Dahlmann smiled uncertainly at this exchange. Then she answered my question. "Mr. Horlig will be right along. He asked me to meet you. My father is Chief Representative for Her Majesty's Government." I later learned that Her Majesty was two centuries dead. "Here, let me show you off the field." She grasped my wrist for a second—an instant. I guess I jerked back. Her hand fell away and her eagerness vanished. "This way," she said icily, pointing to a gate in the force fence surrounding the Pwrlyg landing field. I wished very much I had not pulled away from her touch. Even though she was so blond and pale, she was a woman, and in a weird way, pretty. Besides, *she* had overcome whatever feelings she had against *us*.

There was an embarrassed silence, as the five of us cleared the landing craft and walked toward the gate.

The sun was bright—brighter than ours ever shines over Miki. It was also very dry. There were no clouds in the

sky. Twenty or thirty people worked in the field. Most
were Mikin, but here and there were clusters of Terrans.
Several were standing around a device in the corner of the
field where the fence made a joint to angle out toward the
beach. The Terrans knelt by the device.

Orange fire flickered from the end of the machine,
followed by a loud *guda-bam-bam-bam*. Even as my conscious mind concluded that we were under fire, I threw
myself on the ground and flattened into the lowest profile
possible. You've heard the bromide about combat making
life more real. I don't know about that, but it's certainly
true that when you are flat against the ground with your
face in the dirt, the whole universe looks different. That
red-tan sand was *hot*. Sharp little stones bit into my face.
Two inches before my face a clump of sage had assumed
the dimensions of a vola tree.

I cocked my head microscopically to see how the others
were doing. They were all down, too. Correction: that
idiot Earthgirl was still standing. More than a second after
the attack she was still working toward the idea that someone was trying to kill her. Only a dement or a little Sister
brought up in a convent could be so dense. I reached out,
grabbed her slim ankle, and jerked. She came down hard.
Once down, she didn't move.

Ngagn Chev and some accountant, whose name I didn't
remember, were advancing toward the slug-thrower. That
accountant had the fastest low-crawl I have ever seen. The
Terrans frantically tried to lower the barrels of their gun—
but it was really primitive and couldn't search more than
five degrees. The little accountant zipped up to within
twenty meters of the gun, reached into his weapons pouch,
and tossed a grenade toward the Earthmen and their
weapon. I dug my face into the dirt and waited for the
explosion. There was only a muffled thud. It was a gas
bomb—not frag. A green mist hung for an instant over the
gun and the Terrans.

When I got to them, Chev was already complimenting
the accountant on his throw.

"A private quarrel?" I asked Chev.

The security chief looked faintly surprised. "Why no. These fellows"—he pointed at the unconscious Terrans— "belong to some conspiracy to drive us off the planet. They're really a pitiful collection." He pointed to the weapon. It was composed of twenty barrels welded to three metal hoops. By turning a crank, the barrels could be rotated past a belt cartridge feeder. "That gun is hardly more accurate than a shrapnel bomb. This is nothing very dangerous, but I'm going to catch chaos for letting them get within the perimeter. And I can tell you, I am going to scorch those agents of mine that let these abos sneak in. Anyway, we got the pests alive. They'll be able to answer some questions." He nudged one of the bodies over with his boot. "Sometimes I think it would be best to exterminate the race. They don't occupy much territory but they sure are a nuisance.

"See," he picked up a card from the ground and handed it to me. It was lettered in neat Mikin: MERLYN SENDS YOU DEATH. "Merlyn is the name of the 'terrorist' organization—it's nonprofit, I think. Terrans are a queer lot."

Several Company armsmen showed up then and Chev proceeded to bawl them out in a very thorough way. It was interesting, but a little embarrassing, too. I turned and started toward the main gate. I still had to meet my new boss—Horlig, the Vice President for Abo Affairs.

Where was the Terran girl? In the fuss I had completely forgotten her. But now she was gone. I ran back to where we stood when the first shots were fired. I felt cold and a little sick as I looked at the ground where she had fallen. Maybe it had been a superficial wound. Maybe the medics had carried her off. But whatever the explanation, a pool of blood almost thirty centimeters wide lay on the sand. As I watched, it soaked into the sand and became a dark brown grease spot, barely visible against the reddish-tan soil. As far as appearances go, it could have been human blood.

Horlig was a Gloyn. I should have known from his name. As it was, I got quite a surprise when I met him.

With his pale gray skin and hair, Herul Horlig could easily be mistaken an Earthman. The vice president for aboriginal affairs was either an Ostentatious Simplist or very proud of his neolithic grandparents. He wore wooden shin plates and a black breech-clout. His only weapon was a machine dartgun strapped to his wrist.

It quickly became clear that the man was unhappy with me as an addition to his staff. I could understand that. As a professional, my opinions might carry more weight with the board of directors and the president than his. Horlig did his best to hide his displeasure, though. He seemed a hard-headed, sincere fellow who could be ruthless, but nevertheless believed whatever he did was right. He unbent considerably during our meal at Supply Central. When I mentioned I wanted to interview some abos, he surprised me by suggesting we fly over to the native city that evening.

When we left Central, it was already dark. We walked to the parking lot, and got into Horlig's car. Three minutes later we were ghosting over the suburbs of Adelaide-west. Horlig cast a practiced eye upon the queer rectangular street pattern below, and brought us down on the lawn of a two-story wood house. I started to get out.

"Just a minute, Melmwn," said Horlig. He grabbed a pair of earphones and set the TV on pan. I didn't say anything as he scanned the quiet neighborhood for signs of hostile activity. I was interested: usually a Simplist will avoid using advanced defense techniques. Horlig explained as he set the car's computer on SENTRY and threw open the hatch:

"Our illustrious board of directors dictates that we employ 'all security precautions at our disposal.' Bunk. Even when these Earth creatures attack us, they are less violent than good-natured street brawlers back home. I don't think there have been more than thirty murders in this city since Pwrlyg landed twenty years ago."

I jumped to the soft grass and looked around. Things really were quiet. Gas lamps lit the cobblestone street and dimly outlined the wood buildings up and down the lane.

Weak yellow light emerged from windows. From down the street came faint laughter of some party. Our landing had gone unnoticed.

Demoneyes. I stepped back sharply. The twin yellow disks glittered maniacally, as the cat turned to face us, and the lamps' light came back from its eyes. The little animal turned slowly and walked disdainfully across the lawn. This was a bad omen indeed. I would have to watch the Signs very carefully tonight. Horlig was not disturbed at all. I don't think he knew I was brought up a witch-fearer. We started up the walk toward the nearest house.

"You know, Melmwn, this isn't just any old native we're visiting. He's an anthropologist, Earth style. Of course, he's just as insipid as the rest of the bunch, but our staff is forced to do quite a bit of liaison work with him."

An anthropologist! This was going to be interesting, both as an exchange of information and of research procedures.

"In addition, he's the primary representative chosen by the Australian *gowernmen'* . . . a *gowernmen'* is sort of a huge corporation, as far as I can tell."

"Uh-huh." As a matter of fact, I knew a lot more about the mysterious *government* concept than Horlig. My Scholarate thesis was a theoretical study of macro organizations. The paper was almost rejected because my instructors claimed it was an analysis of a patent impossibility. Then came word that three macro organizations existed on Earth.

We climbed the front porch steps. Horlig pounded on the door. "The fellow's name is Nalman."

I translated his poor pronunciation back to the probable Australian original: Dahlmann! Perhaps I could find out what happened to the Earthgirl.

There were shuffling steps from within. Whoever it was did not even bother to look us over through a spy hole. Earthmen were nothing if not trusting. We were confronted by a tall, middle-aged man with thin, silvery hair. His hand quavered slightly as he removed the pipe from his mouth. Either he was in an extremity of fear or he had terrible coordination.

But when he spoke, I knew there was no fear. "Mr. Horlig. Won't you come in?" The words and tone were mild, but in that mildness rested an immense confidence. In the past I had heard that tone only from Umpires. It implied that neither storm, nor struggle, nor crumbling physical prowess could upset the mind behind the voice. That's a lot to get out of six quiet words—but it was all there.

When we were settled in Scholar Dahlmann's den, Horlig made the introductions. Horlig understood Australian fairly well, but his accent was atrocious.

"As you must surely know, Scholar Dahlmann, the objective voyage time to our home planet, Epsilon Eridani II, is almost twelve years. Three days ago the third Pwrlyg Support Fleet arrived and assumed a parking orbit around the Earth. At this instant, they soar omnipotent over the lands of your people." Dahlmann just smiled. "In any case, the first passengers have been unfrozen and brought down to the Pwrlyg Ground Base. This is Scholar Ron Melmwn, the anthropologist that the Company has brought in with the Fleet."

From behind his thick glasses, Dahlmann inspected me with new interest. "Well, I certainly am happy to meet a Mikin anthropologist. Our meeting is something of a first, I believe."

"I think so, too. Your institutions are ill-reported to us on Miki. This is natural, since Pwrlyg is primarily interested in the commercial and immigration prospects of your northern hemisphere. I want to correct the situation. During my stay I hope to use you and other Terrans for source material in my study of your history and, uh, government. It's especially good luck that I meet a professional like yourself."

Dahlmann seemed happy to discuss his people and soon we were immersed in Terran history and cultures. Much of what he told me I knew from reports received, but I let him tell the whole story.

It seems that two hundred years before, there was a high-technology culture in the northern hemisphere. The way Dahlmann spoke, it was very nearly Mikin caliber—the North People even had some primitive form of space flight. Then there was a war. A war is something like a fight, only much bigger, bigger even than an antitrust action. They exploded more than 12,500 megatons of bombs on their own cities. In addition, germ cultures were released to kill anybody who survived the fusion bombs. Without radiation screens and panphagic viruses, it was a slaughter. Virtually all the mammals in the northern hemisphere were destroyed and, according to Dahlmann, there was, for a while, the fear that the radiation poisons and disease strains would wipe out life in the South World, too.

It is very difficult to imagine how anything like that could get started in the first place—the cause of "war" was one of the objects of my research. Of course the gross explanation was that the Terrans never developed the Umpire System or the Concept of Chaos. Instead they used the gargantuan organizations called "governments." But the underlying question was why they chose this weird governmental path at all. Were the Terrans essentially subhuman—or is it just luck that we Mikins discovered the True Way?

The war didn't discourage the Terrans from their fundamental errors. Three governments rose from the ashes of war. The Australian, the Sudamerican, and the Zulunder. Even the smallest nation, Australia, had one thousand times as many people as the Pwrlyg Spice & Trading Company. And remember that Pwrlyg is already as big as a group can get without being slapped with an antitrust ruling by the Umpires.

I forgot my surroundings as Dahlmann went on to explain the present power structure, the struggle of the two stronger nations to secure colonies in portions of the northern hemisphere where the war poisons had dissipated. This was a very dangerous situation, according to the Terran anthropologist, since there were many disease types dormant in the northern hemisphere that could start hellish plagues in the South World, for the Terrans were still more than a century behind the technology they had achieved before the blowup.

Through all this discussion, Horlig maintained an almost contemptuous silence, not listening to what we were saying so much as observing us as specimens. Finally he interrupted. "Well, I'm glad to see you both hit it off so well. It's getting too late for me, though. I'll have to take your leave. No, you don't have to come back just yet, Melmwn. I'll send the car back here on auto after I get to Base."

"You don't have to bother with that, Horlig. Things look pretty tame around here. I can walk back."

"No," Horlig said definitely. "We have regulations. And there is always this Merlyn, you know."

The Merlyn bunglers didn't frighten me, but I remembered that cat's Demoneyes. Suddenly I was happy to fly back. After Horlig had left, we returned to the den and its dim gas mantle lamps. I could understand why Dahlmann's eyesight was so bad—you try reading at night without electric lights for a couple decades and you'll go blind, too. He rummaged around in his desk and drew out a pouch of "tobacco." He fumbled the ground leaves into the bowl of his pipe and tamped them down with a clumsy forefinger. I thought he was going to burn his face when he lit the mixture. Back home, anyone with coordination that poor would be dead in less than two days, unless he secluded himself in a pacific enclave. This Terran culture was truly alien. It was different along a dimension we had never imagined, except in a few mathematical theories of doubtful validity.

The Terran sat back and regarded me for a long moment. Behind those thick lenses his eyes loomed large and wise. Now I was the one who seemed helpless. Finally he pulled back the curtains and inspected the lawn and the place where the car had rested. "I believe, Scholar Melmwn, that you are a reasonable and intelligent individual. I hope that you are even more than that. Do you realize that you are attending the execution of a race?"

This took me completely by surprise. "What! What do you mean?"

He appeared to ignore my question. "I knew when you people first landed and we saw your machines: our culture is doomed. I had hoped that we could escape with our lives—though in our own history, few have been so lucky. I hoped that your social sciences would be as advanced as your physical. But I was wrong.

"Your vice president for aboriginal affairs arrived with the Second 'wrlyg Fleet. Is genocide the 'wrlyg policy or is it Horlig's private scheme?"

This was too much. "I find your questions insulting, Terran! The Pwrlyg Company intends you no harm. Our interests are confined to reclaiming and colonizing areas of your planet that you admit are too hot for you to handle."

Now Dahlmann was on the defensive. "I apologize, Scholar Melmwn, for my discourtesy. I dived into the subject too hastily. I don't mean to offend you. Let me describe my fears and the reasons for them. I believe that Herul Horlig is not content with the cultural destruction of Earth. He would like to see all Terrans dead. Officially his job is to promote cooperation between our races and to eliminate possible frictions. In fact, he has played the opposite role. Since he arrived, his every act has increased our mutual antagonism. Take, for instance, the 'courtesy call' he made to the Zulunder capital. He and that armed forces chief of yours, Noggin Chem—is that how you pronounce the name?"

"Ngagn Chev," I corrected.

"They breezed into Pret armed to the teeth—fifteen air tanks and a military air-space craft. The Zulunder government requested that Horlig return the spaceship to orbit before they initiate talks. In response, the Mikins destroyed half the city. At the time I hoped that it was just the act of some demented gunner, but Horlig staged practically the same performance at Buenos Aires, the capital of Sudamerica. And this time he had no pretext whatso ever, since the Americans bent over backwards trying to avoid a clash. Every chance he gets, the man tries to prove how vicious Mikins can be."

I made a note to check on these events when I returned to Base. Aloud I said: "Then you believe that Horlig is trying to provoke terrorist movements like this Merlyn thing, so he'll have an excuse to kill all Terrans?"

Dahlmann didn't answer immediately. He carefully pulled back the curtain again and looked into the yard. The aircar had not yet returned. I think he realized that the mikes aboard the car could easily record what we were saying. "That's not quite what I mean, Scholar Melmwn. I believe that Horlig *is* Merlyn."

I snorted disbelief.

"I know it sounds ridiculous—but everything fits. Just take the word 'Merlyn.' In Australian this refers to a magician who lived ages ago in England—that was one of the great pre-war nations in the northern hemisphere. At the same time it is a word that easily comes to the lips of a Mikin since it is entirely pronounceable within your phoneme system—it contains no front oral stops. With its magical connotations, it is designed to set fear in Mikins. The word Merlyn is a convenient handle for the fear and hatred that Mikins will come to associate with Terran activities. But note—we Terrans are a very unsuperstitious lot, especially the Australians and the Zulunders. And very few Terrans realize how superstitious many Mikins— the witch-fearers and the demon-mongers—are. The Merlyn concept is the invention of a Mikin mind."

Dahlmann rushed on to keep me from interrupting. "Consider also: When terrorist attacks are thwarted and the Terrans captured, they turn out to be ill-equipped rumdums—not the skilled agents of some world-wide plot. But whenever great damage is done—say the detonation of the company ammo stores last year—no one is caught. In fact, it is almost impossible to imagine how the job could be pulled off without Mikin technology. At first I discounted this theory, because so many Mikins were killed in the ammo blast, but I have since learned that you people do not regard such violence as improper business procedure."

"It depends on who you are working for. There are plenty of Violent Nihilists on Miki, and occasionally they have their own companies. If Pwrlyg is one such, he's been keeping the fact a secret."

"What it adds up to is that Horlig is creating an artificial threat, which he believes will eventually justify genocide. One last element of proof. You came in on a Fleet landing craft this afternoon, did you not? Horlig was supposed to greet you. He invited me out to meet you on the field, as the chief representative of Her Majesty's Government in Australia. This is the first friendly gesture the man has made in three years. As it happened, I couldn't go. I sent my daughter, Mary. But when you actually landed, Horlig got a sliver from his shin board, or something equally idiotic, and so couldn't go onto the field—where just five minutes later a group of 'Merlyn's Men' tried to shoot the lot of you."

Mary Dahlmann. I stuttered over the next question. "How . . . how is your daughter, Scholar Dahlmann?"

Dahlmann was nonplussed for a moment. "She's fine. Apparently someone pulled her out of the line of fire. A bloody nose was the sum total of her 'injuries.' "

For some reason I felt great relief at this news. I looked at my watch; it was thirty minutes to midnight, the witching hour. Tonight especially I wanted to get back to Base before Demonsloose. And I hadn't known that Merlyn was the name of a wizard. I stood up. "You've certainly given me something to think about, Dahlmann. Of course you know where my sympathies ultimately lie, but I'll be alert for signs of the plot you speak of, and I won't tell anyone what you've told me."

The Terran rose. "That's all I ask." He led me out of the den, and into the darkened mainroom. The wood floor creaked comfortingly beneath the thick carpet. Crystal goblets on wood shelving were outlined in faint glistening reflection from the den light. To the right a stairway led to the second floor. Was *she* up there sleeping, or out with some male? I wondered.

As we approached the door, something much more pertinent occurred to me. I touched Dahlmann's elbow; he stopped, ready to open the door. "A moment, Scholar Dahlmann. All the facts you present fit another theory: namely, that some Terran, expert in Mikin ways, yourself perhaps, has manufactured Merlyn and the rumor that members of the Pwrlyg Company are responsible for the conspiracy."

I couldn't tell for sure, but I think he smiled. "Your counter-proposal does indeed fit the facts. However, I am aware of the power that you Mikins have at your disposal, and how futile resistance would be." He opened the door. I stepped out onto the porch. "Good night," he said.

"Good night." I stood there for several seconds, listening to his retreating footsteps, and puzzling over our last exchange.

I turned and was halfway across the porch when a soft voice behind me asked, "And how did you like Daddy?" I jumped a good fifteen centimeters, spun around with my wrist gun extended. Mary Dahlmann sat on a wooden swing hung from the ceiling of the porch. She pushed the swing gently back and forth. I walked over and sat down beside her.

"He's an impressive and intelligent man," I answered.

"I want to thank you for pulling me down this afternoon." Her mind seemed to jump randomly from one topic to another.

"Uh, that's O.K. There really wasn't too much danger. The gun was so primitive that I imagine it's almost as unpleasant to be behind it as in front. I would've thought you'd be the first to recognize it as an attack. You must be familiar with Australian weapons."

"Are you kidding? The biggest gun I've ever seen was a 20mm rifle in a shooting exhibition."

"You mean you've never been under fire until today?" I saw that she hadn't. "I didn't mean to be insulting, Miss

Dahlmann. I haven't really had much first-hand information about Terrans. That's one reason why I'm here."

She laughed. "If you're puzzled about us, then the feeling is mutual. Since my father became chief representative, he's been doing everything he can to interview Mikins and figure out the structure of your culture. I'll bet he spent half the night pumping you. As an anthropologist, you should be the best source he can find."

Apparently she wasn't aware of her father's true concerns.

"In the last three years we've managed to interview more than fifteen of you Mikins. It's crazy. You're all so different from one another. You claim you are all from the same continent, and yet each individual appears to have an entirely different cultural background. Some of you don't wear clothes at all, while others go around with every inch of their skin covered. Some, like Horlig, make a fetish of primitiveness. But we had one fellow here who had so many gadgets with him that he had to wear powered body armor. He was so heavy, he busted my father's favorite chair. We can't find any common denominator. Mikins believe in one god, or in many, or in none. At the same time, many of you are dreadfully superstitious. We've always wondered what aliens might be like, but we never guessed that— What's the matter?"

I pointed shakily at the creature in the street. She placed a reassuring hand on my arm. "Why, that's just a cat. Don't you have catlike creatures on Miki?"

"Certainly."

"Why the shock then? Are your cats poisonous or something?"

"Of course not. Many people keep them as pets. It's just that it's a bad sign to see one at night—an especially bad sign if it looks at you and its eyes glow." I was sorry when she withdrew her hand.

She looked at me closely. "I hope you won't be angry, Mr. Melmwn, but this is exactly what I mean. How can a race that travels between the stars believe in ill or good omens? Or have you developed magic as a science?"

"No, that's not it. Many Mikins don't believe in signs at

all, and depending on whether you are a demon-monger or a witch-fearer, you recognize different signs. As for how I personally can believe in nonempirical, nonscientific signs—that's easy. There are many more causal relations in this universe than Mikin science will ever discover. I believe that witch-fearers have divined a few of these. And though I am quite a mild witch-fearer, I don't take any chances."

"But you are an anthropologist. I should think in your studies you would see so many different attitudes and superstitions that you would disregard your own."

I watched carefully as the cat went around the corner of the house. Then I turned to look at Mary Dahlmann. "Is that how it is with Terran anthropologists? Perhaps then I should not translate my occupation as 'anthropology.' Before Pwrlyg, I was employed by the Anavog Pacific Enclave & Motor Corporation. A fine group. As anthropologist, my job was to screen the background attitudes of prospective employees. For instance, it just wouldn't do to have a Cannibal and a Militant Vegetarian work next to each other on the production line—they'd kill each other inside of three hours, and the corporation would lose money."

She pushed the swing back with an agitated kick. "But now we're back where we started. How can a single culture produce both cannibals and 'militant' vegetarians?"

I thought about it. Her question really seemed to go beyond cultures entirely—right to the core of reality. I had practiced my speciality within the Mikin framework—where such questions never came up. Maybe I should start with something basic.

"Our system is founded on the Concept of Chaos. The universe is basically a dark and unhappy place—a place where evil and injustice and randomness rule. The ironic thing is that the very act of organization creates the potential for even greater ruin. Social organizations have a natural tendency to become monopolistic and inflexible. When they finally break down, it is a catastrophic debacle. So, we must accept a great deal of disorder and violence in our lives if we are to avoid a complete blowup later.

"Every Mikin is free to *try* anything. Naturally, in order to survive, groups of people cooperate—and from this you get the tens of thousands of organizations, corporations, and convents that make our civilization. But no group may become monopolistic. This is why we have Umpires. I don't think you have anything comparable. Umpires see that excessively large organizations are never formed. They keep our society from becoming rigid and unresponsive to the natural world. Our system has lasted a very long time." *Much longer than yours,* I added to myself.

She frowned. "I don't understand. Umpires? Is this some sort of police force? How do they keep governments from forming? What's to keep the Umpires from becoming a government themselves?"

If I didn't watch out, I was going to learn more about Miki than I did about Earth. Mary's questions opened doors I never knew existed. My answer was almost as novel to me as it was to her. "I suppose it's because the Umpire tradition is very old with us. With one minor exception, all Mikins have had this tradition for almost four thousand years. The Umpires probably originated as a priest class serving a number of different nomad tribes. There never were many Umps. They go unarmed. They have bred for intelligence and flexibility. There's quite a bit of, uh, mystery—which we take for granted—surrounding them. I believe that they live under the influence of some rather strange drugs. You might say that they are brainwashed. In all history, there is no period in which they have sought power. Though they spend most of their lives in the abstract study of behavior science, their real task is to watch society for signs of bigness.

"There's one watching Pwrlyg right now. If he decides that Pwrlyg is too big—and that's a distinct possibility, since there are almost twelve thousand Pwrlyg employees altogether—the Ump will issue an, uh, antitrust ruling, describing the situation and ordering certain changes. There is no appeal. Defiance of an antitrust ruling is the only deed that is recognized by all Mikins as a sin. When there is such defiance, all Mikins are bound to take antitrust action—that is, to destroy the criminal. Some antitrust actions have involved fusion bombs and armies—they're the closest thing we have to wars."

She didn't look convinced. "Frankly, I can't imagine how such a system could avoid becoming a dictatorship of 'Umpires.' "

"I feel the same incredulity about your civilization."

"How big are your 'organizations'?"

"It might be a single person. More than half the groups on Miki are just families or family groups. Anything goes unless it threatens stability—or becomes too large. The largest groups allowed are some of the innocuous religious types—the Little Brother Association, for instance. They preach approximately the principles I read of in your Christianity. But they don't proselytize, and so manage to avoid antitrust rulings. The largest 'hardware' organizations have about fifteen thousand employees."

"And how can a company support interstellar operations?"

"Yes, that's a very tricky point. Pwrlyg had to cooperate with several hundred industrial groups to do it. They came mighty close to antitrust."

She sat silently, thinking all this over. Then she asked, "When can we expect an antitrust ruling against the Australian government?"

I laughed, "You don't have to worry about that. No offense, but antitrust can only apply to human groupings."

She didn't like that at all, but she didn't argue it either. Instead she came back with, "Then that means we also don't have Umpire protection if Pwrlyg commits genocide upon us."

That was a nasty conclusion, but it fitted the letter of custom. Killing millions of humans would warrant antitrust, but Terrans weren't human.

For an instant I thought she was laughing, low and bitter. Then her face seemed to collapse and I knew she was crying. This was an unpleasant turn of events. Awkwardly, I put my arm around her shoulders and tried to comfort her. She no longer seemed to me an abo, but simply a person in pain. "Please, Mary Dahlmann. My people aren't monsters. We only want to use places on your planet that are uninhabited, that are too dangerous for you. Our presence will actually make Earth safer. When we colonize the North World, we'll null the radiation poisons and kill the war viruses."

That didn't stop the tears, but she did move close into my arms. Several seconds passed and she mumbled something like, "History repeats." We sat like that for almost half an hour.

It wasn't until I got back to Base that I remembered that I had been out between Demonsloose and Dawn without so much as a Hexagram.

I got my equipment installed the next day. I was assigned an office only fifty-four hundred meters from the central supply area. This was all right with me since the site was also quite near the outskirts of Adelaide-west. Though the office was made entirely of local materials, the style was old *vimwv*. The basement contained my sleeping and security quarters, and the first floor was my office and business machines. The surface construction was all handpolished hardwood. The roof was tiled with rose marble and furnished with night chairs and a drink mixer. At the center of the roof was a recoilless rifle and a live map of the mine field around the building. It was all just like home—which is what I had specified when I had signed the contract back on Miki. I had expected some chiseling on the specifications once we got out in the boondocks, but Pwrlyg's integrity was a pleasant surprise.

After I checked out the equipment, I called Horlig and got a copy of his mission log. I wanted to check on Dahlmann's charges. Horlig was suspiciously unhappy about parting with the information, but when I pointed out that I was without a job until I got background info, he agreed to squirt me a copy. The incidents were more or less as Dahlmann had described them. At Pret, though, the Zulunders attacked the air tanks with some jury-rigged antiaircraft weapon—so the retaliation seemed justified. There was also one incident that Dahlmann hadn't mentioned. Just five days before, Chev—on Horlig's orders— burned the food supplies of the Sudamerican colony at Panama, thus forcing the Terran explorers to return to the inhabited portions of their continent. I decided to keep a close watch on these developments. There could be something here quite as sinister as Dahlmann claimed.

Later that day, Horlig briefed me on my first assignment. He wanted me to record and index the Canberra Central Library. The job didn't appeal at all. It was designed to keep me out of his hair. I spent the next couple weeks getting equipment together. I found Robert Dahlmann especially helpful. He telegraphed his superiors in Canberra and they agreed to let us use Terran clerical help in the recording operation. (I imagine part of the reason was that they were eager to study our equipment.) I never actually flew to Canberra. Horlig had some deputy take the stuff out and instruct the natives on how to use it. It turned out the Canberra library was huge—almost as big as the Information Services library at home. Just supervising the indexing computers was a full-time job. It was a lot more interesting than I thought it would be. When the job was done I would have many times the source material I could have collected personally.

A strange thing: as the weeks went by, I saw more and more of Mary Dahlmann. Even at this point I was still telling myself that it was all field work for my study of Terran customs. One day we had a picnic in the badlands north of Adelaide. The next she took me on a tour of the business district of the city—it was amazing how so many people could live so close together day after day. Once we even went on a train ride all the way to Murray Bridge. Railroads are stinking, noisy and dirty, but they're fun— and they transport freight almost as cheaply as a floater does. Mary had that spark of intelligence and good humor that made it all the more interesting. Still I claimed it was all in the cause of objective research.

About six weeks after my landing I invited her to visit

the Pwrlyg Base. Though Central Supply is only four or five kilometers from Adelaide-west, I took her in by air, so she could see the whole base at once. I think it was the first time she had ever flown.

The Pwrlyg Primary Territory is a rectangular area fifteen by thirty kilometers. It was ceded by the Australian government to the Company in gratitude for our intercession in the Battle of Hawaii, seventeen years before. You might wonder why we didn't just put all our bases in the northern hemisphere, and ignore the Terrans entirely. The most important reason was that the First and Second Fleets hadn't had the equipment for a large-scale decontamination job. Also, every kilogram of cargo from Miki requires nearly 100,000 megatons of energy for the voyage to Earth: this is expensive by any reckoning. We needed all the labor and materials the locals could provide. Since the Terrans inhabited the Southern Hemisphere only, that's where our first base had to be.

By native standards, Pwrlyg paid extremely good wages. So good that almost thirty thousand Terrans were employed at the Ground Base. Many of these individuals lived in an area just off the base, which Mary referred to as Clowntown. Its inhabitants were understandably enamored with the advantages of Mikin technology. Though their admiration was commendable, the results were a little ludicrous. Clowntowners tried to imitate the various aspects of Mikin life. They dressed eccentrically—by Terran standards—and adopted a variety of social behaviors. But their city was just as crowded as regular Australian urban areas. And though they had more scraps of our technology than many places in Australia, their city was filthy. Anarchy just isn't practical in such close quarters. They had absorbed the superficial aspects of our society without ever getting down to the critical matters of Umpires and antitrust. Mary had refused to go with me into Clowntown. Her reason was that police protection ceased to exist in that area. I don't think that was her real reason.

Below us, the blue sea and white breakers met the

orange and gray-green bluffs of the shore. The great Central Desert extended right up to the ocean. It was difficult to believe that this land had once supported grass and trees. Scattered randomly across the sand and sage were the individual offices and workshops of Company employees. Each of these had its own unique appearance. Some were oases set in the desert. Others were squat gray forts. Some even looked like Terran houses. And, of course, a good number were entirely hidden from sight, the property of Obscurantist employees who kept their location secret even from Pwrlyg. Taken as a whole, the Base looked like a comfortable metropolitan area on the A1 W1 peninsula. But, if the Company had originally based in the Northern Hemisphere, none of the amenities would have been possible. We would have had to live in prefab domes.

I swung the car in a wide arc and headed for the central area. Here was the robot factory that provided us with things like air tanks and drink mixers—things that native labor couldn't construct. Now we could see the general landing area, and the airy columns of Supply Central. Nearby was housing for groups that believed in living together: the sex club, the Little Brothers. A low annex jutted off from the Little Brothers building—the creche for children born of Non-Affective parents. They even had some half-breed Terran-Human children there. The biologists had been amazed to find that the two species could interbreed—some claimed that this proved the existence of a prehistoric interstellar empire.

I parked the car and we took the lift to the open eating area at the top of Supply Central. The utilitarian cafeteria served the Extroverts on the Company staff. The position afforded an excellent view of the sailing boats and surfers as well as three or four office houses out in the sea.

We were barely seated when two Terran waiter-servants came over to take our order. One of them favored Mary with a long, cold look, but they took my order courteously enough.

Mary watched them go, then remarked, "They hate my guts, do you know that?"

"Huh? Why should they hate you?"

"I'm, uh, 'consorting' with the Greenies. That's you. I knew one of those two in college. A real nice guy. He wanted to study low-energy nuclear reactions; prewar scientists never studied that area thoroughly. His life ended when he discovered that you people know more than he'll ever discover, unless he starts over from the beginning on your terms. Now he's practically a slave, waiting on tables."

"A slave he's not, girl. Pwrlyg just isn't that type of organization. That fellow is a trusted and well-cared-for servant—an employee, if you will. He can pack up and leave any time. With the wages we pay, we have Terrans begging for jobs."

"That's exactly what I mean," Mary said opaquely. Then she turned the question around. "Don't you feel any hostility from your friends, for running around with an 'Earthie' girl?"

I laughed. "In the first place, I'm not running around. I'm using you in my studies. In the second place, I don't know any of these people well enough yet to have friends. Even the people I came out with were all in deep freeze, remember.

"Some Mikins actually support fraternization with the natives—the Little Brothers, for instance. Every chance they get, they tell us to go out and make love—or is that verb just plain 'love'?—to the natives. I think there are some Company people who are definitely hostile toward you people—Horlig and Chev, for example. But I didn't ask their permission and, if they want to stop me, they'll have to contend with this." I tapped the dart gun on my wrist.

"Oh?" I think she was going to say something more when the servants came out and placed the food on our table. It was good, and we didn't say anything for several minutes. When we were done we sat and watched the surfers. A couple on a powered board were racing a dolphin across the bay. Their olive skins glistened pleasantly against the blue water.

Finally she spoke. "I've always been puzzled by that Horlig. He's odd even for a Mikin—no offense. He seems to regard Terrans as foolish and ignorant cowards. Yet as a person, he looks a lot more like a Terran than a Mikin."

"Actually, he's a different subspecies from the rest of us. It's like the difference between you and Zulunders. His bone structure is a little different and his skin is pale gray instead of olive green. His ancestors lived on a different continent than mine. They never developed beyond a neolithic culture there. About four hundred years ago, my race colonized his continent. We already had firearms then. Horlig's people just shriveled away. Whenever they fought us, we killed them; and whenever they didn't, we set them away in preserves. The last preserve, Gloyn, died about fifty years ago, I think. The rest interbred with the mainstream. Horlig is the nearest thing to a full-blooded Gloyn I've seen. Maybe that's why he affects primitiveness."

Mary said, "If he weren't out to get us Terrans, I think I could feel sorry for him."

I couldn't understand that comment. Horlig's race may have been mistreated in the past, but he was a lot better off than his ancestors ever were.

Three tables away, another couple was engaged in an intense conversation. Gradually it assumed the proportions of an argument. The man snapped an insult and the woman returned it with interest. Without warning, a knife appeared in her hand, flashed at the other's chest. But the man jumped backward, knocking over his chair. Mary gasped, as the man brought his knife in a grazing slash across the woman's middle. Red instantly appeared on green. They danced around the tables, feinting and slashing.

"Ron, do something! He's going to kill her."

They were fighting in a meal area, which is against Company regs, but on the other hand, neither was using power weapons. "I'm not going to do anything, Mary. This is a lovers' quarrel."

Mary's jaw dropped. "A lovers' quarrel? What—"

"Yeah," I said, "they both want the same woman." Mary looked sick. As soon as the fight began, a Little Brother at the other end of the roof got up and sprinted toward the combatants. Now he stood to one side, pleading with them to respect the holiness of life, and to settle their differences peacefully. But the two weren't much for religion. The man hissed at the Little Brother to get lost before he got spitted. The woman took advantage of her opponent's momentary inattention to pink his arm. Just then a Company officer arrived on the roof and informed the two just how big a fine they would be subject to if they continued to fight in a restricted area. That stopped them. They backed away from each other, cursing. The Little Brother followed them to the lift as he tried to work out some sort of reconciliation.

Mary seemed upset. "You people lead sex lives that make free love look like monogamy."

"No, you're wrong, Mary. It's just that every person has a different outlook. It's as if all Earth's sex customs coexisted. Most people subscribe to some one type." I decided not to try explaining the sex club.

"Don't you have marriage?"

"That's just what I'm saying. A large proportion of us do. We even have a word analogous to your *missus: a.* For instance, Mrs. Smith is aSmith. I would say that nearly fifteen percent of all Mikins are monogamous in the sense you mean it. And a far greater percentage never engage in the activities you regard as perversions."

She shook her head. "Do you know—if your group had appeared without a superior technology, you would have been locked up in an insane asylum? I like you personally, but most Mikins are so awfully weird."

I was beginning to get irritated. "You're the one that's nuts. The Pwrlyg employees here on Earth were deliberately chosen for their intelligence and compatibility. Even the mildly exotic types were left at home."

Mary's voice wavered slightly as she answered. "I . . . I guess I know that. You're all just so terribly different. And soon all the ways I know will be destroyed, and my people will all be dead or like you—more probably dead. No, don't deny it. More than once in our history we've had episodes like the colonization of Gloyn. Six hundred years ago, the Europeans took over North America from the stone-age Indians. One group of Indians—a tribe called the Cherokee—saw that they could never overcome the invaders. They reasoned that the only way to survive was to adopt European ways—no matter how offensive those ways appeared. The Cherokee built schools and towns; they even printed newspapers in their own language. But this did not satisfy the Europeans. They coveted the Cherokee lands. Eventually they evicted the Indians and force-marched the tribe halfway across the continent into a desert preserve. For all their willingness to adapt, the Cherokee suffered the same fate that your Gloyn did.

"Ron, are you any different from the Europeans—or from your Mikin ancestors? Will my people be massacred? Will the rare survivor be just another Mikin with all your aw— . . . all your alien customs? Isn't there any way you can save us from yourselves?" She reached out and grasped my hand. I could see she was fighting back tears.

There was no rationalizing it: I had fallen for her. I silently cursed my moralistic Little Brother upbringing. At that moment, if she had asked it, I would have run right down to the beach and started swimming for Antarctica. The feel of her hand against mine and the look in her eyes would have admitted to no other response. For a moment, I wondered if she was aware of the awful power she had. Then I said, "I'll do everything I can, Mary. I don't think you have to worry. We've advanced a long way since Gloyn. Only a few of us wish you harm. But I'll do anything to protect your people from massacre and exploitation. Is that enough of a commitment?"

She squeezed my hand. "Yes. It's a greater commitment than has been made in all the past."

"Fine," I said, standing up. I wanted to get off this

painful subject as fast as possible. "Let me show you some of our equipment."

I took her over to the Abo Affairs Office. The AAO wasn't a private residence-office, but it did bear Horlig's stamp. Even close up, it looked like a Gloyn rock-nest—a huge pile of boulders set in a marshy—and artificial—jungle. It was difficult, even for me, to spot the location of the recoilless rifles and machine guns. Inside, the neolithic motif was maintained. The computing equipment and TV screens were hidden behind woven curtains, and lighting came indirectly through chinks in the boulders. Horlig refused to employ Terrans, and his Mikin clerks and techs hadn't returned from lunch.

At the far end of the "room" a tiny waterfall gushed tinkling into a pool. Beyond the pool was Horlig's office, blocked from direct view by a rock partition. I noticed that the pool gave us an odd, ripply view into his office. That's the trouble with these "open" architectural forms: they have no real rooms, or privacy. In the water I could see the upside-down images of Horlig and Chev. I motioned Mary to be quiet, and knelt down to watch. Their voices were barely audible above the sound of falling water.

Chev was saying—in Mikin, of course: "You've been sensible enough in the past, Horlig. My suggestion is just a logical extension of previous policy. Once he's committed I'm sure that Pwrlyg won't have any objections. The Terrans have provided us with almost all the materials we needed from them. Their usefulness is over. They're vermin. It's costing the Company two thousand man-hours a month to provide security against their attacks and general insolence." He waved a sheaf of papers at Horlig. "My plan is simple. Retreat from Ground Base for a couple weeks and send orbital radiation bombs over the three inhabited areas. Then drop some lethal viruses to knock off the survivors. I figure it would cost one hundred thousand man-hours total, but we'd be permanently rid of this nuisance. And our ground installations would be undamaged. All you have to do is camouflage some of our initial moves so that the Company officers on the Orbital Base don't catch—"

"Enough!" Horlig exploded. He grabbed Chev by the scruff of his cape and pulled him up from his chair. "You putrid bag of schemings. I'm reporting you to Orbit. And if you ever even *think* of that plan again, I personally will kill you—if Pwrlyg doesn't do it first!" He shoved the vice president for violence to the floor. Chev got up, ready to draw and fire, but Horlig's wrist gun pointed directly at the other's middle. Chev spat on the floor and backed out of the room.

"What was that all about?" Mary whispered. I shook my head. This was one conversation I wasn't going to translate. Horlig's reaction amazed and pleased me. I almost liked the man after the way he had handled Chev. And unless the incident had been staged for my benefit, it shattered Robert Dahlmann's theory about Merlyn and Horlig. Could Chev be the one masquerading as a Terran rebel? He had just used Terran sabotage as an excuse for genocide.

Or was Merlyn simply what it appeared to be: a terrorist group created and managed by deranged Terrans? Things were all mixed up.

Ngagn Chev stalked out of the passage that led to Horlig's office. He glared murderously at Mary and me as he swept past us toward the door hole.

I looked back into the pool, and saw the reflection of Horlig's face looking back out at me. Perhaps it was the ripple distortion from the waterfall, but he seemed just as furious with my eavesdropping as he had been with Chev. If it had been a direct confrontation, I would've expected a fight. Then Horlig remembered his privacy field and turned it on, blanking out my view.

My library project proceeded rapidly to a conclusion. Everything was taped, and I had 2×10^7 subjects cross-indexed. The computerized library became my most powerful research tool. Dahlmann hadn't been kidding when he said that the pre-war civilization was high class. If the

North Americans and Asians had managed to avoid war, they probably would have sent an expedition to Miki while we were still developing the fission bomb. Wouldn't that have been a switch—the Terrans colonizing our lands!

In the two hundred years since the North World War, the Australians had spent a great deal of effort in developing social science. They hadn't given up their government mania, but they had modified the concept so that it was much less malevolent than in the past. Australia now supported almost eleven million people, at a fairly high standard of living. In fact, I think there was probably less suffering in Australia than there is in most parts of Miki. Too bad their way of life was doomed. The Terrans were people—they were human. (And that simple conclusion was the answer to the whole problem, though I did not see it then.) In all my readings, I kept in mind the solution I was looking for: some way to save the Terrans from physical destruction, even if it was impossible to save their entire culture.

As the weeks passed, this problem came to overshadow my official tasks. I even looked up the history of the Cherokee and read about Elias Boudinot and Chief Sequoyah. The story was chillingly similar to the situation that was being played out now by the Mikins and the Terrans. The only way that the Terrans could hope for physical safety was to adopt Mikin institutions. But even then, wouldn't we eventually wipe them out the same way President Andrew Jackson did the Cherokee? Wouldn't we eventually covet all the lands of Earth?

While I tried to come up with a long-term solution, I also kept track of Chev's activities. Some of his men were pretty straight guys, and I got to know one platoon leader well. Late one evening about ten weeks after my landing, my armsman friend tipped me off that Chev was planning a massacre the next day in Perth.

I went over to see Horlig that night. From his reaction to Chev's genocide scheme, I figured he'd squash the massacre plan. The Gloyn was working late. I found him seated behind his stone desk in the center of the AAO rock-nest. He looked up warily as I entered. "What is it, Melmwn?"

"You've got to do something, Horlig. Chev is flying three platoons to Perth. I don't know exactly what type of mayhem he's planning, but—"

"Rockingham."

"Huh?"

"Chev is flying to Rockingham, not Perth." Horlig watched me carefully.

"You knew? What's he going to do—"

"I know because he's doing the job at my suggestion. I've identified the abos who blew up our ammo warehouse last year. Some of the ringleaders are Rockingham city officials. I'm going to make an example of them." He paused, then continued grimly, as if daring me to object. "By tomorrow at this time, every tenth inhabitant of Rockingham will be dead."

I didn't say anything for a second. I couldn't. When I finally got my mouth working again, I said with great originality, "You just can't do this, Horlig. We've had a lot more trouble from the Sudamericans and the Zulunders than we've ever had from the Australians. Killing a bunch of Aussies will just prove to everyone that Mikins don't want peace. You'll be encouraging belligerence. If you really have proof that these Rockingham officials are Merlyn's Men, you should send Chev out to arrest just those men and bring them back here for some sort of Company trial. Your present action is entirely arbitrary."

Horlig sat back in his chair. There was a new frankness and a new harshness in his face. "Perhaps I just made it all up. I'll fabricate some proof too, when necessary."

I hadn't expected this admission. I answered, "Pwrlyg's Second Son himself is coming down from Orbit tomorrow morning. Perhaps you thought he wouldn't know of your plans until they were executed. I don't know why you are doing this, but I can tell you that the Second Son is going to hear about it the minute he gets off the landing craft."

Horlig smiled pleasantly. "Get out."

*   *   *

I turned and started for the door. I admit it: I was going soft in the brain. My only excuse is that I had been associating with the natives too long. They generally say what they think because they have the protection of an impartial and all-powerful police force. This thought occurred to me an instant before I heard the characteristic sound of wrist gun smacking into palm. I dived madly for the floor as the first 0.07mm dart hit the right boulder of the door hole. The next thing I knew I was lying in the cubbyhole formed by two or three large boulders knocked loose by the blast. My left arm was numb; a rock splinter had cut through it to the bone.

In the next couple seconds, Horlig fired about twenty darts wildly. The lights went out. Rocks weighing many tons flew about. The rock nest had been designed for stability, but this demolition upset the balance and the whole pile was shifting into a new configuration. It was a miracle I wasn't crushed. Horlig screamed. The shooting stopped. Was he dead? The man was nuts to fire more than a single dart indoors. He must have wanted me pretty bad.

As the horrendous echoes faded away, I could hear Horlig swearing. The pile was unrecognizable now. I could see the sky directly between gaps in the rocks. Moonlight came down in silvery shafts through suspended rock dust. Half-human shapes seemed to lurk in the rubble. I realized now that the nest was much bigger than I had thought. To my left an avalanche of boulders had collapsed into some subterranean space. The surface portion of the nest was only a fraction of the total volume. Right now Horlig could be right on the other side of a nearby rock or one hundred meters away—the pile shift had been that violent.

"You still kicking, Melmwn, old man?" Horlig's voice came clearly. The sound was from my right, but not too close. Perhaps if I moved quietly enough I could sneak out of the pile to my air car. Or I could play dead and wait for morning when Horlig's employees came out. But some of those might be partners in Horlig's scheme—whatever it was. I decided to try the first plan. I crawled over a

nearby boulder, made a detour around an expanse of
moonlit rock. My progress was definitely audible—there
was too much loose stuff. Behind me, I could hear Horlig
following. I stopped. This was no good. Even if I managed
to make it out, I would then be visible from the pile, and
Horlig could shoot me down. I would have to get rid of my
opponent before I could escape. Besides, if he got away
safely, Horlig could have Chev's sentries bar me from the
landing field the next day. I stopped and lay quietly in the
darkness. My arm really hurt now, and I could feel from
the wetness on the ground that I had left a trail of blood.

"Come, Melmwn, speak up. I know you're still alive." I
smiled. If Horlig thought I was going to give my position
away by talking, he was even crazier than I thought.
Every time he spoke, I got a better idea of his position.

"I'll trade information for the sound of your voice,
Melmwn." Maybe he was not quite so nuts after all. He
knew my greatest failing: curiosity. If Horlig should die
this night, I might never know what his motives were.
And I was just as well armed as he. If I could keep him
talking I stood to gain just as much as he.

"All right, Horlig. I'll trade." I had said more than I
wanted to. The shorter my responses the better. I listened
for the sound of movement. But all I heard was Horlig's
voice.

"You see, Melmwn, I am Merlyn." I heard a slithering
sound as he moved to a new position. He was revealing
everything to keep me talking. Now it was my turn to say
something.

"Say on, O Horlig."

"I should have killed you before. When you overheard
my conversation with Chev, I thought you might have
guessed the truth."

I had received a lot of surprises so far, and this was
another. Horlig's treatment of Chev's genocide scheme
had seemed proof that Horlig couldn't be Merlyn. "But
why, Horlig? What do you gain? What do you want?"

My opponent laughed, "I'm an altruist, Melmwn. And
I'm a Gloyn; maybe the last full-blooded Gloyn. The Ter-

rans are not going to be taken over by you the way you took over my people. The Terrans are people; they are human—and they must be treated as such."

I guess the idea must have been floating around in my mind for weeks. The Terrans were human, and should be treated as such. Horlig's statement triggered the whole solution in my mind. I saw the essential error of the Cherokee and of all my previous plans to save the Terrans. Horlig's motive was a complete surprise, but I could understand it. In a way he seemed to be after the same thing as I—though his methods couldn't possibly work. Maybe we wouldn't have to shoot it out.

"Listen Horlig. There's a way I can get what you want without bloodshed. The Terrans can be saved." I outlined my plan. I talked for almost two minutes.

As I finished, a dart smashed into a boulder thirty meters from my position. Then Horlig spoke. "I will not accept your plan. It is just what I'm fighting against." He seemed to be talking to himself, repeating a cycle that played endlessly, fanatically in his own brain. "Your plan would make the Terrans carbon-copy Mikins. Their culture would be destroyed as thoroughly as mine was. It is far better to die fighting you monsters than to lie down and let you take over. That's why I became Merlyn. I give the rebellious Terran elements a backbone, secret information, supplies. In my capacity as a Mikin official, I provoke incidents to convince the spineless ones of the physical threat to their existence. The Australians are the most cowardly of the lot. Apparently their government will accept any indignity. That's why I must be especially brutal at Rockingham tomorrow."

"Your plan's insane," I blurted without thinking. "Pwrlyg could destroy every living thing on Earth without descending from orbit."

"Then that is better than the cultural assassination you intend! We will die fighting." I think he was crying. "I grew up on the last preserve. I heard the last stories. The stories of the lands and the hunting my people once had, before you came and killed us, drove us away, talked us out of everything of value. If we had stood and fought then, I at least would never have been born into the nightmare that is your world." There was silence for a second.

I crept slowly toward the sound of his voice. I tucked my left arm in my shirt to keep it from dragging on the ground. I guessed that Horlig was wounded too, from the slithery sound he made when he moved.

The man was so involved in his own world that he kept on talking. It's strange, but now that I had discovered a way to save the Terrans, I felt doubly desperate to get out of the rock-nest alive. "And don't, Melmwn, be so sure that we will lose to you this time. I intend to provoke no immediate insurrection. I am gathering my forces. A second robot factory was brought in with the Third Fleet. Pwrlyg's Second Son is coming down with it tomorrow. With Chev's forces on the West Coast it will be an easy matter for Merlyn's Men to hijack the factory and its floater. I already have a hidden place, in the midst of all the appropriate ore fields, to set it up. Over the years, that factory will provide us with all the weapons and vehicles we need. And someday, someday we will rise and kill all the Mikins."

Horlig sounded delirious now. He was confusing Gloyn and Terran. But that robo-factory scheme was not the invention of a delirious mind—only an insane one. I continued across the boulders—under and around them. The moon was directly overhead and its light illuminated isolated patches of rock. I knew I was quite near him now. I stopped and inspected the area ahead of me. Just five meters away a slender beam of moonlight came down through a chink in the rock overhead.

"Tomorrow, yes, tomorrow will be Merlyn's greatest coup."

As Horlig spoke I thought I detected a faint agitation in the rock dust hung in that moonbeam. Of course it might be a thermal effect from a broken utility line, but it could also be Horlig's breath stirring the tiny particles.

I scrambled over the last boulder to get a clear shot that would not start an avalanche. My guess was right. Horlig sprang to his feet, and for an instant was outlined by the moonlight. His eyes were wide and staring. He was a Gloyn warrior in shin boards and breechclout, standing in the middle of his wrecked home and determined to protect his way of life from the alien monsters. He was only four hundred years too late. He fired an instant before I did. Horlig missed. I did not. The last Gloyn disappeared in an incandescent flash.

I was in bad shape by the time I got out to my car and called a medic. The next couple hours seem like someone else's memories. I woke the Ump at 0230. He wasn't disturbed by the hour; Umpires can take anything in stride. I gave him the whole story and my solution. I don't think I was very eloquent, so either the plan was sharp or the Ump was especially good. He accepted the whole plan, even the ruling against Pwrlyg. To be frank, I think it was a solution that he would have come to on his own, given time—but he had come down from the Orbital Base the week before, and had just begun his study of the natives. He told me he'd reach an official decision later in the day and tell me about it.

I flew back to my office, set all the protection devices on auto, and blacked out. I didn't wake until fifteen hours later, when Ghuri Kym—the Ump—called and asked me to come with him to Adelaide.

Just twenty-four hours after my encounter with Horlig, we were standing in Robert Dahlmann's den. I made the introductions. "Umpire Kym can read Australian but he hasn't had any practice with speaking, so he's asked me to interpret. Scholar Dahlmann, you were right about Herul Horlig—but for the wrong reasons." I explained Horlig's true motives. I could see Dahlmann was surprised. "And Chev's punitive expedition to the West Coast has been called off, so you don't have to worry about Rockingham." I paused, then plunged into the more important topic, "I think I've come up with a way to save your species from extinction. Ghuri Kym agrees."

Kym laid the document on Dahlmann's desk and spoke the ritual words. "What's this?" asked Dahlmann, pointing at the Mikin printing.

"The English is on the other side. As the representative of the Australian government, you have just been served with an antitrust ruling. Among other things, it directs your people to split into no fewer than one hundred thousand autonomous organizations. Ngagn Chev is delivering similar documents to the Sudamerican and Zulunder governments. You have one year to effect the change. You may be interested to know that Pwrlyg has also been served and must split into at least four competitive groups."

Pwrlyg had been served with the antitrust ruling that morning. My employers were very unhappy with my plan. Kym told me that the Second Son had threatened to have me shot if I ever showed up on Company property again. I was going to have to lie low for a while, but I knew that Pwrlyg needed all the men they could get. Ultimately, I would be forgiven. I wasn't worried; the risk-taking was worth while if it saved the Terrans from exploitation.

I had expected an enthusiastic endorsement from Dahlmann, but he took the plan glumly. Kym and I spent the next hour explaining the details of the ruling to him. I felt distinctly deflated when we left. From the Terran's reaction you'd think I had ordered the execution of his race.

Mary was sitting on the porch swing. As we left the house, I asked Kym to return to the base without me. If her father hadn't been appreciative, I thought that at least Mary would be. She was, after all, the one who had given me the problem. In a way I had done it all for her.

I sat down on the swing beside her.

"Your arm! What happened?" She passed her hand gently over the plastic web dressing. I told her about Horlig. It was just like the end of a melodrama. There was admiration in her eyes, and her arms were around me—boy gets girl, et cetera.

"And," I continued, "I found a way to save all of you from the fate of the Cherokee."

"That's wonderful, Ron. I knew you would." She kissed me.

"The fatal flaw in the Cherokee's plan was that they segregated themselves from the white community, while they occupied lands that the whites wanted. If they had been citizens of the United States of America, it would not have been legal to confiscate their lands and kill them. Of course we Mikins don't even have a word for 'citizen,' but Umpire law extends to all humans. I got the Umpire to declare that Terrans are a human species. I know it sounds obvious, but it just never occurred to us before.

"Genocide is now specifically barred, because it would be monopolistic. An antitrust ruling has already been served on Australia and the other Earth governments."

Mary's enthusiasm seemed to evaporate somewhat. "Then our governments will be abolished?"

"Why, yes, Mary."

"And in a few decades, we will be the same as you with all your . . . perversions and violence and death?"

"Don't say it that way, Mary. You'll have Mikin cultures, with some Terran enclaves. Nothing could have stopped this. But at least you won't be killed. I've saved—"

For an instant I thought I'd been shot in the face. My mind did three lazy loops, before I realized that Mary had just delivered a roundhouse slap. "You green-faced thing," she hissed. "You've saved us nothing. Look at this street. Look! It's quiet. No one's killing anyone. Most people are tolerably happy. This suburb is not old, but its way of life is—almost five hundred years old. We've tried very hard in that time to make it better, and we've succeeded in many ways. Now, just as we're on the verge of discovering how all people can live in peace, you monsters breeze in. You'll rip up our cities. 'They are too big,' you say. You'll destroy our police forces. 'Monopolistic enterprise,' you call them. And in a few years we'll have a planet-wide Clowntown. We'll have to treat each other as animals in order to survive on these oh-so-generous terms you offer us!" She paused, out of breath, but not out of anger.

And for the first time I saw the real fear she had tried to express from the first. She was afraid of dying—of her race dying; everybody had those fears. But what was just as important to her was her home, her family, her friends. The shopping center, the games, the theaters, the whole concept of courtesy. My people weren't going to kill her body, that was true, but we were destroying all the things that give meaning to life. I hadn't found a solution—I'd just invented murder without bloodshed. Somehow I had to make it right.

I tried to reach my arm around her. "I love you, Mary." The words came out garbled, incomprehensible. "I love you, Mary," more clearly this time.

I don't think she ever heard. She pushed away hysterically. "Horlig was the one who was right. Not you. It is better to fight and die than—" she didn't finish. She hit frantically and inexpertly at my face and chest. She'd never had any training, but those were hard, determined blows and they were doing damage. I knew I couldn't stop her, short of injuring her. I stood up under the rain of blows and made for the steps. She followed, fighting, crying.

I stumbled off the steps. She stayed on the porch, crying in a low gurgle. I limped past the street lamp and into the darkness.

Editor's Introduction To:

THE SKILLS OF XANADU
Theodore Sturgeon

Republics and empires are natural enemies. The late
Herman Kahn once said that the natural state of mankind
is to be governed by an empire, and the natural course of
empire is to grow until it either fills the earth, or is
contained by another empire.

That doesn't always work. In the eternal clash between
republic and empire, the republics don't always win. But
often they do—particularly if the republic is young and
vigorous.

Indeed, young and vigorous republics seldom miss an
opportunity to tweak the nose of empire. As an example,
after the revolution of 1848 was violently suppressed in
Austria-Hungary by Russian intervention, a United States
Navy warship rescued Kossuth, one of the leaders of the
revolution, and transported him in triumph to New York.
When the Austro-Hungarian government protested, Dan-
iel Webster, then Secretary of State, made an eloquent
speech of defiance. "We are," he said, "a nation that spans
a continent, and compared to the United States, the do-
mains of the Habsburgs are but a patch upon the Earth."
Of course there was no possible way that the Austro-

Hungarian Empire could send an army of whitecoats to these shores. The Austrian navy was neither large nor strong nor particularly adapted to blue-water cruises, but it was still much larger than the U.S. Navy. On the other hand, Webster knew he could rely on the British and the Monroe Doctrine to correct our unfortunate lack of battleships.

In later years the American republic grew more vigorous, until by 1917 the United States held the balance of power in the world, and by 1945 was able to field more military power than any empire of history. Both those cases are instructive: before either of the World Wars began, the United States was not really taken seriously as a Great Power. We had the industrial capacity, to be sure. But we had little force in being, and our political authorities were unwilling or unable to do much about that. It was only after we had been drawn into the wars that we mobilized.

It is characteristic of democracies that they seldom have sustained policies, and almost never are willing to make sacrifices *now* to avoid greater sacrifices—even wars—later. How can they? The elected officials are never sure that spending money *now* will prevent the greater harm later, but they are very sure that those expenses won't be popular, and will probably get them defeated in the next election. Better to wait until everyone can see the threat.

Republics, mixed governments, can do better and often have. It was after all the intent of the Constitution that the states take care of most details of government, leaving the federal authority to concern itself with defense and diplomacy. And since the Congress wouldn't have a lot more to think about, nor much else to spend federal revenue on, the national government might do a creditable job of providing for the common defense. There were also those oceans between us and any possible enemy.

Unfortunately, in this era, Congress seems to have a great deal more to think about than defense, and the oceans seem to have shrunk considerably.

Empires can mobilize their resources in time of war or

peace. Empires can design plans that will require decades
to accomplish. Empires are nearly always better armed
than republics, at least when hostilities begin. It would
seem that empires have the advantage.

So they do. But empires always forget what free people
can accomplish.

Ted Sturgeon has said that the theme of this story is
simple enough: your freedom is worthless unless you use
it to free someone else, and the best way to do that is "to
infect locked-up minds with the idea of freedom."

THE SKILLS OF XANADU
Theodore Sturgeon

*And the Sun went nova and humanity fragmented and
fled; and such is the self-knowledge of humankind that it
knew it must guard its past as it guarded its being, or it
would cease to be human; and such was its pride in itself
that it made of its traditions a ritual and a standard.*

*The great dream was that wherever humanity settled,
fragment by fragment by fragment, however it lived, it
would continue rather than begin again, so that all through
the universe and the years, humans would be humans,
speaking as humans, thinking as humans, aspiring and
progressing as humans; and whenever human met human,
no matter how different, how distant, he would come in
peace, meet his own kind, speak his own tongue.*

Humans, however, being humans—

Bril emerged near the pink star, disliking its light, and
found the fourth planet. It hung waiting for him like an
exotic fruit. (And was it ripe, and could he ripen it? And
what if it were poison?) He left his machine in orbit and
descended in a bubble. A young savage watched him come
and waited by a waterfall.

"Earth was my mother," said Bril from the bubble. It

was the formal greeting of all humankind, spoken in the Old Tongue.

"And my father," said the savage, in an atrocious accent.

Watchfully, Bril emerged from the bubble, but stood very close by it. He completed his part of the ritual. "I respect the disparity of our wants, as individuals, and greet you."

"I respect the identity of our needs, as humans, and greet you. I am Wonyne," said the youth, "son of Tanyne, of the Senate, and Nina. This place is Xanadu, the district, on Xanadu, the fourth planet."

"I am Bril of Kit Carson, second planet of the Sumner System, and a member of the Sole Authority," said the newcomer, adding, "and I come in peace."

He waited then, to see if the savage would discard any weapons he might have, according to historic protocol. Wonyne did not; he apparently had none. He wore only a cobwebby tunic and a broad belt made of flat, black, brilliantly polished stones and could hardly have concealed so much as a dart. Bril waited yet another moment, watching the untroubled face of the savage, to see if Wonyne suspected anything of the arsenal hidden in the sleek black uniform, the gleaming jack-boots, the metal gauntlets.

Wonyne said only, "Then, in peace, welcome." He smiled. "Come with me to Tanyne's house and mine, and be refreshed."

"You say Tanyne, your father, is a Senator? Is he active now? Could he help me to reach your center of government?"

The youth paused, his lips moving slightly, as if he were translating the dead language into another tongue. Then, "Yes. Oh, yes."

Bril flicked his left gauntlet with his right fingertips and the bubble sprang away and up, where at length it would join the ship until it was needed. Wonyne was not amazed—probably, thought Bril, because it was beyond his understanding.

Bril followed the youth up a winding path past a wonderland of flowering plants, most of them purple, some white, a few scarlet, and all jeweled by the waterfall. The higher reaches of the path were flanked by thick soft grass, red as they approached, pale pink as they passed.

Bril's narrow black eyes flicked everywhere, saw and recorded everything: the easy-breathing boy's spring up the slope ahead, and the constant shifts of color in his gossamer garment as the wind touched it; the high trees, some of which might conceal a man or a weapon; the rock outcroppings and what oxides they told of; the birds he could see and the birdsongs he heard which might be something else.

He was a man who missed only the obvious, and there is so little that is obvious.

Yet he was not prepared for the house; he and the boy were halfway across the parklike land which surrounded it before he recognized it as such.

It seemed to have no margins. It was here high and there only a place between flower beds; yonder a room became a terrace, and elsewhere a lawn was a carpet because there was a roof over it. The house was divided into areas rather than rooms, by open grilles and by arrangements of color. Nowhere was there a wall. There was nothing to hide behind and nothing that could be locked. All the land, all the sky, looked into and through the house, and the house was one great window on the world.

Seeing it, Bril felt a slight shift in his opinion of the natives. His feeling was still one of contempt, but now he added suspicion. A cardinal dictum on humans as he knew them was: *Every man has something to hide*. Seeing a mode of living like this did not make him change his dictum: he simply increased his watchfulness, asking: *How do they hide it?*

"Tan! Tan!" the boy was shouting. "I've brought a friend!"

A man and a woman strolled toward them from a garden. The man was huge, but otherwise so like the youth Wonyne that there could be no question of their relationship. Both had long, narrow, clear gray eyes set very wide apart, and red—almost orange—hair. The noses were strong and delicate at the same time, their mouths thin-lipped but wide and good-natured.

But the woman—

It was a long time before Bril could let himself look, let himself believe that there was such a woman. After his first glance, he made of her only a presence and fed himself small nibbles of belief in his eyes, in the fact that there could be hair like that, face, voice, body. She was dressed, like her husband and the boy, in the smoky kaleidoscope which resolved itself, when the wind permitted, into a black-belted tunic.

"He is Bril of Kit Carson in the Sumner System," babbled the boy, "and he's a member of the Sole Authority and it's the second planet and he knew the greeting and got it right. So did I," he added, laughing. "This is Tanyne, of the Senate, and my mother Nina."

"You are welcome, Bril of Kit Carson," she said to him; and unbelieving in this way that had come upon him, he took away his gaze and inclined his head.

"You must come in," said Tanyne cordially, and led the way through an arbor which was not the separate arch it appeared to be, but an entrance.

The room was wide, wider at one end than the other, though it was hard to determine by how much. The floor was uneven, graded upward toward one corner, where it was a mossy bank. Scattered here and there were what the eye said were white and striated gray boulders; the hand would say they were flesh. Except for a few shelf- and tablelike niches on these and in the bank, they were the only furniture.

Water ran frothing and gurgling through the room, apparently as an open brook; but Bril saw Nina's bare foot tread on the invisible covering that followed it down to the pool at the other end. The pool was the one he had seen from outside, indeterminately in and out of the house. A large tree grew by the pool and leaned its heavy branches toward the bank, and evidently its wide-flung limbs were webbed and tented between by the same invisible substance which covered the brook, for they formed the only cover overhead yet, to the ear, *felt* like a ceiling.

The whole effect was, to Bril, intensely depressing, and

he surprised himself with a flash of homesickness for the tall steel cities of his home planet.

Nina smiled and left them. Bril followed his host's example and sank down on the ground, or floor, where it became a bank, or wall. Inwardly, Bril rebelled at the lack of decisiveness, of discipline, of clear-cut limitation inherent in such haphazard design as this. But he was well trained and quite prepared, at first, to keep his feelings to himself among barbarians.

"Nina will join us in a moment," said Tanyne.

Bril, who had been watching the woman's swift movements across the courtyard through the transparent wall opposite, controlled a start. "I am unused to your ways and wondered what she was doing," he said.

"She is preparing a meal for you," explained Tanyne.

"Herself?"

Tanyne and his son gazed wonderingly. "Does that seem unusual to you?"

"I understood the lady was wife to a Senator," said Bril. It seemed adequate as an explanation, but only to him. He looked from the boy's face to the man's. "Perhaps I understand something different when I use the term 'Senator.'"

"Perhaps you do. Would you tell us what a Senator is on the planet Kit Carson?"

"He is a member of the Senate, subservient to the Sole Authority, and in turn leader of a free Nation."

"And his wife?"

"His wife shares his privileges. She might serve a member of the Sole Authority, but hardly anyone else—certainly not an unidentified stranger."

"Interesting," said Tanyne, while the boy murmured the astonishment he had not expressed at Bril's bubble, or Bril himself. "Tell me, have you not identified yourself, then?"

"He did, by the waterfall," the youth insisted.

"I gave you no proof," said Bril stiffly. He watched father and son exchange a glance. "Credentials, written authority." He touched the flat pouch hung on his power belt.

Wonyne asked ingenuously, "Do the credentials say you are *not* Bril of Kit Carson in the Sumner System?"

Bril frowned at him and Tanyne said gently, "Wonyne, take care." To Bril, he said, "Surely there are many differences between us, as there always are between different worlds. But I am certain of this one similarity: the young at times run straight where wisdom has built a winding path."

Bril sat silently and thought this out. It was probably some sort of apology, he decided, and gave a single sharp nod. Youth, he thought, was an attenuated defect here. A boy Wonyne's age would be a soldier on Carson, ready for a soldier's work, and no one would be apologizing for him. Nor would he be making blunders. *None!*

He said, "These credentials are for your officials when I meet with them. By the way, when can that be?"

Tanyne shrugged his wide shoulders. "Whenever you like."

"The sooner the better."

"Very well."

"Is it far?"

Tanyne seemed perplexed. "Is what far?"

"Your capital, or wherever it is your Senate meets."

"Oh, I see. It doesn't meet, in the sense you mean. It is always in session, though, as they used to say. We—"

He compressed his lips and made a liquid, bisyllabic sound. Then he laughed. "I do beg your pardon," he said warmly. "The Old Tongue lacks certain words for certain concepts. What is your word for—er—the-presence-of-all-in-the-presence-of-one?"

"I think," said Bril carefully, "that we had better go back to the subject at hand. Are you saying that your Senate does not meet in some official place, at some appointed time?"

"I—" Tan hesitated, then nodded. "Yes, that is true as far as it—"

"And there is no possibility of my addressing your Senate in person?"

"I didn't say that." Tan tried twice to express the thought, while Bril's eyes slowly narrowed. Tan suddenly burst into laughter. "Using the Old Tongue to tell old tales and to speak with a friend are two different things," he said ruefully. "I wish you would learn our speech. Would you, do you suppose? It is rational and well based on what you know. Surely you have another language besides the Old Tongue on Kit Carson?"

"I honor the Old Tongue," said Bril stiffly, dodging the question. Speaking very slowly, as if to a retarded child, he said, "I should like to know when I may be taken to those in authority here, in order to discuss certain planetary and interplanetary matters with them."

"Discuss them with me."

"You are a Senator," Bril said, in a tone which meant clearly: *You are only a Senator*.

"True," said Tanyne.

With forceful patience, Bril asked, "And what is a Senator here?"

"A contact point between the people of his district and the people everywhere. One who knows the special problems of a small section of the planet and can relate them to planetary policy."

"And whom does the Senate serve?"

"The people," said Tanyne, as if he had been asked to repeat himself.

"Yes, yes, of course. And who, then, serves the Senate."

"The Senators."

Bril closed his eyes and barely controlled the salty syllable which welled up inside him. "Who," he inquired steadily, "is your Government?"

The boy had been watching them eagerly, alternately, like a devotee at some favorite fast ball game. Now he asked, "What's a Government?"

Nina's interruption at that point was most welcome to Bril. She came across the terrace from the covered area where she had been doing mysterious things at a long work-surface in the garden. She carried an enormous tray—guided it, rather, as Bril saw when she came closer. She kept three fingers under the tray and one behind it, barely touching it with her palm. Either the transparent wall of the room disappeared as she approached, or she passed through a section where there was none.

"I do hope you find something to your taste among these," she said cheerfully, as she brought the tray down to a hummock near Bril. "This is the flesh of birds, this of small mammals, and, over here, fish. These cakes are made of four kinds of grain, and the white cakes here of just one, the one we call milk-wheat. Here is water, and these two are wines, and this one is a distilled spirit we call warm-ears."

Bril, keeping his eyes on the food, and trying to keep his universe from filling up with the sweet fresh scent of her as she bent over him, so near, said, "This is welcome."

She crossed to her husband and sank down at his feet, leaning back against his legs. He twisted her heavy hair gently in his fingers and she flashed a small smile up at him. Bril looked from the food, colorful as a corsage, here steaming, there gathering frost from the air, to the three smiling, expectant faces and did not know what to do.

"Yes, this is welcome," he said again, and still they sat there, watching him. He picked up the white cake and rose, looked out and around, into the house, through it and beyond. Where could one go in such a place?

Steam from the tray touched his nostrils and saliva filled his mouth. He was hungry, but. . . .

He sighed, sat down, gently replaced the cake. He tried to smile and could not.

"Does none of it please you?" asked Nina, concerned.

"I can't eat here!" said Bril; then, sensing something in the natives that had not been there before, he added, "thank you." Again he looked at their controlled faces. He said to Nina, "It is very well prepared and good to look on."

"Then eat," she invited, smiling again.

This did something that their house, their garments,

their appallingly easy ways—sprawling all over the place, letting their young speak up at will, the shameless admission that they had a patois of their own—that none of these things had been able to do. Without losing his implacable dignity by any slightest change of expression, he yet found himself blushing. Then he scowled and let the childish display turn to a flush of anger. He would be glad, he thought furiously, when he had the heart of this culture in the palm of his hand, to squeeze when he willed; then there would be an end to these hypocritical amenities and they would learn who could be humiliated.

But these three faces, the boy's so open and unconscious of wrong, Tanyne's so strong and anxious for him, Nina's—that face, that face of Nina's—they were all utterly guileless. He must not let them know of his embarrassment. If they had planned it, he must not let them suspect his vulnerability.

With an immense effort of will, he kept his voice low; still, it was harsh. "I think," he said slowly, "that we on Kit Carson regard the matter of privacy perhaps a little more highly than you do."

They exchanged an astonished look, and then comprehension dawned visibly on Tanyne's ruddy face. "You don't eat together!"

Bril did not shudder, but it was in his word: "No."

"Oh," said Nina, "I'm *so* sorry!"

Bril thought it wise not to discover exactly what she was sorry about. He said, "No matter. Customs differ. I shall eat when I am alone."

"Now that we understand," said Tanyne, "go ahead. Eat."

But they *sat* there!

"Oh," said Nina, "I wish you spoke our other language; it would be so easy to explain!" She leaned forward to him, put out her arms, as if she could draw meaning itself from the air and cast it over him. "Please try to understand, Bril. You are very mistaken about one thing—we honor privacy above almost anything else."

"We don't mean the same thing when we say it," said Bril.

"It means aloneness with oneself, doesn't it? It means to do things, think or make or just *be*, without intrusion."

"So?" replied Wonyne happily, throwing out both hands in a gesture that said *quod erat demonstrandum*. "Go on then—eat! We won't look!" and helped the situation not at all.

"Wonyne's right," chuckled the father, "but, as usual, a little too direct. He means we can't look, Bril. If you want privacy, *we can't see you*."

Angry, reckless, Bril suddenly reached to the tray. He snatched up a goblet, the one she had indicated as water, thumbed a capsule out of his belt, popped it into his mouth, drank and swallowed. He banged the goblet back on the tray and shouted, "Now you've seen all you're going to see."

With an indescribable expression, Nina drifted upward to her feet, bent like a dancer and touched the tray. It lifted and she guided it away across the courtyard.

"All right," said Wonyne. It was precisely as if someone had spoken and he had acknowledged. He lounged out, following his mother.

What *had* been on her face?

Something she could not contain; something rising to that smooth surface, about to reveal outlines, break through . . . anger? Bril hoped so. Insult? He could, he supposed, understand that. But—laughter? *Don't make it laughter*, something within him pleaded.

"Bril," said Tanyne.

For the second time, he was so lost in contemplation of the woman that Tanyne's voice made him start.

"What is it?"

"If you will tell me what arrangements you would like for eating, I'll see to it that you get them."

"You wouldn't know how," said Bril bluntly. He threw his sharp, cold gaze across the room and back. "You people don't build walls you can't see through, doors you can close."

"Why, no, we don't." As always, the giant left the insult and took only the words.

I bet you don't, Bril said silently, *not even for*—and a horrible suspicion began to grow with him. "'We of Kit Carson feel that all human history and development are away from the animal, toward something higher. We are, of course, chained to the animal state, but we do what we can to eliminate every animal act as a public spectacle." Sternly, he waved a shining gauntlet at the great open house. "You have apparently not reached such an idealization. I have seen how you eat; doubtless you perform your other functions so openly."

"Oh, yes," said Tanyne. "But with this—" he pointed "—it's hardly the same thing."

"With what?"

Tanyne again indicated one of the boulderlike objects. He tore off a clump of moss—it was real moss—and tossed it to the soft surface of one of the boulders. He reached down and touched one of the gray streaks. The moss sank into the surface the way a pebble will in quicksand, but much faster.

"It will not accept living animal matter above a certain level of complexity," he explained, "but it instantly absorbs every molecule of anything else, not only on the surface but for a distance above."

"And that's a—a—where you—"

Tan nodded and said that that was exactly what it was.

"But—anyone can see you!"

Tan shrugged and smiled. "How? That's what I meant when I said it's hardly the same thing. Of eating, we make a social occasion. But this—" he threw another clump of moss and watched it vanish "—just isn't observed." His sudden laugh rang out and again he said, "I wish you'd learn the language. Such a thing is so easy to express."

But Bril was concentrating on something else. "I appreciate your hospitality," he said, using the phrase stiltedly, "but I'd like to be moving on." He eyed the boulder distastefully. "And very soon."

"As you wish. You have a message for Xanadu. Deliver it, then."

"To your Government."

"To our Government. I told you before, Bril—when you're ready, proceed."

"I cannot believe that you represent this planet!"

"Neither can I," said Tanyne pleasantly. "I don't. Through me, you can speak to forty-one others, all Senators."

"Is there no other way?"

Tanyne smiled. "Forty-one other ways. Speak to any of the others. It amounts to the same thing."

"And no higher government body?"

Tanyne reached out a long arm and plucked a goblet from a niche in the moss bank. It was chased crystal with a luminous metallic rim.

"Finding the highest point of the government of Xanadu is like finding the highest point on this," he said. He ran a finger around the inside of the rim and the goblet chimed beautifully.

"Pretty unstable," growled Bril.

Tanyne made it sing again and replaced it; whether that was an answer or not, Bril could not know.

He snorted, "No wonder the boy didn't know what Government was."

"We don't use the term," said Tanyne. "We don't need it. There are few things here that a citizen can't handle for himself; I wish I could show you how few. If you'll live with us a while, I will show you."

He caught Bril's eye squarely as it returned from another disgusted and apprehensive trip to the boulder, and laughed outright. But the kindness in his voice as he went on quenched Bril's upsurge of indignant fury, and a little question curled up: *Is he managing me?* But there wasn't time to look at it.

"Can your business wait until you know us, Bril? I tell you now, there is no centralized Government here, almost no government at all; we of the Senate are advisory. I tell you, too, that to speak to one Senator is to speak to all, and that you may do it now, this minute, or a year from now—whenever you like. I am telling you the truth and you may accept it or you may spend months, years, traveling this planet and checking up on me; you'll always come out with the same answer."

Noncommittally, Bril said, "How do I know that what I tell you is accurately relayed to the others?"

"It isn't relayed," said Tan frankly. "We hear it simultaneously."

"Some sort of radio?"

Tan hesitated, then nodded. "Some sort of radio."

"I won't learn your language," Bril said abruptly. "I can't live as you do. If you can accept those conditions, I will stay a short while."

"Accept? We *insist!*" Tanyne bounded cheerfully to the niche where the goblet stood and held his palm up. A large, opaque sheet of a shining white material rolled down and stopped. "Draw with your fingers," he said.

"Draw? Draw what?"

"A place of your own. How you would like to live, eat, sleep, everything."

"I require very little. None of us on Kit Carson do."

He pointed the finger of his gauntlet like a weapon, made a couple of dabs in the corner of the screen to test the line, and then dashed off a very creditable parallelepiped. "Taking my height as one unit, I'd want this one-and-a-half long, one-and-a-quarter high. Slit vents at eye level, one at each end, two on each side, screened against insects—"

"We have no preying insects," said Tanyne.

"Screened anyway, and with as near an unbreakable mesh as you have. Here a hook suitable for hanging a garment. Here a bed, flat, hard, with firm padding as thick as my hand, one-and-one-eighth units long, one-third wide. All sides under the bed enclosed and equipped as a locker, impregnable, and to which only I have the key or combination. Here a shelf one-third by one-quarter units, one-half unit off the floor, suitable for eating from a seated posture.

"One of—those, if it's self-contained and reliable," he

said edgily, casting a thumb at the boulderlike convenience. "The whole structure to be separate from all others on high ground and overhung by nothing—no trees, no cliffs, with approaches clear and visible from all sides; as strong as speed permits; and equipped with a light I can turn off and a door that only I can unlock."

"Very well," said Tanyne easily. "Temperature?"

"The same as this spot now."

"Anything else? Music? Pictures? We have some fine moving—"

Bril, from the top of his dignity, snorted his most eloquent snort. "Water, if you can manage it. As to those other things, this is a dwelling, not a pleasure palace."

"I hope you will be comfortable in this—in it," said Tanyne, with barely a trace of sarcasm.

"It is precisely what I am used to," Bril answered loftily.

"Come, then."

"What?"

The big man waved him on and passed through the arbor. Bril, blinking in the late pink sunlight, followed him.

On the gentle slope above the house, halfway between it and the mountaintop beyond, was a meadow of the red grass Bril had noticed on his way from the waterfall. In the center of this meadow was a crowd of people, bustling like moths around a light, their flimsy, colorful clothes flashing and gleaming in a thousand shades. And in the middle of the crowd lay a coffin-shaped object.

Bril could not believe his eyes, then stubbornly would not, and at last, as they came near, yielded and admitted it to himself: this was the structure he had just sketched.

He walked more and more slowly as the wonder of it grew on him. He watched the people—children, even—swarming around and over the little building, sealing the edge between roof and wall with a humming device, laying screen on the slit-vents. A little girl, barely a toddler, came up to him fearlessly and in lisping Old Tongue asked for his hand, which she clapped to a tablet she carried.

"To make your keys," explained Tanyne, watching the child scurry off to a man waiting at the door.

He took the tablet and disappeared inside, and they could see him kneel by the bed. A young boy overtook them and ran past, carrying a sheet of the same material the roof and walls were made of. It seemed light, but its slightly rough, pale-tan surface gave an impression of great toughness. As they drew up at the door, they saw the boy take the material and set it in position between the end of the bed and the doorway. He aligned it carefully, pressing it against the wall, and struck it once with the heel of his hand, and there was Bril's required table, level, rigid, and that without braces and supports.

"You seemed to like the looks of some of this, anyway." It was Nina, with her tray. She floated it to the new table, waved cheerfully and left.

"With you in a moment," Tan called, adding three singing syllables in the Xanadu tongue which were, Bril concluded, an endearment of some kind; they certainly sounded like it. Tan turned back to him, smiling.

"Well, Bril, how is it?"

Bril could only ask, "Who gave the orders?"

"You did," said Tan, and there didn't seem to be any answer to that.

Already, through the open door, he could see the crowd drifting away, laughing, and singing their sweet language to each other. He saw a young man scoop up scarlet flowers from the pink sward and hand them to a smiling girl, and unaccountably the scene annoyed him. He turned away abruptly and went about the walls, thumping them and peering through the vents. Tanyne knelt by the bed, his big shoulders bulging as he tugged at the locker. It might as well have been solid rock.

"Put your hand there," he said, pointing, and Bril clapped his gauntlet to the plate he indicated.

Sliding panels parted. Bril got down and peered inside. It had its own light, and he could see the buff-colored wall of the structure at the back and the heavy filleted partition which formed the bed uprights. He touched the panel again and the doors slid silently shut, so tight that he could barely see their meeting.

"The door's the same," said Tanyne. "No one but you can open it. Here's water. You didn't say where to put it. If this is inconvenient . . ."

When Bril put his hand near the spigot, water flowed into a catch basin beneath. "No, that is satisfactory. They work like specialists."

"They are," said Tanyne.

"Then they have built such a strange structure before?"

"Never."

Bril looked at him sharply. This ingenuous barbarian surely could not be making a fool of him by design! No, this must be some slip of semantics, some shift in meaning over the years which separated each of them from the common ancestor. He would not forget it, but he set it aside for future thought.

"Tanyne," he asked suddenly, "how many are you in Xanadu?"

"In the district, three hundred. On the planet, twelve, almost thirteen thousand."

"We are one and a half billion," said Bril. "And what is your largest city?"

"City," said Tanyne, as if searching through the files of his memory. "Oh—city! We have none. There are forty-two districts like this one, some larger, some smaller."

"Your entire planetary population could be housed in one building within one city on Kit Carson. And how many generations have your people been here?"

"Thirty-two, thirty-five, something like that."

"We settled Kit Carson not quite six Earth centuries ago. In point of time, then, it would seem that yours is the older culture. Wouldn't you be interested in how we have been able to accomplish so much more?"

"Fascinated," said Tanyne.

"You have some clever little handicrafts here," Bril mused, "and a quite admirable cooperative ability. You could make a formidable thing of this world, if you wanted to, and if you had the proper guidance."

"Oh, could we really?" Tanyne seemed very pleased.

"I must think," said Bril somberly. "You are not what I—what I had supposed. Perhaps I shall stay a little longer than I had planned. Perhaps while I am learning about your people, you in turn could be learning about mine."

"Delighted," said Tanyne. "Now is there anything else you need?"

"Nothing. You may leave me."

His autocratic tone gained him only one of the big man's pleasant, open-faced smiles. Tanyne waved his hand and left. Bril heard him calling his wife in ringing baritone notes, and her glad answer. He set his mailed hand against the door plate and it slid shut silently.

Now what, he asked himself, *got me to do all that bragging?* Then the astonishment at the people of Xanadu rose up and answered the question for him. *What manner of people are specialists at something they have never done before?*

He got out his stiff, polished, heavy uniform, his gauntlets, his boots. They were all wired together, power supply in the boots, controls and computers in the trousers and belt, sensory mechs in the tunic, projectors and field loci in the gloves.

He hung the clothes on the hook provided and set the alarm field for anything larger than a mouse any closer than thirty meters. He dialed a radiation dome to cover his structure and exclude all spy beams or radiation weapons. Then he swung his left gauntlet on its cable over to the table and went to work on one small corner.

In half an hour, he had found a combination of heat and pressure that would destroy the pale brown board, and he sat down on the edge of the bed, limp with amazement. You could build a spaceship with stuff like this.

Now he had to believe that they had it in stock sizes exactly to his specifications, which would mean warehouses and manufacturing facilities capable of making up those and innumerable other sizes; or he had to believe that they had machinery capable of making what his torches had just destroyed, in job lots, right now.

But they didn't have any industrial plant to speak of, and if they had warehouses, they had them where the Kit Carson robot scouts had been unable to detect them in their orbiting for the last fifty years.

Slowly he lay down to think.

To acquire a planet, you locate the central government. If it is an autocracy, organized tightly up to the peak, so much the better; the peak is small and you kill it or control it and use the organization. If there is no government at all, you recruit the people or you exterminate them. If there is a plant, you run it with overseers and make the natives work it until you can train your own people to it and eliminate the natives. If there are skills, you learn them or you control those who have them. All in the book; a rule for every eventuality, every possibility.

But what if, as the robots reported, there was high technology and no plant? Planetwide cultural stability and almost no communications?

Well, nobody ever heard of such a thing, so when the robots report it, you send an investigator. All he has to find out is how they do it. All he has to do is to parcel up what is to be kept and what eliminated when the time comes for an expeditionary force.

There's always one clean way out, thought Bril, putting his hands behind his head and looking up at the tough ceiling. Item, one Earth-normal planet, rich in natural resources, sparsely populated by innocents. You can always simply exterminate them.

But not before you find out how they communicate, how they cooperate, and how they specialize in skills they never tried before. How they manufacture superior materials out of thin air in no time.

He had a sudden heady vision of Kit Carson equipped as these people were, a billion and a half universal specialists with some heretofore unsuspected method of intercommunication, capable of building cities, fighting wars, with the measureless skill and split-second understanding and obedience with which this little house had been built.

No, these people must not be exterminated. They must be used. Kit Carson had to learn their tricks. If the tricks were—he hoped not!—inherent in Xanadu and beyond the Carson abilities, then what would be the next best thing?

Why, a cadre of the Xanadu, scattered through the cities and armies of Kit Carson, instantly obedient, instantly trainable. Instruct one and you teach them all; each could teach a group of Kit Carson's finest. Production, logistics, strategy, tactics—he saw it all in a flash.

Xanadu might be left almost exactly as is, except for its new export—aides de camp.

Dreams, these are only dreams, he told himself sternly. *Wait until you know more. Watch them make impregnable hardboard and antigrav tea trays . . .*

The thought of the tea tray made his stomach growl. He got up and went to it. The hot food steamed, the cold was still frosty and firm. He picked, he tasted. Then he bit. Then he gobbled.

Nina, that Nina . . .

No, they can't be exterminated, he thought drowsily, not when they can produce such a woman. In all of Kit Carson, there wasn't a cook like that.

He lay down again and dreamed, and dreamed until he fell asleep.

They were completely frank. They showed him everything, and it apparently never occurred to them to ask him why he wanted to know. Asking was strange, because they seemed to lack that special pride of accomplishment one finds in the skilled potter, metalworker, electronician, an attitude of: "Isn't it remarkable that I can do it!" They gave information accurately but impersonally, as if anyone could do it.

And on Xanadu, anyone could.

At first, it seemed to Bril totally disorganized. These attractive people in their indecent garments came and went, mingling play and work and loafing, without apparent plan. But their play would take them through a flower garden just where the weeds were, and they would take the weeds along. There seemed to be a group of girls playing jacks right outside the place where they would suddenly be needed to sort some seeds.

Tanyne tried to explain it: "Say we have a shortage of something—oh, strontium, for example. The shortage itself creates a sort of vacuum. People without anything special to do feel it; they think about strontium. They come, they gather it."

"But I have seen no mines," Bril said puzzledly. "And what about shipping? Suppose the shortage is here and the mines in another district?"

"That never happens anymore. Where there are deposits, of course, there are no shortages. Where there are none, we find other ways, either to use something else, or to produce it without mines."

"Transmute it?"

"Too much trouble. No, we breed a freshwater shellfish with a strontium carbonate shell instead of calcium carbonate. The children gather them for us when we need it."

He saw their clothing industry—part shed, part cave, part forest glen. There was a pool there where the young people swam, and a field where they sunned themselves. Between times, they went into the shadows and worked by a huge vessel where chemicals occasionally boiled, turned bright green, and then precipitated. The black precipitate was raised from the bottom of the vessel on screens, dumped into forms and pressed.

Just how the presses—little more than lids for the forms—operated, the Old Tongue couldn't tell him, but in four or five seconds the precipitate had turned into the black stones used in their belts, formed and polished, with a chemical formula in Old Tongue script cut into the back of the left buckle.

"One of our few superstitions," said Tanyne. "It's the formula for the belts—even a primitive chemistry could make them. We would like to see them copied, duplicated

all over the Universe. They are what we are. Wear one,
Bril. You would be one of us, then."

Bril snorted in embarrassed contempt and went to watch
two children deftly making up the belts, as easily, and
with the same idle pleasure, as they might be making
flower necklaces in a minute or two. As each was assembled, the child would strike it against his own belt. All the
colors there are would appear each time this happened, in
a brief, brilliant, cool flare. Then the belt, now with a
short trim of vague tongued light, was tossed in a bin.

Probably the only time Bril permitted himself open
astonishment on Xanadu was the first time he saw one of
the natives put on this garment. It was a young man, come
dripping from the pool. He snatched up a belt from the
bank and clasped it around his wrist, and immediately the
color and substance flowed up and down, a flickering
changing collar for him, a moving coruscant kilt.

"It's alive, you see," said Tanyne. "Rather, it is not
nonliving."

He put his fingers under the hem of his own kilt and
forced his fingers up and outward. They penetrated the
fabric, which fluttered away, untorn.

"It is not," he said gravely, "altogether material, if you
will forgive an Old Tongue pun. The nearest Old Tongue
term for it is 'aura.' Anyway, it lives, in its way. It maintains itself for—oh, a year or more. Then dip it in lactic
acid and it is refreshed again. And just one of them could
activate a million belts or a billion—how many sticks can a
fire burn?"

"But why wear such a thing?"

Tanyne laughed. "Modesty." He laughed again. "A scholar
of the very old times, on Earth before the Nova, passed on
to me the words of one Rudofsky: 'Modesty is not so
simple a virtue as honesty.' We wear these because they
are warm when we need warmth, and because they conceal some defects some of the time—surely all one can ask
of any human affectation."

"They are certainly not modest," said Bril stiffly.

"They express modesty just to the extent that they make

us more pleasant to look at with than without them. What more public expression of humility could you want than that?"

Bril turned his back on Tanyne and the discussion. He understood Tanyne's words and ways imperfectly to begin with, and this kind of talk left him bewildered, or unreached, or both.

He found out about the hardboard. Hanging from the limb of a tree was a large vat of milky fluid—the paper, Tan explained, of a wasp they had developed, dissolved in one of the nucleic acids which they synthesized from a native weed. Under the vat was a flat metal plate and a set of movable fences. These were arranged in the desired shape and thickness of the finished panel, and then a cock was opened and the fluid ran in and filled the enclosure. Thereupon two small children pushed a roller by hand across the top of the fences. The white lake of fluid turned pale brown and solidified, and that was the hardboard.

Tanyne tried his best to explain to Bril about that roller, but the Old Tongue joined forces with Bril's technical ignorance and made the explanation incomprehensible. The coating of the roller was as simple in design, and as complex in theory, as a transistor, and Bril had to let it go at that, as he did with the selective analysis of the boulderlike "plumbing" and the antigrav food trays (which, he discovered, had to be guided outbound, but which "homed" on the kitchen area when empty).

He had less luck, as the days went by, in discovering the nature of the skills of Xanadu. He had been quite ready to discard his own dream as a fantasy, an impossibility—the strange idea that what any could do, all could do. Tanyne tried to explain; at least, he answered every one of Bril's questions.

These wandering, indolent, joyful people could pick up anyone's work at any stage and carry it to any degree. One would pick up a flute and play a few notes, and others would stroll over, some with instruments and some without, and soon another instrument and another would join in, until there were fifty or sixty and the music was like a passion or a storm, or after-love or sleep when you think back on it.

And sometimes a bystander would step forward and take an instrument from the hands of someone who was tiring, and play on with all the rest, pure and harmonious; and, no, Tan would aver, he didn't think they'd ever played that particular piece of music before, those fifty or sixty people.

It always got down to *feeling*, in Tan's explanations.

"It's a *feeling* you get. The violin, now; I've heard one, we'll say, but never held one. I watch someone play and I understand how the notes are made. Then I take it and do the same, and as I concentrate on making the note, and the note that follows, it comes to me not only how it should sound, but how it should *feel*—to the fingers, the bowing arm, the chin and collarbone. Out of those feelings comes the feeling of how it feels to be making such music.

"Of course, there are limitations," he admitted, "and some might do better than others. If my fingertips are soft, I can't play as long as another might. If a child's hands are too small for the instrument, he'll have to drop an octave or skip a note. But the feeling's there, when we think in that certain way.

"It's the same with anything else we do," he summed up. "If I need something in my house, a machine, a device, I won't use iron where copper is better; it wouldn't *feel* right for me. I don't mean feeling the metal with my hands; I mean thinking about the device and its parts and what it's for. When I think of all the things I could make it of, there's only one set of things that feels right to me."

"So," said Bril then. "And that, plus this—this competition between the districts, to find all elements and raw materials in the neighborhood instead of sending for them— that's why you have no commerce. Yet you say you're standardized—at any rate, you all have the same kind of devices, ways of doing things."

"We all have whatever we want and we make it ourselves, yes," Tan agreed.

In the evenings, Bril would sit in Tanyne's house and listen to the drift and swirl of conversation or the floods of music, and wonder; and then he would guide his tray back to his cubicle and lock the door and eat and brood. He felt at times that he was under an attack with weapons he did not understand, on a field which was strange to him.

He remembered something Tanyne had said once, casually, about men and their devices: "Ever since there were human beings, there has been conflict between Man and his machines. They will run him or he them; it's hard to say which is the less disastrous way. But a culture which is composed primarily of men has to destroy one made mostly of machines, or be destroyed. It was always that way. We lost a culture once on Xanadu. Didn't you ever wonder, Bril, why there are so few of us here? And why almost all of us have red hair?"

Bril had, and had secretly blamed the small population on the shameless lack of privacy, without which no human race seems to be able to whip up enough interest in itself to breed readily.

"We were billions once," said Tan surprisingly. "We were wiped out. Know how many were left? *Three!*"

That was a black night for Bril, when he realized how pitiable were his efforts to learn their secret. For if a race were narrowed to a few, and a mutation took place, and it then increased again, the new strain could be present in all the new generations. He might as well, he thought, try to wrest from them the secret of having red hair. That was the night he concluded that these people would have to go; and it hurt him to think that, and he was angry at himself for thinking so. That, too, was the night of the ridiculous disaster.

He lay on his bed, grinding his teeth in helpless fury. It was past noon and he had been there since he awoke, trapped by his own stupidity, and ridiculous, ridiculous. His greatest single possession—his dignity—was stripped from him by his own carelessness, by a fiendish and un-sportsmanlike gadget that—

His approach alarm hissed and he sprang to his feet in an agony of embarrassment, in spite of the strong opaque walls and the door which only he could open.

It was Tanyne; his friendly greeting bugled out and mingled with birdsong and the wind. "Bril! You there?"

Bril let him come a little closer and then barked through the vent. "I'm not coming out." Tanyne stopped dead, and even Bril himself was surprised by the harsh, squeezed sound of his voice.

"But Nina asked for you. She's going to weave today; she thought you'd like—"

"No," snapped Bril. "Today I leave. Tonight, that is. I've summoned my bubble. It will be here in two hours. After that, when it's dark, I'm going."

"Bril, you can't. Tomorrow I've set up a sintering for you; show you how we plate—"

"No!"

"Have we offended you, Bril? Have I?"

"No." Bril's voice was surly, but at least not a shout.

"What's happened?"

Bril didn't answer.

Tanyne came closer. Bril's eyes disappeared from the slit. He was cowering against the wall, sweating.

Tanyne said, "Something's happened, something's wrong. I . . . feel it. You know how I feel things, my friend, my good friend, Bril."

The very thought made Bril stiffen in terror. Did Tanyne know? Could he?

He might, at that. Bril damned these people and all their devices, their planet and its sun and the fates which had brought him here.

"There is nothing in my world or in my experience you can't tell me about. You know I'll understand," Tanyne pleaded. He came closer. "Are you ill? I have all the skills of the surgeons who have lived since the Three. Let me in."

"No!" It was hardly a word; it was an explosion.

Tanyne fell back a step. "I beg your pardon, Bril. I

won't ask again. But—tell me. Please tell me. I must be able to help you!"

All right, thought Bril, half hysterically, *I'll tell you and you can laugh your fool red head off. It won't matter once we seed your planet with Big Plague.* "I can't come out. I've ruined my clothes."

"Bril! What can that matter? Here, throw them out; we can fix them, no matter what it is."

"No!" He could just see what would happen with these universal talents getting hold of the most compact and deadly armory this side of the Sumner System.

"Then wear mine." Tan put his hands to the belt of his black stones.

"I wouldn't be seen dead in a flimsy thing like that. Do you think I'm an exhibitionist?"

With more heat (it wasn't much) than Bril had ever seen in him, Tanyne said, "You've been a lot more conspicuous in those winding sheets you've been wearing than you ever would be in this."

Bril had never thought of that. He looked longingly at the bright nothing which flowed up and down from the belt, and then at his own black harness, humped up against the wall under its hook. He hadn't been able to bear the thought of putting them back on since the accident happened, and he had not been this long without clothes since he'd been too young to walk.

"What happened to your clothes, anyway?" Tan asked sympathetically.

Laugh, thought Bril, *and I'll kill you right now and you'll never have a chance to see your race die.* "I sat down on the—I've been using it as a chair; there's only room for one seat in here. I must have kicked the switch. I didn't even feel it until I got up. The whole back of my—" Angrily he blurted, "Why doesn't that ever happen to you people?"

"Didn't I tell you?" Tan said, passing the news item by as if it meant nothing. Well, to him it probably was nothing. "The unit only accepts nonliving matter."

"Leave that thing you call clothes in front of the door," Bril grunted after a strained silence. "Perhaps I'll try it."

Tanyne tossed the belt up against the door and strode away, singing softly. His voice was so big that even his soft singing seemed to go on forever.

But eventually Bril had the field to himself, the birdsong and the wind. He went to the door and away, lifted his seatless breeches sadly and folded them out of sight under the other things on the hook. He looked at the door again and actually whimpered once, very quietly. At last he put the gauntlet against the doorplate, and the door, never designed to open a little way, obediently slid wide. He squeaked, reached out, caught up the belt, scampered back and slapped at the plate.

"No one saw," he told himself urgently.

He pulled the belt around him. The buckle parts knew each other like a pair of hands.

The first thing he was aware of was the warmth. Nothing but the belt touched him anywhere and yet there was a warmth on him, soft, safe, like a bird's breast on eggs. A split second later, he gasped.

How could a mind fill so and not feel pressure? How could so much understanding flood into a brain and not break it?

He understood about the roller which treated the hardboard; it was a certain way and no other, and he could feel the rightness of that sole conjecture.

He understood the ions of the mold press that made the belts, and the life analog he wore as a garment. He understood how his finger might write on a screen, and the vacuum of demand he might send out to have this house built so, and so, and exactly so; and how the natives would hurry to fill it.

He remembered without effort Tanyne's description of the *feel* of playing an instrument, making, building, molding, holding, sharing, and how it must be to play in a milling crowd beside a task, moving randomly and only for pleasure, yet taking someone's place at vat or bench, furrow or fishnet, the very second another laid down a tool.

He stood in his own quiet flame, in his little coffin

cubicle, looking at his hands and knowing without question that they would build him a model of a city on Kit Carson if he liked, or a statue of the soul of the Sole Authority.

He knew without question that he had the skills of this people, and that he could call on any of those skills just by concentrating on a task until it came to him how the right way (for him) would *feel*. He knew without surprise that these resources transcended even death; for a man could have a skill and then it was everyman's, and if the man should die, his skill still lived in everyman.

Just by concentrating—that was the key, the key way, the keystone to the nature of this device. A device, that was all—no mutations, nothing "extrasensory" (whatever that meant); only a machine like other machines. You have a skill, and a feeling about it; I have a task. Concentration on my task sets up a demand for your skill; through the living flame you wear, you transmit; through mine, I receive. Then I perform; and what bias I put upon that performance depends on my capabilities. Should I add something to that skill, then mine is the higher, the more complete; the *feeling* of it is better, and it is I who will transmit next time there is a demand.

And he understood the authority that lay in this new aura, and it came to him then how his home planet could be welded into a unit such as the universe had never seen. Xanadu had not done it, because Xanadu had grown randomly with its gift, without the preliminary pounding and shaping and milling of authority and discipline.

But Kit Carson! Carson with all skills and all talents shared among all its people, and overall and commanding, creating that vacuum of need and instant fulfillment, the Sole Authority and the State. It must be so (even though, far down, something in him wondered why the State kept so much understanding away from its people), for with this new depth came a solemn new dedication to his home and all it stood for.

Trembling, he unbuckled the belt and turned back its left buckle. Yes, there it was, the formula for the precipitate. And now he understood the pressing process and he had the flame to strike into new belts and make them live—by the millions, Tanyne had said, the billions.

Tanyne had said . . . why had he never said that the garments of Xanadu were the source of all their wonders and perplexities?

But had Bril ever asked?

Hadn't Tanyne begged him to take a garment so he could be one with Xanadu? The poor earnest idiot, to think he could be swayed away from Carson this way! Well, then, Tanyne and his people would have an offer, too, and it would all be even; soon they could, if they would join the shining armies of a new Kit Carson.

From his hanging black suit, a chime sounded. Bril laughed and gathered up his old harness and all the fire and shock and paralysis asleep in its mighty, compact weapons. He slapped open the door and sprang to the bubble which waited outside, and flung his old uniform in to lie crumpled on the floor, a broken chrysalis. Shining and exultant, he leaped in after it and the bubble sprang away skyward.

Within a week after Bril's return to Kit Carson in the Sumner System, the garment had been duplicated, and duplicated again, and tested.

Within a month, nearly two hundred thousand had been distributed, and eighty factories were producing round the clock.

Within a year, the whole planet, all the millions, were shining and unified as never before, moving together under their Leader's will like the cells of a hand.

And then, in shocking unison, they all flickered and dimmed, every one, so it was time for the lactic acid dip which Bril had learned of. It was done in panic, without test or hesitation; a small taste of this luminous subjection had created a mighty appetite. All was well for a week—

And then, as the designers in Xanadu had planned, all the other segments of the black belts joined the first meager two in full operation.

A billion and a half human souls, who had been given

the techniques of music and the graphic arts, and the theory of technology, now had the others: philosophy and logic and love; sympathy, empathy, forbearance, unity in the idea of their species rather than in their obedience; membership in harmony with all life everywhere.

A people with such feelings and their derived skills cannot be slaves. As the light burst upon them, there was only one concentration possible to each of them—to be free, and the accomplished feeling of being free. As each found it, he was an expert in freedom, and expert succeeded expert, transcended expert, until (in a moment) a billion and a half human souls had no greater skill than the talent of freedom.

So Kit Carson, as a culture, ceased to exist, and something new started there and spread through the stars nearby.

And because Bril knew what a Senator was and wanted to be one, he became one.

In each other's arms, Tanyne and Nina were singing softly, when the goblet in the mossy niche chimed.

"Here comes another one," said Wonyne, crouched at their feet. "I wonder what will make *him* beg, borrow or steal a belt."

"Doesn't matter," said Tanyne, stretching luxuriously, "as long as he gets it. Which one is he, Wo—that noisy mechanism on the other side of the small moon?"

"No," said Wonyne. "That one's still sitting there squalling and thinking we don't know it's there. No, this is the force-field that's been hovering over Fleetwing District for the last two years."

Tanyne laughed. "That'll make conquest number eighteen for us."

"Nineteen," corrected Nina dreamily. "I remember because eighteen was the one that just left and seventeen was that funny little Bril from the Sumner System. Tan, for a time that little man loved me." But that was a small thing and did not matter.

Editor's Introduction To:

INTO THE SUNSET

D. C. Poyer

Politics is often called a game. This implies that conflict is conducted according to unbreakable rules. Let us follow the metaphor. The best games are those of amateur athletics where winner and loser congratulate each other at the close and chatter gaily on their way to the changing-room. Some of us (as is my case) strongly disapprove of money games. While this is not the attitude of the majority, there are few people who would not regard it as deplorable that a man should hazard his family's keep at a card table.

Now imagine a player so foolish and sinful as to wager the liberty of his children, to be slaves if he loses. Should we be astonished to find this madman cheating to win, and upturning the table if he seems to be losing? Such disregard of rule must naturally follow from inordinate stakes. We must therefore conclude that to keep the game of Politics within the rules, the stakes must be kept moderate.

But here is the difficulty: in case of a game, a man is free to play or not; and if he does, he can limit his stake. Not so in Politics. In a card room, a few people are enjoying a game incapable of ruining them or of bringing misery to a third party. There enters a newcomer who raises the stakes. The old players cannot refuse the higher stakes, and if they leave the table, the intruder wins by default. This is Politics. The "old" parties of the Weimar Republic certainly never agreed to stake civil liberties and the lives of the German Jews on a game of dice with Hitler, but that was in fact what they lost. As this instance illustrates, it is not even necessary for the intruder to name the stakes: "You must play with me," he says, "and if you lose, you will find out in my own good time what you have lost."

—Bertrand de Jouvenal, *The Pure Theory of Politics*

Political change is not always progress. The Roman Republic endured until the evil day when a bunch of Roman Senators fell upon Tiberius Gracchus and slaughtered the tribune on the very steps of the Capitol. There followed, inevitably, Marius and Sulla, fury and passion and relentless slaughter, until Octavius brought peace. Yet, as dearly bought as the Imperial peace was, the rule of law was shattered. Octavius was followed by Tiberias, then Caligula.

Sometimes the game of Politics leaves no choice but to stake everything on the outcome.

INTO THE SUNSET
D. C. Poyer

By Speedletter—Government Use Only
   Penalty for Private Use up to $1000
Date: 19 Sept 2013
From: Director, Special Equipment Development Center, American Sector Luna
To: Secretary of Internal Security, New Washington, 20013

Subject: Resignation.

Dear Mr. Secretary: Hail the First Citizen.

I have received your directive of the 15th, ordering the rapid application of SEDC's recently developed TLCH-PSI scan and interaction sensor to the production of a subconscious aura-triggered anti-subversive-personnel device.

Under my direction, SEDC developed this sensor to enable self-guided infantry robots to discriminate quickly between enemy and noncombatants, thus enhancing their effectiveness and reducing attrition of civilians. Given the trend of Party policies in the last few years, I suspect that the primary purpose of employing the circuit as you direct would be the suppression of internal American dissent.

After due consideration, I have concluded that I cannot in good conscience participate in the development of such a device. I therefore tender my resignation herewith, effective immediately.

I realize that this attitude may have the gravest personal consequences. . . .

> Dr. Michael S. Terhune
> Director, SEDC

The overhead boomed hollowly, at regular intervals, as Dr. M.S. Terhune showed the drab-overalled man to a chair opposite his desk.

"A rather noisy office for the director," Derein said quietly, glancing upward, but leaving his large pale hands flat on the arms of the chair.

Michael Terhune paused, half-bent, and looked at his visitor sideways. Terhune was a tall man, too tall for the low overheads of the Center. Too thin, really, for the Moon, where a stockier body shape had more than once saved a man or woman caught out in Shadow. He might have looked like Lincoln, if he had had a beard and a wen.

"It's the exerciser," he said.

"Exerciser?"

"It's important to stay in shape here. Retards calcium loss. The gym is the next level up."

"I see." Derein settled himself and reached for a brief-case. "Please be seated, Doctor Terhune."

Terhune paused for a moment, looking out the port. At the far edge of sight stars gleamed diamond-hard, then were occulted suddenly by the jagged edge of crater. He knew that edge. He had almost died on it once. Night came suddenly on the Moon. And lasted.

Silently, he dropped into his chair and swiveled toward Derein, concentrating on the situation at hand.

The Party Member had come in on the Station-Luna shuttle early that diurn. He sat now shuffling through his briefcase, a sallow, worn-looking man of medium height who looked as if a few hours a week on an exerciser would do him good. He wore, Terhune noted absently, the Party Cross, the Vow of Silence, and decorations (old ones) from the Jamaican War, two Internal Actions, Manhattan and Chicago, and the first two Mexican Interventions. The blue-drab coveralls were the plainest cotton, not new, but clean. There was a small tear near the knee, which looked as if the Party Member had mended it himself.

Terhune knew then that he faced a dangerous opponent.

"Very good," said Derein suddenly. "Your record, I mean. MIT. What was that?"

"Massachusetts Institute of Technology."

"That was a secular university, as I recall?"

"Most colleges were then."

"Of course. We'll skip the rest of this, it looks dull . . . Director of the Special Equipment Development facility for three years now. Commendations for work on dust solidification, battle laser postoptical collimation, and a theoretical paper on the inhibition of certain types of heavy metal chain reactions. Very good. You've come a long way since your . . . hospitalization."

"Thank you, Party Member."

"Of course I won't pretend to know what all those mean."

Terhune looked deep into clear, direct, fanatical eyes.

It could be true. The Party selected for belief, not knowledge. But it could also be a trap.

Michael Terhune had been told all his life he was brilliant. He had also, all his life, suspected those around him. He had learned that most of his fears were imaginary, paranoid, and he had learned to distrust his own distrust.

But in this case suspicion, he thought, was justified. He was walking, not a tightrope, but the edge of a knifesharp ridge, with a drop on either side far more than enough, even under lunar gravity, to kill. He thought for a moment of the Happy dispenser above his head. There was one in every room of the Center, in every room in America. One needed only to reach one's hand up and touch the trigger for a jolt of the psychentropic drug, removing anxiety and doubt—

"I'll be happy to explain them," Terhune said, not moving in his chair.

The Party Member waved his hand in dismissal. The overhead thumped twice, then began to drum rapidly. Both men glanced up, the shorter with a scowl, the taller with the trace of a smile.

That must be Kathryn, he was thinking.

"Not necessary now," Derein said, speaking above the sound of the exerciser. "It's enough to know that you're a valuable scientist, valuable to the Party, to America, and of course to your family."

Terhune nodded slightly, more to himself than to Derein. By his desk clock he saw that it had taken the Party Member less than three minutes to mention his family, back on Earth.

"Do you understand what I mean?"

"I understand perfectly, Party Member."

"Then explain this trash to me!" shouted Derein, thrusting a piece of paper at him. Meant to be threatening, the motion miscarried. In the slight gravity the letter left his hand rapidly, lost its forward momentum in an earth-normal deceleration—but under a fraction that in the vertical plane, it hovered for a long time before gliding at last to the surface of the desk. Terhune picked it up, glanced at it, then looked at Derein. His face darkened.

"This was addressed to the Secretary. Personally! Not to a—not to you, Brother Derein."

"We don't bother the Leader's deputies with trash. And a refusal of a direct order, an order related to internal security work, in days like these—no, the Party settles matters like that on a lower level. On our level, Doctor. Yours and mine."

"You refuse to forward my correspondence?"

"Oh, on the contrary, Doctor." The Party man leaned back, not smiling. "I'm quite willing to forward an insulting letter from a narrow-minded technician to a man concerned with the highest matters of state, responsible only to the First Citizen! I'm quite willing to let you commit professional suicide, go to the front line in the Yucatan as a private, and see your family split up into Party Age-Group camps! I'm willing enough, you see! But first I would like to make sure, quite certain, that you know what you're doing."

"I believe I do."

"You're making a stupid and futile gesture."

"I think otherwise. Stupid, perhaps. Not futile."

"You have a high opinion of yourself. You think your resignation will stop work on the project?"

"Yes."

"Because your discoveries are so subtle. Because no one else can understand them."

Terhune didn't answer. He swiveled and faced the shadowed corner of Mare Serentatis.

"You're wrong about that, Doctor. You are important, yes; your talents are useful to us, and because of them we have overlooked certain personal shortcomings, certain unwise remarks of yours in the past. But—"

"What remarks? I deny any."

"Deny a digital recording."

"You've bugged me?"

"The Leader has said it: 'Not a sparrow shall fall.' And we have personal reports as well."

"I don't believe that."

"You have dangerous delusions, Doctor. You believe yourself persecuted. You're not; we've put up with your irrationalities, we've honored you. You believe yourself irreplaceable. You are valuable, we all admit that. But no one is irreplaceable in America United."

The two men fell silent. From somewhere outside the room Terhune heard a rocket exhaust. The shuttle? No, he reminded himself; it would not rise till the next diurn. And he would hear it as a rumble in the ground, not as a sound through vacuum. It must be Hernandez, working on his charged engine throats. Hernandez! Could it be he who—

He caught himself and stilled his mind. That was exactly what this man wanted: to sow distrust, suspicion. He trusted all of them implicitly. He always would. Hernandez as well as Hong, Levinson, Kathryn Leah Hogue, every one of the two-hundred-person complement of the Center.

"I will not produce such a device," he stated to the darkened surface of the Moon.

"We'll discuss it tomorrow."

"You're leaving tomorrow."

"I have all the time I need," said Derein. "That shuttle is at my command. I may leave tomorrow, true. But if I do, you're coming with me. In handcuffs."

When Terhune turned around, livid with anger, the chair pivoted idly. The office was empty.

"I dunno what she said, when she left me;
"I dunno what she wrote.
"But the stable was empty, her saddle was missin',
"And I couldn't quite make out her note."

The Saddletramp Saloon was dark, the smell of beer and leather, electricity and whiskey and filtered oxygen-enriched air mingling in a strange blend. He stopped just inside the door, letting his eyes adjust to the gloom.

"Mike?"

She was at the far end of the bar, alone, nursing a beer.

He felt his way toward her past the wooden tables. Or almost wood. They looked like oak, as if they had been made by hand and varnished and shipped west and darkened and scarred by time and cigar smoke and spilled whisky and brawling men.

But made, like everything else in the Center, from the soil and rock and dust of the Moon.

"Sorry to keep you waiting."

"Sit down, stranger. Buy a girl a drink?"

Spike came up to them as he hitched himself up on the stool next to her, fixed the heels of his Texas boots in the rungs where they belonged.

"Whiskey," said Terhune to the bartender.

"What'll you have, pard?"

"Whiskey."

"What'll you have, pard?"

"He said, bourbon," said Kathryn. As Spike wheeled away, its casters grating on mooncrete, she said, "He needs tuning. Aural recognition circuits off."

"Ought to shut the damned thing down. Just get your own."

"Oh," she said, turning to her beer. "Is that how it is?"

"I'm sorry. Had a bad time with a boy."

"That Party bozo who oozed off the shuttle today?"

"The same."

"My condolences," said Dr. Kathryn Hogue, slugging back the remains of a full liter mug. From the rings in front of her it was not her first. Terhune studied her from the side as she whistled loud enough at the robot barkeep to wake echoes in the dome.

Kathryn Hogue was the slinger engineer. With four technicians and one outmoded handling robot she had built the first magnetic accelerator tube on the Moon. She was built strong. Under the Levis and plaid Western shirt her hips and shoulders were solid with muscle. He had once seen her pick up a three-hundred-kilo-mass slinger ring and hold it in position for bolting, a feat made even more difficult by a spacesuit. She could take any man in the Center arm-wrestling, and had. Except him. And he half-suspected that she had let him win.

He remembered the first time he had seen her nude.

"No kisses for a working girl?"

"In front of the help?"

"Spike doesn't mind. Do you, Spike?"

"What'll you have, babe?"

"Same again."

"What'll you have, babe?"

"Coors! Switch to receive, you deaf vacuum-sucker!"

Terhune tossed back his bourbon, a slightly but not significantly slower process in lunar gravity than on Earth, and pulled her to him.

They lay nestled like shadow against dust. He traced the outside of her leg, feeling the roughness of a shave a week old. Was she asleep? His hand moved down the outside of her thigh, caressed the hollow of a well-muscled back. He stroked her for a long time.

"Want 'ta tell me about it?" she muttered, her face to the smooth plastron of her cubicle.

He thrust himself up and groped above them. A switch clicked and the unctuous voice of the Leader surrounded them. The Midnight Party Program from Earth. The Station kept the same time as New Washington, though by treaty Standard Lunar Time was Greenwich Mean.

He pulled back his renegade thoughts as her head rose, close, her eyes focusing sleepily. He examined them at a distance of ten centimeters. Green eyes, a brush-touch of hazel, her cheeks slack and crow-tracked below them. He had painted once, during the revolution, when physics was impossible. A watercolor he had done of Enchanted Mesa hung at home next to his print of *The Howl of the Weather*. The hair that lay curled against his shoulder was brown, rich with veins of silver, but still soft and full and deep with her scent. She was not a girl. She was a woman, full-breasted, full-hipped, taking on her forties the way she took on a new welding setup. With determination, guts, and style.

Bug? her lips shaped the word.

"Could be," he whispered. "That's one of the things he said."

"Slimy bastards."

He groped again and the volume increased. "I think that will mask it," he muttered.

She sat up, half against him, and examined his face. He pulled his attention away from the slope of her belly, her thighs. "Okay," she said. "Now that the built-up charge in the circuit's been dissipated, let's talk."

"They returned my resignation."

She tasted the air, waiting.

"They want the thing built. No matter what. They'll degrade me to the Yucatan. Ship up a replacement. But they'll get it built."

She was silent for a moment. "Your family?"

"Splitup and Party camps."

"Slimy bastards," she said again.

"You sound like Spike."

"He's got more heart than they do. Are you going to do it for them?"

"I don't know." His whisper broke. "I've been trying to think of a choice—any other choice. But they have the power to do it. They have before. I'd like to tell him where to go with this mindsearching tyranny. Like to High Noon it, pack him on the shuttle."

"This is the frontier, baby."

He smiled as he saw what she meant. "Yeah. The outpost of civilization. Funny, how different it is. In those days a man meant something, even alone. If he had right on his side he had power to back it. Now there aren't any sixguns."

"Or at least the Party has them all."

His voice hissed in her ear, then resumed. "The only alternative I have—realistically—is suicide."

"Don't say that."

"No. I won't. Not because of Gwen. She's Party now anyway. Because of you. If I didn't have you, Kath, I'd do it. They'd get it built anyway. They need it bad, from the way he talked. There must be more internal unrest down there than we find out about from the broadcasts. I was bluffing him. There are two guys at Bell Labs downside who could do it and maybe a team at Carnegie-Mellon—I mean, Eternal Praise—but it would take time for them to reverse-engineer Hong's work. And at least I wouldn't have it on my conscience. But as long as I'm alive, I've got to do as Derein directs, or we all lose."

He waited for her to say something, his heart loud in his ears. What she said was important. He had decided that: whatever she would say, he would do.

"I guess . . . that's all you can do, then."

He sighed, not knowing, yet, whether he was relieved or destroyed; Lucifer, or Faust. Suddenly he felt very tired, and very old.

"Have you got family, Wide Load? Downside?"

"Funny you never asked me that before."

"You're not a real communicative type, Kath. Besides, I never cared before."

"No. I don't."

"That's good."

"Maybe," she muttered.

It was as if she went away from him, though neither of them moved. Then she came back. "Maybe. The way things are."

"It can't last forever. Dictatorships can't last forever."

"That's what they said about the Bolsheviks, cowboy. And they're coming up on a century."

"No family, they can't use them to pressure you. It's better not to be attached to anyone."

"I wouldn't say that's my status right now."

He looked at her in the dim light. Her eyes were closed. Her mouth had a strange shape. He looked for tears, but there were none.

"Are you crying?"

"Fuck you. No."

"What's wrong?"

"Nothing. Just hold me."

He turned the program off. They moved together. Not

to merge, this time. Just to hold each other. He listened to the seashell hiss of the ventilator bleeding recycled air through the wall of her cubicle, a hiss that became in his mind the rush of wind across dry empty hills softened with sage the color of dusk.

The next day they stood in the half-sphere of Lab D, looking at a spidery workbench. Five of its eight square meters were covered by a seething assemblage of IC cards, wires, infinite-variable power supplies, and the smelly fluid-bathed trays of bioelectronics and life support.

"This whole thing is the sensor?" said Derein.

"No." Terhune sliced the word short with his teeth. He pointed to one of the trays. "This is the heart of it. The rest is just engineering. Power, support, and tuning."

The Party Member bent over the table. "And that?"

"That's a single-throw relay," said Terhune, staring at him. Again he wondered: ignorance, or a trap?

"Tell me how it works."

"How detailed do you want to get?"

"Just tell me."

"The read function is a modified Fisher psitelechiric regeneration circuit. Field densities of down to two times ten to the minus eight nookies—neural interactions, SI—can be read before noise limit of amplification degrades past the ability of the spectrum analyzer to—"

"Maybe a little more basic, Doctor," suggested Derein quietly.

"You try it, Lo, it's your baby anyway," said Terhune to the short man who stood beside them in nothing but khaki cutoffs, scratching his hairless chest. "This is Dr. Hong."

"You know how lie detectors used to work, Party Member?" said Hong.

"They read heartbeat, skin moisture?"

"That's right. The operator had to infer an internal condition—guilt—from external, physiological manifestations. Sometimes it worked. Kind of. But a man who knew how, or who believed that what he had done was right, often read as innocent."

"I get that."

"Good. Back in the mid-eighties they started to access actual neurological information. Electronically. They learned to read premuscular signals. Speech, before it was transmitted to the mouth and larynx muscles. That's how the embedded transceivers work. You have one?"

"Everyone does now."

"Oh. I haven't been downside for a while. Well, this apparatus—the telechiric-psionic scan, or TLCH-PSI—takes that process further in two ways. First, it reads remotely, by means of an artificial PSI field we generate in this section. The resonance of a living brain repeating, or affirming, a broadcast pattern can be detected by means of the very slight increase in signal strength from that direction. I've got it up to three meters, about ten feet old measure, and I may be able to tweak it up further with a critically-tuned antenna. Twenty feet's the theoretical limit before power output marginalizes against return from other people near the focus. Follow?"

"So far, I think."

"Good. Now the interesting part. There's a delay, if you will, in the repetition of the pattern by a brain, or a mind if you will, if it doesn't *agree* with the signal. If it agrees, the echo is almost instantaneous, on the order of a hundredth of a second or less. If the brain disagrees with the signal, if there's mental resistance, the return is almost as strong as it CFIs—cycles for interpretation—but the *delay* increases about fourfold. It's a slight difference, but we've shown it to be readily detectable, reproducible, and most important, the effect is non-conscious—you can't lie to it."

"Praise the Leader!"

"Uh, exactly." Hong pointed with his chin, Chinese-fashion. "The expert system circuitry here—pretty standard programming, will go well into VHSIC—basically just times it, evaluates and corrects for some other variables, such as sickness or low alertness, by querying with a signal that the brain agrees with—I use "I hope there's some speedmail for me today," which seems to go down smooth with everybody at the Center. The output is a binary decision, go or no-go, that pops this relay. After that, what you do with it is up to you."

"Can I see it work?"

Hong looked at Terhune, who nodded briefly. "Okay," he said. "We'll use you. Stand over here."

The Party Member, looking fascinated despite himself, moved a few feet to the right. Looking down, he found himself in the center of a square chalked on the mooncrete base of the dome.

"Now," said Lo Hong, perching himself in front of a rather archaic-looking keyboard, "Let's see. You're a Party Member, right? What's the current Slogan?"

Derein glanced up. "You don't know, Dr. Hong?"

"I forgot," said Hong, straight-faced.

"The foolish man Leads himself to Doom; the wise man Follows us to Paradise."

"Oh yeah," said Hong, typing busily. "Let's see, better change the bumper, 'cause you probably aren't expecting mail here. You like beer?"

"Party Members do not take alcohol," said Derein frostily.

"Oh yeah. Ice cream?"

"Chocolate chip."

"Got it." Hong typed busily for quite a while. "Got to use hexadecimal, haven't smoothed the front end LISP out yet. Okay." He slid off the stool and stared at Derein.

There was a tiny click.

"Any time you're ready," said the Party Member, his eyes closed.

"That's it."

Derein opened his eyes. "What?"

"Hear the relay close?"

"I . . . thought something, too quick to catch . . . then I heard a click."

"That was it. You believe the slogan."

The Party Member looked confused. "Yes. I do. But then what?"

"As I envisioned the use of this device," said Terhune, his voice controlled, "the query would have been in the enemy language, oriented toward the military; for exam-

ple, 'It is my mission to destroy American battle robots.'
This would have enabled the robot to screen out civilians,
even enemy civilians, and attack only enemy soldiers,
even if ununiformed."

"Would it work on enemy battle robots?"

"They are rather easily identified visually," said Hong,
smiling.

"But this is a wonderful device," said Derein. "Let's try
it with something I disagree with."

"No problem," said Hong, typing again. After a moment he slid off the stool. "Try that?"

The relay did not click. "What did you ask me?" said
Derein.

"The test statement was," said Hong, looking blank,
" 'Human beings who oppose the Party have a right to
live.' "

He had gone to her cubicle without calling on the intercom. He found her in the cleaner. She was nude. The
soap spray clung to her body like lace.

"Done soon?"

"Done now," she said. "Rinse!"

When the shower was finished with her she came to
him wet and naked. He sat on the chair by her cot and
stared at the wall.

"No roundup?"

"What?"

"I said, no roundup? The dogies are restless tonight."

He moved to the bunk and held her close to him. She
felt damp and hard and strong, hugging him back so tight
he found it hard to breathe. He closed his eyes.

"Problem?"

"What?"

"You have a problem, cowboy? Tell me about it."

"I can't do this, Kathryn."

He felt her begin to rock him. She said nothing. He
held her as close as he could, feeling tears bite into his
eyelids.

"What's the matter? Tell me. You can trust me."

"I know . . . that's the only thing that keeps me going sometimes. Kathryn, I can't go through with this."

She turned, reached automatically now. The evening Party Program surged into the room. "We discussed it, Mike. There's nothing else you can do."

"You know what this thing we're building will mean? It'll destroy any hope of a counterrevolution. They can use it to guard government buildings, to stop the Resistance walking in with bombs. Then it'll be in the airports, the sidewalks. And you can't trick it or lie to it!"

"You're destroying yourself over this, Mike. We're out of it, here. We're safe."

"That's not enough. I can't let this loose, not in their hands." He bent closer still, whispering into her ear. "I'm going to change the statement."

"The what?"

"The test statement. I don't care what they do to me. Or my family. Or even to us. There are too many others involved. I've got to change it."

"You can't, Mike. They'll find it."

"I can't do anything else."

"Why? Because of your family? Mike. Forget them." He felt her breathing slow, deepen. "You have me. Don't you?"

"I love you."

"That's right."

"I haven't seen my family for years."

"They'll get along. I think children do that. It's selfish of me. But I don't want you to do it, Mike. Please don't."

"We could stay here together."

"That's right."

"Do you love me?"

"More than anything. More than anything. Christ, Michael. I'm sorry for your kids. But sometimes, oh, Jesus, sometimes I think you don't understand how much a woman can love you."

"I love you too. A lot."

But she did not answer him.

*　　*　　*

Fourteen days later Lab D looked the same. The scientists gathered around the table, however, looked worn. Derein had driven them all eighteen hours, twentyurs a diurn. He had received orders to build and test a complete working model.

The finished prototype was considerably smaller than the square meters of ammonia-smelling bioelectronics that had covered the work table. Hong and Terhune had used the Center's Produktor line to design it, and it had discovered several production shortcuts. Dr. Hogue, pressed into service, had found ways to combine several functions within modules, and had miniaturized the power sources. The five of them stood now looking up at the completed device. The size of an old transistor-model television, it hung shabbily braced from the laboratory overhead, pointing down at a shallow angle. The chalked square was now a rectangle four feet by two.

"Here's the concept of operation," said Dr. Hong, resting himself against the bench, which now gave off the rankness of decay; he had let the breadboard go, and, unshielded, it had caught some random germ and started to rot. "Party Member Derein, you wanted something that could screen in real time. This unit can do it, if people don't come through too fast. You could set it up above an escalator, for example."

"That's ideal," said Derein. Of them all, he looked the best rested, though there were circles under his eyes as well. "The Secretary intends to use the initial installations to screen people going into offices in New Washington."

"Government offices?" said Terhune.

"And Party offices."

"A demonstration, Party Member?"

"Just a minute. Tell me again what happens when they fail."

"When the screeners fail?"

"No, no. I have confidence in your team's technical abilities. I mean, what will happen when the people going through fail."

"We incorporated a wiper," said Terhune. He looked dead. Not dead physically. He looked like a man who had lost his soul.

"Wiping? How does that work?"

"Uh. Dr. Levinson worked that out—he's the psychoradiomanipulator."

A heavyset, balding man stood up slowly. "Well, it's not unlike the wipes your courts order sometimes when somebody gets a death sentence. You know how those operate?"

"Just that they come out without a brain."

"Overstatement, Party Member Derein. It's a traumatic overload, a burnout on the subneural level, where memory and learned patterns are matrixed. The brain is operational, but as far as learning and life experience, identity, it's a *tabula rasa*." Derein looked blank. "A clean slate. Essentially they're no longer a human being, but a newborn. Of course, without the newborn's potential, entirely. Learning is considerably more limited the second time around."

"And this would be better than just firing a laser at them when the disloyalty circuit trips?"

"I believe so, Party Member."

"Why?"

"Because it preserves, at some level, a life." They stared at each other. Before Derein could respond, Levinson added heavily, "Or a soul. The Party would see it as another chance to, uh, *save* that soul, once it had been purged of—antisocial habits and thoughts."

"Of the devil, you mean to say."

"I guess that's the terminology, yes." Levinson sighed.

"That's good reasoning. That's defensible. Yet you seem unhappy about it, Dr. Levinson."

"Do I? How penetrating."

"Are you with the Party, Dr. Levinson?"

Levinson straightened. "Have I said something out of order? I didn't mean to."

"Answer me, Doctor."

Levinson looked at him. At last he turned the collar of his coveralls to show the yellow star. "I think this answers your question."

Derein stared at him. After a moment he turned to Terhune. "Let's get on with it."

"Sure. Step right up," said Terhune bitterly.

"Me?"

"I think you'll agree that you're the best choice for a test."

"Perhaps you'll precede me, Doctor."

"I don't think so, Party Member. You see, this prototype is fully operational."

Derein looked around the circle. "Refusal? That's practically an admission of disloyalty."

"So is yours," said Terhune. "Are you refusing the test, Party Member? It will be difficult. You'll have to terminate all of us to prevent your superiors from finding out you did. And if you do, you won't have the device, will you? The design is in the Produktor. But you can't operate it, can you? If it isn't quite right you can't fix it, can you?"

Derein stared at him. He looked at the overhead. "This is disloyal. This is all recorded."

"I jammed it," said Hong modestly. "Very simple."

"And even if you have a traitor on your side," said Terhune, not looking at Hong or Levinson, "he could produce this model—it's all on the tape—but he couldn't tune or improve it. Not without some months of study. And you don't have some months, do you? You've already notified them the shuttle will instation tomorrow."

Derein stared around once more. He was sweating, visibly.

"I know," he said.

"What?"

"I know what you plan to do to the device."

"I have no idea what you mean," said Terhune.

"Let me tell you, then." Derein looked around at them, all of them. He took a small pistol from the pocket of his coveralls.

"You changed the question."

Terhune's head came up. He felt dazed. Then he saw her eyes. They were wide, but steady on his. Green, with a touch of hazel. He felt his legs begin to tremble.

She was the one person he had never suspected.

After a moment Hong said, "That's absurd."

"Is it? You think he's on the Party's side, fully? Then you step forward, Dr. Hong. Take your place on your chalked-in square. Do it."

Hong looked at Terhune, weighing something in his mind. After a moment he said, "I'm afraid to. I think he is, but—I guess I'm just risk-averse."

"Dr. Levinson?"

"I'd rather not," said Levinson.

"Dr. Terhune?"

Terhune looked at the square. He looked at Hogue.

"No," he said.

"So," said Derein, looking around at them. "You won't do it. Not even if I threaten to shoot you. You know, I believe you. I believe you don't trust each other. And I can see you don't trust yourselves. Do you know how that makes me feel? That makes me feel that everything is right, that I have an operating device. But I'd rather be sure. Dr. Terhune. Step up."

"No."

"Move, Terhune. I'm out of forgiveness. You will prove yourself now. Step up, or your usefulness to the Party ends now." He raised the gun and aimed.

Terhune hesitated. He started to step forward.

Hogue pushed him back.

She positioned herself squarely in the center of the chalked outline. "Turn it on," she said.

"Kathryn!"

"Turn it on, Michael." Her green eyes were steady. Green eyes brushed with hazel. Eyes he had once trusted . . .

"It's too risky," he said. "Do you know what it can do to you? It can—"

"Do you think it will hurt me?"

He stared at her with hatred, knowing himself once

more betrayed. They had all betrayed him, Levinson, Hong—and especially her. She had been the only one who knew his plans. The only one who had spoken the truth to him, bitter and unwelcome as it was, had been Derein.

"No," he said bitterly. "No, I guess it won't."

"You believe I betrayed you, Michael?"

"I know you did."

"Then I guess you'd better turn it on."

Now we know where we stand, he thought. The bitterness turned suddenly into rage: rage at a world enslaved in the name of God; at the men around him, for their weakness in aiding it; at her. But most of all it was at himself, for his foolishness and blindness in believing in another human being.

He nodded to Hong.

The screener hummed for a moment, subaudible, the power supplies she had designed warming up, sending a jolt of subawareness through the half-dead bioelectronics that knew nothing of the mercy of living things, that knew only the programming that men had imposed on their once-human DNA.

Her eyes widened.

She stood still, and said nothing.

"Kathryn?"

She did not answer, simply looked upward, at the blank face of the screener.

Terhune stared at her eyes. The pupils had widened, as they did in the dim light of her cubicle. At her shoulders, broad and strong, slack now under her coveralls in the harsh light of the laboratory.

He stared at her open mouth, at the corners of her parted lips. Lips that he had kissed. They were still there, still whole and firm and warm. Still the same. But not hers, never again *hers*—

His hand crept up for a shot of Happy.

He had believed in her guilt, her treason to him. Yet she had not betrayed him. She had given herself, to convince him of that beyond any doubt.

To show him love that destroyed itself even as it proved itself, even as she parted from him forever.

His hand, numb, was on the trigger for the dispenser when it stopped. His eyes moved slowly up his arm to Derein's hand at his wrist.

"A beautiful piece of work," the Party man said quietly. For once, Terhune noted through the numbness, he looked sincere. "And so appropriate. We've suspected her attachment to the Party's goals for some time. But now"—the hand increased its pressure on his wrist—"she's proven that we have an operating device. God's ways are strange but wonderful! Prepare the plans for full-scale production."

"I don't understand," said Terhune. "It triggered on her. It shouldn't have—unless she was—"

"Disloyal? Exactly." Derein smiled. "You scientists are intellectual children. Competent in your fields, but hardly a match for a trained man. I didn't need a traitor, or a bug, to know that you would try to change that combination. I could see it in your eyes. Why didn't you? You became afraid, at the last minute. Don't worry, Doctor. You're useful. I won't take action against you. But you must accept it. You've been outthought, by me, the Party member you scorn as a bureaucrat, a fanatic, a technological illiterate. What about it, Doctor? Is your intellectual arrogance proof against that?"

Without speaking, Terhune turned and walked blindly toward the hatch.

He sat alone in the darkened saloon.

"Lights?" said Spike.

"No lights."

"What'll you have, pard?"

"Whiskey."

"What'll you'll have, pard?"

"Bourbon. The bottle."

The machine functioned flawlessly.

The three of them, Levinson, Hong, and Terhune, sat at the bar.

"How is she?" said Terhune, after a long period of silence.

"The same," said Hong.

"No change," said Levinson.

"It's noon," said Spike. "Time for the news."

Music filled the darkened bar. "Where's the news?" said Hong. "The Party Program?"

"Must be a minute till."

"Spike don't make mistakes."

"Spike makes lots of mistakes."

The bartender stared at them. It was barely possible to read insult into his molded expression.

Levinson was asking for another beer when the music stopped and a frightened voice filled the room. The two men listened, then turned, as one, to look at Terhune.

"What's going on down there?" said Hong.

"Revolution, I would assume," said Terhune. He slugged back the heeltap in his shot glass and rapped it smartly for the bartender's attention.

"It sounds like it," said Levinson. "But why?"

"I changed the test phrase."

"On the prototype? Impossible—it worked, Kathryn triggered it, and it—"

Hong put a warning hand on Levinson's, but Terhune did not seem to notice. He was already speaking. "No. The prototype worked, all right. I changed it on the Produktor tape. Deep in the hardware, set to override whatever phrase they put in the ROM section after fifteen cycles. They must have gone into full-scale deployment on Derein's word, without waiting for thorough testing."

They listened to the voice. It went on, describing the terror of a nation suddenly left leaderless. "They're panicking," said Hong.

"The Party's not there to guide them any more," said Levinson. "Guide—I guess we'll have to get used to saying what we mean. The tyrants are gone. Null-minded imbeciles, at the mercy of the mob."

"As you sow, so shall ye reap," said Terhune. "Say, Lo, did you leave that prototype set up?"

"If nobody else tore it down," said Dr. Hong.

"Spike. One last bourbon, for the road."

"All out of bourbon," said the bartender, dead-pan. "Next shuttle, maybe."

"I don't think we should expect one for a while . . . Sam, you're next senior after me. We'd better start oxygen rationing, and see if the dust cooker out in Wing One still works. The Center may be on its own till they get things sorted out down there."

The two other men exchanged glances. After a moment Levinson said. "I'll take care of it, Mike."

"What'll it be, pard?"

"Beer. Beer. In a mug. Coors beer. A liter."

"One bronco-buster, coming right up."

After Terhune drank it he got up. He paused for a moment, then shook hands wordlessly with them both. When he left Levinson and Hong did not look after him. They stayed for a while, listening to the news two and a half seconds after the rest of America. After a while another announcer came on. She sounded not frightened, but excited. Angry. And triumphant.

When they thought Michael Terhune had had enough time, they went on in to Laboratory D.

Editor's Introduction To:

SHIPWRIGHT
Donald Kingsbury

Any group would break up of which there was none to take good care. And in the same way the body of man, like that of any other animal, would fall to pieces were there not within it a directing force seeking the common good of all its members. . . . As between the members, it is, whether it be the heart or the head, a ruling chief. In every mass of men there must in the same way be a principle of direction.

—St. Thomas Aquinas, *De Regimine Principium*

No one supposes, when he sees a forester pruning a copse to help the trees to grow, or a gardener hunting for snails, tending young plants under glass frames, or exposing them to the health-giving heat of a conservatory, that these things are done from a feeling of affection for the vegetable kingdom. And yet care for it he does, much more so than cold reason would suppose. This affection, however, is not the motivating reason for his pains; it is rather their necessary accompaniment. Reason would ban all affection from these labours of his. But the nature of

346

man is such that his affections are stirred by the pains
he gives himself.

And so it is with Power. Command which is its own
end comes in time to care for the common good. . . .
—Bertrand de Jouvenal, *On Power*

It is the necessary and sufficient condition of a social
order that there be defenders both powerful enough to
preserve it, and dedicated enough that they want to. This
is of course a truism, but it is one often forgotten.

Some social orders are constructed more on *duty* than
right. For whatever reason, the Oriental model has long
been this way. It is rare that an Oriental society co-opts
outsiders into itself, but that has been done as well.

Until recently, Donald Kingsbury was a professor of
mathematics at McGill University. He is also one of the
best creators of strange human societies in the business.
Herewith, Dr. Kingsbury's picture of a possible future in
which mankind has gone to the stars and beyond.

SHIPWRIGHT
Donald Kingsbury

I am an arrogant man, he thought. *It was arrogance that
brought me out to the Frontier and arrogance that has
given me this ironic reward.*

Throughout the Akiran System, from the mines of in-
most Sutemi to the cold wastes of outer Kiromasho, farmers and merchants and craftsmen and lords were celebrating
with fireworks and dancing. Now the Akirani could forge
an empire out here in the Noir Gulf within this thin wisp
of stars that pointed Solward. They had their own shipyard. They had their first home-built starship, the Massaki
Maru, the First One, the Leader.

I gave it to them.

He stood naked, fresh from the hot pool in the rock garden that mimicked the old wilderness, servants toweling him while two of his children still splashed in the water. His woman Koriru waited patiently for the servants to finish. She had picked out for him a robe of softness, one with black stripes dotted by the crest of the Misubisi. She was a Misubisi. He was not.

For a moment he felt a lonely defiance. He would wear his Engineer's uniform to the celebration, black boots and cling-cloth that protected a man in arctic or desert and, with a helmet, in space. On his chest would be the badge of a shipwright.

I am a Lagerian! The smartest male of the greatest line of engineers in the galaxy.

A burst of white fire exploded in the sky, then turned to red and blue. The blue comets whirled in violent spirals, celebrating his achievement. Somewhere a parade was dancing.

But Lager was 400,000 light days behind him, kilodays by starship, across the Noir Gulf, through a star-fog of worlds. He had thrown away his uniform long ago for the soft robes. He remembered kicking it, wiping his feet on it, laughing as he left it. Putting on the Misubisi robe he smiled at that distant elation. It was too late to regret his foolishness. He was not happy, yet he was proud in the sad way a man is proud when he has disproved a cherished theory.

Well, no matter about the Engineer's uniform. He was not of Akira but the Misubisi were all part of him.

Even fierce little Misubisi Koriru was some kind of relative of his. He'd had their women in his hair for a long time. He looked at her in her formal kimono. A ghost of the caucasian peered thru her Akiran face.

"You should be a Plaek instead of a Misubisi," he demanded impulsively.

Koriru bowed. "I respectfully remind you that you did not marry Misubisi Kasumi!"

He smiled inwardly at her seriousness. "But you're related to me."

She bowed again. "All Misubisi know and cherish how they are blooded to the great Engineer Jotar Plaek."

"Do you know your ties?"

"It is of no consequence. I am proud that a small part of me is you. My life is yours."

"What are the ties!" he insisted.

"For not answering immediately, please pardon me! I am your great granddaughter three times—seven, ten, and forty-one generations back, the last thru Kasumi."

"But of my mad enthusiasm for the machinery of stardrives there is not a trace in you."

Koriru's dark eyes flickered to the floor in embarrassment, showing dark eyelashes. She held her hands in front of her. "My stupidity is inexcusable."

He was inclined to agree. She got mass and charge mixed up and couldn't for the life of her remember whether unlike charges attracted each other and unlike masses repelled each other, or vice versa.

But she nuzzles me in the morning and brags about me to all the powerful people I want to impress so why should I complain? Heredity is strange. Her sister is one of my most brilliant engineers. I suppose I keep her around because I'm lecherous and because she's kind to middle-aged men. She worships me and that makes it easier to be unhappy here out on the Frontier. He smiled at her fondly and sadly. *It won't last. It never does. Koriru will get bored with a man she can't understand. But there will be another. The Misubisi clan takes good care of their Shipwright.*

"Look at me," he said. She half obeyed, not raising her eyes above his chest. "You have the smallness and grace of Kasumi," he mused; Kasumi whom he had loved and treated badly—was that only seven of his kilodays ago? It was amazing that forty-odd generations of Misubisis had lived out their lives since her death. "You are very beautful."

"Arigato." Koriru again dropped her gaze in the conventionally humble gesture of one receiving a compliment but couldn't resist a flash look into his eyes to see if the compliment was sincere. He caught her at it and, flustered, she turned quickly to the servants. "You may go. Take the children."

The garden was still. She followed behind him along the rocky path in the tiny woods to their house that only seemed fragile.

"Goti!" she spoke the name of the robobutler.

"Hai!" answered that invisible machine.

"Call a robocar."

"Immediately, mistress!"

The Engineer turned away in displeasure. "I don't want to go to that fornicating celebration," he grumbled.

"You must be there. Excuse me for my disrespectful manner of disagreeing with you."

His eyes changed to twinkles. "I'd rather be here caressing your soft hand and gazing into your beautiful face and getting drunk!" He walked over to the liquor wall. "What I want is a bottle of Scotch. All of it."

Of the universe of drinks she feared Scotch the most because she did not understand its origin or flavor or effect. In one swift motion she threw herself between him and the devil. "No! The honor of the Misubisi clan requests that you be sober!"

He glared at her. "I'm no Misubisi!"

She stood her ground, did not lower her eyes. "As faithful servants the Misubisi built *your* ship."

"It's *not* my ship!" He shoved her aside. "It's Misubisi Kasumi's ship!" He reached and took the spherical bottle in his palm.

With one chopping motion she sent the bottle flying to the floor where it shattered. Then she was on her knees, her head touching the floor, apologizing and at the same time explaining the necessity of smashing the bottle.

He was enraged. "Sol's Blazes, I have to distill that stuff myself! It takes two kilodays to age properly!" But she wasn't listening to him; she was too busy apologizing for having done what she had to do, so he picked her up under one arm and clamped his other hand over her mouth. "Goti!" he roared.

"Hai!"

"I order you to spank this wench's bare bottom!"

"It is with abject chagrin that your humble servant informs his lord that he is not equipped to spank."

"Well, there must be some fancy service that you can order to come and do it for you!"

Pause. "My lord, I have been incomprehensibly lax in keeping my records up to date and therefore cannot locate such a necessary service. A thousand pardons."

She bit his hand and he dumped her on a pillow. She was wailing.

"It's all right. I'll go to your space damned party and we'll launch that damn ship and bask in all the glory. But after we get home, I get to spank your bare behind."

She began to smile, having gotten her way, and reached out to polish some dirt from his slippers. "If you do, I'll bite your nose!"

"You wouldn't dare. I'd blow it."

"You're impossible to take care of!"

How much she could look like Kasumi, he thought. It was painful for him to watch the way she held her head in that light with that expression. An ancient tanka of the earthbound Japanese came unbidden to mind.

> *Deep in the marsh reeds*
> *A bird cries out in sorrow*
> *Piercing the twilight*
> *With its recollection of*
> *Something better forgotten.*

He even remembered the poet because it was Kasumi who had given him that poem in final good-bye when remorse had driven him to try to renew their love. One hundred generations ago Ki no Tsurayaki had brushed it onto rice paper back on Earth.

She was hurrying along the street that first night they chanced to meet, the light drizzle as damp as his eyes were now, her light robe soaked and clinging to her in a way no wetproof Lagerian cloth ever would. He simply stared at her. She was the first outworlder he had ever noticed. When she passed by she observed his gaze and smiled at him before she looked away.

"Focus on that trick," he said spellbound, nudging his young Engineer friend.

"Exotic!"

"Let's pick her up. It'll save us a trip." They were waiting for a robocar to take them to the Pleasure Basin.

"Maybe she's not horny. This is the business district."

"Tzom!" he exclaimed. "Did you see that smile!"

"She's an outworlder, Jotar!"

"Same race. Women are the same the galaxy over, ready to go nova at the flick of a neutron. They know a good stud when they see one. How could she do better than us? She knows what an Engineer is by now. Look at yourself in the mirror sometime, joker. You didn't get to be where you are by being a weakling. And besides, I want to do the picking for once." Their robocar had arrived, enveloping them. "Follow that woman," Jotar commanded.

The friend was disturbed by this extreme aggressiveness. "There's two of us," he protested.

"That'll make her wheels go round twice as fast. She'll love it." He leered.

"Women like subtle men."

"Grumble, grumble, grumble." The robocar slid to a stop, cutting off the raven-haired exotic but stopping short of enveloping her. Jotar smiled his smile which had been known to send the bank account of a woman flickering in the last two digits. "We've fallen in love with you," he said.

She looked at them without comprehension and her hand went to the hilt of a dagger in her wide belt.

"That's a dagger," whispered Jotar's friend with urgency.

"Perhaps you don't speak Anglish?" added Jotar hastily.

"Excuse myself for speak your language poorly. I hear barbarous intent. I certain I am mistake." Gently she began to edge around them.

"Our intent was to offer ourselves to you for an entire evening of pleasure. Any way you like it."

Her eyes narrowed. She glanced about for possible escape routes, computing the swiftness of the robocar, then looked Jotar in the eyes with great poise and some small trembling. "It would be small pleasure for you rape one as homely as me. Not beautiful at all."

Jotar was taken aback. It wasn't her self-effacement that surprised him, it was her choice of thrill. On a grade F solidio once smuggled into the Monastery when he was a student he had seen an implausible story about a girl who liked to be raped—but he had never heard of such a thing in real life. Maybe they were pretty odd out there among the outworlds. How would he know? "We're pretty good at rape," he said, nudging his friend, and faking a menacing look. Anything to please such a lovely woman. "And I think you are *very* beautiful."

"I struggle hard." She was paling. "I bite."

"Oh, that's no problem. We can hold you down so you can't do any damage," he said, trying to get into her fantasy.

"Please not to harm me."

Jotar smiled broadly. "Harming you would be letting art get out of hand, of course, of course. No bruises. Get in; I know just the place to take you."

She fled, dagger in hand—a short run, then a leap down a staired passage where the robocar could not follow. They watched her disappear into the forested ground floor of a soaring hotel, her graceful stride a composite of motions unknown on Lager.

Tzom turned on Jotar. "I told you; I told you! You'll never get anywhere that way! You have to entice *them* to approach *you*."

"Yeah, yeah." Jotar stared after the lost beauty absently, a remarkable emotion of infatuation puzzling him. "I didn't follow her script."

"You dummy. It was because you overdid it. You've got to remember how women think. They've got to be in control. If a woman wants to be raped, you can't just rape her. You have to be subtle. She has to provoke being raped or she's not going to enjoy it. Everybody knows that about women but you, dummy!"

"Yeah, yeah. I guess it is the Pleasure Basin for us."

They instructed the robocar to take them to the village of dim bawdy houses and terraced restaurants and gaiety.

"How about dancing?"

"Naw," said Jotar, "I'm shorted-out tonight. How about just touring the cafes and getting picked up?"

"Too dull," complained Tzom. "I'd rather get auctioned off at a dance. Get into some clothes flashier than this uniform. Get a sweat up."

"Yeah, but at an auction you have to take who you get. That can be all right except that I'm not in the mood. In a cafe there are easier ways to say no. Go ahead, I'll see you in the morning."

"No, no. We're together tonight."

No youth who entered one of the Engineering Orders stayed a celibate Monk—he either mastered the rigorous mental and physical training and graduated into the ranks of the Engineers or he failed and became a Technician and married if a woman proposed to him. The Engineers were forbidden to marry lest a hereditary caste develop and so an Engineer's name died with him. But not his genes.

All over the planet there were places of rendezvous where any woman might go to meet those men who were the physical cream of the planet and have her sexiest fantasy made real. No matter that she was a simple data clerk, or ugly, or old, the Engineers were hers to buy for an evening of pleasure. Only one out of every thousand citizens of Lager became an Engineer but eight percent of all the children born were seeded by Engineers. And engineering talent abounded on Lager and Lager made its name throughout the human galaxy with its engineering marvels.

The robocar let them off at a cafe called the Lion's Loins. Real male lions greeted you with a snarl at the door. But they were lazy. It was the lioness who pounced from her perch above the door that startled unsuspecting clients. Sometimes a menacing lion or two would grab a shy woman by the wrist and herd her over to an Engineer who would chase the lions away after a mock battle. The animals had computer implants, of course.

There was a central lighted bar which acted as a focus because it was the only place where drinks and food were served. The women could appraise a man here before deciding to approach him. Surrounding the bar were dark junglelike alcoves where privacy was at a premium if you weren't upset by an occasional sniffing lion.

"You'll never guess who picked me up the last time I was here," said Jotar grinning.

"Is she here tonight?"

"No, no. Gail Katalina." Katalina was the Third Director of all Lager.

"You're pulling my ear! What's she like?"

"We ended up spending a ten-day together on her yacht. She keeps herself in good condition for her age. She's always busy. It was like being plugged into a thousand volt line."

"I hear she's kinky."

"Naw. You know gossip. She resonates on photography, that's all. She's a good lay. I felt my innocence, but she wanted to keep me. She was going to set me up in Dronau Hills."

"And you said no?"

"I'm busy."

"You're a brave man to turn down that kind of political connection."

"Come on, Tzom, power is warming but it doesn't rub off. You know that. Once you believe it does, and start chasing powerful people, you end up as a moon, and if you get too close you end up as part of their mass. What do you want to drink?"

Jotar was acutely aware of the women around him. He had to be; Tzom never paid attention until a woman spoke to him and by then it was often too late to control what was happening. One dazzler with bare shoulders stared at him from across the bar. He smiled at her but she turned away and he knew he wasn't going to attract her.

Once they had their drinks he settled on a lady with twinkling eyes who looked like she had had enough of a past to be interesting. She was with a young girl, probably her daughter from the facial resemblance, perfect for Tzom. He smiled at the woman with extra warmth when her eye caught his, and winked at the daughter.

But his mind hardly took the flirtation seriously. While he followed Tzom to a table his imagination put him in the villa of some outworld where his robed stranger was expected. This time he would take her arm gently and be careful not to frighten her.

Their table was equipped with a monitor which, when switched on, indicated to a woman that they were free and allowed any woman to view them and listen to their conversation from the privacy of her table. The two Engineers kept their conversation simple. Jotar's attention wandered.

In the semi-light one distant face seemed to be his mother and he lingered on it for a moment—his beloved, brilliant, crazy, naive mother who had met his genetic father in a place like this and had foolishly preserved her love for him in some corner of her mind beyond reality. She had illusions about the beauty and luxury of an Engineer's life based on one ten day experience. In real life she was a Gardener who was responsible for the ecology of 3000 hectares of land in the Miner's Hills and mother of four children, two of them by her husband. Jotar's only sister was also the daughter of an Engineer.

It was his mother who had decided that he was to become a shipwright. He remembered. When he was not yet two kilodays old she'd taken him for a night hike in the hills and they had slept on the grass beneath the brilliant stars.

"*People* build ships to go to the stars," she said, cuddling him in the sleeping bag. She fastened electronic binoculars on her eyes and slave goggles on his. "See that bright one there?" Cross hairs appeared and disappeared. "That's Gosang. We trade with Gosang in ships we build. See that tiny one there?" The cross hairs reappeared briefly. "Just above Gosang? That's Al Kiladah 43, so far away that no ship yet built has ever reached it. Even though they appear close to each other in the sky, stars may be far apart in space. Someday someone will build a ship that will reach Al Kiladah 43."

"Could I do it?"

"If you became an Engineer."

"Why can't we go there now?" he asked.

She explained to him the problems of the kalmakovian drive in terms a child could understand. "If a starship travels at 200 light speeds, the machinery ages 200 times as fast as normal to fool the gods into thinking it is traveling slower than light so they won't get upset about one of their laws being violated. In fast-time the machinery wears out if you go very far. Engineers have to make it very very reliable. If *you* aged as fast as a starship, you'd be grown up in thirty days."

"Then I would be old enough to run away from home before I'm old enough!"

"Where would you run to?"

"Al Kaladah 43!"

"Oh my. That's far away. I don't think you know how slow 200 light speeds is, young man."

"Some more stars!" he said. "Show me the farthest one we've reached!"

"Hmm." His mother talked to the binoculars and symbols began flashing across the goggles. "Well, I can show you *one* of the farthest." It took her awhile to find Akira. "It's on the Frontier."

"Who went there?"

She smiled. "I don't know. Our binoculars are very stupid. Not much memory."

"Turn up the power and we'll see them!"

"That's a tall order for ten credit binoculars. We wouldn't see them anyway. We'd see Akira before men got there."

"I'll build some good binoculars when I grow up."

"Would you like to be an Engineer?"

"Yes."

"Would you like to build ships? Would you like to build the greatest ship that has ever traveled space?" Her words were more of an order than a question.

She began buying him models of ships to build. He got a modular computer for his birthday and every birthday thereafter it became larger. Its memory eventually held the best private collection of starship materials on Lager. Just to manage the horde of data his mother bought for him obsessively, Jotar eventually developed a cross-indexing system unique in starship design history.

Since physical agility was as strong a criterion for graduation from an Engineering Order as intellectual ability, his mother saw to it that he went to dance school. They were country people looking after forest and grasslands and the nearest dance group was 160 kilometers away but she shuttled him there regularly. She overlooked nothing. Most children could play tag with their robogoverness—Jotar's played mathematical games with him.

Sometimes he had to escape from his mother. He'd put on his waldo leggings and jump across the hill meadows with 20 meter leaps pretending he was on a light gravity planet, or he'd leap to the tops of trees and be an animal. Even then he couldn't always escape her. He'd be pursued by thoughts about stardrives.

Before he entered the Black Horse Monastery, before he was full grown, he already knew what mankind's greatest starship would be like.

Jotar finished his drink. He knew exactly how long it took a woman with a gleam in her eye to make up her mind. Then he ambled back to the bar. It did not surprise him that the lady and her daughter also chose that moment to refill their glasses.

"Would you care to join our table?"

"Delighted," he said.

Tzom never knew why the handsomest women always invited them when he was with Jotar.

They chatted together over a second drink. The daughter had been recently married and was being educated into the wilder side of city night life by her flirtatious mother. The girl hovered between fascination and shyness while the mother decided where to take them to dinner and when they were going to retire for more serious amusement. Two lions blocked their way as they tried to leave. Jotar made the mistake of kicking one of them, and was slapped to the ground. The lioness stood on his chest and licked his face.

"Do you need help?" asked the girl.

"Damn animal show," he said.

Jotar got stuck with the young one. He never let his boredom show: it would have been unprofessional. They went to his apartment and he tried to please her. He let her hold him after their lovemaking while she drowsed, though he was inclined to push her away. To pass the time he thought of his crazy mother's illusions about the life of an Engineer.

She at least had a conscientious husband, a tolerant man who had created a stable home life for his children and generally ignored his woman's waywardness or at least seldom spoke of it. He would just shrug and say, almost with a smile when their mother disappeared for days at a time, "Women have more lust than men." She had the luxury of knowing her husband and sharing with him in a way that is only possible after long contact.

Damn. Jotar couldn't even remember the name of the girl who had picked him up last night. And a week ago he'd been to a pre-wedding party given by the bridesmaids, and the bride and five bridesmaids had had him, one after the other between drink and lavish food and fun—and he couldn't even remember their faces.

It was something he could get angry about. Like he was angry right now at this girl with her legs around him. She'd get pregnant. She'd tell her husband and they'd celebrate. *But she'll never bother to tell me.* Not a chance. *Sol's Blazes, it makes me angry!* He was human. He liked children. He'd cherished his younger brothers and sister. Probably he had seeded thirty children already but he'd never know. They used you and they never came back.

I'll never hold a tiny baby in my arms. The tears were running down his cheeks in the dark and he was furious at his bed partner but he caressed her tenderly. *Little baby girl.*

When she finally went to sleep, he displaced her arm, slowly, carefully, and sneaked out of bed to his workroom.

Without really being aware that an earlier meeting was on
his mind, he sketched the outworld woman's robe onto the
surface of the workroom's computer terminal, rotating
and modifying it, until it matched his memory. Then he
sketched the peculiar racial characteristics of her exotic
face. While he worked, he smiled, wondering what it
would be like to be loved by an outworld woman, pleased
to know already that she was not like Lagerian women.

He put the computer into its pattern recognition mode.
It overprinted his drawings from time to time, asking for
clarifying lines, details. It paused for one hundred seconds before burping out a list of probable worlds. All of
them, it turned out, belonged to a class of solar systems
which could be traced back to the ancient Japanese race of
Terra through a philosophy called the Mishima tradition
that placed strong emphasis on old values and had advo-
cated going into space to preserve them.

Jotar spliced the list into the immigration and trade
records for an intersection-sort. Only one group matched
the available data: a trade mission from Akira, an obscure
Frontier sun. They were here to buy heavy automatic
machinery and starships. Such a trade mission did not
make much sense—Akira was too far away for direct trade.

A detailed examination of the papers of the trade mission members gave Jotar what he wanted. The beautiful
flower who had dominated his senses was called Misubisi
Kasumi and she was the mission linguist.

Elated, he went back to bed, kissing his companion's
rump out of happiness. He did not go to sleep. He began
to plot the seduction of Kasumi by organizing all the
available facts. The central fact was that if they needed
starships, he was the galaxy's greatest shipwright. The
second fact was that she alone of the mission spoke Anglish.

A week of feverish work went by while he prepared and
perfected his plan. Like all good plans it solved two problems at once, allowing him to build man's greatest starship
and to have a steady lover who excited him.

Engineer Jotar Plaek had yet to build a single ship. He
was young, too brilliant to ignore and too brilliant to use.

He was proposing a radical restructuring of the kalmakovian
field guides that scrapped ten generations of engineering
experience. He had solved the new field equations and
shown theoretically that structures of positive mass and
negative mass could be fabricated into the required guides
with impressive inertia-low characteristics. Accelerations
of one light speed per ten seconds were feasible, unheard
of performance for the best of modern drives. Final velocity would only be ten percent greater than with a regular
drive, but that figure was calculated by making enor-
mously conservative estimates of every parameter. Jotar
suspected that velocities of one thousand light speeds might
eventually be squeezed out of the design, where 250 light
speeds was the theoretical maximum for the orthodox guide
configuration.

He was so brilliant that he had never been able to find a
sponsor. He had papers and credits and consultations and
lecture tours that would honor an older man—but no
hardware to his name. He knew some of the best Engineers personally but had few contacts in the government
except for Gail Katalina, the Third Director, and most
dynamic member of the Directorate. As he remembered
her, she was delighted to be seen with young men but had
no interest in starships. In spite of his boasting, she probably didn't remember him.

So his plan was to bypass Lager and let Akira sponsor
the research.

He sent out a feeler to the Akiran mission—terse. He
knew they would check his credentials and when they
found him to be the most knowledgeable shipwright of
Lager, they'd come to him.

Misubisi Kasumi came.

She did not recognize him. He supposed that all Lagerians
looked alike to her. They talked business. He spent the
whole morning with her at a projection table showing her
details of the ship he wanted to build for them.

The table could do anything. It could enlarge or contract the diagrams in its memory, or give you a cross
section through any angle. If you wanted iron in red and

copper in green it would give you that and blot out all else. If you wanted bulkheads, or wiring, or plumbing, it would give you all of those separately. It would give you parts and explode them. It could show you the kalmakovian drive and the field changes as color changes when the drive was "operative". It could run standard simulated voyages that put every part through an extreme test.

Jotar had spent all of his time as a Monk building the plans for this vessel. It was the completed project which gave him Engineer status. He had spent all of his time as an Engineer revising details and trying to sell it to a sponsor.

In all of the galaxy only on Lager was such a monumental one-man project possible. There were myriad computer routines on tap to design almost anything to any reasonable specifications with fabrication cost optimization and maintenance optimization. If he wanted docking gear, a command would generate it.

Where the computers failed he could use the Monks by assigning a project. They enjoyed such projects because they received much credit for solving problems beyond the capacity of the computers. Sometimes he used other Engineers as consultants. It was the drive unit that was uniquely his.

"How fast?" she asked.

"Do you need a fast drive?"

"Yes. We isolated. We live across the Noir Gulf." She paused.

"Never heard of it."

"It is like cosmic moat across the Sagittarian route to the center of the galaxy. It is one of the great gravitic divides. At narrowest between Znark Vasun and Akira, it has width 175 leagues. At other places it has width five hundred leagues. It has slowed human expansion in that direction. Akira is double isolated. We exist tip of stellar wisp called the Finger Pointing Solward. We can trade with Znark Vasun—long trip. But if we go up, down or sideways—nothing. Gulf. We go down Finger toward galactic center—all Frontier, little trade. In future, when all developed, still we be trading along straight line of stars." She gestured negatively. "Much more expensive than trading in volume of stars. We need speed."

"I can't guarantee it on the first vessel but the speed potential is there. A thousand light speeds."

She gasped. "We want that. Explain me your drive."

"It's not mine. It is just a modified kalmakovian. You know the sort of thing—the difference between propellers and jets. I'll show you the differences." He began to put images on the table's screen.

"I am so sorry for my inexcusable ignorance but I not understand physics. There is positive mass that goes down and negative mass that goes up, there are kalmakovs and einsteins and widgets. And momentum and energy are both composed of mass and velocity but they are different. I never understand."

The kalmakovian effect is the converse of the einsteinian effect.

In einsteinian flight an external energy source like a rocket increases the mass of the ship and time slows for the occupants. They can go to a star and back within months of their life and so consider an einsteinian rocket as a "faster-than-light" drive. It is for them. To the people back on the home planet who have lived by a faster time, the einsteinian rocket has never exceeded the velocity of light.

A kalmakovian drive turns a ship into a "falling stone" without an external field to attract it. It can accelerate at thousands of gravities while still in free fall. It uses no obvious energy any more than a falling stone uses energy because it taps into the greatest source of energy available to a ship, the potential energy called the ship's mass. It converts rest mass into velocity. Because the rest mass of every atom in the ship decreases while the drive is on, time accelerates relative to those worlds outside of the field. And because time accelerates for the occupants of the field, it always seems to them that they are traveling below the speed of light. But to the people back on the home planet the journey took only a matter of months and so they consider a kalmakovian ship as a "faster-than-light" drive.

In the early days of starflight shipwrights learned to protect their passengers from this kalmakovian "starship aging" by using related field phenomena to displace some of the rest mass, ordinarily converted into velocity, to the mass field of special slow-time cabins for the passengers.

Deceleration is no problem. When the kalmakovian field collapses, velocity is automatically reconverted to rest mass and the ship stops at rest relative to its starting coordinates. The photon rocket motors on each starship were only used to compensate for the relative velocity differences between departure star and destination star.

"Well," said Jotar, "send your technical expert to me and I'll explain it to him."

"You said you wanted our sponsorship. Excuse me for not understanding."

"You're in the market for ships. I've seen your specs. You want the best. This is the best. If you buy my ships I'll build them for you. If you give me an order for twenty, I'll give you a price comparable to anything else being built. That's what I mean by sponsoring. I need your money."

She looked doubtful.

"You're used to going to a bureaucrat and ordering something that you can already see being assembled up there in some shipyard—the thousandth edition of a standard vessel. You can do that but you won't get the best."

"Honorable Engineer, you are not dealing with ordinary planet. You are dealing with very humble planet of meager resources."

"But not poor because you are lazy or poor because you breed planlessly, but because you are Frontier and isolated. Your people are ambitious and hardworking."

"Yes."

"The best kind to deal with. I'll tell you what. I'll give you a bargain. I'll throw in the ship's plans."

He could see her tremble with excitement. He wasn't going to tell her how useless those plans would be to her people. They were keyed to an inplace industrial plant, a pyramid of crafts and skills that a Frontier planet couldn't hope to duplicate in less than sixty kilodays. Jotar doubted that there were more than ten worlds in the human ecumen that could build from those plans.

"Why you need us? A day's trading on Lager would buy all planets of Akira."

If only I could explain. He sighed. "Getting something done is not easy. It never was for geniuses like me." He tried to think of an analogy to give her and fell back on pre-space Terran history. It was humankind's common background, times and people and clashes that every civilized man related to. "I could have sold aircraft carriers to the Japanese navy in 1925 AD; I doubt that I could have sold flying bombers to the United States Army Air Force in 1925 AD."

She laughed.

"Here. I feel like a snack." He took her away from the table and sat her down on pillows. "I dug up a bottle of rice wine just for you." And he poured her a glass.

"Do you drink rice wine?" she asked in surprise.

"Never touched it before in my life."

"It is my shame that I have never either." She spoke with sadness.

He produced a plate of delicacies—cauliflower with mayonnaise and vinegar, a tofu and tomato aspic, roast peppers which weren't peppers at all but a plant from a world called Tekizei, and raw fish.

"What is this?" she said, tasting it with her fingers.

"You've never had raw fish? I took it from an Akiran recipe book."

"Raw fish on a space ship? I am so sorry but you are out of your mind."

"What are you familiar with?"

"Hard tack." She laughed.

"I see." He paused, reflecting upon the tales of Frontier hardship. "What's Akira like?"

"Ohonshu, the major planet, not need to be terraformed. The plants are *pink*—oh not really, but pink on their bellies. They flower on the ends of the leaves and the seeds form in leaf stem. Terran life not thrive well in wild, except for grass. We have tiny wild horses, real horses. Terran birds have done well, I not know why. The colonists were mostly bushido fanatics caught in the mysteries of a religion their parents not understand and their children not really understand either. They left us strange and beautiful monasteries. It took fanatics to cross the Noir Gulf. They were good people. But I not remember it much. We left when I was small. The captain is my father. My mother not come. It's far away. Living on planets seems strange to me."

"Has being planet bound frightened you?"

"Yes! Oh yes!"

"Eat your raw fish."

"Do you like the rice wine?"

"Oh yes. Sake is in my genes."

He was happy. "You are a pleasant person to be with," he said, trying to draw her into a commitment without being as direct as he was inclined to be.

In response she merely lowered her eyelashes.

It exasperated him. How by the fire of a sun's blazes was he supposed to handle a mannish woman? He paused, then tried again, gently. "Have you been outside of the city?"

"No. But like to. Lager seemed so lush from space!"

"You must have been looking at my parents' place. It is beautiful country. Once you are free of the main burden of your work we could visit them and take a hike along the river. A hundred kilometer walk. You'd love it."

"A hundred kilometer walk would be therapeutic for my soul, but rubber space legs would protest."

"I'll give you waldo leggings. We'll camp out."

The next day he saw Kasumi again. She brought him a small present of dried fruit. He held her at arm's length, looking, smiling. It was good to see the same woman twice.

The next ten days were hectic. Between catnaps, he worked endlessly with the Akiran mission, ironing out the details. They signed a contract. The news spread like a nuclear excursion: Jotar Plaek was going to build his crazy ship. Those were good days.

He found it easy to be with Kasumi, anticipating her grace when he was away from her and marveling in it when she came to him. There was something exquisite about just letting things happen, not investing energy into making them happen. He was good for her. Unobtrusively encouraging her initiative, he brought out a hidden boldness and confidence. Once when they were eating together in a cafe, she struck up a conversation with an Engineer at the next table and took him with her for the rest of the afternoon, letting Jotar fend for himself. Jotar was pleased that because of him she had become more of a woman than she'd even been before in her life. When he was most content he would think that it was a good thing for Lager that they all pumped the blood of their mothers; he imagined Lager as a very quiet Eden with its Eveless men waiting for the apples to fall before they ate.

One day Kasumi was swimming nude at a river bend. She came to him and asked him to towel her off. He smiled at her. She smiled at him. Each felt aroused. Each refused to make the first move. It was like being a Technician. Love. A woman. Contentment. No worries. He took her to the meadow where he had first seen Akira and finally their chemistry drove them to become lovers. They whispered sweet nothings all night and licked at the dew in the morning with their tongues.

When the dew had melted but the grass was still rosily lit, she recited a poem by Akihito from the almost sacred Manyoshu.

> *"I was wandering*
> *Among flowered spring meadows*
> *To pick violets*
> *And enjoyed myself so much*
> *I slept in the field all night."*

The work orders went out, financed by Akiran funds. Countermanding orders were issued by the government's APCT and Jotar flew to the capital to straighten out an administrative mess caused by some lunkhead who couldn't understand an outworld investment in a project which had been turned down by the Lagerian Aerospace Technical Oversee. He got through the fracas by a compromise which required him to hire a watchdog staff to prevent the leakage of Classified Skill and Craft Forms. LATO then issued a Duty Liaison requiring computer-filed abstracts of all progress down to the Work Action Order level.

Within four days of assembling the new staff a minor Liaison Engineer panicked at the new methods of manipulating positive and negative mass fabrications and the project was temporarily halted—Injuncted for a Retro Study. That lasted twelve days. Jotar managed a Reactivation Order but the renewed research had to be transferred to deep space where facilities weren't equipped to handle it. Jotar spent forty days building a new space factory.

Then they ran into real fabrication problems which no simulation could have anticipated. Each glitch was solved but every solution seemed to generate new troubles which had no obvious source. Jotar found to his horror that he wasn't a hardware man. He brought in consultants and that cost money.

Finally some key parts arrived for the drive assembly but they had been fabricated to normal starship specifications which weren't good enough in the new configuration. Jotar sued and was countersued. He won the case but was sued from another quarter for nonpayment because he had neglected to transfer funds, and, alarmed, the government froze funds to cover work orders which had as yet not been issued. He hired lawyers. They sent him a bill.

In 200 days Jotar had gone through all of his Akiran capital. He had promised twenty ships. Not one was remotely finished. In desperation he turned to sex. He didn't think that Third Director Gail Katalina would even remember him, considering her reputation, but he was wrong. She returned his call within two kilosecs.

"Of course I remember you! You're the Engineer with the most beautiful eyelashes on Lager! I'll send an executive plan for you. Can you pack today? I'll meet you at the

Jongleur Gardens. My husband won't be there. I may be late, but that will give you time to make yourself beautiful."

The executive cruiser was prompt and polite and like all high level government roboplanes did not take orders from the passengers. It had been instructed to fly the scenic route through the Lebanor Pass, which it did—skimming the mountains' treetops at a speed never less than 500 meters per second. Jotar kept swallowing his heart.

For all that haste he arrived at the Jongleur mansion to find himself alone. He was put up in the master bedroom with a wooden fire blazing. He was fed delicious food by invisible robocooks and told not to wear his uniform by an invisible robovalet who provided him with lavish clothes of a cut which might be worn on stage but never in public. He swam. He read. He tried on clothes and practiced entrances and lines and charm. That night he slept alone.

Director Katalina arrived late the next afternoon. Her hair was white. Her face was lined by the act of smiling so many times at the victories of her ruthless rise. She hugged Jotar, pinched his bottom and handed him her briefcase. Her two female executive secretaries followed closely to stay inside the shadow of her power.

At dinner she had a videophone beside her wine and continuously interrupted their trivial conversation by answering calls that came in to command her attention. She'd be kidding him about the time he fell overboard on the yacht and switch into an animated discussion with some disembodied voice concerning the credit rating of the Amar Floating Peoples who did not qualify as a solar system, and as quickly come back to comment on the bouquet of the wine.

Once Jotar made the mistake of letting the conversation wander around to the subject of starships. She gazed at him with true adoration while he spoke, so he spoke with increasing fire and clarity.

She cut in. "Your intelligence makes you *so sexy* I can't stand it anymore!" And with that thought she pulled him off to the bedroom where she called up her secretaries, instructing them to handle all incoming communication.

First she undressed Jotar. Then she posed him for inspiration. Then she took out her paints and began to decorate his body while he watched in the mirror-screen. Whenever she asked for his advice he praised her. His ear itched.

She became so enthusiastic about her masterpiece that she called in her secretaries to help photograph him for her collection. They took endless photographs, developing them with different dyes, cutting, distorting, reposing him. He was pleased that she was pleased.

Once her assistants were dismissed, Director Katalina had him carry her to the bed. "Do you remember how I like it, you big beautiful rascal?"

He did. By morning he was suffering a bad attack of anxiety. He had done everything conceivable to please her and she had never given him an opening. In desperation he decided to serve her breakfast in bed. He knew a recipe he was sure the robocooks didn't know because Kasumi had taught it to him, but he got caught in the kitchen by one of the secretaries who hadn't bothered to robe herself.

"Hi, big boy."

"Hi."

She began to fondle him.

"Look, I'm just trying to get some breakfast for her."

The secretary spoke some commands. "Let the robocook do it. I'd like to have you for a moment. I'm much younger than she is."

"The robocook isn't up to this particular dish."

"You don't understand, boy. I'm her *executive* secretary. Everything she acts on goes through *my* hands. You have to please me, too."

"I don't think she'd like that." He didn't dare remove the executive hands from his belly.

"She'll never know a thing, pretty boy. It'll only take us half a kilosec."

He got back to the kitchen while the just prepared breakfast was still hot, and carried it up to the Third Director, cursing the robocook and the secretary. The old woman smiled at him. She pulled him down and kissed him.

"You want something, don't you? What is it?"

Oh thank Newton! He sat down on the bed and composed himself.

"It's about your starship project, isn't it? You're broke. See, I know everything. You want money to continue. Money, money, money—that's all an Engineer ever thinks of."

"Sometimes," he said.

"What makes you think I'll give it to you?"

"All I wanted to tell you was that my starship is important to Lager."

She laughed. "We sell every starship we can make. Your venture isn't important for Lager, it is important for you."

Well, I tried.

She laughed at his misery. "You fool! What would I be if I couldn't do favors? Don't worry. I'll handle everything. It will be all right."

He made love to her in gratitude and she enjoyed his total giving of himself.

Back at his central office, he waited three days. The government put him in bankruptcy to save him from the responsibility for his mistakes. They took over the project of building his ship. The sudden loss of control shocked him: he had an office but no command lines. His faith in the power of sex was shaken.

Then Kasumi timorously announced that she was pregnant.

Jotar did his best to get the State to take over his debt to Akira but the reorganized project refused to underwrite Akiran interests. With that blow Kasumi's father and three of his closest associates committed suicide.

Kasumi called. Jotar refused to see her. He wanted to see her but he couldn't face her. He began to drink heavily. He disconnected his communicator. Finally he put his furniture and library in storage and disappeared. Nobody knew where he was because he was on an island beachcoming with a woman who had run away from her husband but would probably go back to him when her money ran out. They had met at a cafe in the Pleasure Basin and she had coaxed him into chucking it all with her.

One day while this woman helped him carve out an outrigger, the roasting sun at their naked backs, he told her about building the galaxy's greatest space canoe, a tale he embellished with truth, lies, puns, and emotion. The idea seemed hilarious to him, a fantasy laid on him by his mother when he was too young to reject it. The trouble was he wasn't *sure* it was a fantasy. Then for months he didn't think at all. He speared fish.

His woman left him, having learned more about canoes than she wanted to know. He drifted and another woman picked him up. Lusena was a distortion photographer who took pictures and fed them into a special computer. He was fascinated. By playing with the commands and selecting out only those image distortions that caused an emotional resonance the photograph evolved in color and pattern until it became a setting from one's private dream world. Jotar showed Lusena's art to everyone, raving about it for kilosecs. Lusena had a haunting dream world. All that came out when Jotar tried it were pictures of grotesque pinheaded women or elabyrinth long starships that faded complexly into the sky. Time passed.

Jotar was being supported by two waitresses from a local pub in their houseboat when his sister found him. Brother and sister, each seeded by a different Engineer, fought for days. They ranted themselves into a good mood by sunset whereupon he'd cook the three women a sumptuous meal, stews boiled in beer, beer cakes, beered chicken casserole, and the four of them would reminisce about childhood during the cool of the evening. In the morning the fight would start again.

She sneered at his unwillingness to drive ahead against all obstacles. She derided him for being ruled by the considerations of inferiors. She described what they were doing to his ship in his absence. She flattered his genius for seeing the piece of the puzzle that escaped all other eyes. She goaded his pride. She won. He went back to work.

When he returned to the project he was astounded that he was still respected. Genius had its prerogatives. He was astonished that he still believed in his ship with an insane passion. He worked hard. The ship had what he'd always wanted—government sponsorship. He was now willing to be humble when they told him that the fabrication problems needed research and time.

Half a kiloday passed before he realized that, even working, he had no control over the drift of the project. A whole kiloday passed before he saw the trend of the drift.

The project Engineers were solving problems creating solutions closer to something they already knew. As the total solution began to emerge, Jotar panicked. He ran in seven directions trying to trace down the individual decisions. He got passed from Engineer to Engineer to Craft Guild to Economist to Production Manager to Beer Hall.

Finally Keithe Walden took him hunting. Walden was the man in charge since the bankruptcy, an older Engineer, jowls sagging. He could make ten thousand men play choo-choo train in unison. They had it out in a duck blind with bugs buzzing around their heads.

"Keithe, I think you're full of meadow-muffins."

"Jotar, if you were redesigning a woman, you'd take off the breasts for streamlining . . ."

"Would I!"

"You'd take out the kidneys because they smell. You'd . . ."

"Now look! I like women the way they are!"

"No you don't. You'd have a thousand improvements if you thought about the problem for a kilosec. What changes would you make?"

"They'd be practical changes. I'd put in a servomechanism so that a woman could control her ovulation. Shreinhart showed that the immunological system could be vastly improved if it had better data processing capabilities. There's no reason bones should break or get brittle with age—there are much better materials. I think it is shocking that, kilogram for kilogram, solid state devices have more storage and logic capacity than neural tissue. How about an electromagnetic sense? And women certainly should have a penis to piss with."

"You could go on and on, couldn't you?"

"Probably."

"That's what I mean. Then you'd start to fool with the genes so this new woman could reproduce herself—and you'd be in big trouble because of the incredible cross-correlative interdependence of the genetic interaction. Evolution is a slow thing. You can only change marginal things in something as complicated as a woman or a starship—and each change has to be proved out over generations before you can make the next incremental change. A man has 98% of the genes of a chimpanzee, remember that. You want too much change, too soon. You have to start with what you have."

"I'll give you a herd of horses," said Jotar, "and you can start breeding me a flock of birds out of them."

Jotar took up billiards and poker. He danced and wenched. He spent long days playing with his sister's children. Walden built a prototype ship and took orders for five hundred. It hit the news. LATO called it Jotar Plaek's ship and said it was the greatest starship ever launched.

Yeah. We changed the brass doorknobs to silver.

Two days later Misubisi Kasumi followed him home to his apartment. He didn't notice her until he went to close the door. A small girl was clinging to her leg. "Here is daughter you abandoned," she said bitterly.

Shock. "Hi." He went down on his knees but the child turned her face away in shyness.

Kasumi disciplined the child. She held her face toward Jotar. "You must see mean father who abandoned you."

Tears were running down Jotar's face. She was the first woman who had ever brought one of his children to see him. He was touched beyond anything that had ever happened to him.

"A beautiful kid. Your side of the family. Kasumi, come

in. I'm sorry about it all. I got caught up in my own madness. I was destroyed like everybody else."

She marched into the richly furnished apartment, gripping the child's hand. "You seem to be doing quite well."

"I manage."

"You built your ship."

"It's not mine. They changed the grille. It comes in new colors."

"That's good enough for me. Take an order for twenty red ones."

"Sol's Blazes! I wish I owned one to give you! Nothing's mine! I control nothing!"

"You ruined us!" she screamed.

"Yeah, yeah. I ruined you. I won a lot by doing that. How have you made out? Do you still have your ship?"

"Yes."

"Thank Space for small blessings. Why are you still here on this fossilized world when you could be out on the Frontier where people are still alive!"

"The mission must bring back something."

"Have a shot of whiskey. I've got no sake. Some milk for the kid?"

"No thank you."

"So what are you going to take back that you can fill your holds with for free?"

"Knowledge."

"It's a good cargo. They don't sell it for free here."

"Since you left me I have had relationships with many of your Engineers." Her voice flowed like a starlight-stirred wind of helium on a sunless planet. "Each has given me something out of pity. I have enough to build industrial empire. I want you to give me everything you know about starships. You owe it to me."

"I'll give you my head in a pickle jar."

"Don't offend me. I hate you enough to kill you!"

"Sit down. I'm on your side. I'm ashamed. Let me think of the resources I do have." He paused. "I collected a fantastic library when I was a child. I'll give it to you. I'll give you the original plans of my ship." He laughed. "I'll give you the plans for that flying toilet bowl they built in my name. But," he slammed out with careful enunciation, "*it won't do you any good.* Knowledge is only valuable if it can be activated. What can you do with a riddle you don't ken?"

"My people are brilliant."

"I'm brilliant," said Jotar, angered. "If I hadn't grown up on Lager I'd know nothing about starships! Nothing! I could wallow in every computer memory about starships that has ever been recorded and I'd learn nothing!"

She glared at him with hatred.

"I'm not arguing with you. I'll give you all I can. Thank you for bringing my daughter." Impulsively he brought out a toy he'd bought for his sister's youngest. It was a transparent ball, feather light, hard. "Take it for her. She'll like it. It will talk to her and show her pictures that illustrate its story. It is a story kaleidoscope. It will never repeat the same story. Look. What's a wirtzel?" he asked the sphere.

"Once upon a time there was a wirtzel who lived in a cave. . . ." The surface was vibrating. Images were beginning to form. The child watched in fascination.

"Look at it, Kasumi! It would take your Frontier culture three generations just to *understand* the plans for that *toy*. Black Hole, woman. If it's knowledge you want, you need to take a university with you!"

She was crying.

Jotar hung his head. "What could I have done? Tell me. It was a disaster."

"You could have put your arms around me when I cry," she sobbed.

Kasumi left him in a turmoil. He thought all night about her, putting the pieces together. He could not sleep. He sat in a trance on the balcony, bathed in the light of the moon Schnapps, compiling memories. *We are, we are, we are, we are, we are the Engineers! we can, we can, we can, we can, we can swig forty beers!* Memories. The first drunken orgy when they had graduated from the Monastery, their vows of celibacy dead, singing, the mob, the screaming girls chasing after a piece of virgin, rioting, getting carried off by a flying wedge of amazons, to be young, to be proud that one could build anything. A long way from there to the duck blind. *I'll give you a herd of horses and you can start breeding me a flock of birds out of them!* Sarcasm. Maybe if one went back to the common ancestor of horse and bird you could breed a bird. A lot of breeding. Was Akira far enough back on the technological tree? Kasumi crying. *You need to take a university with you!* Why not?

He worked it out because she was leaving and his daughter was leaving and he had an irrational desire to go with them. His images were of them working side by side to build *the* ship on a world that cared.

To accomplish his purpose the ship of the Akiran trade mission had to be refitted. He still commanded that kind of resource. Its holds became a fifty person self-contained college subject to fast-time. He left room for six students in the crew's slow-time protective field. The best students could be cycled through slow-time with him and Kasumi so that he could work with them personally. He intended to breed the best students until shipwright decisions were in their genes. By the time they got to Akira he would be bringing with him a 400 kiloday old university. It would have more tradition and history than Akira itself. With that base he could build a great ship even out there on Frontier.

Jotar was short of students. Who wanted to burn up in fast-time for a goal they'd never live to see? Misubisi Kasumi ordered some of her crew to become students and being good vassals they obeyed. Jotar found four Monks who had flunked out and couldn't bear the thought of becoming mere Technicians. He took them. He took three Technicians and two Craftsmen. He found six women like his mother and took them.

Only when they departed did Kasumi tell him that she was going in fast-time, to die in repentance for failing to carry out her mission. He couldn't convince her otherwise. She said that she wanted to work directly with the college in its infancy, to see that it grew up understanding Akira, the place where the descendants of the first students would work. But he knew she chose that exotic way to commit suicide because she had not forgiven him.

Jotar saw Kasumi only once again while she was still alive. Their first stop was at the small star Nippon where he picked up ten students and bought a quantity of genuine Japanese genes. His original students had inbred and were already looking too caucasian to be received smoothly into the Akiran culture. He had brought with him the frozen sperm of 1000 Engineers but he didn't want to have to rely on such a source.

Kasumi was old and wrinkled. They had communicated, but only through the time barrier where she lived 150 times as fast as he did. He was shy with her, his sorrow at losing her still fresh in his heart. Nor was it real to him that his daughter was older than he was, his grandchildren adult.

Nippon was a red star and consequently the surface of Nippon Futatsu was unnatural to human eyes. Kasumi took him to a mountain inn where she served him tea at a tiny shrine in a ceremony he did not understand. He could feel her warmth. It made him apologetic but she only smiled and pressed his lips gently with her hand.

> *"I have lived so long*
> *That I long for the eon*
> *Of rejected love*
> *When I was so unhappy,*
> *Remembering it fondly."*

She poured his tea to refill the tiny cup. "Excuse my liberties with a poem by Kiosuke. Do you have a poem for me or is your mind too young to partake of such frivolity?"

The twilight inspired him. He did not know how to create a tanka.

> *"Why is the horizon tree*
> *Fixed against the setting sun*
> *When it is the sun that is eternal?"*

Their talk concerned the college. Kasumi worried about the quality of the students. She knew that they were not good enough even to get into a Monastery on Lager. He laughed and reminded her of their different perspectives. What seemed a painful and difficult development to her was a miraculously swift growth to him.

She held his elbow as they strolled along the lake to their solitary cabin which stood half on stilts. The only light she permitted was a candle behind a translucent wall. "Darkness is the friend of age. How fortuante I am. It is an old woman's dream to wake up one morning and find herself in an enchanted land with her favorite long-lost lover, still young of body, potent, and yet not wise enough to have recovered from her charms!"

They made love on the mats, he amazed by her mellowness, she happy to be young again for an evening.

"Remember that Engineer who accosted you in the streets the day you arrived on Lager? You had to run away to save yourself."

"I do! I was terrified."

"That was me."

"Not you!"

"Yeah. That's when I fell in love with you."

"You beast!"

"I was zapped out of my mind. I cooked up that whole scheme to sell you ships just to meet you."

"But you left me!"

"Don't men always leave their first love? They don't have anyone to compare her with to know what they are losing."

"Jotar, you fool. Doesn't it terrify you to find men like yourself out among the stars?"

"The glorious stars gave me you. Is your head comfy on my shoulder? Gods, but I've missed reaching through that barrier to touch you."

When they reboarded their ship in orbit, Kasumi sent him as a gift her granddaughter by her fourth child. Yawahada was a vexing youth who, her grandmother confided in a covering note, coveted Jotar as a lover because he lived in slow-time and she was displeased with the men available to her and wished for a new generation of men to grow up while she remained young. Kasumi was dead and four new generations had risen before Yawahada of the budding breasts, now pregnant by Jotar, found a lover among her descendants who pleased her fickle heart.

By then the college was shaping in ways so fast that Jotar spent his full time monitoring its growth. Every tenth day he checked for cultural deviations that might destroy its purpose. He had the power to change what he wanted. Cultural evolution had elevated him almost to the mystical status of Emperor as provided for in the bushido ethic that came with the college as Kasumi founded it—he was the god from slow-time who awoke at intervals and judged.

After Kasumi's death Jotar began to run the breeding program with an iron hand by the best rules of animal genetics. He never interfered with the natural liaisons which arose among the Misubisis but he alone determined whose chromosomes were carried by every new embryo planted in a womb.

He selected for physical resemblance to the Akirani and for physical perfection—visual acuity that lasted into old age, longevity, coordination, flawless metabolism. You cannot breed for an ability your environment does not require. Jotar required cooperation, craftsmanship, and analysis and so was able to select for those characteristics. The improvement from generation to generation was remarkable.

Part of the improvement was cultural. As the college solved its problems of organizing and transmitting its knowledge it became easier for the less brilliant to do outstanding work.

Part of the improvement was the interaction between culture and breeding. Jotar wanted people predisposed toward fine craftsmanship so he set up a microelectronics industry to build starship brains. He bred the best craftsmen and hardened the electronic specifications from generation to generation until his students were actually selling their extraordinary products in various ports of call. He invented the science of positive and negative mass microstructures to teach kalmakovian fabrications in the limited space available onboard. It was only an exercise in craftsmanship to allow him to sort out his most talented students but they stunned him by producing actual miniature stardrives.

He never stopped delving through his brain for challenging projects. He had only fifty students but in fasttime they were the equivalent of 7500 students. They designed special ships to probe the fringes of black holes, automatic freighters, ships to penetrate regions of dense interstellar gas, ships to sample the atmospheres of stars, ships that could land on a planet, warships to meet the thrust of an alien invasion, tiny robot ships that could carry messages between the stars, a transport vehicle to carry 100,000 colonists. He listed every known ability required by a shipwright, monitored each individual for those abilities, and selected for them.

He seized all opportunities. When they were in some stellar port he sold their services to repair damaged ships of designs they'd never seen before. They had to work with their hands in unfamiliar shops and sometimes right out there in spacesuits. He contracted them out to the hardest problems at the cheapest price. They never complained. They did what he told them to do. They would have died for him.

The strange fast-time culture of the Misubisi took some devious turns. It developed a hedonistic period which produced a literature and spirit that grew up into a wisdom that got lost in a dark brooding upon the Japanese past that gave way to a rediscovery of simple crafts like pottery and multicolored wood block printing that led to a revival of dance and theater which produced a playwright who inspired political revolution and mutiny by twenty students whose places were filled by a new generation of loyalist fanatics whose children adopted the clothes and philosophical games of a passing port of call until their children resurrected an Akiran identity from an almost devout curiosity about the coming Akiran experience.

And so they arrived at Znark Vasun, facing the empty

Noir Gulf, Akira the most brilliant star in a sky forlorn of stars. Eight of the Misubisi jumped ship for passage in a freighter headed across the Gulf. It was the way they chose to reach the Akiran system alive to taste the final triumph of their millennia-long quest. One slender Misubisi woman, filled with a romantic longing for an imagined Akiran paradise, unwilling to die while she was so near to heaven, seduced Jotar and begged him to take her with him in slow-time. He knew the source of her devotion but didn't mind; he liked her company and her body. Another young girl stowed herself away in his cabin, unwilling to grow old and die without building a real ship. He found her nearly starving long after they had left Znark Vasun. She was too afraid of his wrath to come out of hiding.

The remaining Misubisi continued in fast-time across the Noir Gulf as they always had and died there breeding new generations. The very last generation defied "the god beyond the barrier" by birthing a rash of "love children" who took the ship's population past seventy. They knew they were close to home.

Jotar weathered it all. Later he laughed and called himself the longest surviving Japanese Emperor in human history. Halfway across the Gulf they entered the peninsula called The Finger Pointing Solward. No one was happier than Jotar when their goal star showed as a disk.

Akira blazed on the portside.

They were adrift, the kalmakovian velocity reconverted to rest mass. Photon rockets blazed to life, changing their velocity by fourteen kilometers per second so that they could go into orbit around the planet Ohonshu.

They were greeted with incredulous enthusiasm. Akirani wept openly in the streets and on the farms. Two honor shuttles were sent to bring them down and, of course, they were landed at Tsumeshumo Beach where the first two shiploads of colonists had touched down.

Each of the Misubisi were given a torch and they knew what to do. Wild with joy they ran along the beach to the Shrine on the Jodai Hill where they embraced and cried and gave their thanks. Jotar marveled. Now he could build his ship! He went into the Demon's Dance with all of his old Engineering Power. And when he was finished he did a flourish of twenty rapid handsprings.

Panting, he saw that all Misubisis had frozen to watch him. For a second after he finished they stood still, then they bowed. Takenaga's lords were there. They too bowed. The son of the governor of the Rokakubutsu system bowed. Other lords of the outworld systems around Akira bowed.

The first person to move was a graceful child, not yet a woman, who came forward with flowers. She kneeled and offered them, her eyes cast down, as she delivered a prepared speech thanking him for bringing them home. Strange how these people of his called this planet home.

He tipped up her face and kissed her cheek and gave her the smile he had often given to women back on Lager when he wanted to encourage their attention. That was his first meeting with Misubisi Koriru. They became friends. When she was older, she became his mistress.

And so here he was, too old to fight much anymore, philosophical about his last lost battle, going to a celebration that Koriru wanted him to go to when all he wanted to do was get drunk. Why was he starting to do whatever Koriru said?

Ah, those Misubisi. Those scoundrels that Kasumi had planted and he had nourished. They listened with alertness to everything said by the great Jotar Plaek. They hopped to attention and instantly obeyed his every command. But they always came back and, so sorry, they could not do what he requested, and please would he allow them the honor of disemboweling themselves or some such rot. When he refused they humbly offered a second inferior course of action, which, it always turned out, they had already implemented.

The ship had arrived to find a shockingly primitive technology on Akira—*that* was the trouble. Well, not primitive. One's choice of words could not be too strong. Incongruous was the word. Jotar fully expected to find a computer-guided wooden plow one of these days.

Koriru drove him to the outskirts of Temputo, where

they entered the procession that snaked through the city to the Imperial Palace grounds of the Takenagas. Happy people watched. Vendors scurried around selling hot delicacies to the crowd. Children watched from trees. Clowns wearing waldo leggings jumped about the procession to make the crowd laugh. Elaborate paper animals, some of them forty meters long, slithered among the noble daimyo. Computer-implanted birds of paradise added punctuation marks of color to the procession, flying back and forth, resting on the heads of children. Everybody waved paper accordion models of the Massaki Maru on the end of sticks.

At the Palace, lesser daimyo were separated from greater daimyo for the feasting. Jotar was pillowed with the greatest, the nobles of the Akiran tributary systems: red Rokakubutsu, Hodo Reishitsu, desolate Iki Ta, and beautiful Butsudo. All of these men stood to gain enormous wealth from an Akiran shipbuilding industry. Wily old Takenaga himself—the man who had ended Akiran democracy and money wars between the merchant lords— even put in an appearance.

They liked the ship. The talk was all about *Imperial Akira.* Now they could expand down The Finger. At the knuckle end of The Finger was the whole of the Remeden Drift. Power, commerce, glory.

The moment came when the Massaki Maru was tugged from its assembly cocoon in space, already crewed for its maiden voyage to Butsudo. The Captain was in direct communication with Takenaga at the Palace.

"Heika, we await your orders!"

"Do us honor. Launch it!"

"Hai! Suiginitsu! Generate the field!"

"Hai!" came Suiginitsu's reply.

The first starship built on the farside of the Noir Gulf faded from the screen.

Jotar was not pleased. He was ashamed. Even in ancient times, had such an inferior ship ever come out of the shipyards at Lager? The acceleration of the Massaki Maru was shockingly sluggish. Its top velocity was ninety light speeds. Too many compromises had been made with reliability. Fast-time ruthlessly destroyed unreliable systems. He doubted that the ship would last more than five kilodays in service.

The Misubisi collective decision had been that it was more economical to build such a ship than to import a better one from across the Noir Gulf. They were right if they manufactured at least twenty of them. Still he was ashamed. He would not have come to the rim of civilization for that.

Later, as the confusion of the feast brought forth a new course of food, one of the Misubisi women came to him.

"Hanano! You're as nervous as that day I found you starving in my closet! What is it? I know. You're afraid that load of junk will shed its skin all along the route to Butsudo! No matter. Eat! Sit with us! We'll spend an hour here together and afterwards rub pot bellies!"

She fingered his hair affectionately. "If I had only known what a monster you were, I'd have chosen to die in the Gulf rather than throw myself at your mercy. Come." She tugged at him. "I beg of you to come with Koriru and me."

"You will please come," said Koriru.

They took him to one of the Palace gardens where some thirty of the Misubisi clan had gathered. More of them weren't there only because they had vowed the whole clan would never meet in one place at the same time. The handsome hulk of Misubisi Jihoku confronted them.

"Hanano! You found him, the Disapproving One! Welcome. Koriru, you've kept him sober! How do we honor such self-sacrifice!"

"I'm not sober, you pile of shit!" he retorted.

"In my unworthy opinion, Plaek-san, when you can still walk, you are sober!"

There was laughter, but nervous laughter. They knew he despised their ship, had not wanted it built.

"If that junk heap just gets back here, I'll give all gold stars!" Jotar roared drunkenly. "Not for your engineering abilities, but for your monumental good luck!"

Jihoku laughed. "Water on a frog's face! We have a millennia-long tradition of your insight into our inconsequential efforts, threads holding together a history longer than many planets, longer than Akira's, and throughout it all we have learned the joy and profit to ourselves of carrying you, oh noble bag of complaints, on our backs. Complain away!"

The Misubisi cheered Jihoku good-naturedly. They were happy. They were celebrating. It was their day.

Koriru stepped forward. "If I may be allowed to intrude, I have a poem from that tradition. Misubisi Kigyoshin of the twenty-third generation wrote it when the plans of his life's work were cut to pieces by Plaek-san. We were at Kinemon and they had met face to face.

> *Built of my sinews*
> *Flowing over nebula*
> *My crafted starbridge*
> *Pleases not our tortoise god*
> *Whose dreams are swift as wishes*

He's been slashing at us since the mists of our time and his criticism has made us great!"

"Hai!" yelled thirty voices.

Hanano stepped forward, trembling. She had desperately wanted to build ships and had spent her time with him in the Gulf picking his brain. She was his top engineer.

"We wish to give our tortoise god a gift tonight from our hearts and from the hearts of all our ancestors. It will not be good enough but it is our best."

Jotar was sobering. They were afraid of him, really afraid of his disapproval. And yet . . . somehow . . . they were about to give him something . . . if he disapproved . . . they would be destroyed.

It was a wooden box the size of a coffin and he opened it. The model of a starship floated out, glowing bluely. The name on the bow, printed not in their chicken-track script but in Anglish, was *The Jotar Plaek*. It was his ship. But it wasn't.

"The field fins are wrong," he said.

"I am so sorry to disagree," said Hanano, "but they are

a solution to the field equations subject to the fabrication constraints we have assumed."

The robed shipwrights were tense.

"You're telling me that you're building this ship?" He stared about the garden crazily.

"Hai!" said Hanano fiercely. "I have personally checked the entire critical path analysis. We know every problem that will arise, when it will arise, and how to solve that problem. *The Plaek* is to be a fifth-generation ship. We are to build ships of the Massaki Maru class for two more kilodays, at which time the Akiran craftsmen will be ready to build the next generation's prototype. Our fourth generation will be the first significant departure in starship design since Lager produced the Hammond variation. The fifth generation will be your ships."

Jotar stared at her. "And how long is this going to take?"

Jihoku spoke up. "I am very displeased to inform you that you will be dead by then." He bowed to express sorrow.

"I guessed there was a catch."

"We respectfully remind you," lashed out Koriru, "that you have asked thousands of us to die in this adventure. Only a handful of us survive!" She swept her arm about the room. "It does not matter that we die before the summit is reach. Banzai!" Ten thousand years. "It matters only that it is reached!"

"Do you think you can do it?"

"Hai!"

"Why didn't you tell me that this was going on?"

"We wanted to be sure. It was a gift we could not offer lightly. Our honor as shipwrights!"

Jotar Plaek held the model in his hands, turning it about, the tears running down his aging cheeks. He stared at the name printed on the bow.

"Look at that. A fat lot of good that's going to do me! Have you ever met an Akiran who could pronounce my name! Have you?" he challenged them all.

Then he was hugging his Misubisi people, each of them, one at a time.

EMPIRE AND REPUBLIC: CRISIS AND FUTURE

Jerry E. Pournelle, Ph.D.

Professor Richard Pipes of Harvard University reminds us that "One of the salient features of the Russian historical experience has been a propensity for imperialism." In fact, the Soviet Union is the last large colonial empire on Earth. It is not always recognized as such, because unlike the British and French empires, the Russian empire is territorially contiguous, and most Westerners don't realize that much of it was acquired in the last century, long after the age of European colonization had effectively ended.

Pipes continues:

"The second distinguishing characteristic of Russian imperialism is its military character: unlike Western colonial powers, which supplemented and reinforced their military activities with economic and cultural penetration, Russia has had to rely mainly on force of arms. . . . Expansionism of such persistence and an imperialism that maintains such a tenacious hold on its conquests raises the question of causes.

"One can dismiss the explanation most offered by amateur Russian 'experts' (although hardly ever by the Russians themselves), that Russia expands because of anxieties aroused by relentless foreign invasions of its

388

national territory by neighboring countries. Those who make this point usually have but the scantiest familiarity with Russian history. Their knowledge of Russia's external relations is confined to three or four invasions, made familiar by novels or moving pictures—the conquest of Russia in the early thirteenth century by the Mongols (who are sometimes confused with the Chinese); Napoleon's invasion of 1812; the Allied 'intervention' during the Russian Civil War; and the Nazi onslaught of 1941. With such light baggage one can readily conclude that, having been uniquely victimized, Russia strikes out to protect itself.

"Common sense, of course, might suggest even to those who lack knowledge of the facts that a country can no more become the world's most spacious as a result of suffering constant invasions than an individual can gain wealth from being repeatedly robbed. But common sense aside, there is the record of history. It shows that, far from being the victim of recurrent acts of aggression, Russia has been engaged for the past three hundred years with single-minded determination in aggressive wars, and that if anyone has reason for paranoia, it would have to be its neighbors. In the 1890s, the Russian General Staff carried out a comprehensive study of the history of Russian warfare since the foundations of the state. In the summary volume, the editor told his readers that they could take pride in their country's military record and face the future with confidence—between 1700 and 1870, Russia had spent 106 years fighting 38 military campaigns, of which 36 had been 'offensive' and a mere two defensive. This authoritative tabulation should dispose of the facile theory that Russian aggression is a defensive reflex."
—Richard Pipes, *Survival Is Not Enough* (Simon & Schuster, Touchstone Books, 1984)

Anyone making a reasonable study of the history of this century should be convinced that Russo-Soviet imperialism seriously threatens the peace and prosperity of the world. In 1945 republic had clearly beaten empire: the United States had the military and industrial power to dominate the world. That we did not do so is to our credit. But how did it happen that we allowed that power to dissipate, so that now the very survival of liberty and the republic is threatened?

For that matter, why is there any doubt about Soviet intentions? Are they not made clear in hundreds of ways? And why is there "controversy" over something so simple as strategic defense—not over technical feasibilities, but over the desirability of defenses against the ICBM?

Ten minutes' thought will convince you that the West has more than enough technical, industrial, economic, and military potential to overcome the threats of the Russian empire. After all, the Soviet Union is little more than a Third World Nation with weapons. Take away Russia's ICBMs and hydrogen bombs, and she would cease to be a superpower. For a plausible model, think of Bulgaria and Rumania with ICBMs.

Moreover, it's pretty obvious that the glib assertion of the moral equivalence of "the superpowers" is absurd. It isn't that the West is without faults, but the worst horror stories of the West come from violations of Western law and tradition—and don't measure a patch on the standard practices of the Soviet Empire.

Since everyone knows this, why is it "controversial" and "divisive" to say so?

The problem is that while the West enjoys moral, technological, and economic superiority, we have fallen way behind in intellectual resources. In part this is a failure of the schools, but there is considerably more to it than that. Our real problem is that much of the intellectual class of the United States has abandoned the West. It isn't that the intellectuals have gone over to the enemy; a witch hunt to eliminate communists would be about the worst thing we could do. It would also be futile. Intellectuals and academics don't side with the Soviet Union against the United States: they consider *both* to be the enemy.

Richard Pipes lists "a number of factors in Western societies which create an atmosphere favorable to Moscow's strategy of political divisiveness. The resentment of intellectuals and academics of what they consider shabby treatment at the hands of their societies; the desire of businessmen to trade without political interference; the need of politicians and special-interest groups for funds from the defense budget; the quest of climbers for social symbols in a world where these have become scarce—all these combine to make influential segments of democratic society unwilling to face the threat to their country's security and prone to minimize it or even to deny that it exists.

"The power of these groups is much magnified by the influence they exert over the media. That the media, especially the prestige organs, are dominated by people given to anti-anti-Communist views—people for whom the main danger to the United States comes from internal failures rather than external threats—can be in some measure statistically demonstrated. In a 1979–80 survey, 240 editors and reporters of the most influential newspapers, magazines, and television networks in the U.S. indicated that in the preceding two decades, four out of five of them had voted for Democratic candidates; in 1972, 81 percent had cast ballots for George McGovern, a Presidential candidate rejected by the voters in forty-nine of the fifty states . . . Among members of the self-designated public-interest groups in the U.S. (e.g., consumer and environmental-protection societies), the prevalence of such views is higher still—96 percent of the persons polled from such groups stated that they had voted for McGovern; they further expressed preference for Fidel Castro over Ronald Reagan by a margin of nearly seven to one."

Pipes wasn't the first to note the defection of the intellectuals. Eric Hoffer, one of America's genuine home-grown philosophers, noted as far back as 1952 that intellectuals throughout the world were hostile to Western civilization, and that "their search for a weighty and useful life led those of Asia and Africa, as it did their counterparts in Europe, to the promotion of nationalist and Socialist movements.

"Now, although the homelessness of the intellectual is more or less evident in all Western and Westernized societies, it is nowhere so pronounced as in our own common-man civilization. America has been running its complex economy and governmental machinery, and has been satisfying most of its cultural needs, without the aid of the typical intellectual. It is natural, therefore, that the intellectuals outside the U.S. should see in the spread of Americanization a threat not only to their influence but to their very existence." (Eric Hoffer, *The Ordeal of Change*)

By the late 1960s, Hoffer noted that although intellectuals in the U.S. had gained considerably expanded influence and power, they were also increasingly disaffected. "The attitude of the intellectual community toward America is shaped not by the creative few, but by the many who for one reason or another cannot transmute their dissatisfaction into a creative impulse, and cannot acquire a sense of uniqueness and growth by developing and expressing their capacities and talents. There is nothing in contemporary America that can cure or alleviate their chronic frustration. They want power, lordship, and opportunities for imposing action. Even if we should banish poverty from the land, lift up the Negro to true equality, withdraw from Vietnam, and give half the national income as foreign aid, they will still see America as an air conditioned nightmare unfit for them to live in.

"When you try to find out what it is in this country that stifles the American intellectual, you make a surprising discovery . . . What he cannot stomach is the mass of the American people—a mindless monstrosity devoid of spiritual, moral, and intellectual capacities. Like the aging Henry Adams, the contemporary American intellectual scans the daily newspapers for evidence of the depravity and perversity of American life, and arms himself with a battery of clippings to fortify his loathing and revulsion." (*The Temper of Our Times*)

Given the views of those who control most of the media, it's not surprising that TV and the papers will carry plenty of stories about depravity and perversity—possibly more than the public at large really wants.

The problem is not to find fault but to find a way out. That, alas, isn't going to be easy. One consequence of the defection of the intellectuals from Western values—including dedication to scholarship—has been the progressive deterioration of the schools, to the point that the National Commission on Excellence concluded that "If a foreign country had imposed this system of education on the United States, we would consider it an act of war."

The result is that we're losing in a war of words. In fact, it has gotten to the point where it's hard to tell who's talking. As Joe Sobran put it in a review of Soviet America-expert Georgi Arbatov:

> The eerie thing about *The Soviet Viewpoint*, written in the form of several long interviews . . . conducted by Dutch journalist Willem Oltmans, is that Georgi Arbatov seems to be impersonating Cyrus Vance.
>
> What the book stunningly reveals is Arbatov's sophistication about American liberalism. He knows its peculiar gullibility, and he speaks its idiom with near-perfect nuance. No "running dogs" or "Wall Street lackeys" or "capitalist bloodsuckers" here; Arbatov utters the Leninist vision in terms that might have been lifted from *Foreign Affairs*.
>
> Soviet-American relations have need of *reciprocity*. We must seek *mutually acceptable solutions*. Let us avoid *confrontation*, but instead confront *new realities*, eschewing the while any *mood of nostalgia* that might lead to a *new cold war* (much as such a development might please *hard-liners in Washington*, who are fond of *saber-rattling*).
>
> This is a time for *international cooperation*. We face *global problems*, such as the *depletion of natural*

resources, which can't be dealt with through *old percep-tions inherited from the cold war*.

Whether one likes it or not, we are chained together on this planet. We dare not treat the situation as a *zero-sum game*, or *continue to squander our resources through the arms race*. Not *if we are to avoid doomsday*. It is impera-tive that we pursue the *possibility of lessening ten-sions, of lowering the level of military confrontation*.

Despite our *different social systems*, there are *over-riding common interests, that call for cooperation. We are talking of human survival on this planet, of today's increasingly complex, fragile, and interde-pendent world*.

The real issue is the *quality of life*. If we are serious about *building a new society*, we must com-bine a genuine commitment to *social spending* with *a new, broader approach to human rights*.

Remember, *the Vietnam War torpedoed the Great Society*, and in a nuclear war, *there will be no win-ners*. Think of the *human cost!* Not only of *the war threatening humanity*, but of any *new massive mili-tary buildup*.

Any *significant improvement* in the *infrastructure* must be *viewed in the context* of the phenomena of *wide-spread alienation* and *social atomization* stem-ming from *McCarthyist witch-hunts*, and the *long-term trends* that culminated in *Watergate* with all its attendant *pressures for change* in the *military-industrial complex* whose *macho* posturing has thus far pre-cluded *meaningful redistribution . . . social expendi-tures . . . purely internal Afghan development. . . .*

Sobran concludes that, "There's hardly a sentence in this book that couldn't have been picked up on the narrow frequency band between *The New York Times* and the Institute for Policy Studies."

All of which says more about the American intellectual establishment than it does about the Soviet Union.

George Orwell said this about the language of Soviet Stalinists:

"As soon as certain topics are raised, the concrete melts into the abstract and no one seems able to think of turns of speech that are not hackneyed: prose consists less and less of *words* chosen for the sake of their meaning, and more and more of *phrases* tacked together like the sections of a prefabricated henhouse. It consists of gumming together long strips of words which have already been set in order by someone else, and making the results presentable by sheer humbug."

Humbug or no, the war of words is serious. Any time you're tempted to think it isn't, contrast again the relative balance of power between the United States and the Soviet Union in 1945 and today. It is only by self-paralysis that the West has allowed the very idea of a republican form of government to be endangered by an economic disaster area like the Soviet Union.

Jeane Kirkpatrick recognized just how serious it all was:

By calling "autonomous" that which is powerless, "federated" that which is unitary, "democratic" that which is schismatic, "popular" that which is imposed by terror, "peaceful" that which incites war—in brief, by systematically corrupting language to obscure reality— the Communists have made inroads into our sense of political reality. Language is, after all, the only medium in which we can think. It is exceedingly difficult to eliminate all the traditional connotations of words—to associate words like "For a lasting peace and a People's Democracy" with neither peace nor popular movements nor democracy.

Having recognized the problem, we still have to figure out what to do about it.

The first thing is to reject the easy solution of abandoning the virtues of the republic. Not that I wouldn't greatly prefer an American tyranny to any other, but really it's no good becoming like the enemy in order to avoid being conquered by him. Eric Hoffer puts it this way:

"Stalin's assertion that 'no ruling class has managed without its own intelligentsia' applies of course to a totalitarian regime. A society that can afford freedom can also manage without a kept intelligentsia: it is vigorous enough to endure ceaseless harassment by the most articulate and perhaps most gifted segment of the population. Such harassment is the 'eternal vigilance' which we are told is the price of liberty. In a free society internal tensions are not the signs of brewing anarchy but the symptoms of vigor—the elements of a self-generating dynamism."

What Hoffer is saying is that we must be true to our own principles. We must act like free people.

On the other hand, we don't have to be serious about nonsense. We don't have to pretend to be horrified because the President once referred to the Soviet Union as "the evil empire." Why shouldn't he do that? The Soviet Union certainly is an empire under any rational definition of the word, and it's pretty hard to view the slave camps as anything but evil. It's also a pretty tame thing to say compared to what they daily say about the United States.

We don't have to pretend we're in the presence of genius every time someone tries to tell us that international relations are complex. We particularly don't have to act as if someone foolish enough not to see the differences between the U.S. republic and the Soviet empire is wiser than we are.

The first threat to the republic is not so much the Soviet Empire as our unwillingness to see it as a threat; in particular, the willingness of the intellectual class to see the internal crisis as worse than the external enemy.

In the long run they may be right, although I suspect not for the right reasons.

As early as the seventeenth century Sir Roger Twysden said, "The world, now above some 5,500 years old, hath found means to limit kings, but never yet any republique." Alexis de Tocqueville, writing much later, had much the same thing to say. If America were ever to lose her freedom, it would be to a collectivist majority.

Professor Dicey has traced that trend in England. MacIlwain has done the same here. In every case, the root of the problem is the tendency to believe that government can do everything; that there is no problem we cannot "solve" by creating a government agency to deal with it.

A moment's thought would demonstrate that this is unlikely. Certainly it hasn't worked anywhere it has been tried, and few of us have more faith in the man who says, "I'm from the government, and I'm here to help you," than we do that the check is in the mail.

In fact the solution to that problem is simple enough, although politically difficult: we simply must declare large parts of our life off-limits, outside the jurisdiction of government. It is unlikely that we can restrain government power once it is admitted anywhere, but we can prevent it from getting there in the first place. The issue of "Federal Aid to Education" was fought over jurisdiction. The battle was lost, Federal Aid came in, and the result was a school system we would go to war to overthrow if we could only figure out who the enemy is.

It isn't lack of resources.

It was fashionable, in the '50s, to speak of the "Affluent Society." John Kenneth Galbraith made his reputation writing about the coming era of plenty, in which the problems of production would all be solved, so that it only remained to see to equitable distribution of the wealth which would inevitably increase year by year. He saw that era as already upon us.

It didn't quite work that way, and within two decades an American President would tell us of the end of the dream and the era of limits; of national malaise. Oddly enough, John Kenneth Galbraith's reputation suffered not a whit from that, and he remained popular with the Carter Administration. Such are the ways of economists.

In fact, though, Galbraith was more right than Carter and the doomsayers. I doubt that the world will ever come to the point where everyone can have everything, but certainly the era of limits is very nearly over. Energy applied to resources with ingenuity equals production. There are no human economic problems that can't be solved, given plentiful energy and cheap raw materials. Food production is largely a function of fertilizer, and nitrogen fixation is easy if you have electricity. Pollution is merely an energy problem: electric automobiles can banish smog, provided we have the power to run the cars on. And for that matter, given sufficient energy, any pollutants can be taken apart to their constituent elements.

Both energy and raw materials await us in space. One nickle-iron asteroid contains more metals than have been refined since the beginning of civilization. There are thousands of such asteroids. We needn't go even that far. The lunar regolith is about 90 percent useful, and it's already conveniently ground into a fine powder. Meanwhile, the sun pours out a kilowatt per square meter on Earth and Moon alike. Once we have routine access to the space environment, the Affluent Era can begin in reality.

Getting there isn't that hard, or won't be if we don't depend on government, and bureaucracy, and the long, slow, careful "man rating" system NASA uses.

Nineteen eighty-six was a fateful year: it began with the Challenger disaster, which shows that the old ways were ended forever. We are now told that it will take NASA years to fix the shuttle: longer to design O rings than it took to design and build the infinitely more complex bombers and fighters of World War Two.

The year ended with Voyager: with Jeana Yaeger and Dick Rutan and their volunteer help and corporate supporters. No more than a hundred times their effort would plant a permanent colony on the Moon! It was fitting that

1986 ended with Dick Rutan walking around Voyager and saying, "See what free men can do."

That should always be the answer of republic to empire. See what free men can do.

Here is an excerpt from the new novel by Timothy Zahn, coming from Baen Books in August 1987:

TIMOTHY ZAHN

TRIPLET

The way house had been quiet for over an hour by the time Karyx's moon rose that night, its fingernail-clipping crescent adding only token assistance to the dim starlight already illuminating the grounds. Sitting on the mansion's garret-floor widow's walk, his back against the door, Ravagin watched the moon drift above the trees to the east and listened to the silence of the night. And tried to decide what in blazes he was going to do.

There actually *were* precedents for this kind of situation: loose precedents, to be sure, and hushed up like crazy by the people upstairs in the Crosspoint Building, but precedents nonetheless. Every so often a Courier and his group would have such a mutual falling out that continuing on together was out of the question . . . and when that happened the Courier would often simply give notice and quit, leaving the responsibility for getting the party back to Threshold in the hands of the nearest way house staff. Triplet management ground their collective teeth when it happened, but they'd long ago come to the reluctant conclusion that clients were better off alone than with a Courier who no longer gave a damn about their safety.

And Ravagin wouldn't even have to endure the

usual froth-mouthed lecture that would be waiting when he got back. He was finished with the Corps, and those who'd bent his fingers into taking this trip had only themselves to blame for the results. He could leave a note with Melentha, grab a horse, and be at the Cairn Mounds well before daylight. By the time Danae had finished sputtering, he'd have alerted the way house master in Feymar Protectorate on Shamsheer and be on a sky-plane over the Ordarl Mountains . . . and by the time she made it back through to Threshold and screamed for vengeance, he'd have picked up his last paychit, said bye-and-luck to Corah, and boarded a starship for points unknown. Ravagin, the great veteran Courier, actually deserting a client. Genuinely one for the record books.

Yes. He would do it. He would. Right now. He'd get up, go downstairs, and get the hell out of here.

Standing up, he gazed out at the moon . . . and slammed his fist in impotent fury on the low railing in front of him.

He couldn't do it.

"Damn," he muttered under his breath, clenching his jaw hard enough to hurt. "Damn, damn, *damn.*"

He hit the railing again and inhaled deeply, exhaling in a hissing sigh of anger and resignation. He couldn't do it. No matter what the justification—no matter that the punishment would be light or nonexistent—no matter even that others had done it without lasting stigma. He was a *professional*, damn it, and it was his job to stay with his clients no matter what happened.

Danae had wounded his pride. Deserting her, unfortunately, would hurt it far more deeply then she ever could.

In other words, a classic no-win situation. With him on the short end.

And it left him just two alternatives: continue his silent treatment toward Danae for the rest of the trip, or work through his anger enough to at least get back on civil terms with her. At the moment, neither choice was especially attractive.

Out in the grounds, a flicker of green caught his eye. He looked down, frowning, trying to locate the source. Nothing was moving; nothing seemed out of place. Could there be something skulking in the clumps of trees, or perhaps even the shadows thrown by the bushes?

Or could something have tried to break through the post line?

Nothing was visible near the section of post line he could see. Cautiously, he began easing his way around the widow's walk, muttering a spirit-protection spell just to be on the safe side.

Still nothing. He'd reached the front of the house and was starting to continue past when a movement through the gap in the tree hedge across the grounds to the south caught his attention. He peered toward it . . . and a few seconds later it was repeated further east.

A horseman on the road toward Besak, most likely . . . except that Besak had long since been sealed up for the night by the village lar. And Karyx was not a place to casually indulge in nighttime travel. Whoever it was, he was either on an errand of dire emergency or else—

Or else hurrying away from an aborted attempt to break in?

Ravagin pursed his lips. "*Haklarast*," he said. It was at least worth checking out.

The glow-fire of the sprite appeared before him. "I am here, as you summoned," it squeaked.

"There's a horse and human traveling on the road toward Besak just south of here," he told it. "Go to the human and ask why he rides so late. Return to me with his answer."

The sprite flared and was gone. Ravagin watched it dart off across the darkened landscape and then, for lack of anything better to do while he waited, continued his long-range inspection of the post line. Again he found nothing; and he was coming around to the front of the house again when the sprite returned. "What answer?" he asked it.

"None. The human is not awake."

"Are you sure?" Ravagin asked, frowning. He'd once learned the hard way about the hazards of sleeping on horseback—most Karyx natives weren't stupid enough to try it. "Really asleep, not injured?"

"I do not know."

Of course it wouldn't—spirits didn't see the world the way humans did. "Well . . . is he riding alone, or is there a spirit with him protecting him from falls?"

"There is a djinn present, though it is not keeping the human from falling. There is no danger of that."

And with a djinn along to— "What do you mean? Why isn't he going to fall?"

"The human is upright, in full control of the animal—"

"Wait a second," Ravagin cut it off. "You just told me he was asleep. How can he be controlling the horse?"

"The human is asleep," the sprite repeated, and Ravagin thought he could detect a touch of vexation in the squeaky voice. "It is in control of its animal."

"That's impossible," Ravagin growled. "He'd have to be—"

Sleepwalking.

"*Damn!*" he snarled, eyes darting toward the place where the rider had vanished, thoughts skidding with shock, chagrin, and a full-bellied rush of fear. *Danae—*

His mental wheels caught. "Follow the rider," he ordered the sprite. "Stay back where you won't be spotted by any other humans, but don't let her out of your sight. First give me your name, so I can locate you later. Come on, give—I haven't got time for games."

"I am Psskapsst," the sprite said reluctantly.

"Psskapsst, right. Now get after it—and *don't* communicate with that djinn."

The glow-fire flared and skittered off. Racing along the widow's walk, Ravagin reached the door and hurried inside. Danae's room was two flights down, on the second floor; on a hunch, he stopped first on the third floor and let himself into Melentha's sanctum.

The place had made Ravagin's skin crawl even with good lighting, and the dark shadows stretching around the room now didn't improve it a bit. Shivering reflexively, he stepped carefully around the central pentagram and over to the table where Melentha had put the bow and Coven robe when she'd finished her spirit search.

The robe was gone.

Swearing under his breath, he turned and hurried back to the door—and nearly ran into Melentha as she suddenly appeared outside in the hallway. "What are you doing in there?" she demanded, holding her robe closed with one hand and clutching a glowing dagger in the other.

"The Coven robe's gone," he told her, "and I think Danae's gone with it."

"What?" She backed up hastily to let him pass, then hurried to catch up with him. "When?"

"Just a little while ago—I think I saw her leaving on horseback from the roof. I just want to make sure—"

They reached Danae's room and Ravagin pushed open the door . . . and she was indeed gone.

August 1987 • 384 pp. • 65341-5 • $3.50

To order any Baen Book, send the cover price plus 75¢ for first-class postage and handling to: Baen Books, Dept. BB, 260 Fifth Avenue, New York, N.Y. 10001.

"Everybody is asking: How do we knock out ICBM's? That's the wrong question. How do you design a system that allows a nation to defend itself, that can be used, even by accident, without destroying mankind, indeed, must be used every day, and is so effective that nuclear weapons cannot compete with it in the marketplace? That's the right question."

THE MOON GODDESS AND THE SON

DONALD KINGSBURY

The great illusion of the Nuclear Peace is that there will be no war as long as neither side wants war. We have neglected to find a defense against nuclear weaponry—but we cannot guarantee that a military accident will not happen. We argue that defense is impossible and disarmament the only solution—but we know no more about how to disarm than we know how to shoot down rocket-powered warheads.

Exploring these situations is what science fiction does best, and author Donald Kingsbury is one of its stricter players. Every detail is considered and every ramification explored. His first novel, *Courtship Rite*—set in the far future—received critical acclaim. His new novel takes place during the next thirty years.

In the 1990s the Soviets, building on their solid achievements in Earth orbit, surge into ascendancy by launching the space station Mir. Mir in time becomes Mirograd, a Russian "city" orbiting only a few hundred miles above North America. Now the U.S. plays desperate catch-up in the space race they are trailing.

THE MOON GODDESS AND THE SON is the story of the men and women who will make America great again. "Kingsbury interweaves [his] subplots with great skill, carrying his large cast of characters forward over 30-odd years. Neither his narrative and characterization nor his eye for the telling detail fall short. . . . An original mind and superior skill have combined to produce an excellent book."—*Chicago Sun-Times*

416 pp. • 55958-3 • $15.95

TRAVIS SHELTON
LIKES BAEN BOOKS
BECAUSE THEY TASTE GOOD

Recently we received this letter from Travis Shelton of Dayton, Texas:

I have come to assoc te Baen Books with Del Monte. Now what i that supposed to mean? Well, if you're in a strange store with a lot of different labels, you pick Del Monte because the product will be consistent and will not disappoint.

Something I have noticed about Baen Books is that the stories are always fast-paced, exciting, action-filled and seem to be published because of content instead of who wrote the book. I now find myself glancing to see who published the book instead of reading the back or intro. If it's a Baen Book it's going to be good and exciting and will capture your spare reading moments.

Another discovery I have recently made is that I don't have any Baen Books in my unread stacks—and I read four to seven books a week, so that in itself is a meaningful statistic.

Why do you like Baen Books? Drop us a letter like Travis did. The person who best tells us what we're doing right—and where we could do better—will receive a Baen Books gift certificate worth $100. Entries must be received by December 31, 1987. Send to Baen Books, 260 Fifth Avenue, New York, N.Y. 10001. And ask for our free catalog!